Meet
Your

match

OTHER BOOKS BY STEPHANIE FOWERS:

Rules of Engagement

Meet Your

match

a novel

Stephanie Fowers

Covenant Communications, Inc.

Cover design copyrighted 2007 by Covenant Communications, Inc.

Published by Covenant Communications, Inc.
American Fork, Utah

Printed in Canada
First Printing: September 2007

11 10 09 08 07   10 9 8 7 6 5 4 3 2 1

ISBN 10: 1-59811-394-1
ISBN 13: 978-1-59811-394-5

Acknowledgements

(Beware, as this is a long list, but you ALL made this book and other books possible.)

Thank you to Jacqueline Fowers for lending me her name—and no, she's not a squirrelly girl either; Cassie Burgi for loving motorcycles; Vance Bowen for giving me the motorcycle info while Cassie was gone on her mission, and, yes, he is very safe with vehicles in every way; Matt Seeley for going on about the squirrelly girl's evil ways and for showing me how to dumpster dive; and Matt's roommate, Brian, who wasn't afraid to philosophize about little Miss Chief and Miss Creant, though I'm sure I often Miss Understood.

Thanks also to Pete Bradshaw and his roommates for explaining why a nice guy might not ask the girl out (and in a great English accent, might I add); LeAnn Wach for showing us how it's done and beating us all to the altar; Bart Malquist for making midnight foosball such a success; Katie Hansen and Andrea Goates for stealing all the guys and answering all my questions (about baseball and bad dates); Chris Slade for insisting that I use his name (hey, no, I *wanted* to use it!); Bepa (Erika Childs) for sitting on the porch with me and watching our crops grow, and flipping her flatbread with her strange numb fingers; Nate Seeley, who showed us that nice guys really do exist; and Larissa Villers for modeling all the advantages of being short—it made it easier to pick on her.

More thanks to Jay Carr for insisting I put the apple-pie joke in there (hey, it *was* funny); David Blackmer for publishing an underground newspaper (sorry for being such a pest); Dave McNay for his winner's circle T-shirt. They were better marriage notes than I took.

I also appreciate Scott Green for being one of the most relaxed musicians I know; Andy Seeley for showing us the finer points of being cool; Clayton Firth for dedicating all his songs to us and informing us of the jerk guy's allure; Spencer Matsuura for messing with our minds and calling our crushes "The Monsieur"; Mena Seyed-Ashraf for chasing away my boys and feeding me biscuits with jam for dinner; Marcus Green for shrinking my brain and making me think I was crazy; Brian Hansen for pointing out that Sister Childs is grammatically incorrect; and Andy Mott for helping me with my website and designing our fake Mormon adds: "Dating—like hanging out . . . only better." Gratitude to P1, P2, P3, P4, P5, P6 (okay, all of you girls from Pinegar, Moon House, Sherwood House, Banbridge). You rock! You're my real little punk girls.

And thanks to all of my Relief Societies (so far), who are nothing like the Relief Society in the book (thank goodness, but hey, we needed some villains—what was I supposed to do?). Again, more thanks to Moon Apartments for their guys (*seriously all of you*) and their pool. Hey, I think you even took a picture of us playing volleyball for your ad. And of course, I'd like to thank the coolest musicians in the world, Rockwell (the D6 boys: Andrew Cobabe, Conrad Walsh, and David Epenschied), for hanging my articles up on your marriage wall. I'm glad that I could inspire you. Gracias to Erica Okere-Nkimdirim for going off about the Mr. Jerk doll with me; Betsy Huntington, the cutest freshman who's not a freshman anymore—thanks for letting me tease you; and Steve Lahn and fam for hitting my car with a hammer and thereby getting it to work. Thank you!

And gratitude to my brother, Scott Fowers, who rigged my brakes so they would work AND to Stacey Young's family for giving my car its final tweaking (everything I know about cars, I got from you guys!); Crystal Liechty, who wasn't afraid to give me villain tips; Julie Wright for reading my book twice! Also to Vanessa Christensen for looking over my book for me when it was still in its extremely long stages (I know I know, I'm still a slacker); Lily Huntington for explaining law to me; Aaron and Julie Penrod for being the cutest engaged couple I know; and Sandra Barton for crying when she read this (for joy or what?).

And finally, many thanks to Mindy Nelson for telling my character to get over herself; Ashley Fowers for assuming this book will help squirrelly girls everywhere; Bishop Taggart for putting up with our 73rd ward antics; the real Rambo House—I lost a punching bag to you, but it was worth it; *Schooled Magazine* for helping me promote my book; and Bart Seeley for being so incredibly witty and making our lives so much fun (our ship parties were definitely the highlight of the year, nay, our lives)!

And yeah, I know there are a million and two more of you. Thank you so much for being my friend. I will always remember our years together with a smile.

Dedication

To my family and roommates (of course, what did you think?). Thank you for helping me out the summers I wrote this. I would've starved . . . or I at least would've OD'd on cereal and peanut butter sandwiches.

And of course, to my many editors . . . who worked laboriously to help dot my t's and cross my i's and didn't mind my q's and p's. Yeah, yeah, it's wrong I know!

Also to LDStorymakers for all their great advice and love.

And furthermore, a big thank-you to all my friends who read through this and told me to work harder. Ha ha, thanks for making this so much fun!

Make your thinking orderly and free from emotional
overtures, and you will see people and things
as they are, with clarity and charity.
—Sri Nisargadatta Maharaj

Singles Ward Dictionary
(Key Terms)

(Not necessarily in alphabetical order or in order of importance, or, in fact, in any order at all. These terms come from a singles ward; therefore all definitions are irrational, intertwined, and interrelated . . . kind of like plots in a bad soap opera.)

Squirrelly Girl ('härt-brā-kər) *female* **1:** able to make a man's heart putty in her hands **2:** runs from commitment by stringing boys along **3:** puts guys on the back burner while waiting for the perfect one (The Challenge) to come along **4:** gives girls a bad name

Back-burner Boy ('i-dē-ət) *male* **1:** nice guy (finishes last) **2:** unbeknownst to him, is the poor victim of Squirrelly Girl **3:** fed lines to be kept at bay **4:** placed coyly on the back burner (on low heat) as a type of insurance policy in case nothing better comes along **5:** kept interested enough to not give up hope, but not given enough interest to get ideas; destined to become Bitter Boy

Best Gal Pal (ek-'splöit-ed) *female* **1:** willing to do anything for anybody; always listening; always there; always supporting **2:** not a threat (seemingly)

The Challenge ('plā-ər) *male* **1:** the guy Squirrelly Girl cannot resist **2:** the one and only **3:** unattainable (hardly returns calls) **4:** menace to society **5:** (slang) jerk

Bitter Boy ('lü-zər) *male* **1:** has broken heart caused by his antisocial behavior or being left out on the burner too long **2:** jumped out of the game and hopped out of the frying pan and into the fire **3:** hard and cold like burnt toast, charred to a crisp **4:** frosty, jaded, biting, numb—how else can I say it?—cold as ice

Burnt Girl ('nät 'jəs-tə-fīd) *female* **1:** discouraged **2:** just out of a relationship (could be years out); not ready for a new one **3:** played (usually by The Challenge) **4:** can't move on with her life **5:** on the run

Barnacle ('stäk-ər) *male* **1:** has amazing ability to glom onto females **2:** pays so much attention to one particular girl that other guys think she's taken and leave her alone, causing girl to get desperate and issue a restraining order **3:** in times of famine or miracle, aforementioned girl might go for said Barnacle

Claim Staker ('swēt 'spir-ət) *female* **1:** has nasty habit of dibbing guys whether or not claimed guy is interested back **2:** makes other girls back off—if they have a conscience

Safe Guy ('best 'frend) *male* **1:** can also be *harmless* guy, *player* guy, *bitter* guy, *taken* guy, *former* guy flame, and best guy *friend* **2:** you can depend on his noncommittal attitudes to keep you safe **3:** won't make a move **4:** might turn on you

All of them hopelessly flawed, so how will they meet their match—especially if they just *hang out*? Oh, which brings us to:

Hanging Out (fər-'bi-den) *verb* **1:** eternal friends **2:** has replaced dating **3:** will go nowhere **4:** perfect for those with commitment problems (though not even this will save them)

Chapter 1

If there must be hope there must also be charity.
—Moroni 10:20

Tuesday, June 16th, early afternoon

I'm not a squirrelly girl, okay? No matter how much Britton and Christian tell you that I am, don't listen to them. They don't know what they're talking about. If anything, I'm going through a stage. It's called "run," although I'm not *really* running, not exactly. I'm just walking—really fast—from him. It would look too obvious if I actually ran.

I glanced behind me, my shoulder-length red hair whipping against my face. I didn't have time to brush the chunky layers away from my dark eyes. Not now, and not any time soon because he was getting closer. My footsteps quickened.

Garbage. It was June, the month of crazies, especially at BYU. Spring brought love in the air whether we wanted it to or not, with its budding flowers and green leaves and branches that tore at my hair while I ran to escape it.

It's kind of interesting how you mete out your own judgment. Pick the sin and reap the consequences. Yeah, I'd like to extend a special thank you to my favorite sins: fairy tales and chick flicks. Thank you for messing me up. I remember my 150th slumber party vividly . . . Okay, not vividly. What I recall is just the setting of all our slumber parties: pillows and blankets and brownies and popcorn—and the latest romantic comedy.

"He's so cute," my cousin Jade said as we watched the movie. She was three years older than me, so I trusted her judgment with these kinds of things.

"Yeah, I'm gonna marry a guy like him someday," I decided.

She laughed. "Well, they don't really exist. Look at our dads."

"They do too exist!" I was stung. "I will *only* marry a man who is sensitive and sweet, strong, handsome, who will protect me, a good sense of humor, not too bossy, and . . ."

All right, let's get a few things straight, girls. I'm telling you something now so you can avoid the same heartbreak I went through. You will never find a knight who will sweep you off your feet. You will never find love at first sight. You will never be carried off into the sunset on a white horse. I grew up with six brothers, so you'd think I'd have known that myself.

My whole life, I have been cursed for being a romantic . . . or maybe I'm just a victim of Monsieur Romantique, or shall we say, The Challenge. Years after my fierce chick-flick training, he came when I thought I would never find my fairy-tale man who would love me for me. You've got to know that feeling. He was a miracle—so caring, so thoughtful, so sensitive, so different from all the obnoxious guys I knew in Provo. He had poetic blue eyes and curly blond hair. And he was exotic. Not exactly born exotic, but he *had* served his mission in France. That's how he got his nickname.

We had sat next to the canals, the most romantic spot on BYU campus, our legs trailing in the water. Not even the birds dared intrude on our territory. The Monsieur looked deeply into my eyes. "We need a time-out," he said. I could tell this was killing him. "School's just too hard right now. I'm not sure I'm so good for you anyway." He grinned wryly and played with my fingers. "I'm a mess."

No, no! He was everything to me. Why couldn't he see himself the way I saw him?

"I hate this more than you do," he said, "but this has to be. I will never love anyone again . . . not like I loved you."

I squeezed his hand. I felt the same way. "If you need to concentrate on school . . ." *You poor thing. You're really stressed out right now.* It was probably for the best that we were taking a break. And then after he worked things out, I would tell our grandkids the story of how I stood by him through thick and thin, for time and all etern— All right, let's be honest here. I was played, and I should've known better.

After he drove his Harley off into the setting sun, it took me a while to figure it out. He never called. He didn't answer my e-mails. He started dating other girls. And after not really pulling myself back together, I went on the rebound. Well, I *should've* gone on the rebound. After the breakup, everyone wanted to set me up. My gut reaction told me no, but after hearing about the Monsieur's latest fling, I decided to go against my instincts and went on a blind date— my stupidest mistake yet.

"Aren't you a little old for Provo?" he had asked.

I tried to smile at him. He was preying on my insecurities, so I decided to make it a joke. "Yeah, I've been running from the age police for a while now. I'm going undercover as an eighteen-year-old coed." I giggled in the giggliest way I knew how, and swung my legs for emphasis, going even higher on the swings.

"Oh, well, you definitely don't act your age . . . uh, you don't look it either," he said quickly. "I could date you."

"Uh, thanks." I hopped out of the swings.

This one wasn't as smooth-talking as the Monsieur. The next wasn't as tall as the Monsieur. I didn't feel the same way I felt with the Monsieur with the next and the next. It was useless. I couldn't connect. Oh, but before you chalk these guys up to being stalkers or barnacles, as Britton would call them, think again. They're amazing. Some are majoring in engineering and pre-med and law, and every other major that proves they have brains, although that doesn't do *me* any good. *They* usually think I'm an idiot in the end, and I've never managed to change their minds about that.

"I personally think that the equation of *blah blah blah* taken to the fifth degree of *blah blah blah* is highly elementary," my next date said. "What do you think?"

"I like it too."

His eyebrows drew in. *Oops.* My hands twisted over the table legs in the Cougareat. I'd blown my cover. I had no idea what he was talking about.

Construction workers, UPS men, and guys at Gold's Gym love me, but I suppose that's true for every girl, huh? Which is why you can't trust unfounded attention, because it fades just as quickly as it comes, though it's definitely good for a self-esteem boost, since most of the guys are pretty cute . . . like the security guards at the BYU library. But I don't want to talk about *him*. No way. That only brings back bad memories.

My next date was watching me with probing eyes when he said, "He was crazy to let you go." *No, I said I didn't want to talk about him!* But he worked with the Monsieur at the library, so I guessed they had talked about me. All was fair in love. "You're the most beautiful girl in the periodical section. Has anyone ever told you that?"

"Uh . . . all the time?" My smile was frozen to my face. Now we were both liars. This one was too much like the Monsieur. I had to prove there was something more to me than what he saw. "I'm an artist too. I work for a magazine."

"As a model?"

"A photographer and a writer. And I've got ideas, big ideas, of taking over the world." He wasn't listening.

"I should've known you weren't a model. You're a little short. Gorgeous, but short."

After yet another awkward date, I couldn't deal with it any more. I started doing everything in my power to turn guys off. If they liked outgoing girls, I was shy. If they didn't like annoying girls, guess who acted annoying or too career-oriented or crass or maternal? Once I figured out what they hated, I worked it.

"You're a little wild, aren't you?" a guy told me in the printing lab. "I don't normally like that, but . . . can I call you?"

Can we do this again? Again? Again?

I found myself running from seven different guys at once, all of them perfectly nice guys, but . . . Yeah, that's what Christian calls them: "perfectly nice guys, but . . ." They all represented heartbreak to me. I knew nothing would last—not when they didn't really know me or what they were getting into. The world had gone crazy, seriously. Why else would all these guys be going for me? They hadn't before, when I had been idealistic enough to believe they meant something by it. I'm certainly *not* the cutesy little slinky type that you find in chick flicks. I laugh too loud. I've got buff arms, large ribs, and obnoxious red hair that I could easily turn into dreadlocks if I wanted to.

So, uh, as long as I'm pouring my heart out and revealing every ugly little secret I have, don't be offended, guys. I like you, just not in that way. Ugh, this is sticky. I suppose you're all used to those chick flicks that pass off jerks as tragically flawed heroes, and you feel all happy when they get their way in the end, but *I* deserve to be thwarted. Yes, I'm the villain in this piece. Sorry. Although let me straighten this out: I'm not exactly a bad person, just a coward. In fact, I really have nothing against the guys I reject. Other girls can date them and everything will work out just fine.

You've got to believe I don't have a squirrelly bone in my body. I've had my share of brief dating insanity, jumping into bad relationships, giving my all, and stumbling out a burnt girl. This just wasn't one of those times. Nope. Which brings me to my previous state, "run." At least it was good exercise.

I hurried over the uneven sidewalk and barely stopped myself from falling into a gaping hole. It was just the normal, treacherous terrain you find south of BYU campus. Each block of cement juts out as if emerging from an earthquake. I sidestepped the hole and ran into a ten-foot wall. Okay, slight exaggeration. It was just the edge of the next slab of sidewalk, but it still was enough to send me flying.

I managed to stop my ankle from rolling, thank goodness, because there was no way I was slowing down . . . until I stumbled over the chunky soles of my apocalyptic wedge heels and fell in a heap. I muffled a cry of pain. What had possessed me to buy these things anyway?

They made me feel powerful, or at least as tall as everybody else, but they were always tripping me up. *Garbage.* I rubbed my ankle, carefully keeping my eyes on the ground, listening for the unwelcome call of my name.

I got slowly back to my feet, testing my ankle. I had sprained it enough times to know this time there was no damage done, and I knew I could still get away. I was that good.

I chanced another peek behind me, hoping I had lost my newest admirer. Some girls might call this guy a loser, but not me. You see,

I'm done calling guys names just because *I* don't want to date them. Hey, I'm not *all bad*. I just called the lad Lane Bryant—I think that was his name—and I lumped him into the same category with all the other earnest guys who happened to get the wrong idea from me.

The thing is, I don't remember acting interested in Lane in the first place, but no one believes me when I say I'm not really interested in anyone, especially Britton. Christian just warns me that saying I'm not interested will only make me a challenge. It's like guys can sense when I just don't want to play the dating game anymore. And I really don't want to let anybody in, not now, not ever again.

I'll tell you what the real problem is: there are nicer people than me involved here. Take my roommate Maggie for instance. She's my best gal pal—the nicest, smartest person in the whole world, or at least the ward, and definitely the most honest. Of course, she didn't have to point out that I was actually making more money as a flunky flyer girl for *Happy Valley* magazine than writing the actual articles. And she didn't have to throw cookies on Lane Bryant's doorstep either. Once again, I got framed for her good deeds. Maggie was everything I loved and hated about a nice girl wrapped up in one, baggage and all.

Let's just say that I've taken a rather unromantic view of things lately. I've decided to believe that the worst will happen if you give it a chance. Maybe this is in direct response to all those chick flicks and fairy tales. I don't know, but I'm even planning on publishing an article called, "What Are the Odds?" Because the odds are, if something bad happens, it will happen to me.

That was why normally nothing would have enticed me to trespass on Lane Bryant's territory today, except now I was on the job, if you could call it a job. I was passing out flyers for *Happy Valley* magazine. Anything to keep from starving, and I was starving. Well, I would be if my roommates didn't intervene every once in a while. I was an artist. I graduated in art, so I knew starving came with the territory.

I stood up slowly and tried to pass Lane Bryant's apartment. Even now I could feel his eyes behind me, and I hoped it was just my imagination. My back arched unconsciously and I kept my stride brisk, even though my ankle protested. I resisted the urge to look back again. It would look too weird if I looked back now, not that I wasn't acting strange already.

Lane was really just a casualty in my mad dash to "run." And now I found myself doing what I did best—running to Rainbow House (Rambo House, as the guys called it). The dump had been through some major rehashing lately, but my HE brothers still wanted to give it a tougher image. They managed to cover the rainbow on their living room wall, though none of them could explain away the big rainbow painted on the outside. (And no, HE brothers does not stand for He-Men, though I'm sure Christian and Britton might tell you differently. It's just a shortened version of FHE brothers or, for those not familiar with our BYU lingo, they were guys from my family home evening group. And I'm not telling you any more than that, except that the building housed six of my safe guy posse, soon to be five, since one was engaged to my cousin Jade . . . and of course one of them was *you know who*.)

But forget all that. At this moment the Rainbow House just represented freedom. No guy will follow a girl into another guy's place, especially because everyone thought I had something going on with Christian. Like that was very likely. Christian's roommate was the Monsieur, which means Christian's seen me at my worst. No one in that house would ever consider dating me, and no hard feelings, but I felt the same way about them. That's why we could always be ourselves around each other.

"Hey, Red!" I turned the corner just as I heard Lane call his nick-name for me. It looked like he wasn't giving up the chase yet. He was closer than I thought. I kept walking.

"Jacqueline! Jacqueline Childs!" Judging by the urgency in his voice and by the fact that he had reverted to calling me by my real name, I knew he was going to try to ask me out again. I guess you could say, that since the Monsieur, I've gained an overdeveloped radar in this cat-and-mouse game.

My gaze latched on the big oak tree in front of me. It fanned out in front of Rambo House and was covered in ivy and leaves, resembling a big green Grinch hand. This could be my salvation. I scrambled for it. Tucking the flyers under my arm, I reached for the tree trunk and spun myself behind the tree.

I had a bad habit of acting before thinking, and I probably don't have to explain that this was one of those times, because if he had just seen me, he was probably wondering why I had suddenly disappeared. And if he found me? I grimaced, not wanting to think about it.

What is wrong with me? I leaned my head against the ivy and closed my eyes. Why couldn't I just grow up? Well, I guess you could say that I have. Yeah, I'm twenty-six. I've been a menace to society for a whole year. My mom claims that only applies to guys, but I know the truth. I've stayed up nights wondering why I can't get over this. I've counted how many potential futures I've blown, how many kids I could've had, how many minivans I could've totaled.

I sighed, but not too loudly, and after a moment of waiting, I peered around the tree. Sanctuary. I was just steps away from Rambo House, and I knew Christian would protect me. Some people might call this unhealthy. At least Christian would. He's majoring in psychology.

My fingers curled around the ivy. Believe me, Britton has given countless lectures against me to the elders quorum. He's the undisputed president of the Bitter Boys Club in our ward, and no, he has no idea that I call him that, and he certainly has no idea what I'm going through. He's never been chased through Macey's. He's never had to make up a significant other to dissuade a would-be suitor. He's never had to hide behind a tree. And I couldn't believe I was hiding behind a tree.

With a determined grimace, I leaned dangerously far from the tree to peer down the street just as Lane rounded the corner. I ducked. Even though I was nearsighted, I could tell it was him. He was pretty cute in an Abercrombie and Fitch way. I squinted through the leaves. He had completely overdone it with his pre-beaten clothing, and I would gladly let any claim staker have him because the boy completely outdid me in the fashion department. Yeah, plenty of girls were interested, so stop feeling sorry for him.

I was the one who had problems, not that you should feel sorry for me either, except things were about to get worse. I caught sight of my fiend friend walking the other direction. "Charity," I growled.

Charity looked like a gypsy cut out of a magazine. She was wearing layers of cotton shirts without a wrinkle in the fabric, and her light, fluttery Bohemian skirt lifted slightly over her calves in the faint breeze.

I don't know why I didn't like Charity. Oh wait, yes I did. Think Scarlett O'Hara, Helen of Troy, Cleopatra, every horrible squirrelly girl you can come up with (no, not me). Charity Frost was taller than me and perfect model height—a frost-tipped, fake-baked, makeup-caked girl with dark hair and eyes.

She was the new Relief Society president and the ward mystery girl, which is why she drove the guys crazy and the girls mad with jealousy. She was fake polite to the girls and fake scandalous to the guys. She wouldn't hesitate to blow my cover if she could.

Lane was coming closer, and it was only a matter of time before one of them caught sight of me. I tried to think of an escape before Charity ratted me out. If I jumped out from behind the tree, I would look like I was hiding, and I didn't want *him* to know that. Why was my life always a deadly serious comedy of events? Comedy because it was happening to me, and deadly serious because, once again, it was happening to me.

I clutched the flyers and slid down the tree, leaning heavily on my cargo capris. If I was caught, I could look like I was just reading my flyers . . . such interesting flyers. I pretended to be engrossed until I realized where Charity was heading—straight for Rambo House. I frowned. What was she going to do there? I doubted that it was Relief Society business.

Britton could take care of himself, and I could tell the other guys there didn't interest her, but Christian was showing signs of breaking, and he was nice enough to be the perfect back-burner boy for her evil designs. She would toy with him, possibly for months. Now that's a squirrelly girl. My eyes narrowed. Her steps were taking her straight past my tree and—I smiled—towards Lane.

Every girl knows that the best strategy to get rid of a guy is to introduce him to a cuter girl, or, in this case, hide behind a tree until a squirrelly girl comes along. It was the old bait and switch. Yeah, I told you I was a villain. Did you expect me to hide it? At any rate, I feel perfectly safe telling you my plans since you are completely powerless to stop me.

I pulled to the side of the tree away from Charity. It was a bold move because it took me closer to Lane, but at this point I trusted that Charity was attractive enough to keep his attention. Lane would be looking straight at her. True to form, he didn't even glance my direction as he passed.

"Charity!" he said.

Charity smugly tossed back her dark hair. She always looked smug when cute guys talked to her.

"Charity," he repeated. "Man, I thought you were Jacqueline." My nose wrinkled at that. How could Lane possibly mix me up with Charity?

"Are you kidding?" she asked. "You don't see me running from you, do you?"

Rude! True, but rude!

Lane chuckled, a low rumble in his throat. He chose that moment to lean heavily against the tree so that I could smell his Giorgio cologne. I stiffened. He was closer than I wanted him to be. It was only a matter of time before he saw me. "Yeah, she ran like a banshee when she saw me coming. She hates me."

No, he had it totally wrong. I was afraid of him. Big difference, but I couldn't defend myself properly. Fear was worse than hate in my opinion, and I was already miffed that he was onto me.

"Don't take it personally," Charity said. "Jack hates everybody."

I blew out slowly and found myself staring wistfully at Rambo House. Christian walked past the front window into the living room. I recognized his tall, athletic build. His scruffy brown hair looked scruffier than usual. He had probably just woken up. If he even knew what was happening . . . well, he would never say things like that behind my back. He'd say them to my face, and he would probably get away with it because he'd say them with his sweet charm.

It took all my self-control not to pull out from my hiding spot while I listened to Charity and Lane expound on my personality flaws. I just couldn't understand how a guy who thought I was such an idiot could like me in the first place. His affection must have finally started fading.

"Most likely she's running down her poor HE brothers," Charity said, smiling. "She's head of the Christian fan club." I stifled a snort. I was through with being a number. There was no way I'd be part of that entourage of females that followed blindly after Christian. I had better things to do with my time . . . like annoy him.

"Does she spend a lot of time there?" he asked.

"Oh yeah. I don't know why her HE brothers put up with her."
Insulting, but effective. I bit my lip before I could retort. It was best to
make it look like I was interested in someone at Rambo House.
"Britton can't stand her," she added.

I almost choked on that one. I happened to know someone Britton
disliked even more.

"Yeah, well, Britton has the same problem she has," Lane said.
Where was this guy's loyalty? Wasn't he part of Britton's merry band
of Bitter Boys? At least, he was until he . . . until he started breaking
from his secure bitterness to chase me. It was just another turnoff. He
really couldn't win no matter what he did.

Charity giggled. "What, he thinks the world is against him too?"

That was the last straw. Britton was nothing like me, and as much
as I liked to listen to myself being insulted, I had to escape. I took a
brave step towards the Rambo House bushes.

"I would say she's more afraid of the world," Lane mused in true
philosophical fashion.

It took all my social self-preservation not to turn around and show
them just how unafraid I was until his next words changed my mind.
"You play EverQuest, Charity?"

I chose that moment to break free, knowing they'd probably look up
and see me. The odds were against me, but that wasn't going to stop me
from trying to beat them. I dove for the bushes and waited, but they
kept talking casually. After a moment of low crouching, I took the side
path until I found an opening by the driveway. My back was stiff, but I
heard no shouts of discovery or giggles from Charity. I walked swiftly
across the cracked pavement and then, even more casually, strode
through the open weeds, my heart beating heavily against my chest.

"Jacqueline's not a video game girl." I heard the last remnants of
Charity's words trail behind me. "She doesn't have the motor skills
for it."

I grinned wickedly. Charity was a goner. He would ask her out
instead of me. My radar was sending out all the danger signals, and
just as Lane began, I barged into Rambo House without even
knocking.

Freedom! Safety! Sorta. I've always known that I would get what I
deserved in the end, but little did I know that this was the pivotal

moment. You see, I'd never met my match until now . . . or at least I didn't know that I had met my match until now. Okay, now I'm not making sense.

Let me explain. It all started with a wager, though I thought these kinds of melodramatic things only happened in the movies. You know those wagers that characters make in chick flicks and Shakespearean plays? I never believed in them . . . until it happened to me.

Chapter 2

Charity should begin at home,
but should not stay there.
—Phillip Brooks

Tuesday, June 16th, early afternoon

"Help me!" I cried.

I shoved the door shut behind me and locked it, sliding on the chain for good measure. Then I sniffed. There was a nasty stench of fresh paint. I turned and saw Christian staring at me with calm hazel eyes. He was always so composed in the face of danger. Or mabe he was just used to females and their strange ways. Except for his slightly crooked smile, he didn't even seem fazed by my dramatic entrance. He had been changing stations on the radio. Christian had a gift for finding the perfect song, and he flipped past Foo Fighters and Filter until he found something satisfactory: "Here Comes Your Man," by the Pixies.

Garbage. Christian already knew why I was there. I started trying to explain myself, but the only words that came out were somewhat garbled. "They're after me!"

"They?" He crossed his arms across his white T-shirt. It had some band logo on the front, but I rarely recognized the bands he liked. He was covered in off-white paint, so he obviously wasn't too partial to the band. His loose-fitting khaki cut-offs completed his slacker look. "Who are 'they,' Jacks?"

All of them. Now I was in even more trouble than before. Too late I noticed the sheets of plastic draped across the room. Empty paint cans were stacked all over the place, and I realized that I was stuck against the door with nowhere to go.

"They—the guys, I mean—are after me . . . just one guy actually," I stuttered.

"And you don't like it?" he asked. My eyes narrowed. He thought this was funny. "Weren't you going to help us paint?" I had completely forgotten that I had stood them up.

"Excuse me." A greasy redhead pushed past me, rudely unlocking the door to let himself out. He was one of Britton's Bitter Boys. They were everywhere. What was this, a ward activity? Members of our ward wandered back from the kitchen into the foyer, through the living room, into the game room. The living room looked huge because the furniture was all stacked in the kitchen. Forget calling the place Rambo House, it was a regular Rameumptom house, complete with chandelier.

Christian turned back to his painting, dipping his paintbrush in the off-white paint. "So what happened? Did you stand the guy up?" He kept his expression neutral, but I could tell he was trying not to laugh.

I knew what he was getting at, but they had obviously found replacements. I pulled away from the door, still not willing to let my guard down. "I didn't stand you up. I'm just a little late, that's all."

"You going by standard Kolob time now, Jacks?"

"Very funny." I picked my way past Christian, only reaching his shoulder. I'm five feet four inches, well, five feet six inches with the help of platform shoes. Christian smelled strongly of paint. It was smeared in his dark hair, and a line streaked carelessly across his chiseled cheekbone and spattered against his receding hairline.

The boys of Rambo House were trying to get a break on rent. The first on their landlord's list of demands was painting the walls an off-white cream, though it was mostly Britton's idea. Despite his grumbling, I was sure Britton was having the time of his life ordering his minions around, wherever that monster was in this monster of a house.

He had to be somewhere. There was a good showing from the Relief Society. Several of them rushed past me with annoyed glances. The guys at Rambo House always had a large female following. Christian wasn't like the other guys, though. He had grown up in an entire family of girls with the exception of one younger brother on a mission, and he was trained to be the perfect man. Girls were all over him, but he never did anything about it. That was the one flaw in his training. He spent most of his time with his *friends* who were girls, namely me, the ward burnt girl, and Maggie, the best gal pal ever.

He was actually kind of a closet nerd, but I'm not dissing him. It isn't as if I've never considered us an item before. I actually have plenty of times, but it could never go anywhere. Everyone has a Christian in their life . . . the guy that you don't want to mess up the friendship with by dating.

At least, I think that was my reason for not pursuing Christian, although I knew it was different for him. He was a safe guy because he knew me too well to make a move. I guess you could say we took advantage of our safeness, which allowed us to . . . uh . . . hang out. Save the lectures. I know I'm caught.

I headed for the side window. "You've got more than enough people helping you."

"But no one with your expertise, Picasso." It was completely tongue-in-cheek, and he watched me with a curled lip. Christian sweet-talked everyone. He was going to be a shrink so he knew what made people tick, especially me. "Free pizza for everyone who helps," he added offhandedly.

"Really?" *Would I actually get a decent lunch today?*

"Nope."

I frowned, but now I would look selfish if I didn't help. That's probably how he got such an army of do-gooders in the first place. I stiffened when I saw the service project idol on the sheet-covered bookcase. "The service idol," I grumbled. That's what we called them. There were a couple of them floating around the Rainbow Villa and Deluxe complexes—ugly little DI miniatures glued onto stands.

They were the brainchild of the elders quorum, which meant they came from Britton. The rules went like this: if you were stuck with the service idol, you had to hit your neighbors with a senseless act of charity and dump the idol on them to continue the circle of love. It was so unlike Britton, but it was beginning to make sense. He had known he'd need help renovating Rambo House, so he pulled a Tom Sawyer and tricked everyone into working for him.

"Getting more free stuff I see. You've got a gift for it," I said to Christian.

He shook his head. "It's a curse."

Actually, it was the ward scandal. The Rambo House landlord never picked up rent. I mean, why should he come around when that meant he had to fix up the place? So he steered clear. Sure, the place was ready to be condemned, but that didn't stop the Rambo boys from living here. Only this year they'd made a mistake, thanks to Britton's interior designing ways.

They started making repairs, from the hole in the roof to the washer in the basement. Britton wanted everything to be perfect. You would think he was metro with such a calling, but no, he was very manly . . . except when he was being obsessive-compulsive. He'd kill me if he ever heard me say such a thing, which was why I always did.

Christian acted the part of the handyman, and due to his extreme luck (some would call it charm) he always got a free deal, whether it was connections to doting grandmothers, schmoozing with ladies at DI, or dumpster diving. They had scored a dishwasher that didn't quite work, an air conditioner that I would die for since it was a hundred degrees outside, a piano for the Monsieur that someone had left there, and donated couches in tasteful hues of purple and blue.

They had been living there for months, and besides paying a few utilities, everything had been free of charge until the manager snuck by and noticed the place had been miraculously repaired. He was overjoyed when he realized he was free to demand rent, especially back rent. Britton and Christian handled the negotiations—hours and hours of shouting and accusations, with the Monsieur practicing the piano as a soft backdrop behind them—until finally they worked out a deal with the landlord. They would fix the place up to BYU housing standards in exchange for the months of free rent, *and* if the manager remembered, he would pick up a measly hundred bucks from each of them starting in the fall. Not too bad.

"You'd better not be taking the expense out of the ward budget," I mumbled, throwing my stack of flyers next to the service idol.

Christian scowled. "Garbage, what kind of monsters do you think we are?"

I shrugged, looking out the window. I couldn't quite see, so I stood on my tiptoes, using my wedge heels as stilts. I squinted. Were Charity and Lane still out there? There were some figures in the distance. I put my hand on the wall to keep my balance and pulled closer to the window. Suddenly I smelled the paint even stronger than I had before. *Oh no!* I scrambled away from the wall, seeing the paint all over my hands. "Ooh!" I gasped.

Christian's voice invaded my thoughts. "So who are you running from now?"

"No one." I shut the curtains and grimaced at the incriminating white hand mark on the somber drapes. Britton would kill me—or he'd take it out on his roommates. What had possessed them to leave the curtains up while painting? I hid my hand behind my back.

"You said a guy was after you," Christian reminded me. "You only come over when you're running away from someone."

"Whatev—"

But before I could get it out, Christian was saying it with me, "—ever," he finished.

My eyes narrowed. "Ooh." His voice carried along with mine, and I just clenched my mouth tightly until I couldn't resist opening it again. "Excuse me," we said with the same amount of emphasis. I gasped. Who was making fun of who here?

I leaned against the wall and dragged myself down it. As far as I could see, I was surrounded, which meant I was stuck in here. Christian's eyebrow shot up and I gasped, feeling the paint on my neck. It was all over me now, and I leaned my head back in irritation, hitting my head against the wall. *Oh no, my hair!* It brushed against the bottom of the curtains, and I knew I had left my mark.

Christian tightly clenched the paintbrush in his hand. "What are you doing?" He started making his way to my side, dodging the slick plastic with his bare feet in the process.

"No." I stood up, trying to stop him from looking out the window. He stepped back from my paint covered hands. I quickly realized my advantage and thrust my hands out to him. "Unclean," I shouted. "Unclean! Don't you dare try to get past me!"

"Put down the hands." He lifted his paintbrush in defense. "Jacqueline. I don't want to do this, but . . ." I knew that I was going to get painted. I squinted, weighing my odds. As always, they weren't good. He was much too big for me to come out the winner in the end.

"Okay, fine. I'll tell you," I squeaked. "Lane Bryant's after me, okay?"

"Lane Bryant?" By the sound of his voice, I should've known something was up, but Christian was now in spy mode, and he pulled open the curtains before I could stop him. "Let me see." He glanced out the window with an amused grin. "Oh yes, Lane Bryant, here he comes now." He waved at him.

"What?" I ducked away from the window, even though there was really no chance of him seeing me. I couldn't see over Christian's broad shoulders anyway.

Christian turned to me with a dramatic look. He was one to take every opportunity to tease me; it was probably all that time spent growing up with sisters. "He's coming!" he exclaimed. "He's coming!"

"I need a place to hide." I caught sight of the Monsieur's piano. It was covered in plastic and had been shoved safely away from the wall, so there was enough room for me to wedge myself in and spare myself another painting. I squeezed behind it, cat burglar style, keeping my distance from the fresh paint.

Christian stared back out the window. "Mercy, you've got a whole army after you."

"Who else is out there?" I shouted.

"Calvin Klein and a whole army of Tommy Hilfiger's men. They're laying siege to the house!"

Besides the fact that this was starting to sound a little like *The Lord of the Rings*, he was also making no sense. "Those are clothing companies," I accused.

"Yeah, and so is Lane Bryant." He laughed. "Who are you running away from next? OshKosh B'Gosh? Gap, maybe?"

Lane Bryant? That's why it sounded so familiar. Christian was right. I had messed up a couple of consonants. I leaned my head back and laughed, the kind of laugh that makes your insides hurt and turns guys off. I kicked my legs. "Garbage," I said between shouts of laughter. "You never take me seriously!"

He smiled smugly, and I realized my mistake; we had made a pact never to say that forbidden word. "What did you just say?" he asked.

My laughter cut short. "Garbage," I muttered finally.

"Garbage? That's all you can say with a whole army after you?" He pointed to the pink rubber band on my wrist, and I sighed, snapping it. My goal was to cut down on my faux swears, and it wasn't going very well.

"Yeah, well you said it earlier," I said.

"When?"

"Right before you told me that you weren't a monster."

He rolled his eyes and pulled the ugly rubber band around his wrist. "Mercy, I guess I've said stranger things."

"Yeah, like 'Mercy.' What was that?"

Christian smirked. "You stole that one from me too." I had picked up a lot of things from him, including the rubber band. "His name is Raine Lyon by the way," Christian said abruptly. "He's actually not a bad guy." He kneeled next to the bench, and I got a close-up view of his hazel eyes.

I've always been an eye girl, but this really was unfair. He had such amazing eyes with thick lashes and a freckle under one eye accentuating how cool they were. That's when I had to remind myself that guys were nothing but trouble—except Christian, of course, who was perfectly harmless in every way. Maybe that's what made him more dangerous than the rest.

Actually, I really couldn't figure out why we were such good friends. He was an angel, at least compared to me. He was normally very calm, and I wasn't. He was very confident, and once again that wasn't my strong point. But I guess that's the biggest lesson my friends have taught me: you don't have to be perfect for people to like you.

"Did you tell him that you weren't interested?" he asked me point-blank. It was galling that Christian knew exactly what was happening.

"Practically."

"What's that supposed to mean?"

"I told him in every way I possibly could without actually telling him." At his accusing gaze, I threw my hands up. "Look, I know guys say they like it when girls tell them up front, but they don't *really* like it, and then I feel bad because they ignore me after that, so instead I try to make excuses, but they see right through it, and then I try to make them not like me, but then they think I'm a jerk."

"Who's they?" Christian asked mildly.

"Everyone," I spouted.

"So it's you against the world then?"

I smiled at his attempt to make me see how ridiculous I was being. "Who better to take it on?"

Christian leaned back on his heels. "Oh boy." I wasn't sure if he was saying that because of me or because the radio was playing Backstreet Boys. He peered closer at my hair. My hand went up to the red mass. I was sure it was skunk-striped by now, but that wasn't what Christian was grimacing at. His gaze was fixed just above my forehead. Without so much as an explanation, he gave me his paintbrush and reached for whatever had caught his attention.

So you're going to think I'm a crazy for noticing this, but he has those hands. You know, the kind that are strong enough to palm a basketball but gentle enough to cradle a baby? Not that I was looking, but I flinched when he pulled a bobby pin free. It had been hanging on by just a thread of my hair.

"Britton hates these things." He held it up for my inspection.

"He hates anything that reminds him of women."

"Well, you haven't had to listen to the sermons."

"Oh yes I have." I was just glad that he wasn't around. And speaking of people I didn't want to face . . . I glanced at their whiteboard. They had taken it off the wall, and it was now leaning against the piano. Recent phone messages were still on it, including several feminine scrawls meant for the Monsieur from the plethora of girls who had *just happened to drop by* and found him missing. It only meant that he was practicing the piano at school or was with another girl. Either way, it meant nothing to me. Things had been the same when we were dating.

I recognized a particularly familiar scrawl. "Mercy," I said. "Maggie's at it again." Of all the girls on that board, she was the only one who had no ulterior motives. She was so different from the rest of us. I smiled when I read the message under the Monsieur's name. "Maggie gave the Monsieur *one* cookie for his birthday, huh?"

Christian looked sheepish. It was obvious that *one* had been scribbled in and an *s* had been smudged off the word *cookie*. Knowing Maggie, more than a dozen cookies had probably been delivered. Unfortunately, she made the mistake of leaving them with a bunch of hungry roommates. Once the last cookie was gone, I was sure the message would be gone too.

"So, who's all here?" I asked.

"Who do you want to be here?" Christian asked.

"Is, uh, *you know who* here?"

Christian dimpled. "Ah, you mean the one we don't speak of?"

"Yeah. That one."

He gave me a maddening smile, and I felt my stomach clench. There are a few memories that haunt me, and a few that make me smile; unfortunately, a lot of them have happened at Rambo House. I wished they hadn't. How did the Monsieur get past my defenses? Yeah, he was tall and willowy and hotter than sin. Well, he was a security guard at the library, so that should tell you everything. What got me wasn't that he turned out to be a jerk. The problem was that I had actually fallen for him. I wanted to be free of those memories, but even now, just looking at Christian, I thought of the Monsieur.

What were the odds? I'd better get started on that article, because I had more than enough stories exemplifying my bad luck. Who would think that the guys I loved most would live in the same house as my ex? Maybe it was because I spent more time here than he did.

Christian must have sensed my uneasiness, and he put me out of my misery. "Actually, I haven't seen the Monsieur lately. Have you?"

It was a loaded question. I shrugged. "Either the wicked take the truth to be hard or the wicked don't check their e-mail."

He laughed. "Did you chew him out?"

"Not exactly. I just asked him why he was dating other girls when he said he needed a time-out from the dating scene to concentrate on school."

Christian brought his eyes heavenward. "He fed you that line? He wants a time-out? Is that how he broke it off?"

"And the stupid thing was that I believed it. I can't believe I felt sorry for him. Me! I wanted to get back together with him even, as soon as he figured things out!"

His nose wrinkled. "Don't go there. Like a dog to its vomit, kid, like a dog to its vomit."

I bit my lip. He was quoting Proverbs, very Christian-like, and I sighed. "Well, someday I'll find a man with guts enough to love me.

I hate that he was such a coward." I gestured wildly with my hands. I didn't have to tell Christian who I was talking about. I was always talking about the Monsieur. "He was so afraid of commitment, it took him out and crushed him. I hated his fears more than he hated them. They tore us apart." And that's why he was such a jerk . . . because he wouldn't be with me.

Christian cupped his chin in his palm, leaning across the piano bench towards me. "Why can't you just forget him? Go after those other guys."

I shook my head. "The rebound's not working. I can't stand other guys . . . except you, of course."

"Of course," he whispered. He didn't believe me.

"Oh, how tender."

We glanced up like guilty mice who had been caught playing while the farmer's wife was out, or in my case, caught . . . *white handed*. I sat on my paint-covered hands. I'd recognize that deep-throated voice anywhere. It was full of bitter irony.

Chapter 3

Charity sees the need, not the cause.
—German Proverb

Tuesday, June 16th, midafternoon

Britton leaned casually against the door frame between the two living rooms like a panther poised for the kill. He was carrying something that looked like a plastic trident, and he rested it on his shoulder, his other hand in the pocket of his plaid Bermuda shorts. He was hot in every way: tall enough to stand out in a crowd, dark hair, dark eyes, muscular, angry—did I mention hot? Yeah. Too hot, too cold, too bad. What a waste. That's why I spent most of my time at odds with him. But he did fit in nicely with my safe guy posse because he was too bitter against women to make a move.

"Well, if it isn't your bitter half, Christian," I said in an overly bright voice. I knew that would get to Britton more than my acting angry.

Britton nodded at me. "As always, it's a pleasure, Sister Children." I sensed the dark sarcasm.

"Sister Childs," I corrected.

"That's grammatically incorrect, Sister Children."

"Well, Brother Britton doesn't exactly roll off the tongue either, but I still use it. Perhaps you'd prefer Bitter Britton?"

"No, Benevolent Britton suits me much better, I think." He took a good long look at my outfit of the day. "You look like a skater chick. Who are you? Avril Lavigne?"

I scowled. It was probably the blue Hurley skater shirt, my newest acquisition from the DI box. "How about we just call you Bratty Britton?" I said. He swung the trident, looking like the king of the sea, and I decided to get him back. "What's with the plastic trident, sailor?"

"I found it in the basement with a sandcastle bucket. It's a pitchfork."

"Appropriate."

Britton tried not to crack a smile. He opted for prowling around the room instead. Despite our constant battles, I liked him a lot. It was too bad he was so messed up. This Bitter Boy had so much going for him. He immediately interrupted his prowling and gasped, pointing to the ground with the trident. "What's this?"

"What?"

Britton picked up a bobby pin lying on the plastic and his gaze flew to my head. I tried not to grin too hard. He just shook his head, not knowing what to think of this strange girl that wouldn't leave his life. Well, I didn't know what to think of me either.

Christian just rolled his eyes at me. "You see what I'm talking about?"

"You're leaving these things all over the place," Britton said. "I'll thank you to keep them in your hair from now on or you'll be refused admittance to the Rambo home."

I didn't even refute the sentence. I just turned to Christian, who was smiling at me in wry amusement. He then surprised me by winking. Christian and Britton were complete opposites, yet they actually liked each other. "Remind me why you two are friends again?" I asked.

"I ask Christian the same thing about you every night," Britton cut in cruelly. He swung the trident like it was a baton. "That is, when I'm not listening to the extensive list of complaints about you from Maggie."

I sucked in my breath, but not for the reasons that you might think. Britton and Christian's friendship paralleled mine and Maggie's; the bad jaded roommate partnered with the good service-oriented one, both trying to protect the other from the big bad world in completely different ways. "Stay away from Maggie," I said. She couldn't handle him. I could . . . most of the time.

"I'd like to comply," Britton said, "but she can't get enough of me."

What a joke. Maggie was oblivious to all males. "Maggie's not hanging out anymore, so forget ever seeing her again!"

Britton only snorted at that. "That hasn't stopped me before."

Before I could retort, I heard the dirty sound of a 900 cc motor, and I turned in one motion, instinct ruling my thoughts. I listened to the low rumble as it came closer. I stood up.

"What is it?" Christian asked dryly. He already knew.

"A Harley Sportster, streamlined model made in the fifties."

Britton rolled his eyes. "Well, looks like you've found the perfect man."

"I don't want him. I want his bike." I stared out the window. It was grey and black with a chrome finish. "It's a classic." I squinted, not able to see that far. "I want a better look."

Britton motioned emphatically at the door. "Then leave."

"You'd like that," I said, "but I can't."

"Why?"

I hesitated. There was no way I could tell him why I was stuck at Rambo House. First of all, he would think I was trying to brag about my conquests, and second of all, he would give away my position. Britton walked languidly to my side, staring out the window. He suddenly guffawed. "You're running away from Charity? I can't believe it."

Wrong deduction. I shrugged. "So?"

"Is this some sort of queen bee syndrome?" Britton always wanted the latest dirt, and I was ready to give it to him if it meant throwing him off the hunt.

"Sure." This was actually a perfect time to educate these boys. "Look, I know what she's up to. Chalk it up to female intuition or even female superstition if you want. A girl knows a girl, you see." I turned to see their reaction to my warnings. All I saw was Britton's blank look and Christian's knowing one. He knew exactly what I had been running from, so nothing I said would convince either of them right now. Britton just scratched his head with the end of the plastic trident. "Uh, so anyway, I'm not going out there."

Christian picked up the bucket of paint and set it down by my feet. "You need an out." He nodded to the wall. "Make yourself useful."

I dipped the brush in the paint and attacked the wall with vigor. Britton set the trident down by the piano bench and picked up the whiteboard. Giving me a mischievous glance, he put down a tally mark next to a whole group of tally marks. "Hey, what are you doing?" I asked.

"I'm just keeping a tally of all the hearts you break, Red."

I scowled. Britton always used redheaded jokes, so that really wasn't what I was scowling at. He knew exactly who called me Red, and he let me believe that I had fooled him. "I haven't broken any hearts!" I said.

"Hogwash." My head lifted. I've never heard anyone say that who wasn't old. "You're a menace to the male society," Britton hissed as a final insult. "Aren't you due for another birthday? I believe you're getting up there? And with no ring? What will the parents say?" He clucked his tongue.

"Why you . . ." I was really too flabbergasted to get anything out. It was forbidden to make fun of girls for not being married. The problem was he was getting better at teasing me because he knew what got a good reaction from me, and unfortunately for me, I was a reactor—a nuclear one. I tried to play it cool. "Hey, this one wasn't my fault. It's Maggie's. She's too nice! I just wish people would quit mixing me up with her. Those cookies! They were from her, not from me! I've been framed!"

"Yes, very tragic, though maidens in distress are always attractive. Perhaps that's why you're so irresistible. You're a mess."

"Yeah, Jacqueline. If you've got anyone to blame, it's yourself."

I turned and saw Trevor Sykes. He was smiling slightly, looking very angelic, like a blond Peter Pan. He was never found without a big belt buckle and tight pants, even when painting—not because he was a cowboy, but because he wanted to be an alternative rocker thug, probably to spite his sweet ways. He was a safe guy, pretty much because he was harmless in every way. He had plenty of chances to make moves and didn't. Plus, he was a preemie—sorry, girls not an RM yet. Safer and safer.

"Yeah, and how is your dating life?" I retorted.

He put his hands to his hips. "Where should I start? Once I asked a girl out. She said no. The end."

"So then quit giving me a hard time."

"She was a man-eater, just like you! We heard you were flirting up a storm with Raine."

"Who told you that?" I demanded.

Trevor remained silent, protecting their sources.

"Was it Rusty?" Rusty was the only one with access to that kind of information. He was engaged to my cousin Jade, and he was the biggest gossip in Rambo House.

"As your HE brothers," Britton said, "we feel a certain responsibility for you." He put the plastic trident behind his neck, resting his head against it.

"Where's Rusty?" Taken guys were always safe—they couldn't make a move—but that didn't make them completely trustworthy. "Is he here?"

"I'll give you one guess where he's at," Christian said, calmly painting. He was used to our constant bickering, and I had just assumed that he was tuning us out. He wasn't.

"Uh, he's at church?" I guessed, "Repenting of his big-mouthed ways?"

"He's at your place, where do you think?" Britton muttered.

"He's being sacrificed to the wedding gods," Christian said. "His days are numbered." Rusty and Jade had only three weeks, to be precise.

"The redheads are always the first to be sacrificed," Britton said. I pushed my hair back and met his eyes angrily. Britton was really getting into this, wasn't he?

Even Trevor was enjoying the fight. "We made a marriage wall for Rusty. You should see it."

"You didn't!"

"Yep." Britton indicated it with his trident, pointing to the pictures on the wall in the game room. I squinted at it and leaned forward to get a better view. "Normally, I would never allow such drivel on my wall, but I felt this was completely appropriate."

I sucked in my breath when I recognized my articles from my love advice column hanging all over their wall, along with all the cheesy wedding advertisements they could find. "Take those down!" I shouted.

"Our little prodigal," Britton said. "I mean prodigy. I do find it interesting that you wax so eloquently on love when in all reality you have no love life."

"Look, the magazine gives me the assignment, and I write the articles. It's called building your résumé."

"Is everything résumé to you?" Trevor asked. He seemed shocked. "Even love?"

"Well, it's certainly not the pay." I stared at one of the articles.

I had always been very right-brained, which meant that I was good at everything that would never make me money: art, acting, writing. For now I was holding out in the trenches of BYU housing for the summer with no idea what I was going to do in the fall. I was taking random minimum wage jobs while building my résumé kingdom, but let's face it—I was more likely to win the lottery, get hit by lightning, get eaten by sharks, or get married than make money at what I wanted to do.

I flicked the article with my finger. "I only get fifteen bucks for each of these, painful as they are to write." I didn't like bearing my soul to the world, even though I did it with little urging.

"As painful as they are to read, you mean." Britton was relentless. He turned to one of the articles and read it to the room. Several people from our ward continued to walk in and out of the room like we didn't exist.

"'Since man first drew breath to ask girls out,'" Britton read, "'the war has been waged. The cloudy stench of cologne fills the air. The pencil lines have been drawn. The battle of the sexes is on. This is no dating game— this is a dating war. Make your bishop, your momma, your grandma proud, for you are on a mission, men. A mission to get married!'"

"That seems a little sarcastic," Trevor said.

I crossed my arms across my stomach. "It's called satire, and it was aimed at you."

Trevor smiled. "Really? I didn't get it."

"That's because it's too deep," I said, biting down a grin. He had walked right into that one.

"I'm sorry," Britton said, easily coming to his aid. "I didn't realize these were so figurative. What does it symbolize exactly?"

"Idiots like you."

Christian laughed behind us.

"Then this one must be aimed at you, Jacqueline." Britton pointed brutally to my "Get Over the Breakup" article. I tensed as he read. "'Even if you turn that frog into a prince and he dumps you for a prettier princess,'" he read, "'or you've been cursed by some evil witch, don't let that stop you from getting out of your boring tower.'" He glanced at me. "Why don't you take your own advice?"

"I never use my powers for evil."

"Oh, yes you do, but that's beside the point. Oh, here's my favorite, the 'Leave Him Wanting More' series. The girls of *Happy Valley* eagerly followed this mindless saga for at least five issues." He pointed to the articles decorated with little pink hearts. "'Set him at ease,'" he read. "'Make him believe that you're not a threat. Though you visit often enough, keep your visits short. Leave him wanting more.'"

Christian glanced at me. "Is that what you're doing with Britton?"

We both turned red. "I'll never make that mistake," I said.

"Even if she tries," Britton said.

Trevor sat on the edge of their beautiful couch. "If you know so much about guys, Jack, why aren't you married?"

"You just answered your own question, buddy," I said.

"Oh, she's made it very clear what she thinks about guys." Britton widely indicated the rest of the articles, using the trident as a pointer. I had written a lot of that love advice after the breakup. They were a little bitter.

"Oh, I understand," Trevor said finally. "You're an elitist, Jack, aren't you?"

"What? No! What are you talking about? An elitist?" I had a little bit of an idea, but Britton made the meaning abundantly clear.

"Well, let's see," he said. "If you know how to catch a man, as your articles suggest, and you haven't yet, then maybe it's because you're just too picky."

"Whatever."

"Tell that to your unlucky swains. How many do you have now, five? Six? Seven?" I winced and he nodded. "Let's examine our first specimen, shall we? Take this poor barnacle outside, Raine Lyon. Does he have severe hygiene problems?"

I steadied myself, getting ready for the fight. "No."

"He's already married and he wants you to be his next wife?" I shut my mouth firmly. "He's as dumb as a box of hammers?" He pointed brutally at me. "Picky!"

"Picky, picky," Trevor joined him, throwing his hand out to my mouth like he was carrying a fake microphone. "Admit it." Suddenly, I realized that the Bitter Boys' numbers had increased. Spencer Little, their Maori roommate, was at their side calling me picky too, and he didn't even know what we were talking about. His big brown eyes were full of accusation.

"Spencer, you lemming," I accused.

He was a giant of a man from New Zealand, recruited to play football at BYU. Though he had lost his scholarship because of grades, he still wore his football jerseys. He pointed a bulky finger to another one of my articles, reading the tagline, "'Don't let people call you a lemming or you'll lose your focus,'" he said.

I groaned. "I'm sorry, you can't say that. It's copyrighted material."

"Everything I say is copyrighted!" Britton said. "I was the one who said that in the first place! I was the one who even pointed out that you had hit your quarter-life crisis that you so kindly devoted all your 'girl power' articles to."

"Everything we say will make headlines someday," Christian said behind us, letting his brush drip paint everywhere. "Get used to it."

"Picky, picky," Spencer parroted. He lumbered over to the white-board and erased Maggie's cookie message completely. The last birthday cookie had been eaten. Poor Monsieur. I grinned. Spencer came back to me and put his muscular arm around me like the playful bear he was. Yeah, another safe guy. Even if he made a move, he didn't mean anything by it, which threw a lot of girls for a loop. He was the reason behind many of the Rambo House's female guests.

Spencer glanced up at a ship placed carefully on the bookshelf in the corner next to the service idol. It was the USS *Constitution*. Christian had spent months putting Old Ironsides together, but due to one prank too many, the back mast drooped limply. Spencer waved dramatically at it. "You're like a ship. You're not ready to set sail yet."

I think he was trying to be kind, but Britton smiled slowly, suddenly inspired by some evil. "Yes, but what kind of ship is she?

She's a little faster than a tugboat." My stomach dropped, and I knew I was in for it.

"And speedboats creep her out," Christian pointed out. "She's afraid of a falling out."

"No, she's just afraid she won't fall out," Britton contradicted. "Riding off into the sunset is just too much of a commitment."

"That makes her a cruise liner, taking everyone for a ride," Spencer suggested happily.

"Ooh!" I pulled away from him. "No, that's you," I accused. "You're the heartbreaker!"

"The *Love Boat*," Trevor said. "She's out to sea."

"Well, she's cheesy enough to be the *Love Boat*," Britton agreed.

"I learned it from the best," I retorted.

"How about the *Titanic*?" Spencer mused.

"Are you calling me fat?" I tried to put him to shame. I should've known it wouldn't work.

Britton swung the trident like a demented monkey. "The *Titanic* after the shipwreck, sunk to the bottom of the sea, covered in barnacles."

"Is that your problem?" Trevor asked kindly. "The barnacles hang out with you and the other guys think you're not interested?"

I acted like none of this was getting to me. "Nice try, guys," I said.

"How about a ferry?" Spencer asked. "Everyone's invited to the party."

"I'm not a player."

"A houseboat, since you never leave the docks," Trevor said.

My eyes narrowed. For supposedly being a nice guy, that jab almost hurt, but so far they really weren't getting anywhere until Britton leaned against the door, taking me in with a measuring glance. "The USS *Constitution*," he said. It was probably what he had been getting at all along. "Old Ironsides herself."

I turned on him. "What?" Was he referring to my age?

By the self-satisfied smirk, I could tell that he knew he had gotten to me. "A historical icon," he drawled for my benefit, "rotting sails caused by years of neglect, going nowhere, worse than a sunken ship because it's useless."

I could have killed him for that. "Give me that!" I stole his stupid plastic pitchfork and tried to pound him with it.

He easily dodged me. "Old Ironsides," he taunted. The thing about Britton was that he had Simon Cowell syndrome. He didn't mean half the things he said. Well, I'd still get him back!

"You're a submarine, sneaky and low," I retorted.

"You're twenty-six and not married."

My heart sunk at that. Well yeah, I *was* old, at least in Provo. I was gradually coming to terms with the fact that I was no longer a student. The stern hand of graduation had just shoved me into a cruel and bitter world. I had always thought that I'd be happy to be set free, but that was when I actually thought that I'd make something of myself. Now it was becoming painfully clear that I wasn't going to . . . not yet. But that didn't mean that the hypocrite could make fun of me for it! He was just as old as I was. "You want a torpedo to the gut?" I shouted.

"Ah, sink me," he laughed. "Maybe, we'll submit *that* to your magazine?" Britton threatened between beatings. Beating him down wasn't working. He just laughed.

"Do that, and I put this place down as Rainbow House in the ward directory, you broken raft floating aimlessly in the ocean . . . with a hole . . . and sharks swimming . . ." I was so flustered I was drifting. "And I'm the shark and you're gonna get it!"

"Don't threaten the elders quorum president. I can assign you any home teacher I want."

I stilled and threw the trident down. "You're the *Good Ship Lollipop*. Suck on that."

"Nonsense." He held himself up proudly. "I'm simply the ward lighthouse, showing everyone the way."

What a joke. Britton always claimed he was helping me. He didn't like that I was broken. He didn't like that I was running from the world. He didn't like that I had changed after dating his roommate— that I was becoming just as bitter as he was. I wasn't sure how all of his sarcastic comments were supposed to help me, but strangely enough, he thought they would. Yeah, I had a soft spot for him too.

"That's a laugh," I said. "If you're the lighthouse, it's only to spot-light us when we've already crashed into the rocks. That way you can point and laugh. You would think the lighthouse was beyond reproach, but I don't see you dating anyone, you ferry."

"Jacqueline!" Christian was trying to make us be nice to each other. He was staring at us like we had lost our minds, and I guess we had.

"You ferry," I amended, "because you won't stick to one harbor, you hanger-outer, non-dater woman-hater, too afraid to pick up the phone and ask a girl out."

Britton shrugged. He always took criticism well, probably because he did it to himself all the time. "According to church doctrine, gambling is forbidden. Sorry."

"Guys, guys, girl," Christian was trying to distract us from killing each other. "Okay, pick a number between one and ten." This was his favorite thing to do. Britton and I were silent. "Do it or you have to listen to me sing."

"Ten," I said angrily.

Christian pressed ten on the CD player then he turned to Britton. "Your turn, rabble-rouser, pick."

Britton looked mischievous. "Six."

Christian pressed six. "Okay, this song is dedicated to both of you." The strains of hard guitar filled the air. It was catchy until I realized what song it was. It was the Less Than Jake punk version of Dave Cassidy's "I Think I Love You." It was like my mom playing "Love at Home" on the piano whenever I fought with my siblings.

"I think I love you, so what am I so afraid of?" What an opportune, inopportune moment! I liked the song despite the fact that Britton had specifically picked the song to tease me. That thought made my hands itch to pick up the trident again. I sat heavily down on the couch instead. The plastic squeaked beneath me. How long would I be stuck inside with these maniacs?

The door opened and I flinched, expecting another arch-nemesis. I wasn't disappointed. Who else would be found at a guys' apartment? She must have dumped her most recent admirer, but it was hard to tell for sure.

"Ah, sweet Charity," Britton said. (Parents, you know you're asking for trouble when you name your kids after one of the virtues. Every kid rebels against the name, and this particular name was cursed, although you would never know it just by looking at her.) All the Rambo guys backed up, trying to act somewhat respectable for the Relief Society president. Britton gave her a brisk salute. "Her Royal Highness," he said.

"At ease," she said. I couldn't help but notice how classy she was compared to me. Her light skirt fluttered around her calves.

Britton dropped his hand dramatically. "Now all the queen bees are here," he noted in a much too casual voice. "The Relief Society ringleader and the ape leader."

Charity ignored him, her gaze raking across the room, taking in the disorganized service project. She saw me sitting on the couch. "It looks like you're working hard, dear." Her soft voice always made me cringe. Besides Britton, she had no such effect on the guys. She sighed. "It's a good thing I moved into this ward. It needs a lot of work."

"Yes, it is a surprise to see you here," I said. "And hanging out at a guy's house even?"

Charity was left with no doubt of my meaning, though I'm sure the guys were. "Well, guys are so laid-back. They're much more fun to hang out with than girls." She shrugged.

"I wonder why," I murmured into the wall. She was the kind who hated her own.

"Girls are so catty."

I smiled, knowing exactly where that comment was directed. "Oh, I couldn't agree more." Charity was queen of the cats. While I ran from the guys, she led them merrily along, and that's why I had to protect my boys from her. I couldn't stand by and see my friends get hurt by her the same way I had been hurt by the Monsieur. You might argue that everyone gets hurt, but not on my watch.

She had suddenly caught sight of the marriage wall. I winced when she strolled into the game room to look. She read articles silently to herself while I squirmed. She suddenly burst out laughing. "This is priceless."

"What are you laughing at?" Trevor asked, pleased. Of course he was pleased, they were getting attention from a beautiful girl.

"The wall."

"Yeah, she's a little crazy," I explained to the room in general.

"These are so revealing." Charity turned to me with a Cheshire Cat grin. "What wonderful advice, Jacqueline. Secrets to a man's heart. Did this work for you, I wonder?"

There was an awkward silence until Trevor said, "She's had her chances, she just hasn't taken them."

"She wants to find the right guy," Spencer quickly supplied for my benefit. I was grateful that he had stood up for me.

You're probably wondering why I have so much loyalty from these guys. I mean, why on earth would they even care about such a burnt girl? Simple. I told you that I spent more time with them than I did with my former boyfriend. Who do you think helped them with their girl problems? In fact, I have my suspicions that they thought I was a boy until I broke up with the Monsieur. I guess I thought I was one of them too until the Monsieur tried to kick me out of the club.

I looked up to see Charity staring at me. "I suppose some people write about life, some people live it," she mused.

Before she could say anymore, Christian quickly cut in. Rescuing me was second nature to him. "Charity, are you playing on the coed softball team?" I tried not to squirm even more at the change of topic. His calling was intramural sports coordinator, and he had been trying to get me to play on the team forever. I was horrible at softball. I didn't even like to watch it, but if Charity played, I would have no choice but to try and show her up.

Charity smiled sweetly and then she tried to get me where it hurt worst. "Only if you're on the team," she told Christian.

He smiled. "Good, you're in."

I frowned, and she looked as pleased as a purring cat. "How was work?" she asked him. Christian worked at the BYU Bookstore busting shoplifters. He basically pretended to be a customer and trailed people in the bookstore like a stalker. I had always been tempted to come in and make things interesting for him. Apparently Charity had the same idea . . . and she was much more proactive than I was.

"Boring. Nobody's stealing anything."

"So, if I steal something," she said, "will you take me in, or out?"

Spencer laughed approvingly at her joke. I felt like I was surrounded by a traitorous studio audience. Christian just smiled. "Well, it depends on what you steal."

Oh garbage. I couldn't take any more of this. I stood up, knowing I'd have to give Christian a talk against squirrelly girls later. "I have to go, guys." I checked out the window, squinting for any figures in the distance. Nothing. Lane Bryant, or whatever his infernal name was, had disappeared. "See ya, peeps. It was interesting."

"Oh wait, Jacqueline," Charity called. "I was just wondering," she smiled with perfect rosebud lips. "Why on earth were you hiding behind that tree?"

I turned bright red. She had seen me? She had said all those mean things in front of me? On purpose? Mercy, how did I get myself out of this one? Christian watched me with an amused look. *Oh garbage.* He and Britton knew everything. I decided to play along. "What tree?" I asked.

Britton leaned back, thoroughly enjoying my humiliation. "How many trees do you normally hide behind?"

My eyes narrowed. "Why would I do such a thing?"

"I don't know," Charity said. "That's why I asked."

"Well, it was a beautiful day, although I don't know why I would hide if I saw you com—"

Christian interrupted me, knowing that I was probably going to dis Charity. "C'mon guys, can't a girl hide behind a tree without being heckled?"

Spencer's eyes went to his Valentine's Day card on the bookshelf. "Let's find out."

"Don't you dare!" I shouted at Spencer, but already he was running for the bookshelf. It was their favorite game to tease me, but I'd had enough heckling for one visit. "Put that down right now," I commanded, but it was no use. Spencer was already picking up the all-knowing heart card from the bookshelf. My HE brothers had gotten it for Valentine's Day. All you had to do was squeeze the heart on the card and it would answer "yes," "no," or "maybe." It was the meanest invention of all time. "Look, I don't have time for this. We'll do this when I get back." They groaned. They had all heard that one before.

"Will Jacqueline be back?" Spencer asked the heart. He squeezed it.

"No," it said in a sexy voice. Everyone laughed and I rolled my eyes. *Ooh!*

Britton took over. "Was Jacqueline hiding from someone behind that tree?"

"Yes."

"Excuse me!" I shouted.

"Was it a guy?" he asked.

"No."

I smiled smugly. "See! Shows how much you know!"

"Was it a man?" Charity piped up.

"Yes."

I glared. That was the problem with that thing. All you had to do was rephrase the question until you finally got the answer you wanted, which was what these guys always did. I don't know where Charity learned it, unless she had been spending more time here than I thought. My eyes stole nervously to Christian, but he didn't seem to be in her power yet.

Trevor stole the heart from Britton. "Is Jacqueline picky?" he asked. I gasped. He would tease me about that in front of Charity? He was supposed to be nice! What a poser!

"Maybe."

I breathed a sigh of relief, although I wished it had said "no" to vindicate me. Then I would have had the last laugh.

"Does she even have a heart?" he asked.

"No."

I grabbed it from him. "Now, I've got one," I said, trying to keep it from him. I held it tightly and accidentally set it off.

"Maybe."

Britton tried to pull it from my death grip. "Quit trying to steal my heart," I shouted. If anything, I thought that would make him stop mauling me, but it didn't.

"No. Maybe. Yes. Yes."

He unbent each finger from the card until he had it. I didn't care if I was bending the thing beyond recognition. "Ask how I'm still alive if I don't have a heart then!" I shouted.

Britton clicked his tongue. "Yes or no questions," he reminded me in a superior tone.

"Maybe she has a heart, but she just can't control it," Spencer suggested. That was *his* problem, but Britton pressed down on the heart anyway.

"Yes."

"So that's why I have to take preemptive measures," I said, trying to pull it back from Britton. "To stop myself from getting into more trouble."

"Yes."

"So there!" I shouted. "Even if I was hiding behind that tree from a *man*, which I'm not saying I was doing, I'm completely justified."

"Yes."

Now Britton was getting mad, which meant I was winning. Good, but it wouldn't be long until he mentioned the Monsieur the way things were going. "Is Jacqueline the USS *Constitution*?" he asked.

"Maybe."

I felt my face get red. That was low, and he knew it. Suddenly Britton was staring at the curtains, seeing the handprints. It didn't take him too long to see my hands were covered in paint. I met his accusing eyes defiantly and tried not to blink, but I couldn't stop thinking about how unfair this was. "Did Jacqueline—"

Once again Christian came to my rescue. "Will Jacqueline ever set sail into the great ocean of romance?" He dimpled at my enraged look and I pursed my lips. Some kind of rescue.

"Yes."

I don't know who winced more, Britton or me. I couldn't help myself. "Garbage!" Christian pointed at me and I mindlessly snapped my rubber band. I clenched my hands into fists. "I can't believe you guys." I stormed away from them. "I can't take this anymore."

And I really couldn't this time, but there was no way they would know that since I was always blowing off steam. But this time they had really gotten to me. I couldn't believe it.

"I thought that you were going to help paint," Christian said, trying not to laugh. He knew full well that I had had no intention of helping.

"I think she's done enough," Britton said, looking pointedly at the curtains.

I ripped open the door to escape, partly from Britton's wrath, but also from what I was feeling. It was one jab too many, and I felt my eyes welling up with tears. Too late I saw Britton draw back. He hated tears more than I hated pulling them out. Despite everything, he was really a softie, and he looked a little sheepish.

That only made me feel incredibly stupid, which in turn made me angry. I fought back the tears before anyone else saw them. If Christian saw, he wouldn't let me leave, and then I would be stuck here with my shame. And if the Monsieur caught me here after that—I had to escape with what pride I had left.

"Look, I've got institute business," I said hurriedly. Besides working on the ward directory, I was also the institute representative. Practically all of us went to institute in the summer. "I've got some calls to make, unless someone here wants to give the spiritual thought tonight." I turned quickly from them.

Charity just smiled at me, most likely glad to be rid of me so she could work her magic with my safe guy posse. "Don't worry," she told me mockingly. "I'm actually here to help."

I didn't like her predatory look, and I just hoped that she didn't see how unsettled I was, but being a girl, there was probably a fat chance of that. *Well, good luck, honey.* Not even she could get past these guys' shields. They were very safe. Harmless guy, player guy, bitter guy, taken guy, and my former guy—they were all at Rambo House, and I depended solely on their noncommittal attitudes, no matter how annoying they were.

I wouldn't know what to do if they really turned on me. Except . . . my hand hesitated on the door . . . my best guy friend. Christian wasn't afraid of women, wasn't taken, and—most importantly—had a heart to steal. But I couldn't babysit him forever, especially in my condition. Maybe Britton would. I glanced at him. He had on his bored look, but I knew better than to think that's how he really felt. He had made me cry, and it wouldn't be long before I got some sort of reconciliatory phone call that had nothing to do with this afternoon. I knew a better way he could make up for it.

I cleared my throat. "Um, watch his back, huh?"

A single eyebrow went up. Britton had no idea what I was talking about. You would think that a Bitter Boy of all people would know what was going on. How did he become one in the first place? My eyes alighted on Britton's trident on the plastic covered floor and I stole it.

"That isn't yours, Red!"

Yeah, but it would ensure a visit, which would get him close enough to make sure he took his role as Bitter Boys president seriously. "Next time you want to make some sandcastles, you know where to go, Brother Britton."

"Sister Children," he warned. I slammed the door.

Chapter 4

Charity begins at home,
and justice begins next door.
—Charles Dickens

Tuesday, June 16th, late afternoon

I quickly made my way home through the sweltering heat. Every once in a while a soft breeze caught my hair. It was my only relief in this hot weather. I wiped my eyes as clean as I could get them. Christian wasn't the only one I had to worry about. My roommates were impossible when it came to this kind of thing.

"Catch it!"

I glanced up, seeing a football come at my head. I barely had time to drop the pitchfork and catch the ball, falling back at the impact. I welcomed any excuse to break my sad spell, and I laughed, seeing the girls from downstairs. They were my little punks, wearing ugly Lance Armstrong bracelets up and down their arms. It looked like the four had now taken over the street. Cars swerved to keep from hitting them. Music blared from their apartment.

If I hadn't been wearing my clunky wedge heels, I would've kicked the ball right back. There was something about kicking a football that made you feel good, but I just threw it back to the youngest little punk. "Here ya go, Cindy Lou!" That was her nickname. You know, like the little girl in Whoville? Yeah, it was better than calling her the beehive. That's what Britton called her. Betsy was only seventeen, a regular child prodigy attending UVSC.

She was another person lucky enough to earn my protection. I blocked her from all sorts of undesirables. I can't tell you how many players I've scared from her pathway and how underhanded I've been about it. Yep, I told you I was awful, but she had no idea.

"Good hustle," she shouted.

"Thanks." I picked up Britton's pitchfork and passed the hammock on the stairs, running the flight up to our ghetto apartment. We had all sorts here at the Rainbow Villa complex. The cool girls lived downstairs and the gossipers lay in wait on the middle floor—an unfortunate location for us but a most convenient position for them. I nodded to the girls at the window. No one could pass their watchful eye without them knowing what was going on. I dragged myself up the last flight.

The foosball championships were already in full swing on our balcony. Our foosball table really was a piece of work. It was warped from years spent outside. The handles stuck, the table legs were crooked, but it was a guy magnet. I had no idea who the two guys currently playing were. They were a Laurel and Hardy combo—one big and muscular in a Hawaiian shirt, the other skinny and dressed to kill. They worked the bandaged foosball players with nimble fingers. I tried to sneak past, but the burly one scored and began his victory dance. He saw me and grabbed my arms. "Finally! I'm ahead!"

I faked a grin. It was a little watery. "Oh good." I pulled away just as he made a fist of triumph. He hopped up and down on the balcony in his thick-tongued Osiris shoes, barely missing our crops. Well, they were Maggie's crops, which was the only reason they were thriving. Green pots of all sizes lined the balcony: tomatoes, radishes, herbs. It was our own little garden.

"Who's the foosball king now?" he shouted. "Take that!"

"Not so fast, Phil." His skinny friend was a little more reserved. "The game isn't done yet. You afraid to face me?"

The Phil character jumped back to the game. Besides some definite color-coordinating problems, he wasn't bad looking. He scored again, and I quickly ducked into our apartment before he could grab me again. A service idol was stuck in front of the door, and it flew into the living room, bouncing into the pile of wedding presents in the middle of the room.

If it were left solely up to me it would stay there, but I lived with Maggie. The problem was that she never counted any of the good acts she did as service: nursing homes, orphans, the homeless, me. More blessings to her, except that meant we were stuck with the ugly thing.

I fanned myself, then stopped, realizing it wasn't doing any good. It was hotter inside than outside, if that was at all possible. Every fan in the house was on, and they ineffectually blew the hot air around. We had lost two roommates to this heat. No, they didn't die, silly. They simply packed their bags and headed for air-conditioned pastures with empty promises to see us in the fall, leaving us to rot in our oven sweet oven.

I could see the top of my cousin's head in the middle of all the presents. "Jade, is that you?" I felt like I was walking into a land mine. Her wedding dress hung on the door frame. Her baggage was strewn all over the ground. She was getting married in three weeks, and it was indeed a miracle. Once we got rid of her we'd have a clean apartment again. She insisted on storing all her presents here until she signed the lease on her new apartment.

"Am uver here!" she shouted in a muffled voice. "Could yu move summa these boxessss!"

"Man, we'll need a forklift to move all this stuff out of here." I threw the pitchfork safely in the closet and pulled some boxes away from my cousin. I was awarded by a gorgeous smile.

Jade, beautiful Jade in her ugly tailored clothing; the only thing missing was a single strand of pearls. She was pretty much perfect: a studious know-it-all with long chestnut hair and green eyes, yeah, the color of jade. The guys had always been crazy about her, but she had never been crazy about them. Only lately did I see where she was coming from.

"Well, it looks like you're cashing in," I said.

"Or nobody can make it to the reception. Look at all this stuff."

Jade was from Orem, so it was a simple drop-off. "No one would miss such a spectacle. It's not every day a Childs gets married." We were a crazy lot, and our receptions were the makings of horror flicks. Our mothers made sure of that.

Jade was older than me, a twenty-nine-year-old study freak, who professed to want a career more than marriage, but I knew better than that. She said she wasn't ready for marriage. Well, she was ready now . . . right in the middle of law school with loans building up and the internships getting harder. It just took the right guy, or the right girl, to threaten to steal that guy. Let's just say a little Charity did it. I'll explain later.

We were interrupted by a loud round of cheering and trash-talking outside. I tried to ignore it. The big guy must have lost points to his calm companion, and he had completely lost it. That reminded me of something. "Where's Rusty?" That little gossiping turncoat.

"I'm not sure where he is," Jade said with a giggle.

I laughed. Yeah right. If he was here, he'd be right next to her. "Don't try to lie for him," I said, rummaging through the wreckage "Rusty, you're in trouble! Don't think you can hide from me!" Well, at least he couldn't run.

I heard a disembodied voice to my left. "Whaddaya want?" I pulled a box away from him, seeing that Jade had put him to work. He was busy writing down the names of the people who had given them presents. Did they actually think that they would be giving thank-you cards? Such bright-eyed innocence.

He glanced up at me with trusting eyes. His red hair, once buzzed, was undergoing a Jade makeover for the wedding. He was growing sideburns, and he looked good. I didn't think he had it in him, but he was starting to look like one of the Beatles.

"What do you mean by telling everyone I was flirting up a storm with Lane?" I asked.

"You mean Raine?"

"Whatever! I was being nice and actually treating him like a human being. Don't you know the difference?"

"No," Jade answered for him and they kissed. I rolled my eyes. Typical engaged behavior. But I was getting mad. This was serious. Everyone was reading me wrong! Jade held up a framed parchment with bold Japanese figures written down the front. "This is from one of your missionary companions. What's it say?"

Rusty glanced at it and smiled. "I'm a stupid American."

"We'll put it on our wall," Jade said. "It will make us look classy."

"Why are you opening your presents already?" I asked. Jade and Rusty just stared at each other. Was no one listening to me? "I had the hottest trainer at work today," Jade said.

"Really? What was *her* name?" he asked.

My lip curled in disgust. Engaged couple banter was more than I could take. "I would appreciate it if you didn't spread any more gossip about me, Rusty!"

And of course they didn't answer. "You have the cutest laugh."

I stormed into the kitchen. "Hey, wait!" Rusty cried, managing to break free. "I have someone I want you to meet."

Now that I had his attention, I uneasily ignored him and pulled around the fridge, looking for something to eat. I had peanut butter but no bread. I could make biscuits maybe. Anything left on the table was a free-for-all, and I glanced at it, seeing it was covered with Jade's groceries, which were probably a no-no. The bags were piled on top of Maggie's sewing projects. Britton's trousers that she was supposed to hem for him last week were at the bottom of the heap and I snickered.

The problem was that Maggie was the only one in the ward who could sew—the only one who could do anything, really. She had every domestic skill that the rest of the girls were supposed to have and didn't. The ward just took advantage of her, but someday Maggie would stand up for herself, if I had my way. Maggie was another friend that needed me to protect her from the big bad world, mainly because she had no idea how bad it really was.

I realized that someone had left the fridge door open. "C'mon, guys," I muttered. "It isn't like that is going to cool the house down." I tried to shut it and heard a grunt. Maggie? Of course. She was in the fridge. It was the only place that was somewhat cold.

"Let me guess," I said. "They still haven't opened the Deluxe Apartment pool?"

"Nope." Maggie pulled her head out, her blond hair in fashionable disarray over her face. It was funny that the sweetest girl in existence was so very stylish. Her name suited her. She looked like an albino magpie, complete with cute magpie hair cut in jagged layers. It looked like spiked feathers pinned all over with jeweled pins. Actually, everything about Maggie was cute: her pin-striped capris, the bowling shoes, even her surprising sense of humor.

"The Deluxe managers just found a new Provo law. Apparently the pool has to be warm enough before they can open it to the public."

"What? It has to be at least a hundred degrees outside! The manager is just lazy!"

Maggie shrugged. "Well, I talked to the girls at the Deluxe and they're planning a revolt. We'll see how that goes. Maybe we'll just have to find some new friends with a manager that's less law-abiding."

Friends? You call them our friends? I almost asked my questions out loud, but quickly stopped myself before Maggie gave me a lecture. Let's just say that our Deluxe neighbors looked like they could easily fit in a Gap commercial. We were on the other side of the ward, or, shall we say, tracks. Unbeknownst to Maggie there was a cold war waging between our own little Ritz and the ghetto.

"Or at the very least," she droned on, "we should find friends with a manager that isn't as lazy."

I laughed and her face turned red. "Oh, I shouldn't have said that. I really need to be better," she said in her cute little voice.

I bit my lip, feeling guilty for encouraging her to make mean comments, even if I hadn't meant to. "I don't know how you do it," I said, "but you always manage to make me feel guilty for things that *you* say."

"Hey, guess what?" Maggie jumped from one subject to the next almost as quickly as she took things out of the fridge. Was she cleaning it then? "Our landlord took the bait! He wants you to scrub down the apartment next door. The girls there left it a mess when they left. It means free rent for the summer, but you've got to keep it under wraps."

"Maggie Joe Villers!" I shouted. "How did you do that?" Our landlord loved Maggie, but no matter what I did, I could never win his approval. Apparently she had done it for me.

Her blue eyes twinkled. Maggie was one of those girls who gave her loyalty freely, and I didn't know why. I certainly didn't deserve it. At first it made me paranoid that it would go away just as easily as it had come, but then I just learned to accept it. "The info is on your whiteboard," she said.

I glanced at the whiteboard, sorting through the scrawled messages. Not all of them were true. *Jacqueline's a closet Backstreet Boys fan.* It looked like Christian had been here. My family had also called. Then there were messages from a plethora of boys I had no intention of calling back. I groaned when I saw the smiley face under the general announcements. *Please clean the kitchen.* The smiley face meant Maggie was mad.

I glanced sideways at her. "Uh-oh, we're in for it now!"

"What?" Maggie asked, pulling things out of the fridge at an even brisker pace. That was another sign she was angry. How had I missed it?

There was an unwritten rule that we washed our own dishes, but then we just stacked them on the rack to impossible heights to dry. Of course, she might be talking about Jade's groceries all over her sewing supplies too. I erased the smiley face on the board and wrote: *The stuff on the table is free for all.*

"Well, that should take care of it." I opened a bag of Jade's chips and ate one to show her we were serious. If she didn't put away her groceries, we would eat them all.

"Hey, you got an emotional attachment to these eggs?" Maggie held up a carton.

"Are those even mine?"

"Yeah, they're five months past the expiration date. What are they, a remembrance from the Monsieur?" My nose wrinkled in distaste. She was referring to the stash of stuffed animals and other odd knick-knacks under my bed that I just couldn't throw out. My roommates generally shook their heads at me and thought I was crazy. Well, I wasn't . . . that much. I just didn't want to get rid of the memories yet. Maggie threw the eggs into the trash can. "It's time to let go," she said.

Only she could get away with being so bold, and I tried to squash the strange fluttering of guilt in my gut. I pulled a chair from the table instead, scooting it to the cupboard. My fingers barely scraped over the edge of my shelves. It just figured that they would give the shortest girl the highest shelf, but Maggie considered it an exercise of my patience. I began rummaging through my food, not finding much. There were some pickles.

I've learned that what I thought were the staples of life aren't, but cereal is. My fingertips brushed over some Cocoa Puffs. I had forgotten that I had these. Didn't they have all the important vitamins and junk? I pulled them down.

"Your family called," Maggie reminded me. "You need to call them back."

"I will," I mumbled, taking a bowl balanced atop the clean dish pile. I poured the last of the cereal in it and a puff of cereal dust blew a mushroom cloud over the top.

"Your mom wanted you to call as soon as you got home."

"Maggie, how many times do I have to tell you?" I felt like I was explaining this to a three-year-old. "My family is so tight we don't need to talk."

She snorted. "Oh, pleazz." It was her favorite thing to say. "You're just afraid of getting lectured."

I shrugged. *Among other things.* "I'm just afraid my phone card won't take it." One glance in the fridge told me that I needed to find my milk elsewhere. It was on the floor, and I scooped it up, pouring it into my cereal bowl. Chunks of ice landed on the top of my Cocoa Puffs. Apparently the milk hadn't been out of the fridge for too long.

Our escapee roommate had taken all her utensils with her, so I grabbed the measuring spoons out of the top drawer and took a couple of crunchy bites with the tablespoon. I wrinkled my nose. Well, this wouldn't do. I threw the bowl in the microwave and set it for a quick thirty seconds. "Did you get the mail?" I asked.

Maggie just gestured to the top of the microwave where a bunch of bills awaited me. My stomach dropped and I fought the urge to be depressed. "All right!" I cheered. "Just what I was waiting for!"

I stuffed the bills into my back pocket. Now that school was done, I had to pay off my loans. Yet another thing to look forward to. I could only afford to pay the minimum payments, which meant I was only paying off the interest. I sighed. Why couldn't I make money doing something I liked? There had to be some opportunities out there.

I walked into the bathroom and grimaced at my skunk-striped red hair. Maggie hadn't even made fun of me for it. Man, she was so nice she was unbelievable! I began to clean up. Paint and water dribbled down my red hair, and I scrubbed harder, making faces in the mirror.

You see, it's hard to be patient when you're living off peanut butter sandwiches, so right now I was in the business of forcing so-called opportunities to come my way. It was a Herculean task, one where I had to find a better back-up job, which brought me to my original problem. Food. I don't know why everything revolved around food, but it did, and I needed to keep myself from starving.

The microwave went off and, after patting my wet hair back into place, I ran back into the kitchen and pulled the steaming cereal out. I stared at it. It didn't look quite right. Sticking cereal in the microwave had seemed like such a good idea at the time, but now it looked kind of soggy. I wandered into the living room with my cereal and nudged some presents aside so I could sit on the couch.

"Hey, guys," I asked Jade and Rusty, "where did the remote control go?"

They didn't answer, too busy saying sweet nothings to each other. But at least Rusty had forgotten his well-meant pep talk for me. I had no intention of going for his blind date schemes this time. Balancing my cereal on the arm of the couch, I searched around for the remote until I finally found it under the cushions. Typical.

I leaned back and turned on the TV, flipping quickly through the channels because I was afraid that I might land on something educational. It was like playing Russian roulette, and just as I had dreaded, I landed on the news. Now if I were by myself, this wouldn't be a problem. It was just that everyone else wanted to watch the boring channels, and since Jade owned the TV she pretty much had a monopoly on the lineup.

I glanced at Jade and Rusty, but they weren't paying much attention. My conscience said that I should watch the news, but my flesh was weak so I turned it before anyone was the wiser. What was wrong with watching something entertaining anyway? Or *listening* to something entertaining for that matter? Yeah, I couldn't help but hear the heated exchange outside.

Chapter 5

There is always enough self-love hidden beneath
the great devoutness to set limits on charity.
—Magdeleine Sable

Tuesday, June 16th, late afternoon

The guys outside had stopped playing foosball and were now talking about girls. Things were getting way too candid, and I smiled, muting the TV. The reality shows were always much more entertaining anyway, and I needed something to cheer me up. It was tradition. The couch is where we watched the world when the porch was uninhabitable.

"Why don't girls like me? Andrea won't even return my calls. Am I just too nice?"

Same ol', same ol', guys were all the same ol'. I sniffed the soggy, steaming Cocoa Puffs and decided to go for it. I chewed the mush slowly. There was a strange taste to it, but I ignored it. The cereal had been pretty old.

"You, nice? No way," the hyper one said.

"Why do the ones I like run away and the ones I can't stand looking at won't leave me alone?"

"'Cause you're not playing the right game, buddy."

I silently agreed with him, taking another bite. There was no way I'd date such a whiner.

"You've got to be a jerk," he said.

I gagged, but not because of what he had just said. No, I had just glanced down at my cereal. Weevils were floating all over the top.

Ooh! I chased them down with my spoon, seeing more pop up. I felt sick and weak all at once, but I was still hungry! *Garbage!* Institute was just hours away, and what if they didn't even have treats? Then I would have to visit some guys' apartment to scavenge for food.

Okay, so I live off of refreshments, parties, FHE, birthdays, family gatherings, dinner invites, receptions, missionary open houses . . . anything. But right now I just wanted to eat my own cereal in my own house. I glanced down at it. Could I eat it anyway? After all, the weevils were all dead. I could just eat around them. Indiana Jones would, but I finally thought better of it. There were too many of them.

You know, if I were a more sentimental person, I'd cry again, but it was basically my fault that I was stuck in such dire straits. It was because I carried everything to excess. I spent too much money when I had it. I made bad decisions to stay in Provo and build my résumé kingdom when I shouldn't. And now I found myself eating weevils! But I still had a jar of unopened pickles, didn't I? Weevils didn't like pickles. I stood up, heading for my shelf.

"Jacqueline? Are you listening?"

I glanced at Jade and Rusty and they laughed. They were used to my spacey ways.

"What's this?" Jade waved something in front of my face. It was a painting that I had given them for their wedding. They had opened it already? The little vultures!

I threw it back to her. "It's a painting."

"Of what?"

My lip curled. I loved doing this to them. "Guess."

Maggie was sitting on the living room rug with her legs crossed. Rusty turned to her and she turned red. "Oh, I'm not good at this game." That was a safe enough answer.

"Saddam Hussein?" Rusty finally ventured.

I choked. "Very close. It's you actually."

"It is?"

"No, it's just modern. It's a tree, symbolic of your new life together," I made up. "Just hang it up and look classy." They looked dubious. "Look, if you're going to hang up the 'I'm a stupid American' sign, then you need something to balance it out."

"I just don't have your power over the ladies."

We all glanced out the window. The foosball players outside were still deep in conversation.

"What can I say?" the other said. "It's a gift."

Jade and Rusty exchanged a glance that I easily caught. "What?"

"Nothing." Jade knew I was a curious person, and she always liked to play with that because I was always willing to do anything to find out what she was hiding. Thank goodness her fiancé blew everything. He always liked to be the first with a good story.

"We've got someone for you," Rusty blurted. Jade gave him a warning look.

Garbage. "I can't do another blind date." Even if I wasn't desperate, the world was getting desperate *for* me. "You're not going to do that to me again! I won't let you."

"So you got kicked off the horse," Rusty said. "Everybody gets kicked off the horse. You've just got to get back to the game."

Oh no, he couldn't use that card on me again. It was a well-known fact that I was the blind-date queen, which is why I got myself into so many bad situations. And maybe I was curious as a general rule as well. What if this was "the one" and I passed him up? Blind dates had an advantage because I didn't know them. There was always the "what if he's normal?" clause.

"Tell me," he said. "What do you think of the guys playing foosball out there?"

I groaned. "You mean Hunk and Lunk?" I had heard for myself how *not normal* they were, and I didn't want to add either of them to my list of unlucky swains. They were back to their foosball game outside, and one of them cheered loudly. "They sound like real winners," I muttered. Jade groaned. "And who's the lucky one that gets to date me?" I asked. "The one with the emotional problems or the one with the emotional problems?"

"Whichever one you like," Rusty said. Jade gave him an annoyed look. He had just walked into my trap. "But they're both cool," he reassured me.

I laughed. You can say anything mean about anyone and then slap "but he's really cool" after it like a bandage, and just like "bless his heart," it made everything better. "Phil works at the law building with me, and he's a smart one," Rusty said.

"And so good with the ladies," I muttered.

"Okay. So then there's Seth. He's just getting over a really bad breakup, but he's really cool."

I glanced out the window at the two and threw my hands up, knowing I was being dramatic. "I can't do this anymore."

Jade sighed, leaning back. "Maybe you should leave Provo. Go to California. They have lots of available guys there, probably your kind of guy too."

What was that supposed to mean? "Hey, why is everyone trying to get rid of me?"

"There's nothing for you here," Jade said. "You're not going to school here anymore. You're free."

"I'm not free. I have to—"

"Did you know the Monsieur has a new girlfriend?" Rusty interrupted in typical gossipy fashion. Jade tried to give him a warning look, but he didn't get the message. "What?" he said. "I saw him hugging some dancer from one of his classes. They were holding hands." My own hands clenched into fists, and I turned back to the window, looking at Phil or Seth. I actually couldn't remember who was who or who was worse.

I stepped back when Britton came into view. He was here already? His guilt must be eating him up. I really hoped that he hadn't left Charity alone with Christian. Obviously Britton had other things on his mind though, and he approached the two at the foosball table with an evil eye. Even with his bare hairy legs and Birkenstocks, he looked more sophisticated than these two deadheads put together. He leaned against the balcony, acting like he was interested in their game.

Britton saw me watching him, and he nodded my direction. He was full of dangerous class, a natural born leader with a dark Heathcliff expression. By all rights he should be a lady killer, except for one tragic flaw: his ego. I turned swiftly away just as someone knocked on the door and opened it before we could do the honors.

It was a visitor from the second floor, Liza Brinehart, the activities co-chair, and already she was talking a mile a minute, though she couldn't quite get all the words past all the teeth in her small mouth. "Is the directory done yet?" I shook my head and she turned to Maggie. "Got something for you." She threw a white furry thing in

Maggie's lap, and we all gasped for completely different reasons. It was a kitten. A horribly mangy thing that looked like it had a bad haircut.

"Get that thing out of this house!" Jade said. Jade and I both had inherited the allergy genes, and already she was sniffing. It was probably in her head at this point, but for good reason. We knew what happened to us from experience.

"Oh, it's just a harmless little kitten." Maggie nuzzled her nose against it and I stepped back from her.

"Sparky needs a place to stay. It's not breaking the Honor Code," Liza said. "Sparky's a girl, you see. She just needs a good home."

"Not ours," I said. "Give her to Charity."

"Well, Charity told me to give it to you."

It just figured. I knew she had it out for me, but I had no idea she wanted to kill me. Liza turned to Maggie. Everyone in the ward came to her for advice. "Oh, what do I do?" she moaned. "Raine is not asking me out when I know he wants to. Why is he being such a fraidy cat?"

"Maybe he's just intimidated," Maggie said kindly.

I snorted. That was a lie mothers told their daughters to make them feel good about themselves. I found that out the hard way. "No guy is intimidated," I muttered. Especially Lane Bryant.

"This one is." Liza gave me a hard look. She was the kind of girl who noticed the competition for her guy's hand and quickly put a stop to it by claiming him. Nice girls generally backed off. She was just lucky that I wasn't interested, or I'd have no problem claim jumping. Liza noticed her reflection in the window and frowned at her skinny arm. "Oh no, I'm in serious danger of Relief Society arm." I rolled my eyes. She was the reason girls were so anorexic. If she was fat, what were we? She ineffectually tried to tug her small shirt over her low waistband. "No wonder he won't ask me out. I'm obese!"

"What? No," Maggie reassured. I listened to Maggie prescribe all the best workout techniques, all the while assuring Liza that she in no way needed it.

Rusty was standing now, and I tried to ignore his presence at my side. "Just think of it this way," he whispered to me. "You'll get a free meal out of it." I glanced at my uneaten cereal and bit my lip. That was actually a temptation. "I told him that you could go out to dinner with him, so . . ."

"You already told him we were going out?" I hissed. I didn't want Liza to hear. She was from the gossiping middle floor. "Which one? Are you dragging Maggie into this as well?"

Maggie stiffened. "I can't. I've got to find this kitten a good home." She knew none of us would fight that excuse.

"Hey, Liza," I asked. "What do you think of those guys out there?"

"Britton?"

"No, not Britton!" I tried to keep my voice calm. From experience I knew that Liza was the kind of girl who liked to claim every guy as her own, and I was hoping that she'd do me the favor this time with these guys out on the porch. "Don't you think they're cute?"

Liza cocked her head to the side, listening to Britton make rude comments about the girls living inside our apartment, namely me. Old habits are hard to break, I guess. It wasn't long before he began to commiserate with Seth's recent breakup.

"That's cheap," he said.

"She said that she wasn't ready for a relationship," Seth moaned.

"What a line. She just isn't ready for a relationship with you. Sorry to break it to you. Girls are all the same."

Britton glanced up at me and gave a sly grin. It almost appeared he was trying to convert them to his Bitter Boys Club. That wouldn't be so bad either. At least that would make things safer for me.

"Raine," Liza breathed, "is playing EverQuest right now. I was just going to check my e-mail on your computer, but I can just use his, and he might want someone to play him. Later, guys." She passed Britton on her way out, and Britton held open the door. She quickly ducked past him. She was right to be scared of him.

"Call me if you need someone to talk some sense into you," Britton told the guys outside. I half expected Britton to give the foosball players his card with the Bitter Boys insignia on it, but he just walked in, shutting the door behind him. "Poor guy," he muttered. "Some devil woman really did a number on h—oh, kitten!" he cried midsentence. I rolled my eyes. Of course he loved cats. Everyone evil did. "Come to papa!"

Maggie dimpled and flew the kitten into his arms. He scratched it under the ear, but before I could laugh, I remembered the business at hand. "Did you leave Charity alone with Christian?"

"Are you jealous?" He was watching me closely, almost as if gauging where those tears had gone and if they were coming back anytime soon. But he was a firm believer in tough love, which is why he never gave me a break.

I sniffed, trying to rid myself of my embarrassment. I had prided myself on being the only girl Britton couldn't get to, and with some difficulty, I managed to keep myself calm. "This is serious and you know it."

Rusty grinned. He was always eager for the latest gossip. "You're jealous? Of who? Charity or Maggie?"

"I can't believe you just asked that," I said in shocked tones.

Britton was pretending to bite the kitten. "Oh, you can answer that when Maggie leaves."

"Why would I leave?" Maggie asked.

"Because you don't hang out anymore, and isn't that what we're doing right now?" He fixed her with a judgmental stare.

Maggie stomped her foot. "No, you came to my house to visit, and you'll keep it short."

"Who says, Maggot?"

She gasped. "You know I don't like it when you call me that." Of course he did. Britton was bad. Maggie was good. You would think two polar opposites wouldn't get along, but they usually got along great. Until this no-hanging-out policy came into existence. Now it was a constant bone of contention between them.

"C'mon, have mercy," he said. "I need an emergency haircut. I've got to take a test in the testing center." I grimaced, looking at his fancy razor cut. Britton's excuses for hanging out were becoming more and more imaginative. I was sure that he had some sort of bet going.

Maggie hesitated. A haircut was a good cause for a visit, but he had already gotten her riled up with the hanging-out digs. He had really played his cards wrong this time. It was just a good thing that he had brought up mercy. She had a hard time turning that one down.

"Man, for a tough guy, you're real needy all of a sudden," I said. He shrugged and I noticed that Britton held my flyers under his armpit. "Hey, those are mine."

"Nuh-uh." He pulled away. "We're working out a deal for this one."

So he wanted his stupid plastic pitchfork back, did he? "Only if you promise to watch Christian's back," I said. "Charity has designs on that kid."

"Kid?" he mocked. "How old do you think Christian is?"

"Younger than me," I said, "by about a year maybe."

"He's forty?" You'd think he'd have learned his lesson by now. My eyes widened, and I pulled the trident out of the closet and he backed up, holding the kitten out in front of him. "What are you going to do?" he asked, "Hit a defenseless kitten?" It was his sick way of trying to soften me up.

I ignored that. "Here's the deal. You do whatever you do to make Christian see reason, and you get your cute little pitchfork back, get it?"

He laughed. "I'll *steal* it back. In case you haven't noticed, I'm bigger than you."

I glanced at Maggie. "And you'll get a free haircut too." It was the kind of freeloading I despised. "And not from me," I promised as extra incentive. Let's face it. If I did it, I'd buzz *loser* into the back of his head, and since I couldn't cut hair anyway, I would probably do it without even trying.

"On one condition." Britton was clearly enjoying himself. "You can't make Maggie do all your dirty work. I've got a list of demands for you."

"Like what?"

"Old Ironsides goes out to sea."

I didn't like where this was going. "What do you mean?"

"It's simple. It's time to give one of your unlucky swains a chance."

"What?" my voice cracked.

"You heard me."

I glared. Was this his idea of making up with me? I was beginning to believe he was devoid of all conscience. Or maybe he just liked to see me squirm.

Rusty grinned. "Who's it going to be? Seth or Phil?"

I caught my breath. Britton, sensing my angst, decided that this was the perfect solution. "Seth just got out of a squirrelly girl's grasp, we'll give him a break. Go for Phil."

But he wasn't even my swain yet! Fortunately! "You want me to go out with one of those monkeys?" Britton nodded slowly. I steadied myself for the inevitable and turned towards Rusty. "He doesn't dance, does he?" I asked.

Rusty looked surprised that I was even considering it. "No."

"Good." That was one sure way to my heart, and I wanted it to be safe from this Phil guy. He seemed like a snake and a charmer in one, and dancing was my Achilles' heel. "Does he have any tragic streaks? Is he dramatic in any way? Analyze things way too much?" I started naming off all the things that the Monsieur had done.

Rusty looked confused. "No."

"Does he think in grunts?" I asked. Rusty shook his head. "Garbage, that's a strike against him. I want a guy who thinks in grunts." The Monsieur had been too much of a thinker.

Phil made another score outside, and he danced around like a deranged ape. "Looks like we found our winner," Jade said. "He really can't dance."

I steeled myself before I made the commitment that I dreaded. There was no danger of falling in love with that one. "Fine, we've got a deal, Britton." I thrust my hand out to him, and even he looked surprised. Rusty marched outside to inform one of the foosball players of our future together. I squeezed my eyes shut, trying to block out the sight. "Only you've got to find someone to give the spiritual thought at institute. And I *will* be back in time for institute."

Maggie tried to hand me my cereal bowl. She wanted me to wash it before I left. That wasn't going to happen. I took a deep breath and walked outside like I was walking to the guillotine. Seth was stuck behind the foosball table. His eyes searched out his best route of escape—underneath the table or over the railing? He chose the death-defying tightrope act over the railing and I winced, but he made it safely back onto the balcony next to Phil. They both watched me expectantly, and I gave Rusty an uncertain smile. Which one was my date?

"You're Jack?" one asked. I nodded. The football player wannabe must be my date. I directed all my attention on him, acting like this was the most natural thing in the world. Phil noticed the bowl of cereal in my hand. "Have you eaten already?"

I quickly denied it. "No, no, just some weevils." I handed the bowl to Britton and he scowled at it. The kitten started licking it gingerly. Hmm, well, I guess that wasn't such a waste after all.

Britton's eyebrows furrowed when he saw the weevils. "Disgusting. Go and buy some real food, Jacqueline!" He glowered under dark brows, but the worried look in his eyes betrayed him. Well, I didn't want his pity.

"Okay," I told him brightly. Someday I would when I was rich. I tried to think of all the guys that could possibly feed me. Nope, I had burnt all my bridges. Burn, baby, burn! Maybe Phil would feed me. If so, this date wouldn't be so bad after all. Phil smiled at me and we headed for the stairs. Seth followed after us. I hesitated. Who was Seth's date? I glanced at Rusty in confusion, and he just waved me off and went back inside. Maggie? Nope, she wasn't coming. She was getting ready to cut Britton's hair. And Jade was out of the picture. I guess this would be a double date. At least until we dropped Seth off . . . I hoped.

"Let's go play," Phil said. I smiled weakly. What was I doing? My heart was beating loudly and I wanted to die. Christian. I had to keep him safe. Britton probably would've watched his back anyway, but on the off chance that he didn't I could use this against him.

"Remember who you are," Britton said. He looked like he was standing guard at the door as if I'd try to make a run for it.

"And *you* remember what you have to do," I said. Britton had better make this worth it. I would not make this sacrifice in vain.

"As always," he said.

The last thing I saw was Britton heading towards Maggie like a devil trying to get in good with an angel. The door closed ominously behind them. I gulped. He was always trying to get information out of her, but there was no fear there. She didn't gossip unless she was tricked into it, and I was the only one who knew how to do that. Besides, I wasn't hiding anything, right? Well, not that I knew of.

Chapter 6

The worst of charity is that the lives you are asked
to preserve are not worth preserving.
—Ralph Waldo Emerson

Tuesday, June 16th, late afternoon

My two dates and I paraded down the stairs, passing the gossiping floor. I tried not to stand too close to either of the boys. The girls would start spreading the word to the ward that I was no longer available. On second thought, I stood closer to Seth than I should, and he gave me a funny look. I just smiled dumbly at him until we got to the ground floor and I pulled away.

"¿Qué piensas de esta chica?"

"¡Caramba! Está bien buena, pero es una chica fácil. Parece que quiere conseguir marido rápido."

Great, they had been mission companions. I just hoped I wouldn't be stuck with their code talk all night. It was always annoying. "Um, excuse me?" I asked, stopping in front of the line of cars parked on the side of the road. "What did you just say?"

"Justo estábamos hablando de ti, frente a tu cara."

"I know Spanish too, so knock it off."

Phil raised an eyebrow dubiously. "Yeah, what did we just say?"

I turned from him. "I'm not going to repeat that."

Seth started acting superior. "Give us some Spanish then."

"Taco, burrito, enchilada," I muttered quickly under my breath. They both just laughed and I fumed.

"There's my car," Phil said. It was a BMW Z4. My eyes widened. So, he was a richie, was he? His daddy probably gave him this toy for going on a mission. "You're not afraid to be alone in a car with older men, are you?" he asked me.

What? Was he trying to scare me? I was already scared, but that wasn't why. "You're not that old, buddy," I told him. Most likely I was older than him. Phil opened the door for me, and I sat in the front seat. There was no way I was crawling into the back on a date. At least I had *some* respect for myself. Seth looked at Phil, shrugged, and climbed into the back through the driver's side. His shoulders went up to his head and he looked like a henchman.

"*¿La chica no pudo subirse a la parte de atrás del auto?*"

"*Tal vez nunca se ha subido antes a un BMW. No puedes echarle la culpa. Sólo quiere mi dinero.*"

They laughed and I glared. Phil glanced sideways at me. "It's nothing," he reassured me. Sure it wasn't. "So, what are you studying?"

"I've graduated."

"What are you still doing in Provo?"

I looked out the window, realizing this was the perfect time to turn him off. "I'm just looking for a man. You know, one who can show some commitment."

His hands tightened on the wheel and I tried not to smile. "You're just here to get married, huh?"

"Oh, yeah." I was—eventually. So it wasn't really a lie. I actually didn't know why I had stayed in Provo, except for the fact that I didn't want to go home. Could it be independence? No, I was failing miserably at that. Was it friends? No, I loved my family like my friends. Maybe it was because no one was bugging me about marriage here. Well, besides bishops and firesides and Rusty. But nothing could compare to the heat I got at home. I was the only girl smashed between a horde of brothers, four older and four younger. My mom had always wanted a girl. She had always imagined that I would run around in an apron and cook elaborate meals and certainly be married by now.

But even if I was a complete disappointment to her, she actually thought I was pretty cool, and she was enraged that guys wouldn't marry me. How could I go home and have her witness firsthand why that didn't happen? It would be like admitting defeat. That probably was it. Besides, I was tired of moving, tired of a new life. I knew my ship had to come in. Either that or Britton was right and it had sunk already. That would stink.

"What are we going to eat?" Seth asked in the back. I tried to pretend like I didn't care, and I held my stomach before it growled at the thought.

"I don't know," Phil said. "Let's go hunt some pollywogs." That actually sounded pretty fun, except he was probably joking. "They taste like bacon," he said, "only bacon's good."

"Did you ever eat frog on your mission?" Seth asked from the back.

"Oh yeah. And chicken feet and dog and—hey, we could go to the Malt Shoppe." Phil glanced at me. "How much money do you have?"

"I don't."

"Well, there goes the dinner idea," he said in an annoyed voice. I snickered. Just my luck. This would be pure martyrdom, wouldn't it?

"Let's play chicken then," Seth said from the back. *No! Not that kind of martyrdom!*

"Not in my car," Phil said. "Let's go on a scavenger hunt." I groaned. That was even worse than dying. I couldn't take any more magical, creative date nights, and it looked like I really did have two dates. I just hoped that it didn't mean this would last twice as long.

"Let's get people to cuss at us and collect swear words," Phil added as further incentive. *Please.* I couldn't imagine anything worse. Not only was it a scavenger hunt, but a much more uncomfortable one than what I was used to. "Or let's count all the ugly cars in the parking lot at Macey's."

"How about we blow up mailboxes?" I suggested with a glare.

"I know. We can be grave robbers," Seth piped up behind me, completely oblivious to my sarcasm.

"No, no more urns. Not in the BMW," said Phil, and I flinched. "Besides, the spirit of Brad is already with us," he said in a haunting voice. He was obviously bragging.

"You stole an urn?" I was furious. "That's someone's loved one."

"Oh, calm down. We returned it." Phil adjusted his rearview mirror so that he could look at me. "Like you've never done anything bad."

Of course I have. I came on this date. I leaned back, not wanting to play his game. "It's hard to do bad things when you're perfect like me," I told him, trying to act like I was serious.

"Ella es la miedosa. ¡Démosle un susto!"

Phil laughed at Seth and turned to me. "Sounds like you've never had a good time before."

"Well, if you consider throwing tortillas at a football game a good time, no."

Now they were both laughing. "Remember when we hit that girl in the face with that tortilla?" Phil said.

"Man, she was mad."

"So what? She was ugly, all the girls were." Phil glanced at my scowling face. "Oh don't worry, you're hot."

"Oh, that happened to my sister," I quickly made a sister up. "She laughed at some dumb guys' adolescent attempts to pick up on her. And when it didn't work, I think they got pretty bitter and made up stories that made them look like jerks."

They were silent for a moment. "Nice one, Napoleon," Phil said.

"This is like the worst date ever," Seth said behind me.

Phil drummed his hands on the steering wheel. "I love lamp," he said. "I love lamp."

"What?" Were they quoting movies or something?

"Are you just saying that because you saw the lamp?" Seth asked. "Or do you really love the lamp?"

"For he is the Kwisatz Haderach!" Phil shouted crazily.

"What are you talking about?" I finally burst out.

"Have you seen *Dune*?" Phil asked.

"No."

"Stupid movie night." He made a sharp turn towards Macey's. They had a five buck video bin there. "Let's find the stupidest movies we can. How about *Girls Night Out*? I heard that one was a slam."

"Yeah, I also heard it was R," I said in some panic.

"So? What's your problem? You're not some Molly Mormon are you?"

I inhaled deeply. He wanted a fight, did he? I guess it would fit perfectly with my plans of turning him off. "Yeah, what are you going to do about it?"

Seth sighed loudly in the back. "Oh c'mon. If they made the Book of Mormon into a movie it would be R."

"Yeah, well, they *did* make the Book of Mormon into a movie, and it was lame," I said.

"What's wrong with R movies anyway?" Phil asked. He was pretending to be interested in what I had to say, although I had no idea why. He moved closer to me.

I tried not to be too obvious that I was inching away from him. "I don't know. Why don't you ask the prophet?"

"He never said not to watch rated R movies *specifically.*"

I hesitated. I was sure that he had, but there was no way that I could even remotely quote him without Internet access. "Really, well, while we're at it, let's kill each other," I argued. "I don't recall him saying we couldn't do that *specifically* either."

"Okay, let's do that." Phil laughed and started doing donuts in the Macey's parking lot. He turned the wheel abruptly and we spun in tight circles.

I held tightly to my seat belt. "Um, we don't have to do this anymore. I actually want to live through this." Whatever this was. I was getting dizzy. "Knock it off!"

"I say we get the movie," Seth said through clenched teeth. "*She* doesn't have to watch it."

He acted like I would care, but if it meant getting out of this date, then I'd agree to anything. "Sure, Coriantumr," I mumbled. "Go right ahead."

Phil screeched to a stop and I groaned, wanting to throw up. Britton had better fulfill his part of the bargain or I would make sure he'd never forget this night. "Are you judging us?" Seth asked dangerously from the back.

I turned and matched his glare. "What do you think? I'm calling you names, aren't I?" His face flushed, but then again, he could have been choking on his high-necked shirt.

Phil quickly parked in front of Macey's. He must be too good for real parking spaces. "I don't want to get booted," he said. "Someone's got to stay in the car while we get the movie."

He stared at his friend, but I raised my hand and volunteered instead. I figured it was safer that way. I just hoped that the BMW wouldn't serve as a getaway car. "Just don't rob the place, huh?" I told them.

They slid out of the car with the same class as the *Dukes of Hazzard* boys. Phil slammed the door shut and poked his head through the window, his eyes mischievous. "If we get arrested, will you wait for me?"

I smiled. He actually made a good joke. "No, but I'll take your BMW for a joyride. Who knows? I might do that anyway."

"Forget that." He stole the keys and my mouth flew open. There went the air-conditioning! *Garbage.* Why did I have to be such a big mouth? Speaking of which, I was still hungry.

"Hey!" I rolled my window down and stuck my head out of the window, yelling at their retreating backs. "I have to get to institute in about ten minutes." It was a convenient excuse to get out of this, and I didn't care if they saw through it.

"I have to get to institute," Seth mocked in a girly voice.

My eyes narrowed. "*Salúdame al diablo,*" I shouted at them. They both turned quickly on me and I shrugged. "I served my mission in Argentina. Excuse the lisp."

Phil looked intrigued and I fell limply back into my seat. *Garbage.* Why did I have to be so sassy! I didn't want him. It was always during these times of high stress that I did something I regretted.

The Monsieur never would've left me without air-conditioning, and he never would've done donuts. And if he had I would've liked it! He made everything fun. I remembered walking through the canal around the BYU trails with his hand on my back and him walking in that fluid way of his. I had just wanted to see nature. He wanted to experience it, and we splashed all the way through the canal to the other side. What was the appeal of the Monsieur? It was said best in *Anne of Green Gables*: he was a guy who could be bad but wasn't. Phil and Seth would've just thrown me in the canal. And now that I was comparing the Monsieur to other guys, the memories kept popping up when I just wanted to forget him.

So he didn't like me and I had to search elsewhere. I glanced at Macey's and remembered the last time that we had been here together. He was hitting me with a blow-up ball he had found there, and I was really mad. Yeah, see? He was a jerk! Well . . . it had actually been pretty funny. I smiled in spite of myself.

"Do you always park on the sidewalk?"

I glanced over in the side mirror, seeing a cute guy behind me. His blond hair was longish, and he was unshaven. *Garbage.* He had a really nice voice. Too bad I couldn't go for him. He looked like too much of a bad boy. I steeled myself. "I'm waiting for someone," I explained.

"Your boyfriend?" he asked in a gritty voice. I kinda liked it, even though I shouldn't have.

"Oh no, he's not my boyfriend. He's just a guy getting a movie."

He leaned against the BMW and I wondered how Phil would feel about that. "You got one?" he asked in a nonchalant voice.

"A movie?"

He laughed. "A boyfriend?"

I chose honesty for once. I wasn't quick-witted enough to do otherwise. "Not right now." *Mercy.* This never would've happened to me a year ago, before I dated the Monsieur. Why did guys get guts when you weren't ready for it? This one was a little scary in a rugged way. I shouldn't really like him. I wondered briefly if I was on some sort of candid camera and Britton was behind it.

"What's your name?"

I watched him suspiciously, and I felt like a complete idiot for not answering right away. "Jacqueline."

"Beautiful. What's your middle name?"

He must be joking. Would he want my social security number next? Against my better judgment I gave it to him. "Blest." I saw his incredulous look. "It's a family name."

"Good, we're on a middle-name basis, Blest." He shook hands with me.

I wasn't about to let him have the upper hand. I had to have something against him too. "What's your name?" I tried not to be too abrupt about it. It seemed lately I treated everyone coldly, and I wanted to seem normal. It was just really hard for me.

". . . that's what everyone calls me," he said.

Wait. What did he say his name was? I tried to rewind my memory banks, but it was useless. I think it started with a D—? Well, it didn't matter. I was sure I'd never see him again.

"So how old are you?" he asked.

I flinched at the personal question, but I decided I would let my age do the trick. It was easier than turning him down outright. "I'm old enough to be your grandmother in some cultures." He waited patiently until I finally told him. "Twenty-six."

He whistled. "You don't look twenty-six." My mouth fell open. Well, what was twenty-six supposed to look like anyway? Why hadn't that ruffled him? I decided to use my favorite grandmother trick to show him how truly old I was. "Oh, how sweet. Such a nice young man."

"You've got a problem with younger guys?" he cut to the point and I pulled back.

"No." I was disturbed by my honesty.

"I don't normally do this . . ." My eyes widened at the now familiar preamble, and I tried to will him to stop. "What's your number?" Was he serious? I didn't know whether to run, smile like a madwoman, or roll the car window up. "Maybe we can catch a bite to eat sometime," he said.

I tried to think of a polite excuse. He had unwittingly taken them all away from me. And yet, he didn't seem too weird. I stared at him. Was this a guy who would feed a girl? I was hungry and angry, and it made me do crazy things. Yeah, I could give him my number. I knew that I shouldn't, but I was going to do it anyway. Most likely he wouldn't call and it would make for a good story. It might even land in my "What Are the Odds?" article. "You don't dance, do you?" I asked.

"No."

"Got a pen?" I was used to the routine.

He pulled one out from the back pocket of his jeans. "You can write it on my Palm Pilot."

He held out his hand and I smiled. Well, that was different from the routine. That was actually pretty cute. I grabbed his hand and briefly considered putting a wrong number on it, but then thought better of it. I've done some pretty dumb things, and giving out my number in my condition was one of the dumber things I'd done, but not the dumbest. But pretty darn dumb, as you will see later.

Chapter 7

Though I have all faith, so that I could remove
mountains, and have not charity, I am nothing.
—1 Corinthians 13:2

Tuesday, June 16th, evening

Britton stood up behind the pulpit at institute looking very
bored. "Against my will, I've been asked to announce the institute
beach party at the Deluxe pool next Saturday. Although I'm also sad
to announce that, as of today, the pool is tragically still not open."

There were groans in the audience, and he held up his hand to
silence the crowds. He obviously enjoyed the power. I should've
stepped in, but I didn't want to give away how late I was. "We've been
plotting ways to fulfill the city ordinances to make sure the pool will
be properly heated in two weeks. We are accepting donations such as
emergency blankets to reflect the light into the pool, maybe some
pool thermometers we can boil and switch out with the original to rig
the results. And of course, the beautiful Maggie Villers will be
conducting house searches for the desired items . . . in behalf of the
compassionate service committee. I'm sure it's just a good excuse to
make the men fall madly in love with her."

Maggie blushed, almost shaking the curls from her hair to deny
the accusation. There were over a hundred students in the room,
including the overflow upstairs, and everyone turned to look at her.
"We could use some blow-dryers to heat things up," Britton relent-
lessly droned on.

There were some gasps, and I stifled a snort. Did he really want to kill the stake? "Just have a little faith," he told us. The institute teacher's face was red, and he gestured wildly at Britton. He probably wasn't enjoying the announcements like everyone else was.

"Oh yes," Britton said smoothly. "We've been asked to stress modesty in all things. Charity asked me to *discreetly* point out that you all have a problem with it." I watched Charity stiffen, but there was no way the Relief Society president could deny it. You would think she'd know better than to confide in Britton. "So in Charity's behalf, I'm to remind you," Britton said. "No double sins, guys. Actually, I'm just talking to the girls."

I groaned. Not the double-sin talk. Liza from the gossiping floor raised her hand, and I tried to will her to silence. *Don't ask, don't ask.* "What's a double sin?" she asked.

Britton smiled broadly. "Oh, well, it just means that nothing of a scandalous nature should be worn to the pool. And . . . it also means no one, I mean no one, *especially you,* should be wearing that belly-busting, strappy, pop-out thing, pumpkin. That's a double sin." His voice left no doubt of how disgusting he thought it looked. Liza glared up at him, and he met her eyes calmly. He was handling this all wrong, and he was doing it on purpose. Good. All attention was on him. It wouldn't be on how late I was.

I caught sight of an open seat between Maggie and Christian, knowing this would be the best moment to sneak in unnoticed. I dove around the benches and chairs, hopping over some legs. "Excuse me." I smashed a poor girl's toes and almost landed in some guy's lap. He didn't look like he minded.

"Hey, institute rep, glad you could make it," Britton announced to the room in general. Now it was my turn for the unwanted spotlight and I forced my expression into a calm one. "We know it's dollar night at the theater, Sister Children," he drawled, "so we appreciate your sacrifice. I'm sure it was difficult to tear yourself away from such recent and pleasant company."

Thanks, Britton. I guess it could've been worse. I sat limply next to Christian. Charity was sitting in front of us, just to the side, running her fingers through her jet black hair. She didn't even look at me. Brother Baer swiftly took over the microphone as Britton made his casual way down the aisle. "Now we will have a spiritual thought by Raine Lyon," he announced, giving Britton a warning look.

My head went up. Did he mean Lane Bryant? Was this institute going to be dedicated to me? It would be if Britton had anything to do with it. Of course Britton would ask *him* to do the thought. There was no trusting him.

"I thought you were going to stand me up again, Jacks," Christian said in an undertone.

"She was on a date," Maggie whispered proudly.

"We heard she was going out to sea."

"Did Britton announce it?" I asked. He had taken a seat somewhere behind us, and I turned to see a whole army of cold stares meeting mine. I jerked in alarm. The whole Bitter Boys Club was sitting behind me like Peter Pan's lost boys with glasses, zits, intense stares, pale skin—Okay, okay, so none of them actually looked like that. In fact, they were all cute in their own way. It wasn't what they looked like that turned the girls off, actually. It's what they did.

Brock the Bleak, sometimes known as the ward dinosaur, sat next to Britton. He had blond hair and brown eyes. Normally this was a good combination, but Brock just never smiled. He wasn't hot, but he wasn't ugly either. Believe me, I've seen guys succeed with less. He just acted too desperate. At least he had until Britton got a hold of him. Now he wouldn't deign to talk to anyone unless he was insulting them.

And then there was Bryan the Baby, Brock's younger brother. Bryan had inherited his brother's looks except he smiled and it suited him. He had left a trail of broken hearts until the girls got wise, and now they wouldn't give him the time of day. He didn't succeed because he thought he was all that, and sadly, in the end, he wasn't.

Barney of the Unfortunate Name sat at the end of the Bitter Boys pew. He stared back at me with watery eyes. His greasy hair stuck up at the back of his head like a cat had licked it. He was elders quorum secretary. He didn't succeed with the ladies for innumerable reasons, but the first and foremost was that he was way too scared to socialize.

Together with his league of Bitter Boys, Britton held Bitter Boys councils. I called them BBCs. There they discussed ways to overthrow the cold tyranny of women. It didn't matter what we did, these boys were bitter, even if they were the ones to break off relationships. It was a strange phenomenon. I was surprised that I hadn't sensed their glares at my back the moment I sat down. I swiveled away, not wanting trouble.

Raine Lyon brought his scriptures to the podium and set them down heavily. He was also a part of the Bitter Boys ranks. "I would like to talk about marriage." He waited for an audible gasp from the group, which didn't happen, before he continued.

"It wasn't really a date," I quickly explained to Christian. "It was a UDA. It meant nothing."

"A UDA? I've never heard of that."

"That's because you're not a girl. It's an Unidentified Dating Activity, which means I wasn't sure who my date was exactly, or if it was even a date."

"So how was there any pairing off?" Maggie asked in confusion.

"Well, they left me alone for a while to go the store," I said. Maggie just looked at me blankly. "And nothing ever really happened after that. Basically it was just hanging out."

Maggie blanched. Christian crossed his arms across his chest. "Any winners?" he asked.

"Yeah," I said. Christian looked surprised. "Me," I informed him. He rolled his eyes. "Let's just say that I would rather be playing video games with Lane Bryant."

At that moment I glanced up and saw Raine staring at me. "I used to hate the law of chastity," he said.

Christian's lip curled until he fought it down and met my eyes. I guess the topic was appropriate since this summer's institute program was based on marriage principles, but what kind of opening was that?

"Oh, not that I had a problem with the law of chastity," Raine amended. "Not like a lot of other people I know, but I just like to question everything."

"I take it back," I choked.

Christian's eyes danced. "I thought you would."

Raine's voice echoed over us. "I used to think, if I get married, it won't be my fault. I really didn't want to get married, but now I realize that I *do* want to be with one girl, even though she's driving me crazy."

Liza smiled happily in the front, and I just hoped she was right. Raine turned his hopeful gaze on me, and I scooted closer to Christian, who gave me a confused look. I smiled up at him for effect, refusing to change my position.

Raine cleared his throat. "I guess marriage is something that we all have to get over with. You can't just check someone off your list without getting to know them first."

Well, that wasn't a problem. I already knew Raine . . . sorta. Maybe he should take his own advice with Liza. She was looking very hopeful all of a sudden. After exchanging looks with her, Raine abruptly ended his off-the-wall speech and left the stand, and Brother Baer took his place. His finger was on his lips as he stared out at us. Brother Baer was a confident middle-aged guy with a receding hairline. Unfortunately, he was also stuck in the eighties. He had his shirt tucked neatly into his khakis. He always looked so watchful, almost as if he was pondering the very depths of our souls. It made us be quiet.

"Thank you for that brave insight on chastity," he said. "I'm sure we all needed to hear it, though I'm sure no one will tell you that personally." He laughed at his own joke, but nobody got it.

Maggie leaned over to me. "The Monsieur came by to visit while you were gone."

My heart gave a strange leap as my gaze swept the room. "Is he here now?"

Maggie shook her head. "He said something about going to practice the piano. He just seemed really impatient to see you. He waited for at least an hour."

What was with that guy? He always came by when I was gone or when other guys turned up. Just my luck. What did he want this time? I exchanged looks with Maggie, trying to read her look, but I couldn't get it. Neither could Christian. "Save it," he said. He hated our girl telepathy.

Brother Baer was now pacing the room. On the whole he was a sensible guy, besides putting out a bounty on Britton's lips and bribing guys to dance with me at institute dances. And he was always a little crazed about his lessons. Actually, none of us were sure if he was all there.

"Heber J. Grant was a man and a woman much like you and I," Brother Baer said. "I mean, he was a man, not a woman." He laughed. "No, don't worry. I'm not teaching new doctrine here."

I smiled. What was he talking about? I noticed a paper being passed through the pews in front of us and a few snickers followed it. My lip curled. What was that?

"You just can't let it get you down. Sure, you might be having a bad hair day," Brother Baer said, smoothing his receding hairline back. "I have a bad hair day everyday." I cocked my head. So I stopped paying attention for one second. Did that mean I had to lose track of the entire lesson all the time? Of course, I wasn't sure how much everyone else was following him either.

He pointed to a bald kid near the front. He always picked on the front, which is why I never sat too close. "Brother, looks like we're both being translated one hair at a time."

We all groaned. Brother Baer taught in true institute teacher fashion, but I knew the truth. He was just trying to throw us off guard, and I watched him narrowly. Probably no one but me suspected that the madness was feigned. But just like Hamlet, Brother Baer knew a hawk from a handsaw. He knew much more than any of us gave him credit for.

"What makes you think that you need to find some perfect person to marry when there is absolutely no one perfect here?" His hand swept over the room. "With what measure you mete, it shall be measured unto thee. Think about it." He met my eyes, and I tried not to look away.

"Marriage is like rolling down a cliff." He smacked his lips as if devouring each word like a tasty morsel. We all knew his goal in life was to become an EFY speaker, and he was very close. "There are a series of bumps and cuts along the way, knocking off a selfish limb here and an annoying habit there."

"Sounds delightful," Britton muttered behind us. I tried to ignore him.

"There might be someone compatible with you in this very room. There might even be five or six right here," he said. "There is no 'one and only'! There's someone out there for you somewhere. She'd better have been born by now or else you're going to be a cradle robber."

Oh, that was a really good line. I took out the notebook I always kept in my scripture case.

"I married way above me. I never thought that I would find such a girl. Neither of us is perfect, but our relationship is the closest to perfection we'll ever find here on earth. That's because we're working on our marriage. A celestial marriage takes work. At twenty-three I was married. At twenty-four I was having kids."

"Quit rubbing it in," Christian said under his breath.

I chuckled. That was a good line too. It was all good material for an article, though I wasn't sure just yet how I would be using it.

Brother Baer laughed. "I often ask myself why I have such a wonderful marriage. I certainly don't deserve it. But one day a thought came into my head: do you honestly think that God gave you such a marriage *just for you?* And that's when I knew, there's got to be an example of something good out there."

I pulled my head up from my notebook, watching him closely. He had a point, but I wasn't sure how I could weave that into one of my love advice columns. I could give the world a pep talk on dating. I would have to use this junk, since I definitely didn't know from experience. I started scribbling in my notebook. My writing was my equivalent of a nest egg, and I just hoped that someday it would help me live . . . kind of like a retirement plan.

"Guys, ask the girls out."

Raine quickly raised his hand.

"Girls, quit taking your dates so seriously. You don't have to marry everyone you date. At least let's hope not."

Raine's hand went down. The paper that was making its swift way around the room had finally reached him and he had stopped to read it. He suddenly smirked.

Brother Baer always talked in extremes, but it was obvious he was trying to ditch the polite lectures we were all used to, since most of us were beyond hearing until we were knocked on the side of the head, and even then . . .

Was Britton reading over my shoulder? My pen hesitated until I decided to write: *If Britton's reading over my shoulder, he'll be sorry.* There was no reaction to that, and I knew it was really time to test him. *Britton's hot,* I wrote.

"Even if I wanted to read over your shoulder," Britton said, "there's no way I can crack that code. Your handwriting is completely illegible."

"Yeah, well yours isn't that good either."

"I'm a guy. I have an excuse." He leaned in closer. "What did you think of your hapless suitor?"

"We're better off as friends," I whispered.

"You don't pick your friends very well." I glanced behind me. There was a strange smile playing on his lips that I couldn't quite explain.

"I've had my share of dating," Brother Baer said. He went from a whisper to a shout in a second, milking the drama for all it was worth. "So I know what you're going through. The mind games, the rejections, the love triangles, the squirrelly girls, burnt girls, bitter boys, back-burner guys."

I straightened. How did he know that lingo? Who had he been talking to? Maggie shoved the roll in my face, and I flipped through the pages to find my name. Maggie had already marked it for me. Her service knew no bounds, and I guffawed when I saw my description next to my name.

According to this I was six years old. I wondered who had rigged the dates, though I was actually glad that my birthday wasn't there for all to see. Speaking of which, I searched for Charity's and sighed in disappointment. She hadn't even bothered to write her birthday down next to her name. How old was she anyway?

"So what if?" Brother Baer asked us. "What if he isn't the right one? What if she isn't? We can't actually fit two people together like puzzle pieces. To be honest, marriage isn't about fitting two people together perfectly anyway."

I tried to pass the roll to Christian, but I was having a hard time getting his attention. As usual, he was in his own little world, his brows furrowed. I took my pen and poked him in the back of the neck. He calmly wrestled it from me with one hand and glanced at the roll, seeing my name first. "You're six years old, huh?"

"Give or take twenty years."

His lips curled, but he wasn't laughing at me. No, just at the couple straight ahead. The girl was rubbing her fiancé's back, but then she lifted her fingers to stare at her diamond, elbowing Charity next to her. The girl had been doing it all night. I snickered.

The guy part of the couple turned to look back at us with dark eyes and disheveled hair. He played the part of the brooding poet well. Ivan. I called him Hurricane Ivan. Well, it looked like he had found his disaster relief. I laughed and Maggie gave me a warning look.

"I suppose that's possible," Christian muttered. I glanced at him sharply. He gave me a sideways smile. "You act like a six-year-old." He was talking about the roll, and he passed it on to the pew in front.

"Why seek ye the living among the dead?" Brother Baer asked. "You won't find a good living relationship among the spiritually dead, the noncommittal, the jerks. Raise your hand and repeat after me. You can't change *anyone* after marriage."

No one did it, even though he was absolutely right.

"The same spirit that possesses the body will possess you in marriage," he reminded us. "So quit wasting your time. Spiritual girls can be beautiful too!"

I wondered why he even had to say it. I smirked, but quickly stopped when Brother Baer gave me a stern look. Charity was writing furiously in front of me, and I couldn't help but pull a Britton. I spied over her shoulder. Her writing was actually discernable, and I smiled when I saw what she was writing. She was making a list of qualities that she wanted in a husband and was checking them off. She was one of those list writers, was she? *Sensitive, worthy, protective, kind, a great sense of humor.* They were all checked. There was only one guy I knew like that, and I stole my pen back from him. Christian let it go without a fight.

I knew it! She was after him bad. It just showed that girls *did* go for nice guys, no matter how many times guys accused us of going for jerks. No matter how many times Britton said that nice guys finished last, the nice guy would win in the end, or lose in this case if Charity dated him. I decided I would fight for Christian every step of the way.

"What are you writing?" Christian asked. He put his arm around me, pulling me closer so he could see.

I slapped my hand over my notebook. *Garbage.* I had written *that* down. My writing was pretty sloppy, so even if he had seen it, there couldn't have been any possibility that he had been able to make any sense of it, but I wasn't taking any chances. "I'm just . . . if guys think . . . my next article . . . uh, yeah, I just don't want you to read all the tender things I've written about you." I smiled weakly.

"Just when I think you aren't listening, you prove it. I thought you were actually taking notes." *Well, I was, sorta.*

"What are other things stopping us from dating?" Brother Baer asked. *Fear, of course.* No one volunteered the obvious answer. "Uh, this is the part where we raise our hands," he said.

True to form, Maggie raised her hand since no one else did. "Selfishness," she said. I jumped. I didn't expect that answer from her. "We'll never be the kind of person who can honor marriage and take care of children if we don't think of someone else besides ourselves once in a while."

Everyone started talking at once, and Brother Baer nodded at her. "Murmuring is a manifestation of our fear." He cracked a smile.

Hurricane Ivan roughly patted down his fiancé's hair in front of us. He was probably trying to be affectionate, but it was almost like he was petting a cat's fur backwards. I just hoped that he wouldn't pull her hair out. I smiled at the thought, then turned to see Christian's reaction. We always thought the same things were funny. And just as I guessed, he looked amused.

"So, why don't *you* really want to go out?"

"Huh? What?" I stared at Christian. What was he saying? "I'm sorry. I was looking at you, but I wasn't listening."

Christian smirked. I always used that line on him. I was a perpetual spacer-outer. We both had that in common, but for completely different reasons. For me, the world was just too interesting to stay in one place at once, namely the present. For him, it just wasn't interesting enough.

Before Christian could rephrase the question, the paper that was being passed down the pews had finally reached me. Maggie passed it onto me without looking at it. "How swiftly judgment comes to the wicked," Britton hissed behind us. It looked like a newspaper, and I stared down at the column.

Welcome to the first underground paper at BYU, I read to myself. The Bitter Boys were now publishing? I groaned. "Like no one has come up with an underground paper here before," I whispered to Britton behind me. "What's the matter? No one else will publish you?"

"No one dares."

I scanned the column. *She may be fun to flirt with,* I read, *but her intentions are as empty as her head. She'll never take you seriously. Like all BYU coeds, she rejects all guys 95% of the time.* I laughed. "No, just you. She just rejects you," I muttered.

My voice trailed off when I noticed the hostile glares coming in my direction from the majority of guys in the room. Completely untrue news traveled fast, it seemed. I gulped, seeking the headline to see what I was up against. My eyes widened when I found it. *"The Worst Miss from the 73rd ward, A Menace to the Male Society."* It was a counter-article to one of mine, and let's be honest, we all knew who this was aimed at. I read the subtitle, *Woman Causes Miss-ery. Do We Miss-Read, or Does She Purposely Miss-Lead?* This was crazy. I didn't mislead anybody!

What was Britton doing anyway? He knew he had gone too far earlier, didn't he? I found myself mindlessly reading the first paragraph.

Let's not forget little Miss-Behaves, it said. *Sometimes known as Miss-Chief, she borders on the Miss-Fit side. Whether she is putting her interests on the back burner or she's just Miss-Aligned, she excels at breaking hearts. She's the worst Miss on the market. Miss—no, that's too polite of a term— let's just call her the worst squirrelly girl in our ward's history.*

My stomach clenched at that.

She's been taught her whole life to get married, so to avoid the guilt, she goes for jerks like her who won't make a real move so that she is miraculously no longer in the wrong. Someone needs to shove Old Ironsides out to sea or she'll rot on the docks and contaminate the whole lot of . . .

"Uh, so what's this about?" Christian cut off my attention from the paper.

I found myself senselessly thrusting it out at him. "I can't believe your roommate!" He had officially declared war, but why? He knew I would get even. But at the time, I wasn't smart enough to figure out that I was playing into his hands . . . or someone else's hands for that matter.

Christian pulled his arm away from me to look at it, and his eyes got dark with anger. "Britton," he muttered. "Don't take it personally. He thinks *all* girls are devils." He watched me closely, trying to gauge whether I thought it was funny or not.

"I can't believe he's trying to mess with me. I can outwrite him anytime, that punk." I couldn't even bring myself to look at Britton, although I knew he was waiting for a reaction. Once institute was over, he was going to get it. "You have no idea what I can do or what I'm capable of."

"Oh, I think I do." Christian glanced at the articles, and for a moment I thought he was going to laugh. He kept it in, but I pursed my lips as I turned from him.

"We can't be afraid," Brother Baer said. "That is Satan's tool against us."

"Oh, he'd better be afraid," I fumed.

"Banish all fear from your minds. Actually see the people around you. Look at your possibilities. Know that the Spirit speaks to your minds and your hearts."

"That's got to be his fifth closing statement," I growled. I was eager to let loose.

"Dating is the most wonderful thing that you'll never want to do again," Brother Baer said, and with that, he closed the lesson. I was more than ready.

Chapter 8

The highest exercise of charity is charity
towards the uncharitable.
—J. S. Buckminster

Tuesday, June 16th, evening

Everyone stood up, and I waited impatiently for the way to clear. It wasn't happening so I started fighting my way through the crowds.

"Looking forward to refreshments tonight?" Maggie asked from behind me.

Of course. I needed my carbs: cake, cookies, donuts, anything I could bite into. But that wasn't what was propelling me with such energy. I was searching out my Bitter Boys president.

Someone grabbed my arm, trying to stop me. "Hey, is the directory done yet?" It was my favorite freshman, Betsy. Normally, I'd shoot the breeze for hours with the kid, but this time I shook my head, escaping quickly only to get headed off by some guy I didn't even know.

"You look familiar." He grinned at me, and I couldn't return the sentiment. That's the problem when you go on so many blind dates . . . many, many awkward moments. "Oh yeah, I know why," he said finally. "You went on a date with my roommate."

Uh-oh, did he hate me now? What did I do? What number was he? Did I break his heart? I faked a smile. "And how are *you* doing?" I hated my life.

"Well, I got into the art program," he said between bites of Jell-O. Jell-O? What kind of treat was that for institute? That wouldn't fill up anybody!

I heard a smooth voice behind me and my eyes narrowed. "Something to show my posterity." Britton was already bragging to an audience.

It made me forget all sense of propriety. "Excuse me," I told the roommate guy and dove back into the crowd. I saw Britton holding up the Bitter Boys paper to his group of Bitter Boys. They were laughing. *Ooh!* How many of those were out there? "What posterity?!" I shouted. "You actually expect to get married?" I jerked it from his hands. Surprisingly he let it go without a fight, but he still had that mocking expression on his face. "How could you write this?" I asked.

"What? Did you think I would let you have all the fun? You stereotype men, I stereotype women. Opposition in all things."

"I suppose I can *always* count on you."

"Yep."

I sucked in my breath. Very funny. Not really, but that wasn't going to stop me from stapling it to my journal as some sort of sick memento of my life. "The main thrust of your article was dedicated to the 73rd ward squirrelly girl. I don't own that title, you yellow journalist. That's slander."

"Libel," he corrected. "And name one thing I wrote that wasn't true." I hesitated. Anything I said he'd twist, and he made a pout with his lips when I remained stubbornly silent. "Prove me wrong then."

So, this was his way of trying to fix me? Writing a stupid fake newspaper article about me? Was he still feeling bad for making me cry this afternoon? Well, if that was the case, it would've been better for me if he had that heart of stone that everyone thought he had. I couldn't take his meddling anymore. First the date and now the paper. What would his guilt-ridden mind come up with next? I crossed my arms.

"I don't answer to anybody, least of all the president of the Bitter Boys Club," I lashed out. It was the first time that he had heard his official title, and I didn't hesitate to throw it in his face. It was my turn to fix him.

He looked a little startled, and I smirked until he quickly recovered. "Bitter boy?" he asked. "I'm a man, and I'd call it apathetic, not bitter. Big difference. The comforting arms of apathy are quite soothing in a way. I can do anything because I don't care." I wasn't sure how to combat that. Britton always had a way with words.

"Women are nothing but trouble," one of his sidekicks piped in more crudely. It was Brock. "Either that or they're ugly. All of my exes had problems."

"Yeah, *you*, Brock the Bleak." *Garbage*. I was throwing out their nicknames all over the place, and I didn't even care. My hands landed on my hips as I glared at him.

Instead of looking angry, he just looked intrigued. Please tell me that I wasn't doing it again. *It was called rude, not sassy!—why did everyone think it was flirting!* There were two dangers to talking to a Bitter Boy: having to listen for hours about the sins of women or getting asked out and joining the ranks of sinners. I decided to remind him that I was a wicked woman to avoid my punishment. "Even your Xbox doesn't like you, punk," I said.

He frowned, but Britton laughed. "And you would know. You've had plenty of troubles with exes, haven't you, Jacqueline? Perhaps we'll discuss your exes in our next paper: Mr. Examine-his-head-for-dating-you and Mr. Excellent-taste-for-dumping-you-on-your-head."

"Ooh, Britton. We're through. I'm never talking to you again!"

"That's a punishment?" I sucked in my breath and turned my back on him. "Hello, Maggot," he said.

It just figured that Maggie would choose this moment to approach us. She didn't even try to fight the nickname, which meant something was up. I couldn't defend her either because I had sworn my silence against Britton.

"I was looking for you, Jacqueline." I flinched when I heard the crinkle of the paper. How many of those things did Britton print out? "I found this."

"I'll get my revenge on him, Maggie, don't you worry."

Maggie looked a little uncomfortable. She wouldn't quite meet my eyes. I didn't think too much of it, even when she exchanged glances with Britton. I naturally assumed she was on my side.

There were a few snickers. "Well, it appears that Charity never faileth," Britton said. Was he talking about me or someone else? "Looks like she's caught a few men in her man trap." What? Was he trying to drive me nuts? But I refused to look, though now Britton had made me curious. What was Charity doing now? "Looks like she's trying to oust you from your position, Red."

One glimpse wouldn't hurt, and I peeked over my shoulder. The whole Bitter Boys association had already turned as one to watch the latest show. Charity looked like Scarlett O'Hara with her entourage of suitors. She was a regular Southern belle from Southern California—yeah, she had it all. We listened to her battle of words with her latest flirt. "You brat," she said.

Oh, she was good.

"And what is Charity without Faith and Hope," Britton muttered. Well, that's what he called them. Their real names were . . . what were their names anyway? Her blond friends fought over whatever guy crumbs she flung their way. Well, they weren't real blond friends. They were just very bleached, high-maintenance friends with orange legs and blue eyes. How did they all have blue eyes?

Charity enveloped Faith and Hope in warm hugs, a common practice in front of the guys. The one with all the rings on her short stubby fingers acted like we didn't exist. The other girl wouldn't crack a smile when we were around. She looked very elegant with her hair in a twist. She was a dancer, and she never looked at me . . . ever. It was actually amusing. I wondered if I could get her to blink by acting even more like an idiot. I doubted it.

Charity then proceeded to give hugs to all her boy toys. Such a sweet, fake girl. She had fake down to a science: fake tan, fake hair, fake nails, fake smile. I watched her with narrowed eyes. I could just imagine her making notch marks with her lipstick in some secret gaming book she stashed in her purse.

"Look at all those guys she's got on the back burner," I muttered. "Ten at least."

"What? What's that mean?" Maggie asked.

The Bitter Boys knew and they shook their heads angrily at the Relief Society ringleader. "Now, apply the Bitter Boys publication to her and you've got yourself a story," I said. "Let that prove I'm not the biggest squirrelly girl in the 73rd ward." I made sure that the comment was directed at Maggie, and not to *you know who.*

"Just because someone's taking over your job doesn't absolve you from your guilt," Britton retorted. I wasn't talking to him. I pursed my lips. "Does she bother you?" he asked. "Usually people that are carbon copies of you do."

I refused to answer. A hand landed on my shoulder and I jumped. "How disappointing for these young men that you're taken." Brother Baer smiled innocently at me, but I knew better. What was he up to? "Such a shame that you're off the market."

"I'm not off the market," I said needlessly. And he knew it too.

"Oh, then why are you *hanging out* with these losers again?"

I groaned. Now I understood. The institute teacher's plan was to stop us from hanging out. He wanted to shake things up a little bit in his own eccentric way. I saw through his clumsy attempt. "What?" I asked. "You want me to start *dating* these losers?" I'm sure that was his plan.

Maggie gasped at my blatant rudeness. The institute teacher tried to look just as surprised. "Are you saying that you're actually single? And none of these guys has asked you out yet?"

The institute teacher's number one goal was to get everyone married, and I smiled to throw him off. "How is that bounty on Britton's lips coming along?" I asked. "Any takers?"

Now Britton was in the hot seat, and he tried to avoid the institute teacher's free hand as it landed on his shoulder and squeezed him in a death grip. Brother Baer had both of us in his grasp. We were forced to stare at each other just the way he had planned. "Many ladies have applied for the position," Brother Baer said, "but so far, Brother Sergeant has managed to elude them."

"Sounds like he's got squirrelly girl tendencies," I said.

"Maybe you should get together," Brother Baer said in a deceptively innocent voice. We both grimaced. That was everyone's solution to everything. They wanted us to restrict our fighting to home, but Britton and I wriggled away from our institute teacher's grasp.

Brother Baer smiled broadly. Not even he was a good enough actor to repress his amusement. "Marriage is like dying," he told us. "You never know who will go first." He turned to Maggie, who was looking a bit uncomfortable. "At least you have a good friend to keep you in line." I noticed her smile was a little forced. That was probably one job she dreaded. "You've done so much good in this room already." He gazed around the place, most likely tallying all those who had received special help.

Maggie didn't want to be known as a service machine, so I tried to soften the blow. "Yeah, she's plotting to make everyone fat with those cookies so she can take out the competition," I said.

"It's the little Maggot's only flaw," Britton said. "Besides that, she's perfect."

Maggie's lips tightened, and I knew that I wasn't the only one Britton was driving crazy. Britton might as well call her Molly Mormon and get it over with. I wondered if that was his intention.

Maggie turned from us to stare at Charity's entourage of suitors. "Raine seems a little sad," she muttered almost imperceptibly. I doubted she even knew that she was talking aloud. "I'm going to do something for him." She said it mechanically, almost like she was reciting a line. There *was* something wrong, but I never in a million years would've guessed what it was, especially after that alarming statement.

"No!" Her cookies had almost done me in last time. "You might get caught in his video game web," I explained lamely.

"That's a chance that I'm willing to take."

"You're a saint," I muttered. "Why don't you make him fall in love with Liza while you're at it?"

"Making someone fall in love with anyone is quite the undertaking," Brother Baer said. I glanced nervously at him. There was a serious undertone to his voice, like he was actually considering my flippant comment. "Look at Christian and Charity for instance."

I swiveled, my heart in my throat. Now I knew exactly why I didn't like her, especially when I saw Christian stop midstride when she directed a flirtatious comment at him. She was going to make Christian a notch mark.

Well, not if I had anything to do with it. There had to be plenty of girls here who were worthy of him. One who was sweeter than me. I mean genuinely sweet, not fake, and she had to be strong, but not mean like I sometimes was. Witty, but not cruel like . . . uh, you get the picture. I quickly scanned the top floor of the institute building, unable to find this perfect girl.

Britton was shaking his head. "Christian, don't stop to talk to Potiphar's wife." He narrated the scene play by play, like some sort of mad sportscaster. "Flee and get yourself out. Run like Joseph of old." But Christian wasn't running. He had stopped to talk to her.

So far he was polite, but he was flirting back. He was a natural flirt anyway, but by the looks of things, he was saying something scandalous because Charity playfully hit him. I stifled a gasp. Playful hits always meant something.

Charity started comparing hand sizes with Christian. "Your hands are so big." Charity peered over Christian's shoulder and gave me a broad smile. She had caught me staring. Was she purposely tormenting me? How did she know I disapproved of her?

I turned violently on Britton. "You are supposed to be doing something about this."

"I thought you weren't talking to me!"

It wasn't the time to worry about trivial details. "I went through a whole date," I reminded him.

"Oh, you poor thing."

"It's more than *you* would do."

He clicked his tongue. "How touching. The squirrelly girl doesn't like another intruding on her territory?"

I swung viciously from him, my fists clenched tightly. "I'm a burnt girl. Get it straight!"

Brother Baer was catching onto our angst, and, true to form, he decided to play with it. "Let's define why a squirrelly girl is a squirrelly girl, shall we?" Oh no, he wasn't joining the fray, was he? This was certainly not the time. "The last thing a squirrelly girl thinks she wants is protection," he said. "She wants her freedom secured. Back-burner boys provide that security, though she doesn't know it. He's just a guy who's there anytime she wants him. Take it from a former back-burner boy. I cracked the code. My wife was a former squirrelly girl, you know."

Sister Baer? But she seemed so nice! He had to be mistaken. Britton was now staring at Brother Baer as if he had just discovered a very valuable jewel, but I had other concerns. My eyes were on Charity.

"If you won't do something, I will," I hissed to Britton. He had suddenly gone calm, and it was driving me crazy. I gave him a warning look.

"Have some refreshments," Britton said with half a smile.

I glared at him. "I don't like Jell-O."

"Oh, how tragic. You stayed your time and weren't paid properly for it. Perhaps other refreshments will suffice. There are plenty of men here, minus your sweet Christian, of course, but I'm sure there are quite a few of them who can appease your voracious appetite."

I turned swiftly on my heel, leaving Maggie and the Bitter Boys behind with the institute teacher. They could listen to his crazy theories and do nothing, but I had to stop this. I just didn't know how. I was so caught up in my own drama that I barely paid attention to the real drama unfolding behind me. No, it wasn't until later that I realized what I had missed. I had assumed Maggie was lecturing the Bitter Boys, but—well, we'll get to that later.

"Hey, Christian," I said in a saucy voice. "Come here. I've got a sweet nothing to whisper in your ear."

He turned immediately and I gave him a brilliant smile. He was way too good for the likes of Charity. "A sweet nothing?" he asked. "How about a sweet something? You might as well back up your words for once, Jacks."

Charity gasped, not happy that I was intruding on her territory. "You see?" she said in her fakest voice. "You're perfectly scandalous."

No he wasn't! Christian laughed at her. "To the impure, nothing is holy," he said. Charity hit him and he smirked, completely enjoying himself.

Luring Christian away from Charity would be harder than I thought, but when all else failed, I knew I could use the damsel in distress ploy. I had plenty of ammunition. "Christian," I whispered in an urgent voice. "You've got to defend my honor. Britton is taunting me with that paper. Can't you tell him to knock it off? He won't listen to me."

"He's still bugging you about that?" I nodded, trying to keep down my smile, not daring to believe my trick was actually working. I bit my lip. It made me look more pathetic. "What's the matter with him?" he asked.

With one last backward glance at Charity, I followed Christian into the fray. If Britton wouldn't come to Christian's aid, Christian would come to mine. Britton watched him approach with lazy eyes. Maggie was just pulling away from him, her little chin tilted in a determined angle. Brother Baer was nowhere to be found.

"Ah, Christian, cleaving unto Charity I see," he said. "How could you tear yourself away?"

Christian ignored that. "What's going on here?"

Britton merely smiled. "It appears Charity has many virtues. You'd better hurry back to her side or her latest fan will steal her from you."

Lane Bryant had just come in for the kill. He had glommed onto Charity after the tree episode. I didn't feel guilty at all, except for the fact that it might propel Christian to action. What was Britton thinking, taunting Christian back into the arms of Charity? He was seriously bad at this.

"Why can't you leave Jacks alone?" Christian asked.

Britton tugged the paper from my grip. "It's called intervention, so she won't end up like the gingerbread man. Catch me if you can, and then the wily fox gets her in the end. Her own little jerk . . . just what she wants."

"I don't want a jerk, Britton!"

He smirked, obviously enjoying himself. "Are you sure about that? What happened to Mr. Nice Guy?"

Brock jumped to Britton's side and pulled something from his backpack in front of Maggie's shocked eyes. It was a Mr. Nice Guy Doll, our Mr. Wonderful knockoff.

"Hey, that's mine!" she said stiffly. "I was wondering where he was!"

"Whatever," Britton said. "You never tried to get him back. You never wrote. You never called. You never cared."

I laughed, feeling much better now that Christian was in our protective ranks. Was Britton angry that we never caught on to his prank? "We didn't know you had him," I said a little too proudly. Maggie wasn't taking it as well as I was. She seemed a little stiff.

"Who else would take him?" Britton took Mr. Nice Guy from Brock and held it out for all of us to see. It was just like him to bring a visual aid. What did he think this was? Relief Society? "Behold, exhibit A." He pulled the string.

"You smell great!" it piped. Britton smiled and jerked the string again. "Looks like you're losing weight." He began snapping the string like some deranged monkey. "I love *Pride and Prejudice!* It's my turn to cook dinner! Didn't you need some new clothes?"

"Yep, that's just how I like my men." I tried to take it from him but only managed to knock it from his hands. It fell limply to the floor.

All of the Bitter Boys' eyes were on Mr. Nice Guy lying helplessly on the floor. "And that's what happens to Mr. Nice Guy." Britton leaned against a door. "They should make a Mr. Jerk doll. It would be much more popular with the ladies."

"And he needs long Fabio hair," Christian couldn't help adding.

Britton pulled a fake string in the air. "Make me food, woman." He pretended to tug the string again. "Leave me alone. I'm watching the game." Britton was obviously enjoying himself. "No, I don't wanna talk. Do I look like I care?"

"That is not funny," Maggie said. I smiled. It actually was in a sick way.

"Who broke your legs? Take the trash out yourself."

"Britton." Now she had her warning voice.

"You put the kids to bed. I'm not a woman." He was really getting into it, wasn't he? "Don't bother with makeup, nothing will help." He turned to me. "Doesn't that make you feel just tingly all over?"

"Yep." Two could play this game.

Britton stilled, determined to get a reaction from me. "Sure, a woman can have an opinion—if I give her one." The whole Bitter Boys league erupted into laughter, and Britton put his hand down, done pulling the invisible strings and pushing my buttons. "Admit it. You like jerks, don't you?"

"I don't like you, Britton."

I was really proud of that retort, until he said, "You went out with the one who shall not be named." I was silent. He was doing it again, twice in one day. It was a record, even for him. I took a steadying breath. "A nice guy is just the male version of the sweet spirit," he said.

No wonder Britton had such a following. He was very convincing. I didn't doubt that Britton tried to pull this intervention with all his Bitter Boys.

I picked Mr. Nice Guy up and patted his perfect plastic hair. "Let me tell you something, buddy. The only reason I'd end up with a jerk is because they're the only ones who act interested enough to ask us out and make us feel attractive. But nice guys don't even give us a clue of their feelings. As far as we know, they have none."

"Whoa," Christian said. "You almost convince me to be a jerk."

My eyes widened.

"No, no," Britton said quickly. He was getting the opposite response from what he wanted. "Don't give in, get smarter. Become too sophisticated to fall prey to the evil designs of women." Britton's eyes were on mine, gauging my reaction, and I didn't disappoint him. I flinched. Britton wasn't president of the Bitter Boys Club for nothing. He was dangerous.

"You mean join the ranks of the Bitter Boys?" I asked.

He shrugged. "At least we're true to our principles."

Christian couldn't actually be listening to this. My heart thumped uncomfortably. I knew that Britton could be very convincing. He had his share of followers: men who used to walk like men but had let fear overtake them. But if I was the one who convinced Christian to join Britton's ranks . . . well, I couldn't stand losing one of my best friends like that.

"Christian, don't even think about it. If you did that I . . . I wouldn't have anything to do with you."

"Perfect," Britton said with a laugh. "So you're in, Christian?"

Christian smiled wryly and he glanced at me. "Do you really believe that jerks win?" If he meant Charity, yes, but this time I wouldn't let her.

Maggie stepped in before I could. She was adamantly against this. "No, the nice guy *always* wins!"

"In your little world, Maggot," Britton told her.

I snorted. That wasn't true at all. Maggie always went for charity cases. "Look, we get tricked, okay," I blurted. And then I froze, seeing Christian's eyes almost peer into my soul. Some things I've never confided to anyone, most likely because I'm not even aware of them myself: my self-destructive tendencies. There wasn't any help for me, but for him there was. Maybe that's why I was being so open about it. "Jerks are master manipulators. Guys fall for jerks too." He didn't look convinced. "A girl doesn't *really* want a jerk," I told him. "Take it from a girl. I'm a girl, you know!"

"And you don't know what you want," Britton said.

I wasn't ready to give up yet. "Jerks trick us into thinking they're nice guys. That's the only reason it works. It's only later that we realize it isn't real. He's a mirage of what we really want, what all girls want—a nice guy with some guts. You have to believe me."

"Oh, how tender," Britton said in a sarcastic voice, but the Bitter Boys behind him were listening intently. Christian was watching me thoughtfully.

"Hmm," Maggie said. She seemed to be watching me closely. "So, what nice guys do you like then, Jacqueline?"

Maggie was getting pretty smart. Although she hadn't really done it on purpose, she had completely stumped me. Who *did* I like? Mel Gibson, Colin Firth, Orlando Bloom . . . but real guys? I had no idea. I gulped, feeling my momentary control over the argument break.

Christian pulled away from the treat table. "Just promise me one thing, Jacks." He looked serious. "Don't go for any more jerks, huh?"

"What?" Even he thought I wanted a jerk. I didn't want anybody! My fingers clenched.

"Maybe," Britton suggested, "you should write an article on why girls go for jerks, Jack. That way you can write something you actually know about for a change."

Britton was brilliant, did I tell you that? I didn't know it at the time, and that's what made him so dangerous. I just thought he was being difficult.

"How about I write an article on why nice guys really do win . . . if they give themselves a chance!" I said.

"What? You mean if he asked you out?" Britton asked. "You'd just call him a barnacle, or in the words of our friends in Relief Society, a stalker . . ."

Christian stretched. "As much as I'd like to argue about this for the rest of the night, I'd rather go to HB double hockey sticks." That was our acronym for the HBLL, the BYU library. We gave everybody and everything nicknames around here, although it sounded strangely like he meant something else. "See ya, peeps. I gotta study for my test tomorrow."

Too late, I saw Charity waiting for him with a box of Jell-O on her hip. Oh no, honey, not this time. I tried to get between them, but

Britton blocked my way. "I think now it's time for the real treat," he drawled.

I didn't like his tone and I crossed my arms. "What are you talking about?" He nodded at them.

"Hey, Christian," Charity balanced the box on her hip. "Can you hold this for me?" She wasn't that weak, but he smiled and took it for her anyway. "When are we practicing ball?" she asked. Oh great, she was pounding the softball thing to death. She needed to get new material, but to my dismay it worked.

"How about tomorrow?" he said. I couldn't believe it.

"It's a date." I had a feeling she was saying it solely for my benefit, and my eyes met Britton's, but he just looked amused. How could he be so dense? I've seen Charity in action before. She dropped guys on their heads when she got tired of the chase. And that's when they joined the jerk club or the ranks of the Bitter Boys. I couldn't let this happen to the nicest guy I knew. There were enough jerks in the world without adding more to the junk pile.

Chapter 9

If you haven't got any charity in your heart,
you have the worst kind of heart trouble.
—Bob Hope

Tuesday, June 16th, evening

Britton didn't even watch Christian and Charity leave. I might have taken defeat gracefully, but that was before I saw Betsy gallop out the door after them. Charity greeted her warmly and my brows lifted. Was Charity stealing my freshman from me too? They couldn't sense evil, but still it was a double whammy. She wasn't really nice, she was just pretending! Could no one else see that?

"And so it starts," Britton said. "Too bad a guy like him can never win."

"What are you talking about?" I couldn't just stand here and do nothing. "Lots of girls like him," I reminded him hotly.

"Sure, but they'll never go for him. He'll lose out in the end every time. Think about who he likes—the biggest squirrelly girl in the ward." He clicked his tongue. "Nope, he's just too nice to win her."

I clenched my teeth. "I don't want him to win the biggest squirrelly girl in the ward."

Britton smiled at me, conveniently ignoring my outburst. "Do you want to hear what my new experiment is? It's called the broad approach. I'm going to be a jerk to see how many girls I can get." The Bitter Boys grumbled in appreciation behind him.

Maggie's eyes looked like they would pop out of her head. "Now wait a minute, Britton. You never told me about that!" *What had he told her?*

Before Britton could try to defend himself against her, I snorted. "Whatever. It's not as if being a jerk is that big of a stretch for you."

"Yes, but I haven't put my full efforts into being a jerk."

"No, it just comes naturally. And the girls are really pounding down your doors."

"Jacqueline," Maggie said in a warning voice. "Britton, this is ridiculous! Maybe this isn't such a good idea." Neither of us paid any attention to her.

"Of course they aren't," Britton agreed. "I haven't been making false promises yet. I think it's time I show you girls how it's done, to prove to you that the nice guy will never win. Let's make the Monsieur exhibit B, shall we? He rarely makes an appearance, he rarely returns calls, he rarely lifts a finger, yet girls are all over him. Maybe it's the lack of effort that makes a difference?" Britton seemed to be toying with us as if he already knew the answer. "But as you so cleverly pointed out, he makes the girls feel attractive and special."

"A nice guy could do that," I said hurriedly, "if he had the guts."

"Except the jerk drops the girl at the peak of her interest," Britton mused. "He suddenly becomes The Challenge, driving the girls wild in their efforts to win his attention back. Whether he does it intentionally or not, it works every time."

"The girl is just confused," I stuttered. "She thought he was a nice guy, and she's just giving him a chance to redeem himself."

"There's no way to prove your theory," Maggie said with some difficulty. She gulped, glancing at Britton as if the very idea made her squirm. She always was his killjoy. "Unless you get some nice guy going after the same girls a jerk goes after, your experiment is a waste of time." It came out almost reluctantly, but I agreed.

"Of course," Britton said. "Why didn't I think of it before? We need the control specimen in order to experiment with the variable. We'll pit a nice guy against a jerk, and then we'll see who gets the most dates after this is through."

"The nice guy will win!" Maggie said.

"No way," Britton said. "No way."

I was silent, weighing the odds. Britton didn't even know the game. He threw girls off before they could even get interested. But if we could get a nice guy with some guts to represent nice guys everywhere, they might have a chance.

"I think I'll take you up on that offer, Jacqueline," he said. "If the nice guy wins, you can write your optimistic article, but if I win, you'll have to write the truth."

It *was* the truth—nice guys win! And furthermore, I had never made that offer in the first place. But even still . . . "That sounds like a challenge, Britton Sergeant," I said.

"And you're always up for a challenge, aren't you?"

I snickered. "Depends on the terms."

"Mr. Nice Guy and Mr. Jerk go after the biggest squirrelly girl in the ward." His eyes were on mine and they glittered mischievously. "Whoever catches her, wins."

Charity! He'd make her the butt of this wager? My lip curled with amusement. I could just imagine the mayhem that would result when she found herself caught in such a web. Maybe she'd think twice before messing with poor innocents. Plus, it would be the perfect distraction from Christian. In fact, if she could fall for some other guy permanently, I'd no longer have to worry about her. That meant no more pity dates, no more deals with Britton, no more flirting Christian away. I could just relax.

"I wager," Britton continued, "that I'll steal the girl from Mr. Nice Guy even before he has a chance to catch her."

I liked the way that sounded. Of course, the Nice Guy would win, especially if Maggie and I interfered. I knew what tricks to use to get Charity begging, but that didn't take away the fact that Charity would have to put up with Britton trying to win her hand. It would be hilarious.

"That isn't nice at all," Maggie shrilled.

"Oh, Charity deserves it," I said evilly. Britton gave me a wicked grin.

"Yeah, but it wouldn't be nice to mess with Christian that way," said Maggie.

"Christian?" I almost yelled it. They both leaned forward, covering my mouth while the last remnants of institute attendees turned our way. I wriggled free. Why did she have to put ideas like that into Britton's head? "Who said anything about Christian?" I gave her a dirty look.

Britton gave us a moment to consult with our eyes and then he purposely misinterpreted our mind reading. "Done," he said.

"No, no, no!" I didn't want Charity to get together with Christian. "Find another nice guy. I don't want this one to win." Britton's eyebrows shot up. "Don't give me that look," I said. "You know how I feel about Charity."

"No one else fits the bill as well as Christian does," he said.

"Yes," I agreed sarcastically, "and you're the perfect jerk. This changes nothing."

"And who plays the top squirrelly girl in the ward?"

At least now he was admitting that it was Charity. "And he likes her. I still don't care."

He nodded slowly. "The ingredients are all there. What's the matter? Are you afraid that I'll win?"

"No!" Quite the opposite.

"We're not afraid," Maggie said. "She'll love him by his birthday."

The Fourth of July? That was only three weeks away. I couldn't bear to lose him that fast. "Maggie, don't get into this."

But too late, Britton had picked up his cue. "Perfect. A time limit. We'll make it a three-week program! That way I don't have to waste too much time on this."

"No!"

"What? You want longer?" Now, Britton was playing with me.

I rolled my eyes, but I knew how to get Maggie to back off. "I'm sorry. Mormons don't bet. Right, Maggie?"

"That's only when they're afraid they're going to lose," Britton said.

"Yeah, we're going to win," Maggie blurted. My eyes widened. This was so unlike her. "Just think of it as the ultimate Charity case. We're gonna help her fall in love with Christian. C'mon, he really likes her."

She had completely shocked me. Was that why she was joining forces with Britton? "So have you missed the fact that she's evil?"

Maggie suddenly looked uncomfortable. "She's struggling, sure."

I almost went cross-eyed trying not to laugh. "She's struggling," was the worst insult Maggie could give.

Britton's next words sobered me immediately. "Then we're agreed."

"No!"

"Oh, you have no faith in your man, do you?" I still refused to be coerced by Britton's fast-talking ways. "You do realize that it won't be long until Christian joins the ranks of the Bitter Boys." He was now using his new nickname freely, almost as if he liked it. "A nice guy can only take so much, and after so many blows, he becomes bitter. I'd say after he loses this squirrelly girl, he'll be joining the Bitter Boys Club. He'll be one of us."

Britton gave me a wicked grin that only a villain could pull off. "I can't tell you how many boys you've shot off the deep end already. Don't let him be another casualty." I gulped. Was it my fault Christian was turning bitter? How? What had I done?

"He really likes her," Maggie whispered.

"Yes, but Sister Children can't think of anyone but herself," Britton drawled. I stilled. I *was* thinking of him . . . too much lately. "That's what meddling is all about," he said. "What's the first thing you do when you're not happy with your life? Start messing with someone else's. It's called charity."

"But this won't make him happy!"

"Are you sure?" Maggie asked. She looked very earnest, and it confused me. How could she think this was right?

I sighed. Maybe I didn't understand how to make Christian happy. Happiness was an entirely different concept for me. For him, it was finding someone like Charity. For me, that would be prison.

"So maybe the true wager is," Britton said, "will he join the jerks or will he join us? Either way, it's inevitable. I see no one who will break this curse."

If anyone could, it would be me. Who did he drag along to every activity, every concert, every hiking trip? I knew everything about Christian, what made him tick, even his favorite music.

"I've never known you to back away from a challenge," Britton said.

I nodded stiffly. "Except where Christian is concerned."

"Very well, then fight for him. Love is war. Or can't you handle it?" I gulped. Britton laughed. "Perhaps you're just afraid that he'll actually fall for her."

That was the last straw. "He wouldn't," I argued. Britton wanted a war, did he? Well, he would get it. "Christian could win any squirrelly girl any day, especially if he's going up against you."

"Done." Britton stretched out his hand, and I pulled away from it as if he had leprosy. I couldn't believe I had almost played into those hands. I couldn't make Christian into a wager. "Who will win?" he said, completely unaffected by my violent reaction. "The nice guy or the jerk? Whatever happens after that is their business."

No, it was mine. I pulled a bobby pin from my hair and slammed it in his palm. It was the closest thing I could think of to declare war. There was no way I was doing this. No way!

I could hear Britton's echoing laughter as I stormed out, leaving Maggie and the rest of the Bitter Boys behind. What had Maggie just agreed to? I wasn't about to stand idly by and watch the biggest squirrelly girl in the ward win Mr. Nice Guy. And I wasn't about to write an article on why girls went for jerks either. I thought of the Monsieur with a grimace. I would never give him that satisfaction. But Christian wouldn't go for Charity. Not really, not in the end! He was much too smart, right?

I left the institute building in a hurry. Could I trust Christian to do the right thing? Could Mr. Nice Guy actually win the girl and still have the presence of mind to figure her out before it was too late? I wasn't sure. The fact was that I just couldn't trust anyone anymore. It was the very definition of burnt girl. No one could possibly be *that* good. Everyone turned on me, not because they wanted to, but because they just couldn't fight against their true nature. There was nothing for it. I had to find a way to stop Maggie.

Chapter 10

E'en so, in silence, likest Thee,
Steals on soft-handed Charity,
Tempering her gifts, that seem so free,
By time and place,
Till not a woe the bleak world see,
But finds her grace.
—John Keble

Saturday, June 20th, midday

My stomach growled. This was the life . . . sorta. Maggie had left the flatbread to barbecue in her little grill, and the smell was tormenting me.

Saturday's a beautiful day for sitting on the porch. Just the crops and me. I sat in my usual patchwork shorts among the pots of tomatoes and onions, elevated above the world. You might think it's a granny thing to do, but believe me, there's nothing like it, especially on summer days. It was way too hot to go inside, and so what better way to escape it? There was swimming, of course, but the pool was still closed with just a week to figure out a way to get it open for the institute party. The breeze now was perfect. I listened to the Jack Johnson music floating up from the cool girls' apartment downstairs.

I loved watching the world go by. The skateboarders biffing it, the girls from the Deluxe coming in with their stuffy dates, the beehives throwing around the pigskin, the kids hanging out on the porch next door—yeah, real kids.

Everything would've been perfect, except for that stupid wager. I put my screwdriver down next to my hammer and stared at my newest masterpiece resting on my lap: a disassembled blender. The wires inside were amazing. I just didn't know what I was going to do with this wreck when I was done . . . probably tear the wires apart. Yeah, I was that angry.

It was a hobby of mine. My specialty was breaking glass, appliances, and DI findings. It's called modern art, and it gets my aggression out. So does my writing, actually. Some people write angry letters and throw them away, and that's what I should do, except I keep what I write and then publish it and then try not to think about what I did afterwards. This was one of those times.

Maggie stepped outside, her feet bare like mine. I noticed the service project idol was in her hands. "We've got to do something with this," she said.

"Like make Christian fall in love with someone?" I muttered sarcastically. She rolled her eyes but didn't deny it. I fumed. *Over my dead body!*

She plopped the idol down next to me and unfolded a camping chair with some difficulty. "I was thinking of visiting some girls in the Deluxe." I stiffened. Maggie was trying to make me be a better person. Didn't she know it was a lost cause? She finally got the chair open and sat down, propping her bare feet over the railing. Her toes danced. They always did that when she sat too still and I stifled a grin. She pulled a to-do list from the window ledge and began checking things off briskly. She sighed. "I'm not getting anything done."

"I don't understand you. When I make plans, they're usually things I want to do."

She bit down hard on her pen. "Oh, I want to do these," she muttered through clenched teeth.

"Really? What do you have written down about Christian?" She just stared at me, her mind elsewhere. I turned at the sound of a dirty engine. A biker raced by and I quickly stood up, staring over the balcony as it passed. "That's an Indian." The fender covered the front of the bike. My gaze swept over the rear swept fender and saddle bags. It was two-toned, with a red and ivory finish. "I've never seen one in person before. I can't believe someone is driving it in Utah." I sniffed, smelling smoke. "Maggie? I think your flatbread is done."

She quickly stood up and opened her grill, waving the smoke away from her flatbread. It was golden brown, and she reached inside and flipped it with her bare hands.

I jumped. "Don't do that!"

"I can't feel a thing. Don't worry about it."

It was common knowledge that Maggie had no feeling in her hands. It was just some sort of random birth defect, but it still freaked me out. "Yeah, well, there's a reason that people have nerves in their hands, you know! They're supposed to protect them from getting charred off."

She calmly closed the grill and headed back inside, leaving me to lecture myself. I sat back down and picked up my hammer with shaky hands. Maggie always managed to get me riled up. I sighed, trying to concentrate on something else. I couldn't. That stupid love advice column. It was due in a month. Normally I treated these like any other responsibility. I never let myself think about talks or lessons or homework until the night before they were due, but this was different. Suddenly, it held more meaning than it ever had. It was the fight of my life. Well, at least for right now.

Lightning flashed a jagged line across the sky and I drew my knees in, staring at the street below me as the sky grew dark. It was going to be the perfect summer storm, and it looked like it was going to be more violent than the last one. Good.

I tapped my fingers against the iron railing, listening to thunder somewhere in the distance. I could totally prove Britton wrong. Logically, nice guys had a better chance at winning a girl's heart than the jerks did, if the nice guy took some initiative. But in this case, if he did, it would be awful. Christian getting together with Charity? I would lose no matter what I chose. Even if I refused to write the article, Britton would win. He would once again prove that I didn't know what I was talking about. Like Britton would scathingly say, why should these girls follow the blind?

But even worse, was Christian doomed to follow the ranks of the bitter? Would he be the nice guy dumped one too many times? Maybe jerks did have the unfair advantage in love.

A heart was never logical, but that wasn't the main problem. No, the main problem was that the perfect man was never perfect. Even the nerds were jerks in disguise, and when I fell for the act, I fell hard. Even now, I felt I had to strap myself down not to run to *his* side. Uh, yeah, you know who I'm talking about. Monsieur Romantique. Why did he drop by two days ago? I was glad that I had been gone on a date. But I couldn't stop wondering why he had come.

I couldn't help it. My mind kept wandering to a time when we were laughing and holding hands. Like the time when we sat on this very porch and he was talking about breaking up with me. It was one of his failed attempts. Wait, no. Let me think of a better memory.

"Hey, Jacks!" I jumped, seeing Christian in my face. He laughed. "Man, you're spacey. I got you good." He tugged on one of my braids. Maggie had braided my hair to keep the heat at bay, and it made me look like Pippi Longstocking.

"Ooh, watch it," I said.

"What are you gonna do, Red?" I scowled at Christian's underhanded reference to my guy woes. I glanced down at his hands, seeing he held the service idol, and I watched him suspiciously. What good deed was he up to now? I thought about ours and it made me feel guilty that I had even been considering Britton's shady wager.

Christian was in a flippant mood and he leaned down, blending in with the tomato plants like some sort of army dude in his camo shorts. "Your pot is growing weed," he said.

"Watch it. The gossiping middle floor is just below us."

His lips curled up at the side as he started tugging weeds out of the crops. "Yeah, you don't want the neighbors to think you can't take care of your own crops. What scandal!" He was clearly teasing me.

"You know that's not what I mean." I sniffed, smelling something burning. "Maggie!" I shouted.

"Your flatbread," Christian finished for me. He had come at just the right time. Her flatbread was famous. Maggie heard his voice and it immediately flushed her out from the back. She grinned when she saw our apartment boyfriend.

Maggie headed for the grill and opened it. Smoke went everywhere and she reached for the flatbread. "Maggie don't!" I cried.

She rolled her eyes and did it anyway, flipping them one by one onto the plate she carried with her bare hands. Christian stared at her. She was wearing an apron, her short hair swept back. "You look so domest—"

"Don't say it," she warned. Maggie always got mad when we called her that or if I compared her to a Molly Mormon. It was meant as a compliment, but she never took it that way.

"Domesticated," Christian finished bravely. "You are obviously very house . . . bred." The fire alarm went off in the living room. He had just been saved by the bell, except he decided to make it worse for himself. "There goes the dinner bell."

Maggie snorted and turned on her heel, her hair bobbing as she ran into our apartment. She fanned ineffectually under the fire alarm. Christian quickly joined her, grabbing a book. He waved it. "Hey, I have the money I owe you," he shouted through the din.

She shook her head. "No, I don't want it."

"Too bad. It's yours."

"No, I paid for you. It was my treat."

The fire alarm stopped whining and Christian reached into his pocket, pulling out a ten dollar bill. "Take it," he said.

"No. That's even more than I gave you."

"Hey," I shouted out from the porch. "I'll take it if no one wants it!"

"Stay out of this," Maggie said.

Christian just shook his head and set the money on the end table next to some presents. "You can use it on your next charity case, huh Maggie?" I grimaced, remembering exactly who that was. Lightning struck loudly through the sky and Christian leaned on the door frame, staring outside. He dangled the service idol between two fingers. "Well, what do you think? The weather might turn next Saturday."

"For our swimming party? Hopefully not."

He bit down a smile and nodded at the crops. "Well, the rain might could do us a heap a good, I 'spect. Looks like it's gonna be a good harvest this year."

I smiled at his Farmer Brown impression. "Last year we made a pizza with the harvest. This year Maggie's threatening to make a salad."

"Sounds awful."

"She needs her nutrients!" Maggie shouted out from the kitchen. We always kept our window open in the summer. It was a regular NCWO, a noncommittal window. No one had to step in, just drive through. "Pass me the flatbread," she said through it.

Christian passed it through, his eyes not leaving me. "Aren't you eating?"

"Yeah, flatbread." I avoided his eyes, pounding on the blender instead. "I think I'm going to get paid pretty soon for delivering those flyers, and then we'll throw a party."

"Hey, why don't you go shopping in my food storage?"

I stared at him. I couldn't do that. He was poor like me. Jade passed us on the balcony, looking very professional in a tailored jacket for school. We jumped guiltily. She had almost caught us in a deep conversation. "Hi, guys." She walked into the living room, dumping a handful of presents on the almost nonexistent carpet. The pile of presents was getting deep.

I glanced at the service idol as Christian swung it casually. "Look," I said. "This service thing is getting out of control." *In more than one way.*

"Hey, did Rusty call?" Jade asked. She fastened her thick hair into a twist with a pencil.

We all shrugged. Maggie had been gone and there was no way I was going to answer the phone. It was too dangerous. Jade grabbed the phone in the kitchen, putting it to her ear. She gasped. "Don't you guys ever check the messages? Oh my heck. There are seven of them."

Seven? My eyes widened at the significant number. There was a reason that I didn't like the phone. There was no escape. *Please don't let them be from my unlucky swains.* "If you want to do something useful, Christian," I whispered to him, "you can stop her from giving me those messages. I'll let that count as your service."

"Hey, Jacqueline, here's a message for you," Jade told me.

I grimaced. "Now would be the time to save me."

"What? You're afraid of a bunch of dumb males?"

"Junk males," I said. "Big difference. They can talk."

"Our manager is coming Monday," Jade was listening intently to the phone, "and he's bringing his white glove."

"Well tell him he's not wanted," Christian said smoothly. "Michael Jackson impersonators are not allowed here. There, you happy, Jacks? That's your first save."

"That means you have to get it clean by Saturday," Maggie chimed in. No one could keep me safe from Maggie. She was stirring some Kool-Aid in a pitcher.

"Yeah, yeah. Do you have some cleaning supplies I can borrow?"

"Look under the sink."

Jade sighed heavily. "I don't know how you can clean the apartment next door when you don't even clean up around here."

I laughed at that one. "Sorry, I'm not your personal maid."

"Well, apparently I'm your personal secretary." But she didn't give me the phone. She was having too much fun lecturing me. "Here's another one. It's from your editor. Do you know what you're doing your love advice column on, Jacqueline?"

"Not really," I muttered guiltily.

Christian sat down on Maggie's abandoned camping chair. "Tell her Jacqueline wants to get paid more before she starts writing for them again." He glanced at me. "That's number two."

"résumé, Christian," I reminded him.

"Here's one from your mom."

"Tell her," Christian hesitated and I looked up, "her daughter is fine."

I laughed. "You want my secretary to lie to my mom?"

"It saves *you* the trouble. Besides, it wasn't a lie. You're one fine woman."

"Uh-oh." Jade was listening intently to the phone. She glanced at me with a delighted look and I felt my heart drop to my knees. "I think one of your stalkers called."

"Not a stalker," I automatically corrected, especially after Britton's accusations, "just some poor boy cursed with liking me."

"Yeah, yeah. Are you free tomorrow night?" Jade asked.

I glanced at Christian, gauging his reaction. I didn't want him to think I was a jerk. It was a sore subject. "I'm not sure."

"How about the night after that? Or the night after that? After that?"

I scratched my ear. "Yeah, I'm probably busy doing something."

"You don't even know who it is," Christian sputtered.

"Well, then whoever it is can't take it personally." It was like the guys could sense I was unattainable. It was why girls who say they're going on missions ended up getting married and the girls setting out to get married ended up going on missions. I couldn't take any of this personally either. These phone calls had nothing to do with whether I was fun or good-looking because it certainly didn't happen before, when I was open to such things. "It's called the 'other' syndrome," I muttered.

"What?" Christian was playing with the wires on the blender that I had been tearing apart.

"That's why these guys keep calling. I just have to figure out how to beat it."

"Get married," he said in a way too innocent voice. He knew exactly what my reaction would be.

I sucked in my breath. "Just run into marriage when I don't have feelings for anybody? I can't even date someone on such false premises. Besides, dating only makes the 'other' syndrome worse."

"What are you talking about?" He was trying not to smile. I had played right into his hands, but I didn't care. He loved my dramatic soliloquies. They made no sense to him.

"Well, just the fact that people become really *attractive* when you can't have them. Like if a guy starts going out with someone, all of a sudden he's hot. And it works the other way too. Like when you're dating someone and all of a sudden everyone else looks a whole lot better."

Maggie walked outside. She had covered the flatbread with honey and she began passing it out on napkins. "Thanks." I had been wondering what I would do for dinner.

Christian put down the blender, accepting the flatbread gratefully. "You seem to know a lot about this, Jacks."

Maggie and I exchanged looks and she smiled secretly. It was probably why I had thought Christian was so attractive when I was going out with the one we don't speak of. Of course, Monsieur Romantique had it worse than I did. Well, at least he couldn't control it.

"Hey, knock it off," Christian said. He waved his hand between our faces, trying to break the lines of communication between us. "Just say it. You know I can't read girl telepathy."

That's what we counted on. Maggie pulled away from us, leaning on the balcony. The wind was picking up and we watched it blow debris across the street. "Look," Christian said, "forget about your stupid theories. You're just scared."

Before I could retort, Jade called for Maggie outside the window. "You've got a message!"

I sighed in relief. "Finally."

"What?" Jade said. "You didn't think they were all for you, Jack, did you?" Well, I hoped they weren't. Jade turned to Maggie. "It's Britton. He wants to talk about business. Whatever that means. He wants a full report."

I knew what that meant. Why couldn't he just leave us alone? I couldn't do this, but that wouldn't stop Maggie. Christian finished the flatbread, his hands sticky. "Maggie, I've got to do some service around here. Jacqueline won't give me anything real to take on."

"We don't need another service idol around here," I retorted. "Especially with your half-baked ideas of service. It just isn't worth it."

Christian stood up to go wash his hands. He gingerly picked up the service idol with two fingers and kicked off his leather flip-flops before entering our apartment. *Garbage.* Britton had him well trained. I followed him in, holding my hands at an awkward angle, trying to avoid getting honey all over everything.

He glanced around the kitchen. There was stuff all over the place. Jade's groceries. My threat hadn't worked. Maggie's sewing projects were still on the table with Britton's trousers under the heap, still not hemmed. "Even Britton can't put his stuff away," Christian muttered. He washed his hands. "I feel like I'm just getting my hands dirtier."

The phone rang and we all turned as one to stare at it. My heart went to my throat, but Jade stomped over to it. "Hello?" Jade listened then glanced at me. "Which boyfriend are you?"

I buried my head in my hands, trying to keep myself from running. "Who is it?"

She handed it to me, forcing me to be strong and deal with whoever it was. "He's asking for Blest. I assume he's talking about you."

I gulped. *No, not him.* It was the middle-name guy. Could I even remember his name? No, I realized, I couldn't. He'd told me, but I hadn't been paying attention. Judgment was too swift. My sins were coming back to haunt me. I answered it, forcing my voice into happy tones. "Hello?"

"Hey, Blest, guess who this is?"

I stared at Jade and Maggie. Jade watched sternly, Maggie with concern. *Oh great.* Christian was picking at the flatbread, pretending he wasn't listening—the big eavesdropper. I sighed. Was I ready to do this again? I mean, what if he was cool? It's the big *what if* that kills me every time, you know? It's like jumping off a bridge into the water. Someone keeps telling you that some day you'll have the perfect dive, but you keep belly flopping. Still, you're curious because *what if* this time, he's the one? *What if* this time you dive in perfectly and win the medal—or whatever analogy would work for this? Curiosity kills me every time. It was a wonder I was still breathing.

"So, you still want to grab a bite to eat?" he asked.

Well, of course I wanted to do that, but not with him. "Uh, yeah."

"Well, I'm not sure if I can make it."

I smiled. This was a whole lot easier than I thought. "Okay."

He laughed. "Just kidding." My brow wrinkled. He was a wily one. How in the heck was I supposed to outdo him? "You didn't sound too upset," he said after an awkward pause. Probably because I wasn't.

"Oh no, I was really upset. I would've cried myself to sleep tonight."

"Okay, you've convinced me. How about dinner on Friday? Anything you're allergic to? Any foods you don't like?"

"Weevils," I said. "And rats and chicken feet. That's about all I can think of right now."

"Gross. I'll see what I can do. See ya on Friday."

"Bye." I stared at the phone.

"See, that wasn't so hard," Maggie said.

"The first date never is." Jade stared out the window at the flailing trees. The wind was really picking up outside. "She usually gives them a first date."

"So what's his name?" Christian asked in a formal voice.

"Uh . . ." I didn't want to admit that I hadn't even listened for it. I was sure that it started with a *D*. "Doug or Dan or David or something like that. He told me his middle name though."

"What?" Maggie asked.

"I can't remember that either." I collapsed on a chair, burying my face in the mess on the table.

"Wow, Jacks," Christian said dryly. "It sounds like you really like him."

I laughed. "No, I'm just senile." I smiled, realizing my out. "Yeah, I'm getting way too old for this. And he is way younger than me." If anything, that would get me off the hook if I needed to wriggle out of the date. "Probably two years or something."

He laughed. "So he's as old as I am? Let's see. When you're eighty-two, he'll be eighty. When you're a hundred-and-two, he'll be a hundred. What a baby."

The phone rang again. "I got this one." Christian picked it up. "Rainbow Five's answering service. If you would like to make an appointment for a date, we have operators standing by."

"Give that to me!" I tried to grab it from him, but he easily wove out of my grasp.

"Yeah, this is the right number. Yeah. Yeah." He put a hand on my head, keeping me in one place. "Yes, Jack's just fine. She's kicked the habit, and we're just glad she's starting to come back to church, bless her heart."

Maggie laughed. "That's my line."

"Who is that?" I demanded.

"Your mom."

"What?" I renewed my efforts to grab the phone from him, tugging down the layers of my shirts at the same time. No matter how hot it was, everything had to be layered. I could never find anything high enough or long enough. At times like these, it made things really inconvenient.

Christian turned his back on me. "Yeah, she's real eager to talk to you too. I know what you mean. No one can catch her. She's been real busy lately. Maybe she just can't stand the phone." I stomped my foot. Why was he making it sound like I didn't want to talk to my family? I loved talking to them, but then my ear hurt. I've never figured out how to get around that. "Oh, she hasn't told you?" Christian said. "Well, things are getting pretty hot around here." He listened for a little bit and then his lip curled up. "Oh, I'm always hot."

What? Christian had served his mission in the Philippines. His blood had thinned there. He didn't ever get hot. And then I realized what he was saying to my mom. "Quit talking to her! Give her to me."

"No, Jacks won't have me."

I gasped. "Mom, what are *you* telling him?"

Christian inanely went on as if I hadn't said anything. "She's got all these other boyfriends in the way. Yeah. Oh, she hasn't told you about them? Well, there's the one who shall not be named—"

"Mom!" I cried desperately. "Don't listen to him!" I grabbed Christian around the neck and tried to use him as leverage to get to his hand. My fingers stretched out to full capacity, but I still couldn't reach.

"Well, it looks like she wants to tell you all about it. Yeah, we'll talk to you later, Sister Childs. Love you too." He held the phone barely above my reach. "Apparently you're hard to pin down in more ways than one." He laughed, finally handing the phone to me. "Here ya go."

"Thanks a lot." I had a lot of things to undo. "Mom!" I said. "He's a total liar."

She was laughing. "Now that sounds like a fun boy. You should marry *him*."

My nose wrinkled. Christian? Marry him? She obviously had no idea what she was talking about. "Uh, he's not interested," I muttered, hopefully out of Christian's earshot or he'd give me an even harder time.

"How do you know?"

Christian was making his own spot on our whiteboard for messages. Since he lost his cell phone, he had apparently decided that gave him the privilege of sharing our phone. Now who was whose answering service?

"Hmm, well, maybe you should go to Texas. There are some great singles wards there."

I bit my lip. Who was she talking to now? "There's a girl in our ward," she continued. "She went to Texas to be a teacher and she found the guy she wanted to marry. Apparently guys are desperate there."

"Mom!"

"I have the invitation right here. It's SaraLynne. Didn't you used to babysit her?"

Now Christian was sitting at our community computer. It belonged to Maggie, but everybody used it. I squinted to see what he was up to. He was changing our screensaver. I twisted the phone cord around my fingers. "Mom, I have something serious to ask."

"Yes?"

"Have you been praying to humble me again?" It was the only explanation. My mom's prayers actually worked. The woman's faith was like dynamite.

"Uh . . ."

I knew it. "Can't you tone it down?"

"Well, it sounds like it's working. You've found a nice boy."

"I did not find him!"

"What? Did he find you? How romantic. Well, I won't keep you long. It sounds like you're busy. You'd better be."

Mom." I was whining now, but she had already hung up. I slammed the phone back on the cradle and turned on Christian with a growl. "You're in big trouble, buddy. I thought the lectures about marriage were bad before! That's nothing to what I'm going to get now!"

"Hey, just take what advice you can get," Christian said. Little did he know what advice I had just been given. "Oh, and I guess I'll be screening your dates from now on," he added nonchalantly.

"Forget it."

"Sorry, it's your mom's orders since your dad's not here and all. She wants me to look out for you." He pulled away from the computer, and I wondered what vile thing he had written on the screensaver now. I made a mental note to check it once he left.

"My mom would never tell you to limit my dates. If anything, she would try to get you to lobby in elders quorum to get guys to date me."

"She mentioned that."

The lightning flashed outside the window and the thunder boomed loudly in reply. Jade went to close the window, and just then someone grabbed her from outside, pulling her onto the balcony. I jumped when he kissed her. "Was that Rusty?" I squinted, trying to see.

Maggie and Christian laughed. "I sure hope that was him," Maggie said.

"Well, it is a NCWO," I said.

"A noncommittal window?" Christian asked. "No way. Those two are way too anxiously engaged. Just two weeks to go now. How are they going to do it?"

Rusty was talking excitedly, and Jade reached over to him and hugged him. He swung her around in one exhilarating movement and then reached for her hand. She just laughed and pulled away, making him chase her down the stairs. He quickly caught up to her and she surrendered her hand to his. He spun her on the way to his car. I guessed they were going.

"Sick," I muttered.

Christian glanced at me. "Yeah. Doesn't that make you want to find someone?"

The wind picked up outside and I shrugged. "Well, I am going on a date on Friday."

"You won't like him anyway," Christian said firmly.

Was this reverse psychology or what? Probably, because it was working. "You never know!" I railed. "It's not like I'm sabotaging myself on purpose. I like to have fun just like anybody else."

"Unfortunately, your very touch is toxic." He headed for the door, and I followed him through the present-packed living room. "So, what's a good way to impress a girl who's not easily impressed?"

I froze. Was he talking about me? Maybe he was trying to make me see the error of my ways. Well, I'd show him. "Don't try to impress her, for starters. She's tired of it."

"Where would be a good place to take her?"

"Avoid fancy restaurants. Don't look like you're trying too hard, but still have fun. Do something crazy, but not too creative. Let her drive your car. Buy her a Slurpee at 7-Eleven." That's what I wished this guy would do on Friday, but he probably wouldn't. It was too low-key and spontaneous. "Why?"

"I'm just trying to figure out what to do with Charity on Friday." I clenched my teeth. I had just given him advice for Charity? He reached up, playfully slapping the top of the door frame on his way out the door. "I've got plans, too."

Maggie gave me a triumphant look, but I felt far from triumphant. It had only been a week and we hadn't even done a thing. No way was this happening. "And you didn't tell me?" I groaned. "Didn't you go on a date with her already?"

"What, the softball practice? She got sick."

I grinned. I knew it. Well, Britton did. "She stood you up?"

"Nope, she was sneezing the whole time. She had to get her allergy medicine. I took her home and put an ice pack on her head. Maybe I should send her flowers or something."

"No, no, don't send her flowers. That would ruin it." What was I saying? I didn't want it to work out. "Well, maybe some long-stemmed roses," I modified. That was way too serious and for sure would freak such a squirrelly girl out.

"No, daisies are her favorite flower. I've got to think about what I'm going to put on the note." He leaned on the balcony between the tomatoes and onions. "I enjoyed softball," he dictated to the air. "Hope you had a good time, you and the pollen."

"Wow," I said. "That was quite poignant."

He laughed. "Yeah, forget the note. I'll tell her in person."

"No, uh . . ." That was too cute, but a note might break her. "Make the note really deep and long." To my relief, Maggie agreed with me. She had no idea what she was doing either.

"I know better than to listen to you," he said. I was stung. "C'mon, Jacqueline. You and Charity are two different girls. She likes attention, you don't." Christian looked down at his watch. "Oh, speaking of which, I've got to go." He turned, his foot catching on the smallest herb plant. It toppled over the balcony to the ground below, spilling all over the grass.

"The crops!" I turned on him. "You've ruined this year's harvest!"

He laughed. "I'll get you a new tomato."

"That's fine, except that was . . . basil!" *I think.* I pretended to be outraged to keep him there a little longer. What did he mean, Charity liked attention? Was he going over there now? This couldn't be happening.

Christian held his hands out to Maggie. She had on her patient look. "I'll get you a new basil." He started heading for the stairs. "I'll see you later. I'm late."

"That's not good enough!" I shouted. He didn't even slow down, and I got desperate. "You can't leave." He *was* going to Charity's. He was headed her direction. "Hey, not without your idol!" Not even that worked.

He just waved back at me through the darkened air around us. "I did my service. Your mom's real proud of you today. See ya, peeps." The sky grumbled ominously. The streetlights had turned on even though it was the middle of the day.

"It's going to rain on you! You'll get soaked." I leaned heavily on the balcony, watching him go to his doom.

"Bye, Christian!" Maggie shouted with a happy smile as he disappeared through the canopied entrance at the Deluxe apartments. I pulled away from the railing and sat back on the porch, crossing one leg over the other. "Poor fool," I muttered. "She'll break his heart in ten different ways. She'll feed it to the fishes when she's done. She does it to guys all the time."

"Like him?" Maggie asked.

What did she mean by that? "Yeah, guys like him. I can't just stand by and watch this happen." Maggie was quiet and I realized how I sounded. Maybe she thought I was against this wager for entirely different reasons. Was that why she had no pity for Christian? "I mean, if she meant something by it, then maybe I wouldn't care as much," I tried to explain. "It's not like I'm jealous or anything." A flash of lightning cut across the sky. How could I explain this once and for all? "Christian and I, we're like brownies and orange juice."

She crossed her arms. "It's apples and oranges."

"No, brownies and orange juice. And they're both really good separately, but not together. Have you ever tried to down brownies with orange juice?" The thunder crashed loudly behind us. "It tastes awful."

The rain started pouring down, and I pulled away from the balcony before I got soaked. And Charity and Christian were like . . . uh, bad apples and orange juice. Yeah. One was nice, the other wasn't.

Chapter 11

I hate nobody: I am in charity with the world.
—Jonathan Swift

Sunday, June 21st, midmorning

I slid next to a girl with a huge diamond ring. Was she engaged? I glanced at it and my eyes widened. It was a gold CTR ring inlaid with diamonds. "Whoa," I blurted. "What's that stand for? Climb the Rameumptom?"

She glared at me. Of course, it made sense in a way. If you didn't expect a ring by spring, you could give it to yourself or get Daddy to supply the goods. If you were from the Deluxe, that is.

The princess sporting the ice glowered, but this time it wasn't at me. Betsy stood self-consciously near us, looking for an empty seat, and the girl was trying to discourage any ideas. I smiled purposely at Betsy. There was always room in the inn for my freshman. "Hey, Cindy Lou. Over here!" She smiled gratefully and brushed past the ice princess, taking a window seat on the other side of me.

With a nod from Charity, Maggie stopped playing the prelude music and made her way to her seat, looking very chic in her school-girl outfit. Tube socks and baby doll shoes showed off her skinny legs. I expected the ice princess to glare at her like she had at Betsy, but instead she smiled and picked up her scriptures, which had served as a barrier between us. Everybody loved Maggie, didn't they?

Maggie sat down beside me and gave me back my scriptures after accidentally sitting on them. I took my quad, my heavy coat swishing.

Yeah, I brought it especially for air-conditioned Sundays. Besides the chill, the room was a little unconventional for Relief Society. It was downstairs from the testing center with four long tables stretched from one side of the room to the other, complete with laptop plug-ins and Internet hookups. Don't ask me what it was used for.

"Man, we thought you'd never stop playing," I whispered to Maggie.

She was thrown a little off guard. "What?"

"We couldn't start Relief Society until you stopped showing off your fancy new hymns." Maggie knew that was a lie, but it still was funny to imagine that we were actually waiting for her, and she burst out laughing just as Charity made her way to the makeshift podium at the front of the room. Charity flipped her hair and began tapping the podium with well-manicured nails. Maggie stopped abruptly when everyone turned toward her, and she gave me a reproachful look once they turned away. That only encouraged me. "Fine, we're all impressed with your piano playing skills. Happy?"

She covered her mouth, managing to keep the laugh in this time. Her eyes watered. I glanced around the room of blank faces. To be honest, I couldn't really tell all these blonds apart. I smoothed my plaid skirt. It poked out from my heavy coat. "Man, you've got a tough crowd here. Not even a golf clap. I guess you're just not good enough for the church crowd. Of course, no one clapped for the musical number in sacrament meeting either."

Maggie quickly turned from me, using the last bit of her self-control. The fact that it was forbidden to make a noise made everything doubly funny. Now Charity was staring at us, her sculpted eyebrows raised. "Does anyone have an announcement?"

Jade did. She stood up and made her way to the front, exuding professionalism. Her crisp white collar was folded down perfectly. "Last week I announced the blood drive at ward prayer, and I could tell it really made a difference with all the people beating down my door just to sign up." We watched her uneasily. "Oh wait, that didn't happen," she said dryly. "So, I just wanted you to know that I met my fiancé doing this. Yeah, so now we'll see who beats down my door." And with that bit of bad psychology, she abruptly went back to her seat. She certainly did not meet Rusty that way, although she did drag him to a few of those to get his veins drained. He'd do anything for love.

"Liar." I covered it up with a cough.

Maggie quickly stood up, taking the attention away from me. She tried to escape her seat, but every angle she tried was blocked. "You can go under the desk," I suggested.

She refused to look at me, deciding to just stay put. "On Wednesday, July first, we're holding Home, Family, and Personal Enrichment." Maggie was the only one who could say the whole Enrichment title without stuttering. She was that good. "We'll be learning how to use our talents to serve others, and maybe we'll brainstorm ways to pass around the charity idol."

I couldn't believe that she had just called it that. She had been spending way too much time around Britton . . . or was it me? "We can't let the priesthood beat us," she said, swinging her fist for emphasis. With Maggie at the helm, there was no danger of that. She flopped down in her seat as the door opened.

Christian popped his head through the door and about half of the Relief Society came to attention. As I told Britton, he had his entourage of females, and for some reason Christian was easy on the eyes today. His tan looked really good against his white shirt, and I watched the girls' reaction with fascination. It never ceased to amaze me how nice they all became at the sight of a male.

The fact was, we didn't really have a lot of guys in our ward. But what we lacked in quantity, we made up for in quality. Well, that's what the bishop always said. I never agreed, but maybe that was our problem. Guys. Not enough of them.

"Is it okay to make an announcement?" Christian asked Charity.

She nodded, suddenly perched at the end of her seat like an eager vulture. "Go right ahead," she said in a throaty voice. I wondered how long it took to perfect that.

"Oh, I can wait until you're done." Christian strode easily into the room, but instead of looking for me, he sat down next to Charity. Sitting in the front with her, he could see the drooping heads. Some of us looked like we were drugged. "What's this, a slumber party?" he asked.

Charity giggled and I sat up in my seat, watching closely. I was more paranoid than ever. I had been watching Christian all day at church, looking for some sort of sign that he really liked her. And maybe this was it. Another girl stood up to announce . . . oh forget it. I wasn't really paying attention. Nope, I was too busy spying.

"How is the plot to take over the ward going?" Christian whispered to Charity.

She whispered something back and he smirked. I couldn't hear what she was saying, but I was sure it was clever. I drummed my fingers on the desk. It was too dangerous for Christian to be in Relief Society. "He couldn't trust any of us to announce this for him?" I murmured.

Liza's sidekick, Sara, raised her hand behind us. I turned to look at her—a dour-faced brunette from the gossip floor. She had kicked off her shoes, most likely as a sign of being unconventional. Her bare feet were propped on an empty chair beside me. It was the new fad. Everyone wanted to be an individual, which kind of defeated the purpose. Granola girls. She was saying something about visiting teaching. She only got my attention when she started talking about the afterlife and how we would be going to some bad place if we didn't do it. Was she being sarcastic? If not, it was interesting motivation.

"Well, not exactly . . ." Maggie started to defend the sanctity of visiting teaching, and I elbowed her before she started a fight for right.

"I want you to report your stats early this month," the sarcastic girl said. "And if you don't," once again she drove in her point, "we all know where you're going."

Christian had finally caught sight of me and scooted closer, amused at our discomfort. "Speaking of," he said with a grin.

"Yes, just think of how lucky we are," Charity skillfully interjected. "As sisters, we get visiting and home teachers. Poor guys don't get as much attention as we do."

Christian looked up at her. "Well, there have been requests for visiting teachers in the elders quorum," he pointed out.

"I'll volunteer." Liza raised her hand. "I'll help the poor guys out."

"Leave that to the compassionate service committee," Christian said, looking at Maggie. She turned red, but not because she was embarrassed. I was afraid she was going to tear his head off if he didn't watch himself.

"I think you'd better go ahead and make your announcement," Charity said, "before you introduce some new doctrine into the 73rd ward."

"Yeah, I'm scheduled to corrupt the guys today instead. I'd rather be teaching Relief Society. The smell alone is worth it."

I rolled my eyes. So, it was the Christian show today. I could hardly wait to hear what he came up with this Sunday. He was known for putting the smack down on the priesthood. He stood up. "Intramural softball starts in two weeks, and I want to see every sister on the team. I know you all have a mean swing, so don't hide your talent under a bushel." He glanced at me. "Or your dress. Where'd you get that huge coat, Jacqueline?" I groaned, hiding my face while everyone got a good laugh.

Charity smiled, rubbing her tan arms. "It *is* cold in here."

"You're cold?" he asked in sudden concern.

I stood up, knowing I had to distract him from offering his dark suit jacket to her. "Hey, I have an announcement!" Everyone was still laughing and talking at once. I turned to Jade in desperation. She was folding her arms tightly, combating the cold. "I like how reverent Jade is being," I said.

Instead of getting everyone's attention, it did the opposite. Now the laughter turned to a loud roar. Jade scowled. "So, institute is on Tuesdays," I told the room in vain, "in case you haven't noticed. Seven o'clock." I locked eyes with Christian. Instead of gallantly offering his suit jacket to Charity, he was laughing at me. He liked to see me stuck in situations like these, especially ones he thought he'd started.

"Sorry," he mouthed.

Betsy raised her hand. "Hey, what about the directory? When's that coming?"

Of course she had to ask that, but I forgave her when it did the trick. Everyone went silent and turned to me in suspense. There was nowhere to run and I cleared my throat. "Uh yes, I have a few more pictures to take, and if you think you've escaped me, I will root you out."

Charity finally tore her attention away from Christian, most likely because his eyes were still on me. "Oh, you're having such a hard time, bless your heart," she said.

I stared at her closely. Was she insulting me? I wasn't sure. I bit my lip.

"That's your cue to leave," Charity told Christian in an undertone. "We have to teach our lesson. It's controversial."

"Good luck," Christian said. "Remember, if ye are prepared, ye shall not fear."

"So, why am I so scared?" she murmured.

"Don't blame yourself. Maybe it's just the peanut gallery." With a final look at me, Christian left. I bit my lip again. Where was Britton when we needed him? It didn't even look like he was fighting for Charity at all. Was this what he meant by being a jerk? Doing absolutely nothing?

Charity took her place at the front. "If that is all for announcements, we'll go ahead and start our lesson. MaryBeth will be giving it. The bishop assigned us a special topic. MaryBeth?"

A girl with spiky, medium-length hair walked to the front, and even though she wasn't wearing her Lance Armstrong bracelets, I recognized her as one of the little punks from the Rainbow Villa downstairs.

"Brothers and sisters," she smirked at her own mistake. "I mean, not brothers. Uh, sisters, you may have noticed the lack of a centerpiece. I did that on purpose," she said in a hard voice.

Did we ever have a centerpiece? Not that we were morally against it, but who cared? "Rebel," I whispered. Maggie shushed me.

"Maybe," MaryBeth said sternly, "we'll just have to concentrate on the lessons from now on and not on—"

"Something that was abolished centuries ago," I muttered. Maggie pursed her lips, determinedly ignoring me in her dogged support of the teacher.

"On an elaborate ice sculpture," MaryBeth finished. Everyone laughed at what they thought was a joke. There hadn't been a centerpiece since . . . well, maybe since Maggie taught. Maybe we should resent her for it. *Poor kid!*

MaryBeth looked taken aback, not expecting anyone to have a sense of humor about such a serious issue. The little punk was new to Relief Society, wasn't she? It was probably why she had been made a teacher. She was still stuck in the myths reinforced by spoofs on Mormon culture.

Sure, it was touching to see someone put a lot of energy into their lessons like that, but something truer to life might actually be funny . . . like maybe all these sign-up sheets. I signed Maggie up to make brownies and passed the sheet on to her.

"This won't go over very well with the underground fellowship of the Relief Society," I told Maggie in an undertone. "I say we shun her."

Maggie gave me a warning look, not appreciating the joke. "Would you pay attention?" she said harshly.

"To what?" I said, "There's no centerpiece and we're stuck here for a whole hour."

Maggie ripped the sign-up sheets from my hand and shook her head, seeing that I signed her up for brownies. She took her pencil to it and signed herself up for cookies too. My eyes widened. Man, she always beat me in the shock category.

MaryBeth paced the front. "I don't mean to be rude, but"—this was always a preamble to someone being rude—"this Relief Society has a big problem."

Everyone's eyes widened. I smiled, leaning forward. Garbage, this girl was uptight. I made a mental note to ask MaryBeth after the lesson where her centerpiece was. Even Charity looked a little strained, and my smile broadened. Just what topic had the bishop assigned? Probably repentance. I wondered if Charity had expected MaryBeth's take.

"The question is, do we value each other as sisters?" she asked. I could answer that. *No.* But she had silenced even me. "Just what are we doing here? Can someone answer that?"

Everyone stared at each other, and after an awkward silence, Maggie raised her hand to bail the teacher out. "The Relief Society Declaration says that we should delight in service and good works, so—"

"Yeah, yeah, I'm not talking about that."

Maggie looked stung, and I chuckled at MaryBeth's blunder. She had just lost her pity supporter. Now who would answer her questions?

"Are we just here to make casseroles and cookies, or what?"

There was an awkward silence broken by a few giggles, but Maggie was made of sterner stuff than we were. She raised her hand like she was sticking it out in front of a firing squad. "I don't know if this is what you're looking for, but—"

MaryBeth cut her off, "I'm not looking for anything. This is an open discussion."

"That's not what I got," Jade whispered behind me.

Maggie humbly took it. "Maybe it's about being happy for each other when something good happens," she said. "Or just being there when someone's having a problem. Help each other feel comfortable maybe."

"Instead of trashing someone's outfit," MaryBeth added in her gruff fashion. *Why? Did that just happen to her or something?* "When's the last time you talked about someone behind their back? A week ago? Yesterday? Two minutes ago?"

She might as well ask us for a repentance story. Who would admit that? Without thinking, I pretended to raise my hand. MaryBeth saw me, and I quickly tucked my hair behind my ear. "When is the last time you helped someone take their groceries in?" she asked. I frowned. Well, Christian helped us all the time, and Maggie was always at hand, but I was sure that MaryBeth didn't want to hear any of that.

"And I'm not talking about 'projects,'" MaryBeth said. "We gotta quit making people into projects. Projects are for school."

Maggie turned red, and I met her eyes, raising an eyebrow. "See," I mouthed.

"Let's flip to chapter 15 of 2 Kings. Jecholiah—"

"I'm naming my kid that," Jade muttered.

MaryBeth's head went up, and I flinched. She had heard that for sure. Jade had no idea how to make her heckling discreet. "Her son was given leprosy. What does leprosy mean?" she asked. It was obvious, so no one answered. Her eyes hardened. "Corrupt and unclean," she told us condescendingly. "Why was he given leprosy do you suppose?"

"Because he was corrupt and unclean," Jade whispered, purposely parroting the teacher's answer.

A girl to the side of us raised her hand. "Because he was corrupt and unclean."

I quickly looked down, concentrating on my breathing. I couldn't laugh. I looked like a jerk already. "He was doing what he needed to be doing," MaryBeth said, "except . . ."

Oh great, I couldn't even listen now. I grabbed my pen and shot Jade a warning look. She knew that I was a writer! She just couldn't say things like that around me. I couldn't concentrate on anything else when someone said anything remotely clever. I quickly scrawled it down before I could forget.

"Amlici was the perfect example of someone who used the world to measure success. Can someone please read Alma 2?" It sounded more like a threat than a request. By now everyone was afraid to talk, and I blew my breath out. Generally, I was really bad at making comments . . . quality comments. The only way I could participate was by reading. With a final glance at the uncompromising room, I raised my hand in surrender, giving Maggie a break.

MaryBeth nodded at me. "Jacqueline, read verses 11 and 14," she said.

"'Now the people of Amlici were distinguished by the name of Amlici, being called Amlicites . . .'" The sarcastic girl behind me sniffed loudly. It took some effort, but I didn't give her a look, glaring down at the words instead. "'And it came to pass that Amlici did arm his men with all manner of weapons of war of every kind; and he also appointed rulers and leaders over his people,'" I continued, "'to lead them to war against their brethren.'"

"War against their brethren? Do you think it was worth it?" MaryBeth asked. "You can always find someone smarter, better looking, more talented." MaryBeth glanced at me and I flinched. "Yeah, really." As if I doubted that? She seemed as if she was talking to me specifically.

The dour-faced girl behind us raised her hand. "I believe the correct pronunciation is *Amlicites* with a soft *c*." She gave me a pointed look, and after meeting Maggie's calming look, I smiled at the walking dictionary.

"Why, thank you," I said in exaggerated politeness.

MaryBeth ignored that. "Now look at verse 35." She caught her roommate with a look. "Betsy, read it."

Before I knew it, Betsy had wrestled my scriptures away from me. "'And it came to pass that when they had all crossed the river Sidon that the Lamanites and the'"—she glanced at the girl behind us in worry and spelled Amlicites out—"'began to flee before them, notwithstanding they were so numerous that they could not be numbered.'"

"The Amlicites outnumbered the Nephites," MaryBeth said, using the hard *c* version. The dour-faced girl's hand shot up. "But that sort of thing didn't make a difference when it really counted, did it?" Her eyes finally alighted on the dictionary Nazi behind us, most likely because she had started to wave her hand back and forth. "Yes?"

"Amlicites is pronounced with a soft *c* according to the pronunciation guide." Was there such a thing as a pronunciation guide?

MaryBeth froze her with a look and thrust a quote roughly at the ice princess beside me. "Clara, read this, will ya?" She actually knew our names? How could that be?

The princess cleared her throat. "'This is in regards to a traveler passing through Salt Lake City in September of 1849,'" she read. "'I have not met a citizen, a single idlet.'" The Nazi raised her hand but no one looked at her. Clara sniffed. "That's what it says." It was obviously a typo, and MaryBeth gestured for her to go on, "'Or any person who looks like a loafer. It is incredible how much they have done here in the wilderness in so short a time.'"

Jade leaned across the table, and I knew I was in for trouble. "Hey, idlet." Ooh, a new nickname? I felt a smile stretch across my face, and I forced it down. Now was not the time. Besides, I think she was calling me lazy.

"So, Liza," MaryBeth said. "What are your thoughts on this?"

"Uh . . . I think it's interesting that . . . uh, the pioneers were . . . uh . . . there. It's just pretty interesting." Obviously she hadn't been listening.

Betsy fixed me with a mischievous grin. "Would you say it was interesting?" she asked in an undertone. My eyes widened at that. This was a tough crowd. Even I wasn't such a jerk.

"Yes, but how does it apply to us?" MaryBeth asked. How didn't it? It was becoming more obvious how much we needed this lesson on being nice. We were out of control.

"Oh, um . . . what was the question?" Liza asked in resignation.

"I think what she's trying to say is that we should make Relief Society a safe haven," Charity cut in. "A place where we feel comfortable." Well, that was a watered down version of it anyway. "So come ready to make friends." She didn't look at me.

"If not, don't come," MaryBeth said harshly.

Maggie's hand shot up. "If I might interrupt."

"Please," Charity said. I was sure there was a double meaning in that.

"Okay, so, maybe you're new and that's your excuse for feeling uncomfortable in a new Relief Society. Well, we're all new. This really reminds me of a story . . . actually, Jacqueline can tell it much better than I can." She turned to me. "Remember the one about your dad and how he visited that ward when you were on vacation?"

I gave her the you're-gonna-get-it look. "Thanks for thinking of me." She smiled, not getting it. I cleared my throat. "Uh yeah, and my dad was kinda mad because no one was introducing themselves to him. He's a bishop and he was sure his ward would never treat a visitor that way, so he finally decided to show this ward how it was done. He introduced himself to the guy next to him. That's when he found out that guy was visiting too. And the other guy next to him had just moved in that week. I guess they were all wondering why no one was introducing themselves." I glanced at Maggie's expectant face and just shrugged.

"So," she said, wrapping it up. "If you're waiting for someone to be friendly to you before you get friendly, you're wasting time because most likely they're waiting for you to do the same thing. You might as well just go for it. I mean, how many times have you judged someone at a first glance and then later found out you were wrong?"

I avoided looking at Charity. No, not too wrong.

MaryBeth seemed to be in deep thought, and I almost wondered if she was thawing towards Maggie. Everyone did eventually. "I guess we're developing our ability to have good relationships now," she said. "It's all about getting out of a comfort zone that might be too comfortable. When Sarah laughed, she was told, 'Is any thing too hard for the Lord?'"

I brushed my hair from my face and MaryBeth glanced at me. "Comment?"

"No."

MaryBeth let it pass and I wondered why she was suddenly having pity on me. "In Ezekiel, the Lord promised Israel He'd give them a new heart and take away the stony heart. If we suffer from stony heartitis, we need to learn to strengthen those love muscles. We are sisters, and we are daughters of God, and our goal is to have a heart like His."

"If not, you'll be thrust down—" the girl began behind us.

"Yes," MaryBeth finished quickly, "to a place where the less valiant visiting teachers dwell."

I smiled at that one. This girl really wasn't that bad.

Charity stood up. I had never seen her move so fast. Well, in Relief Society. "Thank you for that lesson. I never thought of it that way before." And that very interesting rendition was the unspoken message. A very interesting rendition. I tried to forget it.

Chapter 12

Cold is thy hopeless heart, even as charity.
—Robert Southey

Friday, June 26th, evening

"Oh good, you're here!" Jade looked like she was being tortured. My date was sitting on the couch next to her, looking very stiff. He had the slacker rebel edge with his loose-fitting jeans and Vans. Normally I would think he was really cute, but it was almost like he was trying too hard for the bum look, like he was some sort of Christian counterfeit. Why did I just think that? What was wrong with me? I tried not to think of where Christian was right now, and I still couldn't remember what this guy's name was. "Um, we're on a middle-name basis," Jade told me quickly.

"I'm so glad to hear that." And that middle name was? Before I could ask, my date stood up and bowed low. I blinked a couple of times.

"Blest, I'm blessed to know you." Uh, if only he really knew me.

Jade was eager to get rid of him. The traitor. "Well, have fun, kids."

He put his hand on my back and I tried not to recoil. Where did he get off touching me already? "You look just as amazing as I remember you." I gulped at his quick rundown on my looks. If you dress too unattractively on a date, the guy will start putting on airs like he can control you. But if you dress too attractively then you've lost the game. That's why I always made sure I dressed well, but not too well. The stitches on my shirt made it look like it was inside out, and the Converse shoes did not go with my capris at all. It was kind of the hobo chick look, which I was sure scared guys off. At least I did my makeup.

"Your eyes are so dark," he said. "They look great with your hair."

I frowned as he led me to the door in his smooth fashion. I tried to quicken my steps to avoid his hand. I felt like he was leading me to a guillotine, and it was not the right way to start a date. I had to prove to Britton that I was more grown up than this. *Girls go for nice guys. Girls go for nice guys.*

"Remember who you are," Jade called out the door. It was the roommate ritual. "Wait," she amended. "Don't do that."

What was that supposed to mean? My date closed the door on Jade's relieved face, and we passed the gossipers on the second floor. I'm sure we were a sight with his hand on my arched back. I waved to the faces in the kitchen. Maybe this time I would be good. I was just picky, that's all. And really afraid. But I wasn't a coward. I could do this. He led me to his car. It was a black convertible. I forced my eyes not to narrow. Just because he was in the money didn't mean he was a bad person. I had to give him a chance . . . for everybody's sanity.

"Where'd you get the car, your parents?" It came out before I could bite it off.

"It's mine." Sorta better, but then again, no, not really. He clicked on his keys, and it made a clean unlocking sound, and he stuffed me inside. The leather seats squeaked. He climbed in and leaned across me. I tried not to flinch. "Everyone wears a seat belt in my car." Before I could react, he clicked mine on.

"Thanks," I said belatedly.

He smiled, used to being charming. "I've got the perfect place to eat."

"Great!" I stared out the window, wondering if I could jump out. Being hungry wasn't so bad. I was kind of used to it by now. "So, uh,"—*what's your name?*—"What do you do?" I asked.

"I'm studying chemistry at UVSC." He was used to the "get to know you" game, except it was completely one-sided as he rattled the facts off. "Who knows? Maybe I'll learn how to make lightsabers and blasters someday."

Hey, that was interesting. "You're going to make weapons for the military?"

"No, weapons for me." Suddenly I noticed his eyes weren't on the road. They were on me. I looked pointedly at the street so he would take my cue, but no such luck. His eyes wouldn't leave me, and his mouth kept moving. It made me think of ducks. Ducks with beady eyes. The Monsieur and I were feeding them. It was duck night at the botany pond. We fed the ducks, wrote duck poetry, got chased. Those ducks were vicious, but it was so cute when the Monsieur grabbed my hand and helped me get away.

My date touched my elbow, and I jumped back to attention. His hand was on the stick, and every time he shifted, he bumped a muscular arm against mine. I sucked in my breath. He definitely kept me on my toes. Every sense tingled from the danger, and I tried not to be too obvious about pulling away. It took me a moment to realize what he was saying.

"The telephone isn't safe for establishing lines of communication because you never know who could be listening. The Internet isn't much better. They're always watching." He parked and leaned toward me until I was leaning the opposite way against the door. He smiled. "No, I'll get that."

He jumped out of his car and opened the door to free me. I felt relieved until he gave me his hand. I squinted up at him before I accepted it. "Thanks." He pulled me out, once again bowing low. I managed a smile until he put his hand on the small of my back again and guided me to the restaurant. *Oh no.* Eat-O-Rama. It was the most expensive restaurant he could find. It would be a complete waste of money. How could I lead him on like this? He wasn't going to try to buy me, was he?

"I guess we all have our price, don't we?" he said.

"What?" I hadn't been listening again. He opened the door and ushered me in, and I couldn't think of a socially acceptable way to wriggle from his grasp. A waiter turned and smiled, his mischievous eyes crinkling. I melted. Now he seemed like a cool guy. Maybe because I wasn't on a date with him.

"Table for two?" the waiter asked, giving me a funny look.

"Yeah, my girlfriend and I want a secluded spot," my date said. "You know, romantic, soft lights." My eyes widened and the waiter nodded in understanding, his eyes on mine with an unspoken question.

I quickly turned away. I could barely handle one guy. "We're exclusive," my date reminded him as we followed him into the dining area.

What? Garbage! What was he talking about? The waiter gestured grandly to the back of the room. My date pulled my wicker seat out for me, and I quickly sat down before I decided to strangle him. The waiter gave us our menus and left.

"So, uh, why did you say we were exclusive?" I whispered.

He leaned heavily towards me on the glass table. "To keep you safe."

"From what?"

He laughed. "Okay, okay, we'll drop the girlfriend talk. You're not ready for that yet."

No, I wasn't! Girlfriend talk? What was he saying? And that's when I saw Charity and Christian at the front. Christian's hands were in the pockets of his shorts, but Charity's bejeweled fingers were on his arm. I stiffened as Christian leaned against the counter. She looked up at him, her thick lashes lowered over doe-like eyes. What was she doing? Christian wasn't going to fall for that, was he? Did she mean it?

"You know what would be hilarious?" I heard. "Let's pretend we're married." I swung around to face my date. He had a funny way of bringing my attention back to him.

"What? No . . . uh . . . it would never work. I don't have a ring."

"I can take care of that."

I ignored that, quickly covering my face with my menu, scanning through the prices. Too expensive, too expensive. Everything meant some sort of commitment. It would look weird if I ordered salad.

"So, your parents bug you about marriage, huh?" he observed.

My head came up from the menu. Maybe he was right; I was being watched. "How did you know that?"

He shrugged, thoughtfully stroking the stubble on his chin. "It's the usual thing you get here."

"Well, I'm like a diamond: the more pressure I get, the stronger I get."

He leaned closer to me. "I can help you with that."

I stared at him and quickly dismissed playing the hungry-for-marriage girl. Maybe the career-oriented woman was the better angle for this kind of situation. "I don't need help," I said. "I've got better things to do with my time."

"That's because you haven't met the right man yet." He kicked my feet under the table, and I quickly folded my legs and sat on them. The waiter came back, his pencil poised. I wasn't surprised to hear my date order the most expensive thing on the menu. He turned to me, and I gaped like a fish, my mind definitely not on the food. "Get her the same thing," he said firmly.

The waiter nodded, stealing the menu from my cold grasp. I forced a laugh, suddenly desperate to turn him off. "Oh, that's what Christian would've done."

"Who's that?"

I tried not to cringe. Britton was right. I was a jerk, and I couldn't stop myself. "Oh, some guy. He's on a mission." I saw him relax, and I quickly backtracked. "I write him all the time. He always lectures me. So protective, you know? We're very good friends."

My date leaned back, his dark, mesmerizing eyes bearing into mine. I tried not to turn away. "Will you wait for me?" he sang.

He stopped singing. "Have you ever thought that you've met your love in the preexistence? The first moment I saw you . . . well, there was something about you."

My smile was frozen on my face. "Uh well, no. Actually, that's a fallacy. There isn't a one and only." Finally, institute was coming in handy.

My hand was on the table and he reached for it. Luckily, I saw his intention and clasped my drink in a death grip and started drinking nonstop. Maybe he would notice that I didn't want to be touched, but he really didn't. He just stared at me, completely oblivious. He even made me wish Lane Bryant was here instead. Maybe I just wanted what I couldn't have.

"When I saw you, I just had a feeling, you know? I just knew we were meant to be together."

I started giving up. There was no way to keep him off this topic, but if I could just shame him out of it. "What? Did you have a revelation we were meant to be together?" I asked.

He laughed. "I'm not that spiritual. No, I just thought you're so pretty and cool and . . ." He started naming everything he liked about me, but since he knew nothing about me, it was pretty shallow. It was beginning to sound like a business proposition, and I half expected him to pop a ring out—tucked neatly in his pocket, nice and handy for moments like this—just to finish the deal. I'm sure it didn't matter who the girl happened to be.

The waiter saved me by bringing the food to our table. There was enough to feed a pig. Wait, it *was* enough to feed a pig! I put my elbows on the table and began shoveling the rice into my mouth, which was hard considering my appetite was gone. "Man, I'm so hungry. I haven't eaten for probably an hour." The waiter stared at me. "I might want seconds," I told him.

He laughed, but my date didn't seem to notice. Could I do no wrong? Surprisingly, he waited for the waiter to leave before he continued. "You know, Nephi didn't have a lengthy courtship with his wife."

"Hey, do you like dumpster diving?" It was the most random thing I could think of. Christian did it all the time, but everyone thought it was awful.

After a moment he nodded, and I thought I had beaten him until he beat me back. "I only like to do it when it's dark like the fathomless seas. What do you think of the dark?"

"Uh, it's okay."

"Most people think of it as intimidating, maybe even a little scary. I think of it as a warm, velvety blanket." He leaned closer to me and confided. "I don't tell my deepest secrets to just anyone, you know."

No, just to a random stranger he happened to meet in a Macey's parking lot. "You know—" I began.

His cell phone rang and he put his finger up to silence me. He held the phone to his ear, and I could hear the other person jabbering on the other side. It was a girl. Maybe an angry girlfriend, I hoped? He didn't really react but just watched me in silence. I glanced at the clock on the wall. 7:32 pm. A watched clock never moves. I quickly turned away.

"Okay, bye." He clicked the cell off and stared at me until it got uncomfortable. He must be one of those guys who didn't mind silence. In fact, the intent look on his face swallowed all conversation.

"So," I tried to ease the situation, "where are you from?" He just stared at me until I wondered if he was all there. "Oh, I see. It's a guessing game," I said. "California? Colorado?" I started naming off states while he calmly sipped his drink.

"I already told you," he said reproachfully.

"Oh." I shoveled another spoonful of food into my mouth.

"It starts with a *C*," he said.

"Christian!"

Christian walked past the aisle with Charity, the hem of her white skirt dancing around her ankles. I flinched at the evil look she gave me, but even that wasn't enough to make me back off. Christian looked startled until he realized the significance of my outcry. His eyes ran from me to the guy lounging on the seat opposite me. "So *this* is your date?" he said.

It was the moment that I had feared. I couldn't introduce them. Suddenly I cursed my stupidity for bringing attention to myself. What was his name? Daniel, David, Doug? "This is D—" I coughed.

"What?" Charity asked.

"Oh, garbage," I said. "My mind is totally elsewhere. We were just talking about . . . uh, I mean . . . I'm still trying to guess where he comes from. Can you believe it? He won't tell me. Actually, he already told me. I just forgot. Yeah, isn't that funny?"

Obviously Charity didn't think so, but at least everybody else was nice and confused. Christian's lips curled up at the sides and he threw his hand out to my date. "My name is Christian, and yours is?"

He just stared blankly back. "Back from your mission already, Christian?"

"Four years now."

"And still getting in the way?"

Christian stilled and Charity tugged on his arm. "You're right. Ice cream sounds really good right now," she said. Christian might as well have been a boulder for all the good it did.

"Hey, Jacqueline, Maggie wanted to be sure that I told you . . ." Christian glanced at my date. "Excuse us a sec." He leaned next to me, whispering into my ear. "Need help?" My date's eyes were steadily on me, and I shook my head. "Oh, so you didn't tell him about the baby?" he said in a louder voice. With an annoyed jerk, Charity managed to pull him away. "Um, Jacks, did you know your shirt's inside out?" Christian called as a parting shot.

I stared after him, the corners of my lips turning up. I met my date's eyes and shrugged. "He's kinda crazy." The waiter passed and I held my hand out to him. "Can I get a body bag?" I flinched. "I mean, doggy bag." Now that I knew that not even Christian approved, I was completely justified to escape.

I piled the rest of my food into the box. "Let me." My date pulled closer to me, his hands guiding mine.

"No, no, I've got it." This time I stood up quickly, trying to avoid the hands on my back. I sped out the door, talking a mile a minute. If I could outtalk him, I could keep his mind off things. My hands landed on the car door, but the handle wouldn't move.

He laughed, catching up to me. "You're locked out." He put his hand on my back, unlocking the door, and he shoved me in with an efficient push that only a gentleman could get away with. He got in the driver's side and put the key in the ignition, and the power locks went down. I tried not to panic.

As he started driving, I leaned back against the leather seats with a sigh. He was being too quiet. Anything could happen in that silence, and I turned to see him staring at me. And that's when I started talking about everything. Everything except what really concerned me. I was one big loud mouth. Blah, blah, blah. I barely listened to what I said. The more words between us the better. It kept him at bay.

"Did you know that I saw a motorcycle accident on this very road? Yeah, it was crazy." He couldn't even get a word in. "I love bikes though." He parked outside my apartment with a long sigh. "Huh, we're here," I said. "Well, bye."

His brows furrowed. "I'll walk you to your door."

"Oh, yeah." I tried to shove my own door open.

"I'll get that for you." He leaned over me, and I flattened against my seat so he couldn't touch me. Once he got it open, I scrambled free. He smoothly got out his side, and I waited for him. It would look ridiculous if I ran, especially with the gossiping middle floor lying in wait. We passed them up the stairs, and as we neared my door, I tensed for the inevitable hug. Maybe I could get away with a handshake. Except even I wasn't that cruel.

"Well, bye." He pulled me into a hug and rubbed my back. I felt like a cat trying to escape water, and I managed to wriggle free, patting him loudly on the back as a last measure. It was the one signal to a guy that you just weren't interested.

"We'll have to do this again," he said.

I pushed away, staring at him. I couldn't even politely agree with him. I just couldn't do it this time. He'd get the wrong idea, and I was tired of giving the wrong idea. I put my hand on the doorknob. "Well, bye."

"Are you doing anything tomorrow?"

"Yeah, an institute party. I'm kind of in charge."

"How about next week?"

Oh no, please don't force my hand. I didn't want to see the look on his face when I told him I just wasn't interested. What if he got mad? And he had wasted all that money! And I never even gave him a chance. I turned towards him, trying to be brave. "Um, actually, I can't get over my missionary. I'm sorry. This was a waste of your time and . . . you want my leftovers?"

He took the box that I shoved into his hands. "Is it Christian?" he asked darkly.

I got nervous. What if he chased him down? "What? That moron you met tonight? No, my Christian's off in the wilds of Africa." It wasn't a lie. I was sure there were Christians in Africa.

"You? Waiting for a missionary? Wouldn't he be a little young for you?" *Ouch!* That was a low blow. He bowed low over my hand. "Until we meet again, Blest."

"Yeah, yeah." I shoved through the door and saw Jade and Rusty wrapped up on the couch watching TV. I sped through the living room.

"Well, you're home early," Rusty said.

Jade snorted. "I didn't think she would make it this long. Before he looked at my ring finger, he was picking up on me! Her roommate!"

"What?" Rusty was incensed, but I could barely hear him.

"He didn't really match her wit anyway," Jade said. "He just kept talking and talking."

I walked into the kitchen and stared at all the new messages on my board. Phil, Lane . . . I squinted. Oh, Raine and Paul and Ryan and Nigel. Uh, yeah, you haven't heard of them all yet. The number of suitors was up to eight! Eight! That's what getting back on the saddle was doing to me. I had to get rid of them. All of them! I was finally cracking under the pressure. There was something wrong with me! They didn't deserve this. But I couldn't handle any of them!

My hand landed on the phone. I could call the Monsieur. Of course, I wasn't sure what he would do. Protect me like some knight in shining armor? He never even protected me when we were dating. I put the phone down. Christian would save me, but he was on a Charity date. Britton would just rub it in my face that he was right and I was wrong. Then he would tell me I was mental. *Maybe I am mental.*

"I need help," I whispered.

I listened to the high-pitched sound of a cruiser bike outside, and I peeled open the window, feeling the warm evening wash over my face. I desperately wanted to escape, so I pulled myself halfway out the window and tried to thumb a ride—anything to get me out of this place, to be free. The guy on the bike slowed down, leaning over his windshield. *Wait, no! This is a bad idea,* I told myself. I loved his ride, though. It was a bullet bike, a Kawasaki Ninja. *No, don't do this, absolutely not!* I pulled back, slammed the window shut, and slid down the wall to the floor. I heard the guy on the bike speed away.

"Jade," I called. "I'm no longer here."

"What?"

"I'm cleaning. Yeah, I'm cleaning." I crawled to the cupboard under the sink and began pulling out the cleaning supplies. "I've got to scrub down those floors next door. I can't be interrupted no matter what."

"What do you want me to tell these boys that keep calling?"

"I don't care. They don't care about me," I said to ease my conscience, "and I don't care about them. Get rid of them. I'm cleaning!"

Chapter 13

We need more spontaneous compassion and charity.
—Glenn L. Pace

Saturday, June 27th, morning

I scrubbed down the linoleum in the kitchen, squeezing the soap out of the sponge. Bubbles slopped onto the floor. I tell you, the things I did for free rent. Well, actually to hide out. The radio was on, and though I had given up on finding a good station, every once in a while a good song came on. I was surrounded with cleaning supplies, and no, I don't know what chemical I'm supposed to use with what, so I just used whatever and hoped I didn't die.

There was a whole bucket overflowing with ragged towels and washcloths that I found in the living room closet. I had started from the top down in the kitchen, scrubbing everything in sight. Then when everything started looking a little musky, I polished it. I guess you're not supposed to use soap on wood. My bad. Suds covered the oven and the fridge. They streamed down my arms, knees, and hair.

They were the only thing cooling me down in this heat. My red hair curled until I looked like Medusa. My red sweats were rolled to my knees, my shirt didn't match, and I was barefoot. I swear that was the real reason we have morning curfew, because if a guy saw me like this he would turn into stone. And I didn't care. I wanted him to.

I sucked in my breath at the loud thump at the window and ignored it, scrubbing harder. I had very good very bad friends. They wanted me to play, but I couldn't. I had to work like a banshee. I had to earn my keep somehow. I heard another thump on the window and saw the pinecone before it dropped out of sight. I determinedly turned from the window. Couldn't they just leave me alone?

"Knock it off!" Maggie ducked the pinecones and she peeled the window open to confront me. All I could see was her impossibly optimistic face. "You're wanted." She tried to shove a phone through the window.

"I'm supposed to be cleaning!" I shouted. "That means I have to stay away from the phone."

She sighed heavily and left, and I scrubbed even harder. I was through. No more. I don't know how I even got started with this crazy dating whirl. It was the Monsieur. But how had he gotten through my defenses anyway? No one could get through before. I had to make sure that I'd never make that same mistake again, even if I had to give some guy a black eye. I'd take them all on if that's what it took.

Christian tapped on the window, interrupting my dark thoughts. I sighed, seeing his hazel eyes watching me searchingly. No, I didn't want to give all guys a black eye. Christian always made me think logically, even if he didn't mean to. Why was I such a meanie anyway? He wasn't. I grimaced, wondering how his date went. Christian poked his head through the window. "Jacks," he said. "You stood me up again."

"What are you talking about?"

"The swimming party. Britton built stairs with cinder blocks to get over the gate at the pool. It's open rebellion."

I glanced at the darkening sky behind him. "In ice cold water? Sounds like a lot of fun." I wasn't prepared for the shock I'd receive going from my hot condition to a frozen one.

"And this looks like a lot of fun too." His eyes were steady on mine, and I quickly turned away, scrubbing even harder.

"Why don't you go bug Jade? She's not going either."

"Yeah, she's getting married in a week. What's your excuse?"

"I feel like I've been hit with a ton of bricks."

"You look like it too," he said wryly.

I glanced up quickly. What? Did he mean the strange sweatpants getup? "I can't find a good pair of pants. They're either dumpy or sleazy. You can't get something good with a shape like mine." I was too curvy.

"No, no, I suppose not," he said. I pursed my lips at his tone. I didn't care what anyone thought of me. My eyes narrowed at his laughing expression. "What? Is it my hair?"

"Let's just say that it has a life of its own . . . this whole place does. What happened here?" I guess it was a pretty strange sight. There were suds all over the place, and with the smell of chemicals it was like a war zone. "You would think Maggie would be all over this," he said.

I shrugged. "She wants me to do it by myself. It's a learning experience. She's all about tough love, you know."

"You should take a break and come to the swimming party. There will be food there."

Not even that could entice me. "I'm not really in the mood for a polar bear swim."

Christian interrupted my rejection. "What are you listening to?" He disappeared from the window, and before I knew it he had kicked off his sandals and was kneeling next to me in the suds, the hems of his long shorts getting wet. It was only then that I was aware the music was in Spanish.

"What? Did you fall in love with this stuff on your mission or something?" he asked. "No wonder you're in a bad mood." He turned the station without my permission, and I knew it wouldn't be long before he found the perfect song. He had the magic touch, and true to form, he landed on a Foo Fighters song. "Times Like These" blared boldly through the speakers, perfect background music for such a dramatic scene.

I groaned. "This song is dedicated to you," Christian said. He began to sing off-key with it, and I hid a smile. It was so cute. He was a shower singer, he claimed, and I always told him to keep it there. "You know," he said, repeating the words of the song as if he had just come up with it off the cuff. "It's times like these you learn to love again."

I laughed. "Knock it off."

"So, why are you so mad at the world?"

"What? Me? I'm not in the world, I'm of the world, so I couldn't possibly."

"Okay, let's go then." He stood up, playing with the suds at his feet. He was really good at ignoring my bad moods. "There are plenty of fresh RMs at the swimming party."

"Whatever! At my age? I don't want to date fresh RMs."

"Yep, fresh as paint." His lips curled into a smile.

"I don't even know how you want me to take that." Suddenly I matched his smile with my own. "Come to think of it, your brother is coming back from his mission in about two weeks. Is he cute?"

That wiped off his teasing look. "Don't even go there."

I smiled broadly now. I knew that would shut him up. "Isn't he coming home around your birthday?"

"Nope, the Fourth of July is mine. He's coming home the fifth. Wow, do you even know what you're doing?" Christian got down on his hands and knees next to me and stole the rag from my hand, his strong hands briefly brushing mine. "Let me help you. We've got to get you to your ball on time, Cinderella. We don't want to disappoint your many admirers."

I sat back on my toes. *I'm sure they hate me by now. They'd better.* I gave Christian a warning look. "I don't have any admirers."

"Oh yeah, you do. I know because they can't stand me. Watch their expressions when we get there. In fact, let's do an experiment. We'll go together and I'll count how many guys glare."

"Sorry, your plan isn't going to work. I'm not going."

"Hmm. You know, Britton is accepting dating applications for your hand." He looked at me innocently. "What? Your mom did put me in charge of your dating life. I didn't approve any of them though."

"Good."

"Your date went that well, huh?" He knew very well it hadn't. He had witnessed weirdo for himself. "Did you ever figure out his name?" I shook my head. "So what did you do after dinner?"

"He took me home."

"Ow ow!"

Christian looked really cute right now, covered in suds, his hair curling in the heat, the hems of his khaki shorts and knobby knees covered in suds. "You're a man-eater," he said.

"Don't you dare feel sorry for him!" I tried to justify myself. "He wasn't really interested in me in the first place."

"I saw it differently."

"How could he possibly be interested after a half hour? Especially after he had gotten to know me, for crying out loud? It only means one thing."

"What?"

"When I grow old or gray or fat and pregnant, he'll lose interest, and he'll wonder why I can't immediately slim down like all the supermodels do."

"What if he doesn't?"

"That's a lot of trust to give to a stranger. I don't want some guy dragging me off by the knot of my hair like some caveman, okay? I want a little more control than that."

Christian slid across the linoleum in the soup of bubbles, grabbing a rag, and then he pushed himself back, giving me a light push to the right for good measure. "So why did you give him your number?"

"I'm a bad judge of character. That's why I've got to protect myself when I actually come to my senses." I sighed. "Each crazy date like this just brings me one step closer to getting married to some borderline maniac."

"Oh brother."

"Don't you 'oh brother' me. I tried everything to turn him off, and I still couldn't shake him." I slid across the floor to the fridge and started scrubbing the sides down. "I had a gift for it before, but now it seems no matter what I do, they keep coming. I'm losing my touch. Me!"

He snickered. "Look, you really don't have to worry. I really don't think that he was after you for a long-term commitment."

"He told me Nephi didn't have a lengthy courtship with his wife."

Now it was Christian's turn to look startled. "Let me get this straight. You can't remember his name, and he's still proposing?" I nodded slowly. "You do go out with psychos."

"That's what I was trying to tell you. I'm surrounded! You know how Benjamin Franklin had a girl in every port? Well, I'm running from a guy at every port, and I'm through with it. There's nowhere to run now. " I scrubbed harder, caught up in my words. "Some girls go on the rebound. I tried it, but I can't replace the Monsieur that way."

"That's why you upgrade," he said firmly.

"Yeah, except I just can't trust myself." I had been going at the fridge for a while until it was completely lathered in soap, and I wasn't quite sure how we were going to get rid of all of these suds all over the ground. I say *we* because now that Christian was here, I'd make sure he finished this with me.

Speaking of, he was being too quiet. "That's your cue, Christian. You can call me a coward and a player now. Go ahead, slap any name on me you want, but I'm putting my foot down." I slipped on the suds, and he reached out to steady me, a serious look on his face. "Short of moving, I'm not sure what I'm going to do," I said. "I'm just tired of running, you know?"

"And then what? You either graduate from the singles ward or you flunk out."

I smirked at that. "I'm not getting an MRS degree, that's for sure. I'll get a bachelors." I laughed at my own joke. "Yeah, I'll be a bachelor-rat. That's what I'll do."

His hand was still on my arm and his warm fingers slid down until he found mine. He squeezed my hand. For some reason it felt so natural. That was the thing about Christian. He could do anything he wanted and I never got worried, but if he had been some other guy . . . ? "What's the matter?" he asked. "You too hip to get married or something?"

I looked up into his worried eyes, and tried to put his mind at rest. "Heck no! I'm not a loser, I'm just taking a break." I smiled and Christian frowned. A break? Yeah. Even Christian couldn't fight that. A break from guys—the wrong guys. If there were some right guys, I could deal with them—except there weren't. Only one guy was right— the Monsieur. Except even he wasn't *exactly* right. Anyway, I needed a hiatus, a reason not to break guys' hearts. Freedom. That sounded so good right now. "I'll just take a sabbatical from guys," I said, not believing my own brilliance.

"What lucky men," Christian said under his breath.

I grinned. Nothing could ruin my good mood now. "It's perfect, Christian. I'm tired of being fake! I mean, these guys like me because I must be putting on some sort of act. But I can't be entertaining all the time. I can't be smooth all the time!"

"No, you can't."

I smiled, feeling perfectly content with the world now that I had made my decision to abandon it. Christian didn't think I was serious, but I was. "I can't stand any more, Christian. I just can't."

He studied me. I knelt on the kitchen floor, suds all around me. "Then don't stand. You're already kneeling anyway. Maybe you just need to ask for some help."

I laughed. "You're crazy, you know that?"

Christian was silent for a moment, watching me. "That's an understatement," he said finally. He stood up. "C'mon, let's clean this place up. If you want to take a sabbatical, then take a sabbatical, but I'll only believe it when I see it." As soon as he found his feet, he slipped, almost falling. I laughed until he grabbed the sprayer.

"Watch where you spray that—" He sprayed me full in the face.

"Just cleaning," he said with an innocent voice.

I wiped my face off, grinning. That was the thing I liked about Christian. He loved life. He always treated it like a gift. I wanted to be like that. "Ooh, you're getting it!" I tried to get to my feet and slipped back to the ground.

"What are you going to do?" His strong hands landed on my back, and he pushed me around the kitchen floor like I was a human mop. "Once this place shines like the top of the Chrysler building, we can go have some fun!"

I laughed. "What? This *is* fun! Besides, I can't go like this, not with my hair all greasy!" I grabbed the squeegee, starting to round up the bubbles.

"It's fine. C'mon, Monsieur Romantique won't be there." *Of course.* That went without saying. Music majors had no time whatsoever. "And Charity might be there," he added as further incentive. I glared, seeing the mischievous look on his face.

"Oh yeah! We get along great. Almost as well as the two of *you* get along." It was a pointed remark. I wondered if Maggie and Britton had tried to work their magic yet.

Maggie stuck her head in the window. "Hey guys! I brought you some biscuits and jam."

My eyes lit up. Maggie always knew how to make things better. She passed the food through the window and Christian and I both settled on the wet floor. This would be the best feast I had had in a long time. "You're not here on your own, you know," Christian told me.

He was right. I wasn't. I felt like I had been given friends to help me through times like these. I cut the biscuit in half, trying to catch the crumbs before they fell on the clean floor.

"Look," I said. "I'll go, but only if you protect me." I spread the jam over the biscuit.

"Against what?"

"Against being social."

"Boring."

"Yes, but maybe I can make you my pretend boyfriend or something, and . . ." My voice faded when he shook his head. I sighed. He had Charity to think about.

He shoved the rest of the biscuit into his mouth and stretched to his feet like he was getting ready to leave. He stretched out his hand. "You mind giving me a hand?" he asked.

I stared at him. "No. I mean, yeah. I don't know the answer to that one."

Christian waited for me to decide if I would go. *Well, why not?* He helped me, and now I would help him. Charity wasn't the only one who lay in wait for him now. There was only one week to go with this stupid wager, and I'd make sure I thwarted Maggie and Britton every step of the way.

"Fine." I surrendered my hand and he helped me up, his fingers entangled with mine.

Chapter 14

Charity creates a multitude of sins.
—Oscar Wilde

Saturday, June 27th, afternoon

"It's time for the polar bear swim," Christian said firmly. He pulled the towel from his freckled shoulder and slapped me with it before I could tease him about his farmer's tan. It was our tradition. "Let's play some volleyball," he said.

With only a backwards glance, I followed him eagerly to the edge of the cold water. Lane Bryant had been edging towards me since the moment I arrived. Nothing but a male could tempt a woman to plunge into the water just to escape him. But even then I hesitated at the water's edge, my toes dangling just above its crystal depths.

Charity swam to the side, shivering delicately in her red suit with the Marilyn Monroe straps. She leaned against the warm white cement, folding her arms under her. It looked like only our ward showed up to the institute activity. *Typical.* Charity's posse of high maintenance girls sunbathed on the roof and she called to them. "Girls, the game's on!" Without putting down their cell phones, the blonds slid on their flip-flops and dropped from the roof like tanned spiders.

"And what is Charity without Faith and Hope?" Britton said as the two girls approached. I turned to him hopefully. Was he going to do what he was supposed to do? Flirt her away from Christian? He lounged on a beach chair in black swimming trunks, soaking in the rays over his already tanned back.

The girls giggled at their nicknames, but Charity wasn't amused. I was disappointed. "That's getting old," Charity snapped at him. "If you think you're going to get a date that way, you're going to have to actually work on your material."

Britton clicked his tongue at her. "Remember, Charity is love." She scowled until he completely threw her off guard. "Just leave me out of it," he told her with a disarming grin.

I sucked in my breath. He knew the jerk role well, and it certainly had blown off Charity's defenses. In fact, he had completely dumbfounded her.

"C'mon, let's start the game," Christian said quickly. I dipped my toe in the water and quickly pulled it out. If there was any way I was going to get in there, I would have to take it slowly. Spencer cannonballed in, football jersey and all, and I ducked from the huge splash. He pushed out of the surge of self-made waves, treating me with a broad grin. Christian turned to me. "You going to survive?"

"Why do you ask?"

"You had that smile again, the nervous one."

Trevor peeled off his shirt and dove in wearing his skinny jeans. Only a preemie could get away with that. And obviously he was much too cool for a suit. "You're not supposed to dive!" I said, flinching away from the angry surge of water. His head broke out of the water just in time to hear my furious lectures. "You could break your neck or something!"

Charity flipped on her back, her legs paddling elegantly through the water. "If we wanted his mom to be here, we would've invited her," she said softly.

Faith and Hope giggled, jumping into the pool and making synchronized patterns in the water in their matching blue swimming suits. Okay, I'm exaggerating.

"You're dissing his mom?" I asked sarcastically.

"No, you."

I turned to Christian. "What do you see in her again?" I whispered.

He smiled crookedly. "Well, she did get Jade and Rusty together."

Would he never take this seriously? I took another step into the water. It was now up to my knees, and my pink board shorts soaked up the water. I squinted in pain, feeling like a cat. Besides poor beached Britton, I noticed that I was the only one not in the water. Even Maggie and Betsy had passed me and were making a powerful whirlpool around us like happy little seals until Betsy lost her Lance Armstrong bracelet in the current.

"Hey, Jack!" Spencer yelled from the farthest side of the pool. "Need some help?"

My eyes got wide with fear. The last thing I wanted was to be dunked. "No, I don't want that kind of help." But too late—they were all coming in like sharks. I felt Christian's hand on my back, and I weighed the odds. They didn't look good. Christian might have mercy, but Raine had already dove in and was getting too close for comfort. I took a painful lunge off the steps into the shallow end. It hit a little above my waist. I tried not to scream like a girl. "See," I said through gritted teeth, "I'm in the water. Now leave me alone."

"You're not all the way in," Spencer pointed out. What was he, the pool Nazi? But everyone else nodded in agreement.

"It's as good as it's going to be," I said, giving him a stern look. It didn't work, and he still came for me. I quickly plunged into the water, making sure my hair got good and wet so that he wouldn't decide to dunk me for good measure. I whipped my ponytail out of the water, slapping him in the eye with it. Good. He deserved it. I shivered involuntarily. "Quick, let's start this game. It's the only way to stay warm."

"Raine is right behind you if you're chilled," Britton teased above us. My head jerked up to face him. The baby still hadn't gone in. Or maybe he was the only guy with any sense of self-preservation around here. "Watch out for barnacles," he warned, and I scowled at him, grateful Raine didn't know what that was.

"Christian!" Charity threw the inflatable ball at him and he easily caught it. "Wow, good catch. You've got to be on my team."

I pursed my lips, recognizing her ulterior motives. I called for the safest guy I knew. "Trevor, come play on my team. We'll show them who's better." Trevor dove to my side of the pool, and I tried to ignore the dangerous move. He didn't care if he got hurt, did he?

"Then we'll take Spencer," Charity said, her expression hard. Somehow, we had become the unofficial team captains, and she would try to hit me where she thought it hurt me worst, steal all my safe guys. Well, I wouldn't let her get away with it.

My eyes lit on the only other guy in the pool. "Raine," I chose.

Charity smiled evilly. "Maggie."

I tried to cover my gasp as Maggie innocently swam over to her side, her little pool skirt fluttering in the water. I wondered how much they had bonded since the ill-fated bet. Their eyes met and they grinned. My eyes narrowed. "Hope," I said, deciding to steal her best gal pal too.

Charity tried to play it cool. "Faith," she said, before I could take her other friend.

"Betsy!" Betsy tried to stop in the middle of her man-made whirlpool and tried to swim against it. "Betsy," I called again.

"I can't escape it!" It pushed her to our side, and we dragged her out of the current. "Thanks," she said breathlessly. I bit down a grin.

"Hey, freshman." Britton pointed to the shallow part of the pool, leaning over the water like some cool Cheetos cheetah stalking his prey. He even had the shades. "That's where the kiddies stay." She glared up at him. He shook his head. "No need to thank me, Cindy Lou!"

"Watch it!" I warned him. Nobody else could call our little punk baby that, least of all Britton.

"Oh, are you afraid I'll corrupt your little protégé? Just what we need, a bunch of beehives following the squirrelly girl around."

"Who are you calling squirrelly girl?" *We decided I wasn't.*

Spencer interrupted Britton's sinister ranting with a shout. "We're the happy team!" Charity jumped when he pushed her, trying to get her to join the cheer. "Happy, happy, happy!"

"Well, isn't that ironic." Britton had picked up a novel . . . some *War and Peace* kinda thing, as if he actually had a brain or something. I knew it was all part of his devilish plan. "Does that mean that Jacqueline is on the bitter team?" He casually flipped a page as if he hadn't just said that.

"Britton," I reminded him. "Keep out of it. You're not playing!"

"Let me guess. You're the team mascot?"

I brushed the hair that had escaped my ponytail from my eyes. "No, I'm the team manager. Big difference." I made my way to the front of the net, my head barely above the water. Raine took the front with me, looking like a tower next to me. Christian smiled on the other side of the net, not impressed with my size.

"Good luck getting past me," he said.

"That sounds like a challenge, Christian. I'm always up for a challenge."

"Are you?" Charity went to his side and I turned determinedly from them, seeing Spencer taking the middle. Maggie and Hope took the back. I hated playing an evil turn on my Maggie, but I was sure she was their weak spot. She would definitely miss it if I hit it to her. She stood there, her wet hair hanging over her face, the blond ringlets actually straggly for once. Betsy was getting ready to serve, but I knew my telepathy wouldn't work on her—she couldn't read my mind like Maggie could.

No matter, our little punk would be blind not to see it. She threw the ball up and slapped it through the air. It was one of those hard serves where you smash them or you smash yourself. In this case, she smashed the net. I ducked before it could hit me too. For once I was glad for my height.

"That's some power, Betsy," I laughed and she shook her head at me, her eyes twinkling as I continued to tease her. "Why don't you direct it at the happy team? Like so!" I hit the ball to them with my fist. Christian easily blocked it from Charity's face and tossed it back to Faith. She bit her lip, picking it up. She was tall and willowy, and I didn't expect her to give us much of a fight. I was wrong. She served it neatly over the net and consequently over my head. I scrambled up just as Betsy dove for it, splashing us all hard.

"Sorry," Betsy said.

"No problem." Raine threw it back to the happy team, and Faith got ready to serve again, acting like she still didn't have the capability to show us all up. "1–0 service."

"Wait," Trevor said. "Do we—" The ball slammed him hard in the head and we started laughing.

"Faith!" I accused. "You've played before, haven't you?"

"High school varsity," she told us in a matter-of-fact voice. Apparently, Faith had discovered our weak points too. The ball sailed over my head yet again and flew past Betsy and Trevor, going straight for Hope. Even if she had the same capabilities as Faith, she was much too short for it to do any good. Her head barely poked out over the water. Hope made a halfhearted twist for the ball, but it was much too high for her, and it bounced off the edge of the pool and rolled across the white cement. I sighed. Too bad I didn't think of her height when we were picking out our teams.

"Please don't judge me too harshly," she said. I suddenly felt bad that I had. Poor Hope tried to retrieve it, but her fingers couldn't quite reach it. She stood on her tiptoes. Britton just watched dispassionately.

"Would you get that for us?" I shouted angrily at him.

"Why? I'm having too much fun watching. On your tiptoes, woman," he tried to direct Hope. "Nice and easy, kind of like how you string *all* your men along." Hope gasped, and Britton finally kicked the ball back with a long hairy leg.

I grumbled to myself. How could I show Charity up if her friends worked against me? Faith served it to Hope again, and I tried to reach it in time only to have it scrape past my fingers. Hope splashed through the water with an angry grunt. I had to give it to her; she was actually trying now. "Faith, quit serving it to me!" she cried.

"I'm just giving you a chance to get me back. 4–0 service." Hope did it again and I jumped for it, trying to intercept. Raine got it instead, but he just knocked it behind us. It bounced off the white cement and rolled back to the other team. I leaned my head back, feeling the water against my neck. We couldn't even get the ball over the net. "5–0 service."

Britton laughed at our clumsy attempts. "All right. Get back on the sidelines, sport," he told me. "Your job now is to make the team look good, nothing else." I determinedly didn't answer. "On second thought," he said after my silence, "leave that to me."

"6–0 service." I had definitely picked the wrong Charity pal for my team, except now I wouldn't have it any other way. Hope was the underdog, and I always rooted for the underdog. Besides, Faith was much too arrogant. If we won this, it would be purely as scrappers. "7–0 service." They were murdering us. Hope looked desperate, which just made me more determined. "8–0 service."

My fingers curled over the ladder, and I got ready. Faith served it and it shot over the net. I dug my feet into the lower rungs of the ladder, using it to propel me high into the air. I might not be tall, but I could jump. I gave a battle cry, my hands coming in contact with the ball, and I slapped it back. It smacked Spencer hard in the face and he grunted in surprise.

I made a fist. "Ha! Not so happy now, are we, happy team?"

Christian grinned. "Finally, we can start the game." He tossed the ball to Raine who rotated to the serving position.

He executed a beautiful serve. The only problem was that a human wall got it. Christian and Spencer jumped up as one and I winced, but there was no way I was going to let them intimidate me. I jumped up with them, paddling my legs through the water. Spencer hit it to the side of me where Betsy was supposed to be, and she ducked. I watched to see if it would go out of bounds, but it just landed dully in the end of the pool. Trevor just watched it dully. *Garbage!* I slapped the water. We were making this too easy for them.

Raine stretched his hands out to me. "You need a hug, Red."

"Yeah, just not by you," a disembodied voice rasped above us. I tried to ignore Britton.

The other team rotated and Christian rolled the ball in his hands. "8–0 service, right where we left off." He served it over my head and Raine got it. He aimed it straight for Maggie. She wasn't paying attention. She was gesturing with her hands, but it somehow bounced off her fingers and flew back to us. What? What were the odds?

"Oh, Maggie, you're nice," Britton began, "or shall we say fine?"

Maggie blushed. "Thanks, cheerleader," I growled, but as long as it demoralized the other team, I was fine with it. Betsy jumped up, slapping the volleying ball back with her forearms. It bounced through the air, hitting Britton squarely in the arm. "Good shot!" I cried.

Both teams clapped. It left a red mark on Britton's bicep, and he curled his arm, flexing his muscles to get a better look at it. Except that really wasn't his intention. Nope. Charity was looking, and he gave her a disarming grin, almost as if he had caught her staring. She swiveled away and I just rolled my eyes. There was no way that was going to work.

"Someone needs to keep him on his toes," Christian said. He began rubbing at his eye, blinking rapidly. "Time-out. I've got something in my eye."

Charity was immediately at his side, her fingers light on his face. "Let me check it out."

"Maybe it's a mote," I grumbled.

He smirked at that and wiped carelessly at his scratchy eye. "9–0 service." He popped it over the net. He had somewhat miraculously recovered, unfortunately. I dove for it, and my foot slipped. I fell under the water instead, coughing up water.

Christian swam towards me. "You okay?"

"Fine."

"10–0 service." This time he didn't serve it to me, and Hope tried to get it with the same tragic results. Trevor just laughed at her. "11–0 service." It sailed in Raine's direction. Good! Raine hit it every time, except the human mountain of Spencer and Maggie—okay, just Spencer—hit it back Betsy's way. "Man, I'm starting to feel bad," Christian muttered. "12–0 service." He hit it back over.

"Betsy, get it! Oh, good try!"

Christian shook his head. "13–0 service." It deflected off my head and he hid a grin. "This is pathetic. 14–0 service. Game point."

My lips twisted in determination. There was no way I was going to let this slip past me. Not after that "pathetic" comment. Betsy and I both went for it and ran headlong into each other. It felt suspiciously like a clown act, and I rubbed my head. Our defeat was complete. It was a total shutout.

"Okay," Christian said looking sympathetic. "Let's switch up the teams a little."

"Oh no you don't." Trevor pushed off the side of the pool where he had been leaning the whole time. "We're beating you next game."

"Yeah, right."

I pulled my hand from my head. "What? Are you afraid?" I taunted, though it hurt my head to say it. "Whoever wins two out of three games rules the world! I think that's fair enough."

Britton leaned back, crossing his arms over his lean stomach. "Ah yes. Always one for impossible wagers." I glared at him. As far as *that* was concerned, I was not doing it.

"So, you want us to crush you again?" Christian asked in a way too innocent voice.

"Uh-oh, don't do that," Maggie warned. "The other team will probably play better when they're angry."

Christian was in a teasing mood and he grinned crookedly. "You think that will actually help them?"

"No, 'cause I just reversed the curse," Maggie explained. Her beautiful blue eyes twinkled. "Once they're aware that we know what's happening, they can't be as angry, and then they won't stand a chance."

My brows furrowed. It was disturbing that Maggie knew what made the bitter team tick. Christian swam to the front of the lines and handed me the ball. I tried to grab it under the net, but he wouldn't let go. "Don't make it too easy on us," he said softly. I scowled. He was trying to make me angry on purpose, but Maggie was right. Once I knew he was doing it out of pity, it took the fight right out of me. I tried to pry his long knobby fingers from the ball.

"Mercy, Jacks," he said. "Your hands are freezing."

"No, they're numb. There's a difference."

"Let me warm them up for you," he said in a teasing voice. He was on one today.

"No, that's my job," Britton interrupted us. I gave him a look. What was he doing? Was this part of his plan too? Even Christian looked confused, but before he could react, Charity splashed Christian from behind.

He splashed her back. "Watch it," he said. "We're on the same team."

I dove forward, stealing the ball before Christian could even react, and he let me have it without a fight, taking his place by Charity's side with a wry look at me.

She poked him playfully in the arm. "You never know when I'll turn." Wow, she was being incredibly honest.

"Okay, bitter team," Trevor said. He actually looked like he was going to take this seriously. Maggie was right. The goads *had* gotten to him. We made a circle with our team. "There's no such thing as unnecessary roughness. We're gonna kill happy team!"

Raine snickered. "That seems a little violent."

Christian laughed behind us. We were anything but secret about our plans. "As long as Jacqueline resuscitates me. I'm fine with that."

I almost stumbled at his words. I thought he refused to play the fake boyfriend?—but I quickly gathered my wits and took the ball to the back and tossed it. "Don't let them sink you, Ironsides!" Britton called out. "This time I want less talk and more action."

I clenched my teeth and slapped the ball harshly over the net. It landed between Christian and Charity, and I laughed. "Oops, I guess you're just not fast enough for me."

"I told you not to make them angry," Maggie said. Count on Maggie to make me feel good. I called the score and smacked it through the air. It slapped the water next to her.

"That was yours, Maggot," Britton said.

"Oops."

"Hey, happy team," Raine called. "Life's not so bad! Smile." Even he was getting into it.

They straightened angrily, and I aimed it for Faith. "This is for you, Hope." It flew for Faith's head and she ducked. I smirked, and so did Hope, though she tried not to.

Charity breathed in angrily. "Oh, you want a piece of me too?"

"Yeah." I aimed it for her and she gasped. Her fist caught it, but it flipped behind her. Much to my amusement, it rolled out of bounds where she couldn't reach it. She tried to slide halfway out of the pool, her legs kicking in the water.

Britton was just inches from her face and even closer to the ball, though it wasn't a surprise that he didn't bother to help her. He made a pout with his mouth. "Did Charity fail?"

"Of course not," she snarled. She finally got a hold of it and slid back into the water and back to Christian.

"You're fired," he told her. She forced a smile, passing the ball to him, her fingers lingering on his. He passed it down the line until it got to me, and I took the tainted goods.

"4–0 service." Charity was still smiling at Christian when I aimed the ball at her again, catching her off guard. I laughed when it landed dully in the water, splashing her in the face.

"Pay attention to the game," Christian teased her. He moved closer to her and I frowned, even though he was just trying to position himself to get the ball. I was too smart for that trick.

"5–0 service." I aimed it at the spot Christian just vacated. He twisted back, but he couldn't get through the water fast enough. That would teach him to stay too close to Charity.

"Ha," I shouted. "War's like love, wouldn't you say?"

"And I daresay, in your case, a bit of cheatin' too," Christian said. "How did you catch up so fast, hot stuff?"

Spencer couldn't believe it. "She's killing us." He was probably trying to make me cocky. The kid played enough football to know the strategy.

"Well, as long as she resuscitates you," Charity said sarcastically, "apparently you don't care, you turncoat." I think she was trying to shame Christian, but it didn't work.

"What's a matter?" Trevor asked. "You want in on the action too?"

Charity gasped. "What is wrong with this ward?"

"6–0 service." I aimed it for her, but this time she was ready. Charity got it over the net, and I knocked it right back. She tensed, lunging through the air, hitting it over with an efficient snap. We volleyed it back and forth, neither of us aiming for anyone else. So maybe it was the queen bee syndrome, but I'd prefer to call it the "I was really annoyed at her" disease. I was just afraid I wouldn't be able to keep it up much longer. If I could just outlast her . . . She smacked the ball right at me. It glanced off my hand. I spiked it over the net with all the strength I could muster and hit Charity in the head way too hard. *Oh garbage.* The boys groaned.

Her hand went to her head, her eyes squinting shut. "What is this, dodgeball?" she asked furiously. "What were you thinking?"

"I'm sorry. I was aiming for Spencer."

Spencer bit down a grin. "You monster." I tried to bite one down too. It wouldn't do for me to look like a complete jerk here, especially when all of a sudden Charity had become a helpless maiden. It didn't take me long to figure out why. She fell into Christian's arms, and he had no choice but to help her out of the water. Double oops. It didn't matter who won the game, the wounded always received the most attention.

"Ah," Britton said, "did Charity get a break?"

For just a second, Charity dropped her weak act. "Don't you think about cracking any more name jokes!" she snarled.

"Poor Charity. It hurts." A hand landed on Britton's shoulder, cutting him off. He jerked to attention when he realized it was Brother Baer.

"How's the love life, Britton?"

That would take some explaining. I sighed, leaving my teammates to their knowing looks and tiptoed to Charity's side. I felt bad in a way. Like always, Christian read my nervous smile. "It's okay, Jacks. I think she'll live." Christian pounded Charity on the back for good measure, and she looked up at him reproachfully. "You're tough, right?"

"Not as tough as Jack," she hissed. "She's quite the player . . . and not in a good way."

I grimaced. She was calling *me* a player? She waited for my response. "You're not jealous, are you?" I asked before it got too awkward. Charity's eyes widened.

"Sure, she is," Christian interrupted us briskly. "But she'll get over it. Wickedness never was happiness, you know."

I broke into a smile, trying to ease the situation. "Until now." Perhaps it wasn't the wisest thing to say.

Charity watched us scathingly. "Grow up, Jack. How old are you supposed to be anyway?" I froze. Was she referring to me flirting with guys younger than me? Namely Christian? I knew one thing: whenever my age was used as an insult, it only meant my opponent was desperate to cut me.

My cold smile matched hers. "Oh, I will grow up . . . when I'm eighty and can't move."

"Will that be soon?" she asked sweetly.

"Ouch," Christian said. I was surprised he even knew we were fighting. A guy normally didn't pick up these undercurrents. "C'mon, girls, be nice."

Charity stretched. "What? Are you worried about your *old* girlfriend?"

"We've never dated." His eyes were cold.

"Neither of you have dated? Not anyone?" Charity joked, purposely misinterpreting him. Perhaps she sensed he wasn't too happy, but true to squirrelly girl fashion, she knew being mean only added to her allure. Well, maybe later. Christian actually looked annoyed. "No, I guess not," she said. "That would force you to abandon your desperate fan club, Christian. We can't have that."

My expression hardened. She had gone too far, acting like he was some kind of player. Nobody insulted Christian. Hope unwittingly saved her. "Oh my gosh!" she leaned over Charity. "You're getting a burn, sweetie!"

"Oh no," I intoned in a bored voice. "Her perfect skin."

Charity flipped through the towels and flip-flops on the ground with furious fingers, trying to find her sunblock. "I don't like to bake my skin to a fine cancer like some people."

"Who?" I asked. "Your friends?"

She tilted her head to the side, giving me a look. "There are worse things than being high maintenance," she told me. "There's deferred maintenance." My lips twisted.

Maggie handed me a bottle, most likely trying to force me to be kind. "Here's some sunblock."

I turned the lotion over in my hand. Jade's sunless tanning lotion? I smirked. It was some awful off-brand that turned everything orange in a matter of minutes. Last time Jade's weird orange legs hadn't faded for a week. Maggie must've thought it was the real stuff.

"Maggie," I joked, "how could you be so cruel?" My words faded off when I saw Charity looking up at Christian through incredibly thick lashes. "Christian," she said in a sweet voice, "help me with my sunscreen. It's the least you can do. I can barely move my head."

"What a baby," he said, though it was a little too flirtatiously for my taste. He was already softening towards her?

I sucked in my breath. A person can only get pushed so far, especially a person like me. Charity's sunblock was at my feet. All I needed to do was kick it out of the way and it would be out of sight and out of mind. Then her evil designs against Christian would be thwarted.

Maggie wasn't looking, and with a stealth that surprised even me, I kicked the sunblock under the lawn chair. I turned quickly away before they started looking for it, so my smirk wouldn't completely give me away. My gaze rested on Maggie. She had ripped Britton's book away from him, and they were talking earnestly. It could only be about that stupid wager. How could Britton actually believe that he could win Charity over with that stupid jerk act?

I felt something slide from my hands, and after a moment of watching the two conspirators, I turned to Christian. Too late I saw him applying Jade's sunless tanning lotion to Charity's face.

I choked, but I wasn't sure if it was on a laugh or what. I mean, even I wasn't that evil, right? Right?

"Just wipe it all over my face," Charity said, closing her eyes. Oh, don't worry, Christian was. The orange gunk streaked nastily across her face.

I should really do something. "Uh, guys . . ." Charity gave me a snotty look and I hesitated. What were the odds that something like this would happen? I could only consider it a sign really. I was like a hapless Lamanite, and my job was to be a scourge to the Nephites, bringing them back to repentance—even though I really hadn't meant to do it. The only thing I felt bad about was that Christian's hands would be orange after this escapade, but sometimes the innocent must suffer with the guilty.

"Oh, you missed a spot here and here and here." She giggled. Her face was already turning orange, and I hoped nobody would notice. Not that it would do Charity much good, unless someone had some lemon juice on hand.

Chapter 15

In faith and hope the world will disagree,
but all mankind's concern is charity.
—Alexander Pope

Monday, June 29th, afternoon

"You're cheating!" Britton threw a dart into the dartboard, hitting the bull's-eye. He scooped up another handful of darts, looking like the perfect villain in his frayed jeans. It didn't take too much of my imagination to picture him brooding in some wild moor in an Emily Brontë novel. "Are you trying to be a jerk on Christian's behalf or what?"

"It's the newest scandal in the ward," Maggie said.

Britton nodded at Maggie, his eyes lingering on the sandal ribbons tied around her trim ankles. I thought they were pretty cool too, but I couldn't take her seriously with that bright pink scarf on her head. My nose wrinkled. "What are you talking about?"

"Oh, you know very well, twinkle toes!" Britton cruelly reminded me. "You're the reason that Charity is little Miss Orange Face for the next couple of weeks."

"I didn't touch her."

"Everyone knows you're to blame, even the stupid ones." Only he would make such a mean point. "Rumor is you did it in a fit of jealousy."

"What?" I tapped out a nervous rhythm on the polished wooden floor at Rambo House. I should've known better than to show my face at FHE, but Maggie made me come . . . and early, too!

"Who put that sunless tanning lotion on Charity?" I spouted. "Christian, not me! I demand to meet my accusers."

"That only works in a court of law, honey, not in Relief Society." Britton threw another dart into the board and it reverberated. Bryan snickered on the couch. He was playing a mean game of EverQuest. His fingers worked quickly over the controller. Britton's Bitter Boys posse was all at Rambo House, lounging on the stadium seating. The sheets of plastic were all gone, and the place looked pretty good . . . for a guys' apartment. Except now it looked sinister. Were they holding a council or something? None of them were in our FHE group. An opened box of Costco muffins sat on the table.

"Jacqueline, what were you thinking?" Maggie flopped down on a chair. "We just had a lesson in Relief Society about being nice. You couldn't even stick to it for a week!"

I bit my lip. I knew that I was going to get it for not interfering with Charity's face job. Even now I couldn't understand why I hadn't said something, so I excused it the only way I knew how: charity, sweet charity. "You wanted me to make her fall in love with Christian, so I did it. We're just throwing them together faster. We only have a week left to work with, you know."

"What?" Now she was gaping, but not for the reasons I thought. "You weren't supposed to make her your mortal enemy! That wasn't the deal. Now how will this work?"

"I've just upped the challenge. She hates me." Just the fact that everyone suspected I liked Christian would be enough for her to act. Even now I was cursing myself.

"Who said you could interfere?" Britton asked. "The deal was to see who would win the squirrelly girl, the nice guy or the jerk."

"Shh!" Maggie threw her finger to her lips with a pointed look at the Bitter Boys. They were completely absorbed in the video game, but it didn't matter. They all knew about this crazy deal anyway. I was surprised the rest of the ward was still in the dark.

"You never said how," I hissed.

Britton smirked and threw another dart. "Do you have Charity's picture for the ward directory yet?" We all grimaced, imagining her orange face in the dating line-up.

Maggie sighed and stood up to pace the room. "Didn't you say Spencer had a sliver in his thumb?"

"He told you that? Is that why we came early?" I glared at Britton, grateful that I wasn't the only guilty party. It was Britton's plot to get her to hang out against her will. He was an evil one.

"Yep, and that's not the only activity we have planned. Forget the USS *Constitution*, this is even better." I pushed away from Britton, not wanting to hear it.

"What's going on?" Christian walked into the living room in his worn vintage jeans. He wore a short-sleeved shirt unbuttoned over a white T. I met Britton's eyes nervously, but Britton didn't look worried. He had no trust in his roommate's eavesdropping abilities.

"Oh, so people like you do come to FHE?" Britton said.

Christian smiled briefly. It looked like he was just coming back from work. He looked tired. He had one strap of his backpack slung over his shoulder, and he collapsed on the couch next to Bryan, watching the TV blankly. His eyes were a little red. "The old lady next door complained about us to the cops again," he muttered. "She wants our garbage picked up."

"It isn't our fault that the garbage men won't take our garbage," Britton said.

"It is when we don't take it to the sidewalk."

They groaned, but Christian was good at talking his way out of things, so it was probably smoothed over, at least for now. The last thing they needed was trouble with their landlord. He'd probably try to charge more rent for misbehavior.

Christian wasn't quite looking at me, and I wondered if he was mad at me. "Where's that big lug with the sliver?" I searched the room desperately. "Spencer!" I shouted. "He's got a sliver, that's why we came," I explained needlessly. "And for FHE and all that too." Christian was only half listening, and I watched him nervously.

Spencer trudged out from the kitchen in his white football jersey, practically hanging his head. Maggie went to his side and efficiently snapped her fingers at him, making him hold his hand out to her. She winced at the huge splinter lodged deeply in his index finger. The skin around it was turning strange colors. "We have to operate immediately," she said. He started whining, and she soundly shushed him. "Jacqueline, make yourself useful. Sit on him."

"What?"

Maggie pushed the big guy on the couch, and I obediently sat on him. "I don't really think this is going to do anything," I said.

"Then put a pillow over his head or something so he can't see what I'm about to do."

"That's worse," I sputtered.

Maggie was relentless. "Get me a needle, Christian." Christian got up reluctantly from the couch.

"I hate needles," Spencer whined.

I rolled my eyes and threw a couch cushion over his head. "Big baby."

Britton now had a captive audience on the couch, and he mercilessly shut off the games, sticking a DVD into the player. "Hey," Bryan complained. "I was on level eighteen!"

Britton ignored him, holding the remote with deadly accuracy. "Let's display Jacqueline's adventures at sea, shall we?" He laughed to himself. "This one's my favorite." It was *The Truman Show*. He skipped to the end where Truman was sailing on a glassy sea. "Ah, freedom," Britton narrated. "Nothing like sailing the open sea. And just when you think you're going somewhere . . ." Truman's ship crashed into a wall in the middle of the ocean and Britton laughed. "Last year. With the one we don't speak of."

I gasped, exchanging glances with Maggie. She just shook her head and grabbed Spencer's bulky finger. He tensed and I leaned on him with all my might. I'd take out my aggressions on him, but there was no way I'd be able to keep him down if he decided to fight.

Christian handed Maggie the needle from the kitchen. "It's sterilized, doctor." She grinned and he quickly joined me, pinning the other side of Spencer down. He smiled, though he looked really tired. "You realize this is dangerous, don't you?"

I lifted an eyebrow at him. "Only for a guy. Spencer wouldn't dare touch me."

"Youb kibb me," Spencer said under the pillow.

Britton was still at it. He threw another DVD in. It was *Cutthroat Island*. "This is you, Jacqueline. After your reign of terror is over." A keg of gunpowder exploded and a ship blew up. He rewound it, showing us again. Splinters flew through the air in slow motion.

Christian groaned, finally realizing what was happening. "You're unbelievable, Britton."

"Yep, this one's even better." The next clip was the Red Sea being parted in *The Prince of Egypt* and the "suitors" being wiped away in the aftermath. Christian laughed and I gave him a warning look. He stopped abruptly.

"That hurts!" Spencer's hands flailed and Maggie tried to catch the one with the splinter.

"It will hurt worse if you don't hold still."

He shouted out in fear, just as Britton played another clip, a happy little cartoon of a tugboat. It made figure eights in the water and everybody loved it and it saved the day . . . I actually snickered at that one. It had nothing to do with me. "Britton, I think you put the wrong one in."

"Oh, that one's for the Maggot," he replied flippantly. "It's *perfect*."

Maggie turned briefly from her grisly work. "What? Oh pleazzz!"

Spencer moaned just as Trevor came out from the back room, his hair sticking up. He looked like he had just woken up from a nap, probably because we were fighting so loud in here. We were worse than an alarm clock. "Hi, Dad," we chorused in a round of guilty voices.

His eyes were wide and blinking. "Who's making all that racket?" Bryan set the muffins down on the table and Trevor could see that half of them were gone. "Hey, who's been eating all the treats?" he shouted. He took his job as FHE dad very seriously—probably because it was his first time with an FHE group. "Those were for FHE! What are you doing? Is this talent or something?" We were the only group that did talent. It was kind of a joke because we didn't have talent. "Who did we assign last week?"

We stared at each other. If no one talked, then we were free. "We were just planning the activity." Even Britton seemed cowed. "We're just putting in DVD clips that remind us of each other."

"Lame," I mouthed to him.

"The family that plays together, stays together," Britton said, and under Trevor's narrowed eyes, he put *Pirates of the Caribbean* in. I braced myself, digging my elbow into Spencer's side. It was a dramatic moment with Elizabeth standing on the end of a plank. She stared down at the water for an interminable amount of time. There was no way she was going to jump. A dirty pirate approached her. I glanced at Christian and he met my eyes knowingly.

"Too long," the pirate growled. Britton religiously mouthed the words just as the pirate knocked the girl off the plank and into the water. Britton joined the pirates in their raucous laughter. Weirdo. He turned to me. "At this rate, you won't even be able to hold onto your stalkers."

"I won't even be alive," I exploded, though at the same time I was strangely flattered. What kind of time did he put into this? "According to you I'm going to crash into a wall and get blown up! Did I miss anything? Oh yeah, I'm going to drown my suitors! Tell me you have a point. Please!"

"Nope, you covered it. Wait, you'll also be left all alone on an endless ocean of vanity. Where's that clip?" He picked up *Castaway*.

"Mayvee, she's indecissssiv," Spencer mumbled under the couch cushion. That was something he knew about.

Christian smirked. "No, I'd say she makes her decisions fairly quickly." I met his eyes. I knew he was referring to the sunless tanning lotion incident.

Britton copied my voice. "No, no, and always no."

"Hmm," I said dryly. "I guess you can read my mind then."

"Just like a cheap romance novel."

"Fine!" Trevor shouted. "We'll count teasing our brothers and sisters mercilessly as our activity. Why not?" Despite myself, I laughed, and Trevor's eyes narrowed. It was just like a real FHE at home with the dad getting mad. "Can we please do this right?" Trevor angrily stormed into the kitchen. "Family, get in here! It's time for FHE!" Of course Rusty was nowhere to be found. He must be with Jade.

Maggie jabbed the needle into Spencer's finger harder than she intended. "Ow!" Instead of tackling Britton like I wanted to, I quickly jumped to Maggie's aid, pinning my shoulder against Spencer's side. "Don't you dare move, big guy!"

But Spencer couldn't take any more. He knocked both Christian and me off, and we went sprawling to the carpet. Our heads collided, and I grunted in pain. Instead of holding my head, I quickly tugged my skirt over my knees. Christian grinned wryly. "I told you to be careful." He wrapped his arm around mine and interlocked my fingers with his, pulling me up with just his arm. I was astounded at his strength. Why did I never think he had it in him?

"Hold out your hand," Maggie ordered Spencer. "C'mon, be a man about it."

"Yes," Britton drawled. "Take it like a man. We men have to be so brave nowadays in the face of conspiring females."

Maggie tugged Spencer's finger closer to her. "The first time a Deluxe girl bats her eyelashes at you, you're a goner." I glanced at Christian. I knew that from experience.

"I think we're a little stronger than that," Britton said.

Spencer screamed out in pain. Maggie pulled away, the sliver on the end of her needle. "See, that wasn't so bad." Spencer's expression said otherwise.

I got ready to argue, but Maggie just shook her head at us. "We've got better things to do than argue about exploding ships."

"Yeah, like baking cookies."

We were interrupted by "Love at Home," and that's when we broke into a musical. Okay, not quite, but "Love at Home" is very catchy when you're not the recipient of it. Christian plucked the tune out on the piano with one finger. FHE had officially started. For a guy who liked Foo Fighters and Pixies, he wasn't very musically inclined, but it did the trick.

Trevor pointed to the elevated couches. "Sit down, family, and sing. It's time for FHE." After receiving one stern look from him, I landed on the couch next to Britton and we began singing in stiff voices.

We sounded like a choir of Frankensteins, especially since the piano had a stuttering problem. Since the Monsieur had disappeared, Christian had just learned to play for FHE and was still in the extremely syncopated stage. "When . . . there's . . . love . . . at . . . home."

The Bitter Boys sat stiffly in the back of the stadium-seated couches, not quite knowing what to think of us. We were all clinically crazy, but I suppose we deserved it. It's the number one rule, you know. You never complain about your FHE group. If you complain, then you get the worst group ever. Look what happened to us.

"Okay," Trevor said as soon as the song was done. "Once again Mom has deserted us for another man." Of course, he was referring to Jade. "So once again, I'm in charge. Anybody have the spiritual thought?" After that little activity, there was no way I could.

Christian quickly intervened. "Hey, I got the spiritual thought. You want me to give it?" Trevor nodded regally. Christian pulled his scriptures from his backpack.

"You carry a quad in your backpack?" I asked. "No wonder you're so tired."

"I'm not tired. I got sprayed in the eyes with pepper spray today." My eyes got big. "It was a part of work," he explained, flipping open his scriptures. "Okay, many of you are familiar with the 'Choose ye this day' speech."

I was still stuck on the pepper spray thing, but at least his eyes weren't red because of me. "Why did they spray you with that stuff?"

Trevor soundly shushed me. "Let him do his lesson."

"Thanks, Dad." Christian squinted up at us with red eyes. "Where are your scriptures?" he asked. It was slightly tongue-in-cheek, slightly not.

"Uh."

Britton, Trevor, and Spencer sprung to their feet to get their scriptures. They came back and thrust them at us. "Thanks, Britton," I said, not taking them from him.

"You need more religion in your life," he told me, not budging.

"I know someone else who's lacking."

Having received a warning look from Trevor, Britton sat next to me and we turned to Joshua. "Slightly less known is Caleb's 'Bring it on' speech," Christian continued as if he hadn't been interrupted. "The children of Israel didn't think they could take the land from the Anakims. Those were giants that possessed the promised land. If you read this verse, the spies were 'as grasshoppers' compared to these Anakims."

"Cool," Spencer said.

"Yeah, they probably looked just like you," Britton muttered.

"And the people even threatened to stone Moses if he tried to make them fight them."

Spencer frowned. "Not cool." I hid my smile.

"And of course, you know the curse. Everyone over twenty who had murmured against the prophet would never see the promised land."

"That meant that a lot of time passed before they had a chance to take the Anakims on again. Only this time, Caleb said, 'Give me this mountain.'"

"That's what you said when we got lost between Slate and Rock Canyons," I said in an accusing tone. It *had* been the only thing that kept me trudging through that hot summer day.

Everyone groaned. The ill-fated family hike. It had been someone's bright idea—and most of the time Maggie remains nameless—to hike up Rock Canyon and find the "secret passageway" to Slate Canyon. We never found that "secret passageway." Just one wrong turn, and we were scaling the mountains, instead of taking the easy hike that we had counted on.

"Garbage," Rusty called from the kitchen. "We were lost forever." He peered around the corner. He must have come in through the back door trying to evade FHE. But the memory was too much to keep him quiet. A lot of things were too much to keep Rusty quiet.

Christian shrugged. "It wasn't that bad."

"Eight hours is bad!" Rusty carelessly swigged a carton of chocolate milk in his hand.

"What are you complaining about?" Britton said. "The children of Israel wandered the wilderness for forty years." Unlike the rest of us, I think he enjoyed it. He was always up for any physical challenge.

"Give me that mountain," Christian said, and I grinned at the memory. But that's where it belonged—in my memories. There was no way I was doing that again. "Caleb was eighty-nine years old and still fighting," he said.

"Like you?" Britton whispered to me. I trod over his foot. "Ouch."

"And as you all know," Christian said, "the children of Israel got their promised land when they decided to fight for it. So, make this your new attitude. When God commands, that's your cue to say, 'Give me that mountain!'"

The door flew open. "Why aren't you at FHE!" Jade's head popped around the door and her eyes grew wide. She tucked a glorious strand of hair behind her ear. Her accusing tone quickly changed. "Oh." She stared at the group piled around the living room. Her voice was strangely deflated. "It's here."

"Hi, honey," Rusty said. Jade sighed. It was obvious that she had thought she had caught him skipping, even though she had tried to skip too. Now she had to join us or she would look like a sluffer. She stormed into the room, looking quite dignified in her tailored work clothes.

"Mom," Spencer said brightly, "you've decided to come."

She flopped down next to Rusty on the love seat. Appropriate. "I was just rounding up some tardy children." She didn't quite look at Spencer when she said it.

Trevor sighed. "Well, thank you, Mom, for coming. We appreciate it, since you and Rusty only have a week to live. And thank you, Christian, for that lesson. Deluxe Seven was in charge of games, but they're a no-show, and since you already had your activity—"

"Then FHE's over!" Jade clapped her hands decisively.

"Let's go." Maggie seconded the call. That was unlike her. But she *had* been unusually quiet, and when Britton tried to wave her to his side, she ignored him, her back stiff.

Jade and Rusty were already whispering sweet nothings to each other. "Let me walk you girls home," Christian said quickly. Maggie tried to stop him, but he took one glance at Trevor's wounded look and left Britton behind along with Spencer the invalid. He opened the door for us and we stepped into the Monday twilight. The moon covered the sky in its yellow brilliance. You would think that it wouldn't be as hot, but we still could find no relief in the darkness.

A light breeze cooled the sweat on the back of my neck. Dark trees shadowed us overhead. Someone was pounding on something. A car? It wouldn't be surprising, since nobody's car worked around here. Here and there a scream echoed through the night. You would think we were in a war zone, but it was just Provo.

"I made something for you." Christian pulled something from his back pocket. "Maybe this will help you in your quest for bachelor-rathood."

He handed me a CD, and I held it up under a streetlight. He had drawn dancing stick figures all over it, and I pocketed it with a faint grin. Any music was priceless if it came from him. I took a deep breath, knowing I had to face this sooner or later. "So, I'm sorry for uh—"

"Making me dye Charity's face orange?" I nodded, feeling guilty. It was a familiar emotion lately. He sighed, running his hand over the bushes. He plucked out a wild flower and tickled my nose with it. I pushed him away. "Well, I'm sure it just adds to her attraction."

"Yeah, about that . . ." I wasn't quite sure how to word it. "Um, off the record . . ."

He watched me closely. "That means it will be a headline," he said. "Go on."

He wasn't making this easy on me. I really didn't want to know, but it was time to face the truth. "So you like her, don't you?"

"Who? Orange face?" Christian smiled at the memory, and I suddenly felt miserable. Who was I to stop him if he really liked her? He gave me a look, and I knew that I was in for it.

Maggie's cell rang just as we reached Rainbow Villa, and she answered it. I hesitated on the steps, grabbing Christian's hand before I changed my mind. "So about her . . . I'll help you." It came out a croak.

"Oh no, you don't. I don't want your help."

"What's wrong with my help?"

"Nothing." Christian playfully stuck the flower into my hair. I felt the warmth of his strong hands as he tucked it under my ear, and I tried not to get too distracted. It meant nothing to him. "If I want something, I'll get it myself," Christian told me. He smoothed my hair around it. He was laughing a little to himself. The flower didn't want to stay.

Maggie snorted into the phone. "Talk to her yourself. I'm through making deals."

She shoved her cell at me and Christian pulled away. "Don't worry, Jacks. I'm fine." The flower fell from my hair and he caught it just in time. He put it in my hand and crushed my fingers over it with a snicker. "Man, it's just like you, stubborn."

Well, I didn't mean to be. Before I could get the words out, he left. I watched him go like he was dying. I was losing him. So, what did I prefer? Having no say in his destiny or actually taking matters into my own hands?

I put the phone to my ear. "Are you having second thoughts?" It was Britton. For once I wished I could talk to an unlucky suitor instead.

"I don't run away from anything."

"Au contraire. I want my 'Jerk Wins' column nice and poignant."

I sighed. Charity didn't deserve Christian, but if that was what it took to make him happy, fine. And if things turned out the way they should, it would just be one week of tormenting that squirrelly girl. I could handle that, right? I stared at the crushed flower in my hand. "Let's lay down the ground rules," I said finally.

"Good. Interference seems to be second nature for you, so I'll consider it fair game. Second, this will be a 'love him or leave him by his birthday' program. Sparks will fly on the Fourth of July . . . uh, hi, Christian."

I smirked, almost wishing that Britton had blown his cover. He lowered his voice. "I'll just get his Bitter Boys card ready and throw in a complimentary gift bag. Perhaps I'll reserve a spot for him as vice president. I'm sure you'd like that."

"Not so fast, Britton." I nervously plucked a yellow petal from the flower and let it flutter to the ground. I jerked. *He loves her.* "Normally when you have a wager, there's something at stake," I said.

"Oh, I'd say there's plenty at stake."

"Not for you." I plucked off another petal. *He loves her not.* I breathed out. "If I win, you have to ask someone out for real. Then we're even."

"Well, seeing there is no possible way I can lose, I have no problem with that."

He hung up on me and I glared at the phone. There was more at stake than Britton's love life and some measly article I was morally against writing. Besides, if I wrote my column lousy enough, it could easily be cut from the magazine.

Still, no matter how I looked at it, there was no winning this wager. Another petal rushed to the ground. *He loves her.* Once again, I crushed the flower in my hand, unwilling to let fate have a hand in this. No, now it was my turn to interfere. It was Christian's happiness, wasn't it? What were best friends for anyway? If I could just remember.

Chapter 16

Charity isn't a good substitute for justice.
—Jonathan Kozol

Tuesday, June 30th, evening

Girls, don't do this at home. What I'm about to do would push a guy away so fast you wouldn't know what exit he took. With that daunting thought, I stepped into the Manavu Chapel for institute with Maggie beside me. Of course, I had nothing to lose, right? Well, I could lose my best friend with this fake boyfriend finding, but then again, Christian was so oblivious he would never know what was up, even with my sudden transformation.

I had resisted the urge to pillage the DI boxes and had raided my roommates' closets instead. I wore Jade's delicate white blouse and Maggie's jaunty plaid skirt. I actually looked cute in all my borrowed clothes. Maggie's wannabe ballet flats were the perfect touch. What? I only had a week to work with here, don't give me flack.

I leaned on the doorjamb, looking into the classroom. Charity had to be in here, orange face and all. And sure enough, she was sitting next to Christian . . . sort of. A chair was wedged safely between them. She was being coy. Well, you snooze, you lose, honey. At least that's what I would teach her.

"Do we have a volunteer for an opening prayer?" Brother Baer asked. He looked around the room. "Going, going, gone. Sold to Britton Sergeant."

"I didn't even raise my hand." I took careful note of Britton's placement. He was sitting in front of Charity in perfect jerk fashion, his white shirt a dramatic contrast against his dark-washed jeans like some fifties rebel without a clue. He had situated himself where Charity could stare at him but he could be just out of reach. He'd have to do better than that.

Christian laid a tan arm around the vacant chair, the short sleeves of his blue shirt bunching over his biceps. My lips curled. Even if Christian picked up on my sudden advances, he would never take me up on them. The most he would do was avoid me for a couple of months. That would make us even.

Maggie was starting to look nervous. "How are we going to do this?" she asked.

"Just be here." That's all it would take to make Charity jealous. "She'll do the rest." I watched Charity perform her magic. She crossed her legs in her fitted capris, swinging her pointy-toed high heels. The look was lethal. She had the sign-up sheet in hand. Just like me, she used her resources. She had actually managed to tone down the orange face. She must keep her plastic surgeons handy . . . or at least her concealer.

"I like that she never loses her cool," I whispered to Maggie. "It makes it much more fun to break it."

Charity flipped to the dessert sign-up and leaned closer to Christian, mouthing to him with perfect red lips. "What should I make? Brownies?" He shook his head firmly and I scowled. What was he dissing brownies for? That was the only thing I *could* make. "What's your favorite then?" Charity pulled closer to Christian. "I didn't catch that?"

Oh, she was trying to make him work for her . . . leap over the obstacle of the chair between them. Every challenge he overcame would bring her closer to him—literally.

"It's time to throw down the gauntlet." I strode boldly into the room. The point was to come fashionably late, much to Maggie's dismay. And I had to act flirtatious, which was basically how I always treated Christian, but this time I had to step it up. Before Charity could do anything about it, I brushed passed Christian, running my fingers through his already disheveled hair.

He glanced up at me with a puzzled look on his face, and to be honest, it felt pretty weird on my part too. He grinned dubiously. "Looks like Jack's back."

I ignored that, pointing at him. "This seat taken?"

He put a hand up in surrender. "You chasing some guy away?"

"No." I took the seat between Christian and Charity. Normally this was a dangerous place to sit because Christian liked to read over my shoulder. Of course, I didn't like to be too close to Charity either. But today I wouldn't have it any other way. She was my star witness. Christian pulled his arm from my seat, and I turned to him mischievously. "No, don't move on account of me." I threw his arm back around me. He couldn't help but grin at that.

Maggie brushed past him, taking Christian's other side, He looked at her smiling upturned face. He was flanked on both sides by this deranged Charity organization, and he turned to me in confusion. "So, what is this? A bet or something?" With some difficulty, I kept my face impassive. Like this was so out of character? "I thought you were going to be a Mormon nun?"

"Not yet," I whispered, my lips very close to his ear. It was a good thing I didn't care what he thought of me because after this, he'd have no respect for me. He gave me a nervous glance and I bit down a smile, not realizing it would be so much fun to mess with him. For once *his* feathers were ruffled.

Too late, I noticed Britton was sitting with Lane Bryant. Raine chose that moment to look back at me with a longing look. I froze, knowing Britton too well to think it wasn't a setup. Sure enough, Britton smirked. Raine's face was flushed. It was probably the sweater. He was one of those guys who wore the latest style in the wrong season. It was way too hot for that sweater, but there was no way he'd take it off because it was too cool. I leaned closer to Christian and he gave me a knowing look. "You could've asked if you wanted a fake boyfriend," he whispered.

"I don't know what you're talking about," I said sweetly.

Christian glanced at Maggie, who once again smiled brightly up at him. I sighed. She was completely useless. She'd better be grateful she had me on her side or her little charity program against Britton never would have worked. She had wasted two weeks doing almost nothing. I'd make this last week the clincher.

The opening hymn had already started, and I kicked my hymn-book all the way under my chair. Christian pulled away, searching for his. "Can I share a hymnbook with you?" I asked him.

"Oh, I'll share one with you," Charity interrupted in a much-too-sweet voice. I sniffed, smelling her strong dose of perfume. It was effective in more ways than one—a draw for the guys, a repellent for me. I really hoped my allergies wouldn't kick in.

"Are you sure? It looks like you might have to share your hymn-book with Hope." Hope heard her nickname and grinned back at me. You know, that girl was too good for the likes of certain company. I should probably steal her from Charity too.

"She's got one already," Charity said through gritted teeth. The music started and she thrust her hymnbook at me. Before I could argue further, the singing started and our voices noticeably changed from catty to sweet. The war had begun, and we soon were trying to outsing each other. "Shall the youth of Zion falter in defending truth and right? Yes!"

Maggie winced, and Christian elbowed me. "Knock it off," he said, but then he broke into a grin. "You just said 'yes.' I'm pretty sure you're supposed to say 'no' after that line."

I giggled and met Charity's challenging eyes just as the song ended. She slammed her hymnbook shut. The sign-up sheets threatened to fall off her lap. "Oh, let me get those for you." I stole them from her, scanning the desserts to see what she put down. "Oh, mud pie," I glanced up at Christian and said dryly, "Your favorite."

He shrugged. "Too bad those sign-ups are for Enrichment."

"Oh really?" I shrugged. "Who knows? Maybe we'll invite you as a guest speaker." I gave Christian the sheets and he passed them along.

Maggie flipped to the attendance sheets. She first marked off Christian and then looked for me. "What's with your birthday?" she asked. "You put yourself as five years younger."

Charity's head shot up at that, and I gave Maggie a false smile. At least she hadn't picked up the roll I was six years old on. "Christian made me do it," I said in a warning voice. She was forgetting the mission. I couldn't look bad in front of the competition.

"Actually, you can thank Britton for that," Christian said. "He thinks he's funny."

I tried not to look surprised. All this time I had blamed it on Maggie's misguided deeds. "Well, how sweet." Britton didn't even turn at the inference. He was really good at ignoring us, most likely plotting his next move.

Brother Baer was warming up to his marriage prep lesson. "Turn to Philippians 1:3."

Christian opened his scriptures and I leaned over them. He teasingly pulled them away. "Forgot your scriptures again, huh?" I smiled in response.

"Do you ever read them?" Charity mumbled.

My smile didn't waver. "Yep, that's why I lost them."

Christian finally relented. Garbage, I really needed glasses. I found myself practically resting my head on his shoulder just to see the verse—and not just for effect. Girls, that's another one to remember. Never take your scriptures to institute. "Would someone read this?" our teacher asked. "Anyone? Anyone? Britton, go ahead."

True to form, he hadn't raised his hand, but Britton sat up, leaning casually against the bench in perfect jerk fashion. "'I thank my God upon every remembrance of you,'" he read in a remarkably velvet voice.

My head lifted. I hated to admit it, but that was really romantic, especially the way he had just read it. I turned to Charity to see her reaction, but she was biting her lip in irritation, still looking at Christian. *Good.*

"You're treating the dating scene totally wrong. It's about getting to know the other person," Brother Baer said. "You can't do that unless you date. That doesn't mean that you have to accept someone you won't be happy with." My fingers stilled and I started paying attention. "You've got to choose. After all, we don't practice polygamy anymore."

"Don't we?" Britton asked casually. He glanced back at Charity and me and poor Christian in the hot seat. I stiffened at the insinuation; so did Charity.

Lucky for him, Brother Baer was in the mood to play. "See me after class and we'll discuss the finer points of our doctrine," he said with a conspiring wink. "Seriously though, don't become a professional investigator like on your mission."

Christian glanced down at my notebook. It was uncharacteristically blank. "You haven't written anything down yet?"

"Yeah, I got distracted by the lesson."

"It takes a miracle, but God is in the business of miracles," Brother Baer said.

"I can't read your writing anyway," Christian muttered.

With some difficulty, I tore my attention away. This called for a handwriting contest. I printed out my name in my best hand and thrust it at him. "Try this."

Christian squinted. "What's that supposed to be? Egyptian hieroglyphics?"

Garbage! I tried to write my name in legible cursive. He still couldn't read it. I pursed my lips and printed it all out in caps. Christian stole my pen. "Give me that." He wrote my name in print unusually good for a guy. "Now, that's legible."

"Hey," Maggie asked suddenly. "Are you guys paying attention?"

Sure. My eyes met Christian's. I had his full attention. So far, so good. Charity was stiffening beside me, but now I had to step it up. I was never touchy-feely, but it was for a good cause, and suddenly I didn't really mind that much. "Look, your writing is just as bad as mine." I put my hand over Christian's and wrote my name with his hand. The oblivious kid didn't even notice how brilliant the move was, but Charity did.

Maggie leaned over us. "Do you even know what our teacher is saying?"

I glanced up at her, my eyes sparkling. It was as if she didn't know why we were here. "I don't know. Christian distracted me." I tried not to laugh, taking advantage of the fact that Christian just thought I was joking.

"Now is the time to talk intimately with the Lord," Brother Baer stated. "Develop a personal relationship with Him. Tell Him how your day was. Ask for help when you need it."

"What's the point?" Britton asked. Apparently he never had to raise his hand, even when he wanted to speak. "If God already knows what's in my heart, why pray?"

The boy loved playing the devil's advocate, and Brother Baer humored him. "Well, if God knows everything and He asks you to pray, then I guess He knows what He's talking about, huh? Maybe it's not for Him, it's for you." We all laughed at that. "My point is, you need the help. Man was not meant to be alone. The man is not complete without the woman. She's got your rib, for crying out loud."

"False doctrine." Britton quickly raised his hand, though he shouldn't have bothered.

"I'm trying to be symbolic," Brother Baer explained slowly. "So when you find the right one, get down on one knee and ask for your rib back." His eyes dared Britton to retort.

"So women don't just steal hearts, they steal ribs too?" It took Britton a while, but he delivered. The teacher just ignored him this time.

"So." Christian leaned over to me. "Whose rib did you steal?"

"How should I know? I'm a perpetual rib stealer. Is yours up for grabs?"

"Heck yeah." I didn't even have to glance at Charity to know she was glaring at me.

"Marriage should be honest," Brother Baer said. "That means dating should be honest too." And that's when the worst thing happened: my eyes started watering. It must've been Charity's perfume. It had finally fulfilled its evil purpose. *Garbage.* Now everyone would think our teacher had hit a soft spot. If anyone needed a lecture on honest dating it was me.

Brother Baer wrapped up the lesson, and we once again found ourselves searching out the refreshments. I don't know why they bothered. It was just Jell-O again. Maggie stepped in front of me, blocking my exit. "What are you doing?" she asked. I could ask her the same thing. She was letting Christian escape. "You're supposed to make her jealous, not make it impossible for her to make a move."

I swiveled, seeing Charity was long gone . . . and most importantly out of earshot. "Oh, she's industrious. She'll find a way." Speaking of, she'd have Christian by now. I quickened my steps and Maggie tried to keep up with me. "It makes it more of a challenge," I explained, hoping she'd buy it. I could tell by her eyes that she didn't.

I heard a shriek. It was Charity. "Give me back my scriptures!" she cried. Britton was already working his magic with the ladies.

"Do you know what it means to be more exothermic than a supernova?"

I didn't even want to know what Britton meant by that. Engineering come-on lines. What would he think of next? I wasn't sure how well it would work, but I headed full speed for them anyway just to be intercepted by Raine. "So tell me, Red. Do you want to eat Jell-O for dinner or do you want something real?"

I gaped. "Who told you that—"

"You were living off weevils?" I stared at Raine. You know, he was actually starting to act normal. "Britton told me a little story," he said.

"Don't listen to Britton, he's . . ."

Evil came to mind, especially when I overheard his conversation with Charity. "You have enough ambient molecular kinetic energy to turn an igloo into a six-alarm fire. You're a hot . . . head."

Charity sucked in her breath angrily. "Would you just give me my scriptures!" Girls, didn't I warn you not to bring your scriptures to these kinds of things?

"So, Raine," Maggie came to my rescue. "I hear that you're planning on playing on our softball team?" She nudged me away, and suddenly I was free.

"Let me explain the law of universal gravitation to you," I heard Britton drawl. "Every single atom in me is attracted to every single atom in," he held up the scriptures before Charity could hit him, "these scriptures."

"Oh, is that why you're acting like such a stalker?" Yep, I knew if I threw in that title he'd kiss all chances with Charity good-bye. I wrestled the scriptures back from him.

Britton looked surprised to see me. He turned to find Raine and flushed when he saw Maggie's interference. "Hmm, your stalker, someone else's Prince Charming, I see."

"No, he isn't. Not for Maggie." Though I suppose he actually wasn't that bad, but Britton was distracting me from my purpose. I smiled at Charity. As far as she knew, we were still supposed to be bitter friends. It was time to claim my territory. I hated claim staking above everything, which is why I enjoyed doing this to her. "If it wasn't for Christian," I told her, "I would never go to Rainbow House, not with this kind of rabble around."

"Do you go there often?" Charity asked.

"Well, when Christian isn't over at my place or when we're not at the movies. Last time he insisted he pay for me. He always does."

Okay, so here's the unwritten rule. You never build up a guy in front of a squirrelly girl or she'll go for him too. Don't talk about him too much, don't pay attention to him too much . . . that is, if you don't want the other girl to go for him. But with one glance at Britton I plunged ahead. "He is the sweetest guy ever, always so considerate. I could tell you stories . . . such a good friend."

"Just friends?" she asked. I smiled in response and she called my bluff. "Next time you hang out, be sure to invite me then."

"Sure, if I remember." I gave her a look like I wouldn't and she stomped off in Christian's direction. With difficulty I stopped myself from going after her.

Britton was shaking his head. "Your pitiful attempts are futile."

I snorted. "And you think your pernicious plan is going to work? You only have a week left."

He shrugged. "It's called the attention grabber. The lines are inconsequential; the fact that I will be on her mind for the next day is."

"She's just going to think you're a weirdo."

"In the beginning all women think men are weirdos. The difference between a stalker and Prince Charming is that the girl likes one, not the other. In the end, it's the one who makes the biggest impression on her mind that counts."

Whatever. Christian would be the only thing on Charity's mind tonight, and I gulped. "Stop pretending you know so much about girls," I said. "None of my stalkers made that much of an impression on me."

"That's because they just shower you with compliments. Where's the challenge? I'll ignore Charity for the rest of the night." His attention drew back to Maggie and Raine and his expression softened. "I'm a softie, aren't I?" Before I could argue, he left me abruptly, going to Maggie's aid.

Chapter 17

Real progress is progress in charity, all other
advances being secondary thereto.
—Aldous Huxley

Wednesday, July 1st, morning

"I'm about to turn this ward on its head," I announced to Maggie. She was starting to look nervous about it, but since this was her idea, she couldn't say a thing. I had the guy skills, but I had never chosen to use my powers until now.

It was a fine Wednesday morning in front of Rainbow Villa lawns. A cool breeze swept through our hair. Maggie tugged on the end of her hoodie. "Look," she whispered, trying not to disrupt Hope, our diminutive Enrichment speaker. "Don't cause too much trouble, okay?"

I shrugged. The theme for Enrichment was about using your talents, and I had every intention of doing so. "I'm just giving Charity more competition. There's nothing wrong with that." I had gathered my hair into pigtails. Christian liked them, and true to our word, he was our guest speaker. Crossing his arms across his stomach, he looked a little out of place. You'd think he'd be in his comfort zone surrounded by females.

He smiled ironically at me when it was time for me to introduce him. "Our first guest," I announced, "is Christian Slade, bachelor extraordinaire. When he's not fixing cars for girls, he's serenading them from their balcony. He also works undercover as a spy at the bookstore."

"Uh, thanks for blowing my cover," he said. The Relief Society laughed at that one.

"But don't call him a stalker," I said hurriedly. "Any girl would be more than happy to be caught stealing by him, especially if it's his heart."

Charity looked positively annoyed that I stole her line, and I smiled. Well, maybe it was at her faux velvet pink jumpsuit. I turned a grin on Christian and before he could stop me, I felt his biceps through the flimsy material of his white T-shirt. "Wow." I fanned myself. "I'm sorry. I can't remember what I was saying." The girls giggled and Christian rolled his eyes. He didn't believe me for a second. There was no way I could embarrass him, which was why this was so easy. "Can you believe he's still single?" I asked.

"And what's your special talent, Jacks?" Christian asked in an undertone. "Auctioneer at a bachelor auction?"

I kept my determined smile. If truth be told, I was pretty crazy, but you've probably guessed that by now. "What are you talking about?" I said.

Hope stood up, her dancer feet unconsciously going into ballerina stance. "Uh, thank you for the introduction, Jacks. Britton will also be showing us the basics of car maintenance."

My eyes went unwillingly to Britton. Why did Maggie invite him again? He stood dangerously close to Charity, seemingly not a threat. "Um, yeah. Britton Sergeant is desperate for a mate, girls, and to quote *Lord of the Rings*," which I was sure only he would appreciate, "if you want him, come and claim him!"

Britton cocked his head at me in grudging salute, still managing to look hot in his angry way. It would take a little bit more than a lousy introduction to make him appear desperate, but it was worth a try. I saw how he flirted with Charity before opening prayer, and I couldn't let him win that easily.

The laughing procession of girls hurried to keep up with Britton's long-legged stride to Charity's yellow bug convertible. It was my dream car. Further proof that she had everything I'd never get. Britton lifted the hood with the ease of a true man and pulled out the dipstick to check the oil, showing us the desired quantity and quality of the texture. Of course, Charity's cute little VW had both.

Christian leaned forward, inspecting the car from another angle. A deep dimple showed at the corner of his mouth. "Oh, here's the real problem," he said, pointing to the New York Yankee sticker on the bumper. "I can get rid of this for you if you like."

Charity grew red. "Excuse me?"

"Oh, I just figured you weren't a sellout," he said. That was the one thing I knew about baseball. Yankee fans were die-hard and anyone who was not a Yankee fan was against them, hated them even. I could play with this.

"At least they're not losers like the Diamondbacks," said Charity.

"Only because you stole Randy Johnson from us."

I smiled. They were fighting? But then, it was a form of flirting too. I frowned, trying to remember that it was what I wanted. "Like that makes a difference," Charity said. "You couldn't even make it to the division series. We did."

"We? You're not even from New York, pumpkin."

"My grandfather was a Yankee. My dad was a Yankee. I'm a Yankee too."

"I see, so you're stuck in the wicked tradition of your fathers." I tried to hide my snicker. It was like Romeo and Juliet, and I could use it against them.

Unfortunately, Britton saw the danger too. He had been silent for too long, almost as if he were determining his best strategy. The jerk role? The hero? He decided to follow his instincts and feed the fire first. He picked on Christian's favorite team. "Yeah, but then there are the Cardinals. They were a sore disappointment."

"Don't even start, Britton," Christian said. "You're a Kansas City Royals lover."

Oh, but Britton was only just beginning. "How can I not be? Yankees are destroying baseball. Babe Ruth, Lou Gehrig, Yogi Berra, Joe DiMaggio, Mickey Mantle, and they just picked up Johnny Damon. Yeah, they're awful players."

Charity cast him a grateful look. I wasn't sure how she understood he was on her side. "They just picked up Johnny?" Christian sputtered. "That's what I'm talking about!"

My nose wrinkled. What was Britton talking about anyway? "Red Sox fans are obsessed, not loyal." I heard Charity say.

"So, you could never lower yourself by marrying a Red Sox fan then?" I asked her, trying to salvage this the only way I knew how. I made sure I was wearing a broad smile.

"No," she said slowly. "I can always flirt to convert."

Britton met my eyes surreptitiously while he fiddled around with the battery. He pointed out everything obvious that we were all supposed to know if we owned a car. The girls *oohed* and *ahhed* like he was showing them magic tricks, since, like me, they had no idea what he was talking about. "Thank you, Britton," Charity said, clutching his arm affectionately. She cast Christian a mean look at the same time. "At least someone is a gentleman around here."

With some difficulty, I kept from rolling my eyes at Britton's smug look. *Whatever.* That was not a score. It was the kind of touch that was supposed to make someone else jealous. Any jerk would know that.

Maggie raced over. So far she had been completely useless, but now she gave Christian a flirtatious hug. She really made it cute. She did everything cute, and for some reason it made my hackles rise. "Christian, you're always the gentleman," she said, trying not to look at me.

Christian was caught off guard. "Thanks, Maggie. You're . . . the most polite girl I know."

Britton snorted, putting the hood down on Charity's car. "Okay, Christian, that's as far as my expertise goes. Take over."

Christian smiled. "Well, first I'll need a beautiful assistant." Charity smiled prettily. "Jacks, get over here." I stiffened, knowing it wasn't a compliment. This was for revenge. "I think we should look at a car that might need a little more attention," he said. "No offense, Charity."

"None taken."

Of course not. Christian turned to me. "I'll volunteer Jack's." He put a conspiring arm around my shoulders. "Do you know how to change a tire?"

Was this a trick question? Was there something wrong with them? I could see Britton slashing them when I wasn't looking. "I've never tried," I said.

Christian dropped his arm and led the girls over to my minivan. It was a sorry sight in comparison to Charity's convertible. He shook his head when he caught sight of it. "When's the last time you changed the air in your tires?"

I wrinkled my nose, trying to think. "I don't know. About six months ago."

He grinned broadly. "Are you sure?" I shrugged. "If this is the way you take care of the things you care about, no wonder you have so many problems."

Was there a double meaning in that? "Why? Is it bad not to change the air?"

"Yeah. You can get some pretty hot air stuck in there. I suggest you change the air immediately. Take it to Macey's. They'll know what I'm talking about." I wrinkled my nose. Did they change air at grocery stores? He prowled around my car, hiding a smirk. "When's the last time you realigned the hubcaps?"

Britton was laughing, and I glared at him. "Never."

Christian shook his head. "They're on backwards." The girls flocked in for a closer look and he flicked the side of the minivan, quickly diverting their attention. "You haven't recharged these windows lately, have you?"

I crossed my arms in front of me. "Nothing in this car is automatic. See for yourself. I only have rider participation locks."

"Okay, let's check the engine." With the ease of a skilled mechanic, he jacked up my car and pulled himself underneath. I heard some banging and then, "Garbage!"

"Hey, what's going on?" I tried to peer beneath.

Christian rolled out just long enough to give me a serious look. "Better check this out for yourself." I shifted reluctantly. It was the perfect excuse to look cozy with Christian, but I was afraid of what I would find down there. I wasn't ready to see the sorry state of my car firsthand.

"I'm not going down there with you," I spouted. "There's no room."

"I can't believe what I'm seeing," he groaned. "The transmission!"

"What?" From what I knew, the transmission was supposed to be important. I flattened to the ground and crawled under the car, glad that I had reverted back to my hobo look. I couldn't care less about the clothes I was wearing. The whole Relief Society watched me go in. If I wanted to start a rumor, now would be the time. We were all alone with dozens of spectators. Britton wouldn't have it any other way, especially if it meant he could steal Charity's attention from Christian. "What are you talking about?" I asked.

"I don't know who's been working on your car, but they put the transmission in the wrong place." My eyes widened. "It isn't even supposed to be under the car," he explained.

I snorted. "You can't just . . ." I stuttered under his serious look. "My brothers worked on it once. They might've . . . does it make a difference where the transmission is?"

He rolled his eyes. "Yeah! It's not used for aesthetic purposes like some passengers I know. I can't even think of anything worse! Except your NOS tanks are almost out, and it looks like someone stole your muffler."

I kicked him hard. Now I knew he was playing with me. Sure my car was loud, but it wasn't that bad. No wonder Britton had been laughing. Take it to Macey's, huh? I could just imagine what a cashier at the grocery store would say when I gave him a list of those off-the-wall complaints. "Ouch," Christian said between laughs, and I kicked him again. On the upside, Charity would think we were playing footsies, but I was way too irritated for that.

I decided to get Christian back. "Well, I'm so glad that you got me under here to check the transmission," I said in my most flirtatious voice. "That's what you were trying to do, right? Get us alone. It's so nice and cozy here, just the two of us. We could make the sparks fly. Ever play the spark plug game?"

He grinned, not flustered in the least. "Not with you." He had oil all over his hands and he wiped some on my nose. I gasped, swatting at it. By the amused look on his face, I could tell I had only made it worse. "Don't start a war, Jacks. I can outshock you any day."

"Oh yeah? How about this?" I moved in closer to him and he backed away, knocking his head on the bottom of my car. He let out an "Oof!" and held his head gingerly. I twisted my lips into a pout. "Huh, look at that. I don't even have to touch you to cause damage. I'm magic." And that's when I thought of the lamest pickup line I knew. "Wanna see?"

"I'm not sure."

I propped my elbows onto the ground, deciding to beat him at his own game. "I bet you a quarter I can kiss you without touching you."

Britton's head appeared out of nowhere, almost as if his ears had been pinned to the hood. I really was too wily for him. The eaves-dropper knew he had to do some major damage control. There was no way he could steal Charity if I had Christian's full attention. "Don't fall for that, Christian," he warned.

"Yeah." Christian's smile suddenly turned mischievous. "Who cares about the quarter? Right? That's pocket change for a kiss."

I tried not to look too alarmed. I didn't mind being the attacker, but when it turned? "Yeah," I pulled away. "Let's make a different bet. I bet I can get the whole Relief Society to fall for you." Christian sobered at that and Britton cast me a warning look. I modified my words somewhat, "And I won't even need to bribe them a quarter."

Before he could question me, I scrambled away from my car. Christian tried to follow me out, but Betsy and her little punk rockers were ready. I let them take him without a fight, and I tried not to hide my face at the look of understanding that spread across his face. What had I been thinking? Normally I was so calm in these situa-tions, but I had completely lost my cool and had practically given everything away. What was I doing even mentioning wagers? Now, he'd see right through us.

Even now, Britton was making his arrogant way towards me. Before I knew it, his hand was on my arm and he tugged me behind the nearest tree. "What was that all about?" he asked. "You remember the deal. He wasn't supposed to know."

"You know I can't keep anything from Christian," I said. "I don't know how he gets things out of me. And besides, he doesn't know everything."

"You'd better keep it that way."

My hands landed on my hips. "Yeah? Well, what's with your Mr. Nice Guy act? Are you trying to get yourself translated?"

"'Course not. You'd miss me too much."

"You'll never win her that way. She wants a challenge." I had no idea why I was giving the enemy tips. Well, I had a little bit of an idea, and I tried to fight it. "You're supposed to be a jerk."

"Welcome to the world of the jerk," he explained smoothly. "Bursts of gentlemanlike behavior are vital in the beginning until the jerk slips into the picture. She spends so much time trying to resurrect the man she used to know that she forgets to question why she ever liked him in the first place. It's how the Monsieur works, and the ladies still can't let him go." I scowled and he wiped the grease off my nose. "Now if you'll excuse me, I've got to go taint Christian's reputation."

"There's no such thing as bad publicity," I shouted at his back. "Make him as bad-boy as you like. It won't do you any good."

"Is that what you're trying to do?" he asked, turning back to me. "I'd be careful. You don't want to turn Charity off completely." He swaggered away and I poked my head from the bush. It didn't take me long to spy the object of our contentions.

"Oh, Christian." Just as I had predicted, the little punks weren't the only girls who were surrounding him. Engage him in lively conversation, and now all the girls wanted a part of the action. Christian tried to get to me, but a cloud of chatter and laughter stopped him in his tracks.

"Girls, girls, you have to pay money for these kinds of skills." He tried to distract them from himself. "Yes, her car's made a miraculous recovery, although I can't say as much for her tongue. There's no filter there." His tone was flippant, but his eyes were hard when they met mine. They took it as a joke, and I forced a laugh too. It was a part of showing how great he was. It was getting tiring, especially with all those random girls draped all over him.

Maggie stood a little to the side, and I tried to force myself to be calm about this. "Let's take a head count, shall we?" I told her glibly.

Her lips were pursed, almost white. "How many of these little flirts were assigned?" she asked.

Oh, just the little punks, but they were only to fill in the gaps. I don't think we needed them. "He's looking pretty irresistible right now."

"To you?"

"Uh, to everybody. To Charity mostly! Of course, now she's just one of the number of his female admirers." Charity wandered outside of the circle and much to Maggie's alarm, suddenly backed off when she saw Britton. She approached him instead, her voice flirtatious.

"It's not a surrender," I reassured Maggie. "It's only retreat."

"Are you sure?"

Charity laughed loudly at something Britton said. *Oh yeah. Dead sure.* That was a laugh entirely for Christian's benefit. The only problem was that Betsy followed the sound of laughter and soon they all looked like they were having a great time. Christian would flock to them soon, but he shouldn't. Not yet. Not if he wanted to seem a little unattainable to the squirrelly girl. I hoped that the other girls could hold him back long enough.

"Well, well, Jack." Liza's hand was on my arm. I had been waiting for the queen of the gossips. Sarah stood sullenly behind her, her silent shadow. "What's this all about?"

I faced her. There are two types of girls: those who follow the current and those who despise the current and seemingly go the opposite direction. I say seemingly because they were just annoyed that they weren't the center of attention for once. I knew they secretly plotted ways to get ahead of the current. Well, that was my theory anyway. Let's face it, I never could read these particular girls.

I forced myself to relax enough to work my magic. "Oh, Christian. The girls just love him, don't they?"

"I don't!" MaryBeth said determinedly.

I hid a smile at the vehement reaction from our little Relief Society rebel teacher. *The lady doth protest too much.* "That's what we all tell ourselves," I said.

"It looks to me like he's turning into a player."

"Yeah." I nodded my head solemnly. That's just what I wanted the gossip chairs to think. It was the necessary element for Charity to go for him. She'd want to tame 'the challenge.' "He broke my heart too."

Maggie gave me a shocked look and Sarah looked angry. "I always knew that you two had a thing going," Liza accused.

My eyes narrowed until I remembered myself. "No, we were never like that."

"Yeah, then why does he save seats for you and stop Britton from teasing you?"

Really? I was curious. Was that a sign that he liked me? "Well . . ." I couldn't give in to self-gratification right now. I had a job to do. "Perhaps it might've been that way once, but he's not ready for a relationship. His parents haven't been very good role models for him, you see." I started to outline a completely untrue tale of his tragic, yet heroic life. Anything to get their nurturing instincts involved. "He doesn't even know what love is. He's never experienced it."

Now they all turned to look at him. Even MaryBeth's gaze softened just a little. Just a few right moves. I hated myself. "He's so brave despite it all," I said. "Like one of those guys you know would be some white knight in shining armor if he had been born a few centuries earlier." Okay, so maybe that was going overboard, but the girls didn't seem to mind. "He's just so friendly and kind and sweet and sensitive." I hesitated, reminding myself that I was talking about a guy here. "And he doesn't even know it."

They were silent.

"He told me that you had a beautiful pitching arm, Liza," I said.

"He did? Well, he's a really good athlete."

"Yeah," they all agreed. "I don't even know why he's still single."

"Maybe I'll still go to his game today," I said with a show of reluctance. "He needs the support."

They nodded and started making plans to go. Maggie gave me a scandalized look, and I turned to leave with a determined look on my face. Hey, she started it. I would just end it. There was no reason for her to look like I had just stabbed my best friend in the back. I mean, what were friends for anyway? This was in his best interests—right?

Chapter 18

Lady, you know no rules of charity, which renders
good for bad, blessings for curses.
—William Shakespeare

Wednesday, July 1st, afternoon

It was a vulture free-for-all. You never know what you'll find in the DI boxes: yellow plastic cups, a BYU Barbie doll, a black shirt. "Yeah!" I hugged it to me. The DI boxes were thrown haphazardly into the corner of our laundry room. Everyone threw whatever they were tired of in the bins, and it was how we survived. They were just like the missionary barrels in *Pollyanna,* and I rummaged through them looking for long pants for the softball game. I was already wearing the baseball T-shirt Christian gave me. He owed me big time. This was the ultimate sacrifice.

I lifted a pair of jeans out. A little worn in the seat, but they'd do. Supposedly our landlord was supposed to pick these "gently used" articles up and give them to charity, but he never did, so we charity cases ended up pillaging the boxes instead.

It was tradition to throw our weirdest finds on Maggie's bed, and since I was soon to be the last of Maggie's motley lot of roommates— starting tomorrow after Jade's wedding—the duty fell to me. I pulled out an apron. "Kiss the Chef." Well, that would never get used. "Trespassers Will Be Shot." I smiled. That could replace our "Bless this Home" sign, and I could throw this plaster of Paris pig onto Jade's pile of wedding presents. Silverware with flowers? There was potential there. I could imagine Britton's reaction if we replaced his silverware with this stuff. Or even better . . . I threw the utensils back into the box and snatched out a poster of Paris Hilton. I bet I could get Spencer to hang that up on Britton's wall. I threw it in my laundry basket with a wicked laugh.

But it just wasn't enough to break Britton's spirit. I pulled a cap from the box. Red Sox. Was there a way to deliver this to Charity, compliments of Britton? It still wasn't enough to sabotage things with those two, and it might even help with his jerk image. I shoved the cap onto my head, thinking hard. This was maddening. What did Charity hate? I mean, more than me? Well, Britton of course. So how did he even think he could win her over?

I grinned. And would he even want to once I was through with him? Especially if . . . bobby pins. I picked them up, black ones. They would be perfect for Charity's hair. I pulled a corroded perfume bottle out. It looked suspiciously like old lady perfume, and I sprayed it into the air. My nose wrinkled, confirming my suspicions. Ugh, it was perfect. Charity always left her layers of clothing lying around. Maybe I could spray some at the baseball game when she wasn't looking. It would be sure to repel Britton.

The door to the laundry room opened and I jumped when I saw Christian. Trust him to come in when I was about to do something diabolical. He had changed from his leather flip-flops to Nikes, though he still had on the Bermuda shorts. I quickly threw the perfume into my pocket. "Hey, what's going on?" I smiled disarmingly at him, hoping he had forgotten about this morning.

He wasn't about to be thrown off, and I tried not to edge away as he approached me. It would just make me look as guilty as I felt.

"Oh, I thought I was doing great until I heard the most tragic tale. Apparently some guy in our ward is afraid of commitment, but don't worry. It's through no fault of his own." I squirmed as he began to describe what I had said about him to the gossips "Poor man. It really brought tears to my eyes. His parents are struggling, see."

"Rusty," I breathed. He was worse than the girls. You would think he'd have better things to do with his wedding tomorrow than spread gossip to Christian. It belonged with the girls. "Oh, where did you hear such a sad tale?" I forced my voice into placid tones, realizing Christian had me cornered.

"It's interesting you should ask. Britton, of all people, happily informed me of it after Enrichment." Was nothing below him? Well, nothing was below me either. I wasn't sure what I thought about that.

"How insensitive," I mustered, carefully keeping the anger from my voice. I was still working out my take on this. "Did Britton actually think it was funny?"

"No, of course not." Christian leaned against the DI boxes, trying to read my expression. I purposely kept it blank. "As always he was very concerned." I sensed the sarcasm in that one. "He was afraid the Relief Society would deem this poor guy a player."

"They like players," I said quickly.

Christian watched me closely, and I tried not to give anything else away. He tried a different tack. "The cookies have got to stop," he said finally. "My roommates are getting fat."

"Oh, you're having cookie troubles, huh? Maybe someone's trying to get rid of the service idol."

"Well, some do-gooders left about a dozen plates on our doorstep this past week. The numbers just doubled this afternoon, along with some heart-attacks and candy bar notes. This is not the work of the service idol."

I smiled. Most of the cookies had been Maggie's doing, but the rest must have been the Relief Society. *Garbage, I'm good.* "Huh. It looks like you have some admirers." I shoved the DI box back into place, but unfortunately he still managed to block me. No, he didn't physically stop me. He just leaned too close, and there was no escape for me unless I touched him. I wasn't sure if I could handle that right now, and I didn't know why.

"So," he said, "you ran away so fast yesterday, I didn't get a chance to ask you something." I was silent and he reached across my bubble. I sucked in my breath, but he just tugged playfully on my solitary braid, trying to ease the mood. He must've seen my nervous smile. "I know my girls, and they've been acting pretty weird lately, especially you." I reached for my laundry basket, but his next words stopped me short. "Where'd you get that Red Sox cap?"

"The DI boxes."

"It's cute on you." He tugged it off my head, catching some strands of my red hair with it. "Is it for Charity's benefit?"

I bit my lip and decided to play it dumb. "Well, yeah. The DI boxes are for charity, but we figure that we need them just as much."

His eyes glittered with sudden mischief. "You've decided to join the team then? That's great."

I hesitated. It was a sacrifice just to watch the game, but to play? I squeezed my eyes shut. "Yeah, yeah." I nodded violently before I could give myself away.

"I knew it. There's no way you'd play softball just like that! You *are* up to something, and I'm going to find out what it is!" *No, he really wouldn't.* "This is about Charity, isn't it?" My eyes suddenly opened, seeing his arms crossed. "C'mon, I know you well enough to know you're not interested in me," he said.

"What?" That took me off guard. Why wasn't it a possibility? I mean, it wasn't, but it could've been.

"You're acting different, and I don't like it," he said. I tried to smile but found it hard. Losing Christian was going to be harder than I thought. "Weren't you going to be a bachelor-rat?" he asked.

"Well, yeah," I sputtered.

"Then quit flirting with me." He glanced down at my laundry basket of clothes and ill-gotten items. "If I find any of those things in our house . . ."

"You won't find them."

"Forget bachelor-rat, you're a bachelor-brat with a capital *B*. What are those bobby pins for?" Darn his hide. He had too many sisters.

"They're not mine," I said quickly.

"Of course not. You don't have dark hair." He cocked an eyebrow at me and slid the cap back over my head like he was crowning me with it. After a moment, he pulled away. I watched him leave with some alarm. What was wrong with me? I had been the one considering escape, but now that he was doing it for me I was experiencing separation anxiety. Maybe it was because he was taking away my dramatic exit. Sure, that's what it was.

Christian's hand was on the door. "If you keep this up, I just might take you up on that quarter deal." I seriously doubted he would do that. "You wouldn't like that."

I doubted that. Brownies and orange juice, I told myself quickly. Brownies and orange juice. Good separately, not together. I just had to remind myself that this was good for him. He would never end up in the Bitter Boys ranks, and I would publish an article that would blow the Bitter Boys' theory out of the water. The nice guy was about to win.

Christian closed the door between us. "See you at the softball game, punk."

Chapter 19

The charity that hastens to proclaim its good deeds,
ceases to be charity, and is only pride and ostentation.
—William Hutton

Wednesday, July 1st, evening

Peaceful clouds swam in the blue sky. Bagpipes wheezed dramatically in the background. It was a beautiful day in the intramural fields, so why did we have to ruin it by playing ball? I tossed the bat in my hand. I looked the part with my baseball T and DI pants, but that was about it. "Let's get this stinkin' baseball game over with," I said.

"Softball," Christian reminded me with a grin. He practiced his swings on the sidelines.

I rolled my eyes. "Whatever." I couldn't play baseball either. Maybe I hated the thought of losing my teeth after someone made the perfect hit. But who was I kidding? Everything about it drove me away. The slowness, the outfits, the spitting. Well, actually I liked the spitting. It made things interesting, but there generally wasn't too much spitting during intramural softball, except when Spencer brought sunflower seeds.

I just couldn't take the constant competition. Except this time the other team didn't all show up, including the Monsieur, which wasn't a big surprise, and they forfeited. We were in the middle of a scrimmage. Now that we were divided into teams, the gathered fans (all girls), headed by Betsy, had no idea who to cheer for. They tried, but it was difficult and they just started trash-talking everyone.

"We want a catcher, not a belly scratcher," Betsy said between bites of her hot dog. MaryBeth ground some ice down to make snow cones. "We want a pitcher, not a glass of water!"

I couldn't have paid for better fans. Well, I did pay for them in a way, although I felt a little bad for Christian. He was looking forward to a good game and now it would just be a flirt fest, especially since the umpire left.

Britton chased after Maggie with the ball and I laughed. "What is she doing?" She ran back and forth between the bases yelling, her hair flying around her red face.

"Maggie, you can't do that!" Christian shouted. He put a hand through his already disheveled hair. Well, he deserved it for recruiting greenies.

Maggie finally put her hands up in surrender. "Britton was chasing me!" she cried, retreating back to us. She kicked the dust angrily with her Skechers. "I couldn't let him get me."

"I know the feeling," I said. Charity glared at me, and I bit down my words. What was that one about? It was the jealous reaction I wanted, but for the wrong guy. I turned suspicious eyes on Britton. What had he been up to? He stretched like a lean tiger. His baseball getup accentuated his broad shoulders and narrow hips. Britton really was too good-looking for me to go up against him in this operation. And where'd he dig up the stupid Yankees cap? It matched Charity's baggy T-shirt.

"You've got to be kidding!" Britton called gamely at me. He was playing it relaxed and cool—a great cover for what was really going on inwardly. "The only time I touch you is when I'm fighting you off me."

Liza sucked in her breath at that one, tucking her mousy hair into her cap. It was just what she expected from a boyfriend stealer. Basically everyone who hated me was on the other team, except for Trevor. He pounded his fist into his mitt with a broad smile. "Let's get this game going, huh? Batter up!"

Raine went to bat and I avoided his backward glance at me. As soon as he was out of earshot, I turned to Christian. "So have the cookies stopped yet?" He gave me a sideways glance and I smiled. One call to Liza had taken care of that. The word was that Christian was allergic to cookies, but he sure loved apple pie.

"Let's just say that we're running out of room in our fridge," he muttered.

"Hmm, maybe you can start giving your leftovers to charity," I said offhandedly. Charity wound up the ball. I noticed that Charity's orange face was fading somewhat, and I popped my gum loudly. I could never kill the habit. I glanced at Christian's tan face, not able to resist. "My, you look nice today," I said loudly.

Charity's pitch went in flat and Raine swung. He popped it up and over the fence behind him, nearly hitting a car in the nearby parking lot. Christian shot me a warning look. What? Apparently she wasn't the only one affected by my trash-talking. Raine's jaw had tightened.

Raine steadied himself for her next pitch. Charity tended to pitch fast and hard, and she didn't disappoint him. Raine hit it right on. Trevor dove for it, missing, and Britton scooped it up and threw it to second, getting Rusty out.

"My deepest condolences," Britton called out in his throaty voice. "On the marriage tomorrow, that is." We groaned and Rusty just shook his head. Jade was finishing off the last of the wedding details with her mom, but he needed to work out his nerves. Raine slid into first, taking advantage of the commotion.

"All right! Get on the Raine train," Spencer said. He stole my bat. "Choo choo!"

I acted like I didn't know what he was talking about. I indicated his football jersey with my chin. "Hey, Spencer, this is baseball, not football."

A slight twist of the lips was the only indication that he heard. Charity pitched it high and long, but Spencer smashed it over her head. Liza sprinted for the ball, but Trevor beat her to it, quickly throwing it back to Charity.

"Well, finally we're at least getting on base." Christian slapped Rusty heartily on the back when he got back to us, not able to resist teasing him. "Keep your mind on the game." *Yeah right–he's getting married tomorrow.* Christian took the fallen bat and marched to the plate. First and second bases had men on them. "Get ready to run like little girls," he muttered, "because you're running home, men."

Our fans were out of control behind us and my lip curled. "Hey, batter, batter, batter, swing!" I glanced back at Betsy. Last time I checked there were no cheerleaders in baseball, but she was having a blast. "Go Christian!" the little punks shouted. Sarah handed them snow cones. It was a regular fan club. Christian tried to ignore them.

His hands tightened on the bat, and he hit the ball. It landed in the outfield. One of the players from another intramural team scooped it up. Christian's foot landed on first base just seconds before Britton caught the ball. Raine and Spencer had only advanced one base, so now the bases were loaded. *Garbage.* It was my turn to bat.

Feeling like I was stuck in slow motion, I peeled the bat out of the dust. I knew that guys liked sporty girls, but I had no idea how to show Charity up in this game. It left me no alternative. I lowered the bat and played helpless. "Okay, what are the rules?" I asked.

Charity groaned. "You've got to be kidding."

"They're lame," Christian shouted out from first base. "You can't steal and you can't lead off. Just try to get a base hit or an RBI." Blah, blah, blah is all I heard.

Britton and Liza came in closer from the outfield. "Easy out," Britton called.

"Get back out there," I shouted irritably. They just laughed and my eyes narrowed. I'd show them. "So, Charity," I said. "I heard that you're a closet Mets fan."

She started her windup. "Don't listen to gossip."

"That's what I found out when I was out with your boyfriend. We had a fun time at dinner last night, by the way."

Charity gave Britton an angry look, and I was taken aback. *That's not who I meant!* "Let's hear some chatter out there," she shouted behind her. "Come on. Let's talk it up out there."

"Hey, batter, batter, batter."

How was that even insulting? "Hey, fielder, fielder, fielder," I mumbled under my breath. She chucked the ball at me and I swung at it. It nicked the top of my bat and went bouncing over my head into the crowd behind me. "Heads!" Everyone ran, ducking. Maggie easily caught it. "Maggie, you're on my team!" I cried.

"Like it counted." She pulled to my side before she threw the ball back to Charity. "What are you doing?" she asked in an undertone.

I tried to explain myself, "I'm just upping the odds of our success."

"By making Charity hate you even more?"

"Yep."

"You're going to get what you deserve. I can't watch."

"All right, bat brat, show us what you got," Britton called. Charity's hand tightened over the ball and she slung it at me. The bat made contact with the ball, stinging my hand at the impact. I watched it sail through the air. At least I hit the ball in front of me this time, but they were right. Easy out—except no one was going for it. Were they actually going to let me through? It bounced off the ground and then Britton had it in his nimble fingers.

Too late I realized their strategy. They weren't just going to take me out with my lousy hit. They were going to take out my whole team. It was complete humiliation. Britton threw it home, making Raine the first casualty. Then the home baseman threw it to the third baseman. Liza easily tagged Spencer. He shouted angrily. Without a moment's hesitation, she threw it to Charity.

How many outs did we need anyway? The other team just wanted me to pay, and I quickened my steps, almost tripping over my feet, seeing Charity was about to cut me off. Suddenly she was in front of me, but she wasn't about to stop and neither was I. We collided, her arm clipping me through the air, and I went rolling through the dirt.

I groaned, pulling to my knees. "That's what we real softball players call biting the dust," Charity said. Her jeans were dusty, but she was hardly hurt. "Maybe next time you'll stand with the fans where you belong. Leave the game to the professionals."

My nose wrinkled. Man, she was mean! Yeah, I was too, but at least I was acting most of the time. Of course, maybe I had driven her to it. I watched my team go to the outfield with slumped shoulders. Before I could rise from the dirt, Britton picked me out of it, swatting the dust off of me. I was surprised at the foreign gesture of kindness. "You just need some more practice, Jack. I'll pencil you in for Saturday night at seven?"

Yeah right, but it wasn't a question . . . it was a proposition. Britton grinned disarmingly at me, and I was confused. He didn't do that. "What are you doing? Playing the field?" Charity asked him.

"Nope, just the fielder." Britton was enjoying this, wasn't he?

"And they say guys can't multitask," Charity spouted. "I suppose you're planning on penciling her in after we go geode hunting?"

"Oh, good idea."

Geode hunting? Oh no he wasn't. No way would he steal all my hard-earned work. He was playing on the fact that she couldn't stand me. By flirting with me, even a jerk could have her in no time. The competition was too much for her to bear.

"Does anyone have a right glove?" I asked them quickly. "I'm right handed."

"Then you'll need a left glove," Charity said in an irritated voice. "You throw with your right."

"Take mine." Instead of throwing the glove, Britton handed it to me, his fingers lingering over mine. *Garbage.* I couldn't let him use me as his dummy. First of all, it hurt my case with Christian. No one could possibly think Christian was a player if it looked like I was playing him. And second of all, I liked flirting with Britton too much and it worried me. I pushed Britton away. I always did have a soft spot for him, but this was too much.

Britton didn't act like he minded. In fact, he just looked more devilish. I tried not to think about how cute it made him look. I didn't know what was more amusing to him, messing with me or with Charity. "Let's just hope it brings you more luck than you've been having," he said.

I flinched at that, knowing exactly what he was talking about. It was apparent his jerk act was working, but on who? Me or Charity? I shook my head. If I had anything to do with it, it wouldn't work for long.

"Come here. I'll give you some luck," Charity grabbed Britton's hand and blew gently on his fingertips. He stilled, watching her closely and I hid a grin. It was hard for him to keep the act up when she outplayed him. "It's called blowing on the mitt. Works every time."

"You gotta actually have the glove on to get some luck," I said in my most sensible voice. I tried to tug mine on but couldn't quite get it right. I spied Christian. It was a perfect excuse to distract them. "Christian, fix this for me." Normally my incompetence would embarrass me, but I had a job to do.

For a second Christian looked confused, but then he smiled. I recognized his mischievous look and gathered my courage. "Oh sure," he drawled. I had expected him to be clumsy about throwing it over my hand, but he slid the mitt over my fingers as if he were slipping on a pair of delicate kid gloves. His fingers brushed over mine and I met his hazel eyes. He had warned me what would happen if I kept flirting with him. A sudden dimple showed over his lips as he lifted my hand, kissing the air above it like I was some sort of fair maiden. He put Charity to shame.

"Take notes," he murmured so softly that only I could hear him.

It took me a while to answer. "What are you talking about? I wrote the book."

"It's outdated."

I didn't even try to understand what he was saying. All I knew was that we had Charity's attention. He must have realized it too. "You ready to pitch?" he asked in a louder voice.

I opened my mouth to complain, but Charity was already clutching to Britton. "You realize you owe me a date now for all my good deeds." What was the geode thing on Friday then? Obviously, she was scrambling to make Christian jealous.

Britton realized it too, but he hid it well. "I'd be too scared," he said smoothly. "But who knows? Maybe if you keep blowing on my mitt our luck will hold out." The flirtatious comment sealed the deal and he left abruptly. Charity stared after him. The girl wasn't used to being rejected. The world was a confusing place for her right now. She stomped to the fence.

"Just remember not to pitch like baseball," Christian said. I turned back to him. Was it possible he hadn't noticed that exchange? He didn't seem jealous at all.

"Look," I argued. "No matter how many times you make comparisons between softball and baseball, I'm not going to get it." I hesitated, suddenly realizing what he was asking me to do. "Did you just say you wanted me to pitch?"

"It's an underhanded pitch. Don't worry. You're good at that." There was a double meaning in that, and I tried not to let it get to me. "Look," he said. "You've got a good arm. You've hit me enough times for me to know that."

My forehead wrinkled. Sometimes I wasn't sure why Christian believed in me. It put me in a lot of difficult situations. I pulled away from him, pounding my fist into my mitt, waiting for the other team to shuffle back to the home plate. This was going to be a disaster.

Apparently Christian wasn't the only one with fans. They cheered Britton like a returning hero. I wasn't sure what he was doing, but judging by the evil looks Charity kept giving him, it was working. The girls were suddenly mad for him because he was such a jerk. That wasn't much of a change, except now he was working it. What was wrong with my kind?

Trevor was the first at bat, and he smiled at me in a friendly fashion. Now why didn't more girls like him? Because he was too nice? No, impossible. Maybe it was just the huge belt buckle or the skinny pants. I tried not to get bitter on his behalf. I pitched the ball instead. It cracked against his bat and flew over my head, past the infielders, past the outfielders, clear to the other baseball field.

Uh-oh. Our team went scrambling for the ball, but there was no hope of getting it in time. Trevor took an easy jog around the bases in his flip-flops and had enough time left over to do three front hand-springs before reaching home. I groaned. *Thanks for rubbing it in.* We were really losing here, and it was because of me.

Liza took the bat and hit a solid ground ball that ricocheted to the side of me. Once again, I missed it, and she took first base before Christian could get a hold of the ball. It was a conspiracy. They were trying to make me look bad, weren't they?

Britton was next and his fans went crazy. I pitched it, hoping that I could transfer all of my negative energy into it. No luck. He hit it right at me and it landed just short of me. It was so obvious that he had done it on purpose. I dove for it, but it rolled under my legs. Britton ran past me.

"Get that article ready, hot stuff," he said, passing me on his way to second. He swatted me on his way. My fingers fumbled with the ball until I finally got a hold of it. By then it was too late. Liza was on third and Britton was safely on second, not even breathing hard. I couldn't say the same for myself.

I sighed, glancing at Christian on first base. This was ridiculous. Did he still want me to pitch? He gestured for me to go on like he didn't care we were losing so pathetically. But now Charity was up to bat, and just my luck, she was good. Well, at least she acted like it with her cool expression. Everyone stepped back and I gnawed on my lower lip, thinking hard. I threw the ball and hit Charity hard.

She gasped, rubbing her arm. "What are you doing?" she shouted.

"Okay," Christian said slowly. "Bean balls aren't allowed." He gave me a suspicious look like I had done it on purpose and I just shrugged. Maybe I had.

"Sorry, I can't keep the rules straight from baseball."

He snorted at that and quickly glanced at second base. "No leading off, Britton, or we'll change the rules and pick you off," he warned. "Jacks, watch him."

What was I supposed to do? I guess I could bean him. If anything, that would be amusing. I pitched again and Charity swung early, the inertia twisting her completely around. Our catcher was from the other ward, and he flinched as the ball bounced behind home plate and hit him soundly in the face.

"What happened to your good luck charms?" I shouted. "I guess the ritual just doesn't work with every guy you come in contact with, huh?"

I pitched it again and she grunted angrily when it flew past her. "Get me a real pitcher!" she shouted. "That's an outside ball."

"That's a strike. Face it like a man. You swing like a sissy."

Her expression hardened and I saw Liza leading off third base from the corner of my eye. I glanced at Raine on third base and threw it to him to pick her off. Before Liza knew it, she had been tagged by her man. Well, the man she had claimed, at least.

"You can't do that," she told him. For once her anger was directed at the right party.

"Well you can't lead off, so I guess we're even," Raine said.

Liza stormed off and I pitched it one last time to Charity. She hit it straight at me. I lifted my mitt to cover my face and it smacked into my glove and knocked against my chin. I brought my throbbing hand down only to realize the ball was in it. I rubbed at my chin.

Did this mean I had redeemed myself? Did I actually get her out? I better have because my chin was killing me. "Jacks," Christian called. "Britton! Britton! Get him!" Britton was running home, and I threw the ball to Spencer. He caught it just seconds before Britton ran into him.

"No score for you, Britton," I taunted. "Is that a sign, I wonder?"

It was their third out and Britton left his adoring fans to reclaim his mitt for the last inning. "Good thing it's just a game," he said smoothly, sliding the glove off my hand. He met my eyes steadily. "I wouldn't want to disappoint the ladies."

I jerked away from him. "Don't worry about it."

His eyes wouldn't leave my face. "Too bad you're in a wedding tomorrow. Looks like you've marred that beautiful face." My hand went to my throbbing chin. Beautiful? Had he just called me beautiful? Charity was nowhere to witness it, so why had he done it? I made my way back to home plate just as Maggie was coming back from the bathrooms.

"What happened?" Maggie was slurping on a snow cone. Her eyes were on Britton and his newfound fans. She looked a little dismayed, and it wasn't too hard to guess why. I had witnessed for myself how good Britton was getting.

Spencer pointed viciously at Maggie, reclaiming her attention. "Get back. You're bad luck. I don't think it's a coincidence we got our game back after she left, Christian."

Christian laughed at that, but Spencer was serious. It must be a football thing. Man, I wished that I was deemed bad luck; then I could get out of here. Charity was glaring daggers at me, and I knew I'd be getting beaned for sure . . . if I didn't get kicked out soon. Maggie went up to bat. I turned to Rusty. He was testing the bat, swinging it.

"So," I said. "Have you heard the latest?"

"What?"

"Oh, never mind."

It was the cruelest thing I could do to him, which was exactly why I did it. I knew he would try to get it out of me. Maggie swung at the ball and hit a line drive over their heads. It was far enough to get her to first base. Apparently she wasn't *that* bad of luck.

Rusty was next, and after I informed him of the latest, he held the bat tightly, glancing at Charity with a sincere look. "So," he asked her, "are you really part of the evil empire?"

Her eyes went to me at the Yankees slur, and I snickered. She knew exactly where that came from. "Just checking the grapevine," I said. "Making sure it works properly."

Charity shook her head with an even harder look. "You need help . . . just have to keep reminding myself . . ." And with that rather mysterious side note, she pitched. Rusty drove the ball past the rover and it skidded over the ground into right field, advancing everyone one base. Christian watched Spencer go to bat, and he started getting antsy.

He turned to me. "Jacks, you're going to fake bunt."

"I can't even real bunt."

"And that's why you're the only one who can do it." He picked up a bat and handed it to me. "All right, hold the bat up." I did it wrong and his eyes went up to the sky. "No, like this." His arms slid around mine and I gulped. This time he wasn't acting. It was the perfect move to make Charity jealous, so why wasn't I working it like I should? I was too nervous. What was wrong with me? "As soon as Charity begins her windup, pivot your body and move the bat into position. Then as she releases the ball, pull back. Got it?"

"Yeah, sure." I pulled away, realizing my heart was beating quicker than it was supposed to. This was crazy. I didn't like Christian, right? I could still smell the faint scent of his cologne, and I tried not to think about it. Spencer crushed the ball into the outfield, and true to form, they quickly brought it infield just as he made it to first base. Just like before, the bases were loaded and it was up to me.

"Bring it in," Britton called. They pulled in and my eyes narrowed.

Christian nodded at me. My grip tightened over the bat. Charity pitched it, and I had no idea how to follow Christian's instructions. I swung, missing the ball completely. I glanced sheepishly at Christian.

"C'mon, Jack Mormon." With that term of endearment, I knew he was in earnest. "Don't you play with me now. Get serious."

I breathed deeply and concentrated on the ball. Charity pitched a perfect pitch and I swung. "Slam it!" Christian ordered.

I felt the bat make contact and I felt the power behind it. And then I saw the ball fly outfield past Trevor. He collided with Liza, who was also trying to catch the ball, and it rolled towards the other intra-mural sports game and into their group of fans.

Score! I landed on first base, then second, then third. I blew a kiss to Britton for good measure and rounded the bend to go home, completing a perfect grand slam. I slid to home plate, the dust billowing up around me.

"Well, looks like you're making your way to stardom . . . or some kind of dumb," Britton called out.

There was no way he could get to me. I felt too good. "Well, you're the lighthouse. I guess you've shown me the way."

Christian took the bat. "Well at least someone has."

"Too bad she's too blind to follow my lead," Britton said.

"More like deaf," I retorted. "I can't hear anything when you talk, Britton. You're worse than a foghorn. You've got one of those sports-caster voices. It sounds like—"

"That's it," Britton cut me off before I could take it even further. "Get her!"

It was a bench-clearing brawl. Well, symbolically. There were no benches in the BYU intramural fields, but if there were, they would have been emptied. Everyone ran for me and my eyes widened. "What? Nobody does that in an intramural game!"

But our ward thought they were so funny. The game was about to end anyway, and so they just had to end it with a bang. "Get her!" It was the baseball equivalent of ripping down the goalposts.

My breath came out with an "Oof" when Britton pulled me off my feet and threw me over his shoulder like I was some kind of trophy. I kicked my legs, seeing the ground speed past my eyes. "Good game!" He started slapping hands with my team as they lined up, almost as if he had forgotten I was there.

"Let me down!" I shrieked, but he had just stepped up the game, and I knew it. He looked very flirtatious now. If I didn't know better . . . but I did. "Hey, do we have some water here?" he asked impishly. "We've got to cool Red down."

"Don't you dare!" What were they thinking? This wasn't the World Series! The fans pulled dutifully forward, and I gave Maggie an evil eye. She worked for me, not him, but I should've known this would be too fun for her to resist. With the help of Betsy and the other little punks, Maggie dragged the water pitcher to home plate. Christian was more than happy to pick it up. I should've known he would turn on me, especially after what I had put him through.

"Hey, you're on my team!" I shouted.

He rested the pitcher on his shoulder "Yep, good game." He doused me and I screamed under the cold water, my shrieks mingling with Raine's. Everyone turned to him. Apparently he had been crushed in the melee. He twisted on the ground in utter pain. I was more than happy to relinquish the attention to him.

Liza ran to his side, hoping to nurse him back to health. "Are you all right?" Spencer was holding his head, and suddenly it was obvious what had happened. The two had knocked heads.

Britton let me down and I glared at Christian, the water dripping down my hair. "Oh, I'm sorry," Christian said. "You need a *Y* hug, don't you?"

What was that? Some sort of BYU thing? I watched him stubbornly. "*Why* hug when you can kiss?" he asked with an impish glint to his eye. My mouth fell open. *Great.* He had just succeeded in reversing our roles, and I didn't know what to do, especially in the midst of all that gasping from the infield. I glanced at Maggie for help, and she gestured for me to continue the act. Had she no conscience?

"Well, I don't want your lips to atrophy," I retorted. Now it was Christian's turn to look shocked and I lifted an eyebrow.

Christian called me on it. "So then what are you going to do about it?" he asked.

Betsy shoved the baseball into his hand. "Hey, can you autograph this for me?"

I felt Charity's eyes on us, and I was forced to continue our game. I was glad for the distraction. "Give that to me." I stole the ball and wrote on it. *For a good time, call Christian.*

Christian laughed, snatching it from me. *For a better time, call Britton,* he wrote.

I guffawed at that. It was pretty clever, but there was no way I'd let him outdo me. I pulled it from his hands. *For an even better time, don't,* I wrote.

Christian tried to wrestle it from me, but I wouldn't let him have it. Betsy's eyes went back and forth from us. "Um . . . am I ever going to get that back?" she asked.

Like she cared. "Of course. It's the only way Christian will behave himself. I don't want him throwing it around in my car."

He finally tugged the ball from my grip. "Who says I'm going with you?" he asked.

"What? Are you afraid we'll break down?"

"Maybe."

"Then I'll need a mechanic on hand."

Christian grinned at that and tossed the ball to Betsy. She caught it with a laugh, and he playfully jerked the bill of my Red Sox cap over my eyes. I jerked the cap up, watching him run out to retrieve his mitt from Charity, who had been trying to get his attention anyway.

Britton had been a silent shadow up to now. "Well, you shameless little flirt," he said with grudging respect. "Another job well done, although your efforts are for nothing."

He sighed, watching Christian and Charity exchange a few words. Christian had tucked the mitt under his arm and she was touching his arm, until he finally broke away from her. "Poor Charity suffereth long," Britton said. "Perhaps I shall ease her sufferings."

He jogged towards her and started to make her forget Christian with a few smooth lines. With a final glance at Christian, Charity went with Britton. I snorted. She wouldn't be happy with him. A squirrelly girl never was. She just liked the challenge, and I wasn't sure if Britton was enough of one. Of course, he might be if he didn't care about her . . . and I wasn't sure about that yet.

Maggie's face was red. You'd think she'd be happy with this turn of events. It was obvious that Christian was driving Charity crazy. But it was that tiresome conscience rearing its ugly head. It always got in the way, and I had supposed she had squashed it by now. She never believed that the ends justified the means. I didn't know what I believed. I just did things.

Chapter 20

It is religion to be thus forsworn, For charity itself
fulfills the law, And who can never love from charity?
—William Shakespeare

Thursday, July 2nd, evening

"Is that her?"

Jade was dressed in an elegant white dress with ribbons in her hair.
Rusty couldn't stop looking at her. The girl was gorgeous. Her hair was
swept up, and she held a simple bouquet of long-stemmed roses in her
hands. I stood next to her, predictably wearing black.

"Yeah, I think that's her."

I bit my lip, pretending like I couldn't see the accusing stares as
they made their way through the reception line. Cousins, close
family friends, relatives of every degree. I had rejected their favorites.
In fact, I wasn't aware of one person here who hadn't tried to set me
up. I almost wished that my car had broken down on the way here.
It was a miracle that I had gotten here. It kept threatening to break
down on me. So inconvenient, but what were the odds? Yep, always
against me.

"This is your fourth time as a bridesmaid, isn't it?" My uncle
enveloped me in a hug.

"Yep, I'm pretty much cursed by now." I pulled back. "You would
think my friends would stop asking me to stand up with them. It's
like they don't want me to get married."

He laughed heartily, slapping me on the back.

Maggie was next to me, her blond hair standing out against all the black like an angel's. She gave me a reassuring smile. My aunt stepped away from Maggie and went for me.

"You look so gorgeous," she said. "How could a girl like you still be single?"

"Uh, I don't know." That got a couple of snorts from the rejected ones, and I avoided their eyes, especially the pitying ones. Don't forget those ones. There was some understanding mingled in that pity, though sometimes that was worse. I forced a smile to my lips to put everyone's fears at rest.

I wasn't the only one to suffer at a wedding reception, but it wasn't for the reasons they supposed. It was guilt, plain and simple. I wasn't worried about marriage right now. I had started worrying at an early age and then got it out of my system. It wasn't my fault that everyone I knew was still in that stage and everyone just assumed that I felt the same way. I supposed I could use it to my advantage.

It could've been worse. At least I wasn't the frazzled mother of the bride. My aunt was running around like a chicken with its head cut off. All the dresses had needed to be altered. Apparently none of us were as skinny as we had said we were. Relatives had come in from out of town. The flowers needed to be reordered. Delicate white Christmas lights decorated the basketball hoop and the wedding arch like little stars. And the wedding cake? Thank goodness Spencer had stepped in at the last minute to help make the fondant. Who would've thought he had it in him?

All the presents from our living room decorated the side tables, and little nieces and nephews wandered the room handing out punch, sitting at the guestbook, holding the feathery pen. The bride and groom couldn't care less. They held each other in a hug, not daring to separate.

My younger cousin smiled coldly at me and gave me a hug. "Joey got married. He's off the market now." She shook a bejeweled finger at me.

Oh no, her husband's older brother? I guess I missed out. There was nothing left to live for now. "Don't worry," her husband told me. He held himself up with dignity. "You'll be next."

Was that a threat? "That's what you said last time," I told him. He patted me on the head, and I laughed when his finger accidentally caught a hold of my hair. Once I freed myself, I turned to their mother and she crushed me in a tight grip. I fought for breath against her flowered shirt.

"How could such a jewel be alone?" my aunt cried to the room in general. "You just haven't found the right setting, my dear."

I met my cousin's sharp eyes behind her back. "Yeah, sure." I forced a smile and tried to look very jewel-like. It was hard with Monsieur Romantique pounding a dramatic fugue on the piano.

No, I couldn't see him, thank goodness. His piano was carefully maneuvered to the side, and I wondered if Christian had something to do with that. We were mercifully out of each other's way. He was just like the neighbor on *Home Improvement*—always behind the gate, never seen, but always heard.

"Don't worry," Maggie leaned over to me. "He's so far gone, he won't notice anyone."

"Oh good." My life consisted of pretending I wasn't in the present. But really, what was a little unhappiness in the face of such happiness? Jade was smiling. Rusty was trying to concentrate on his new family and friends, but his gaze kept slipping to her. Jade had found someone to love and that gave us all hope. I just could've done without the guilt line.

"Who knows?" My answers were starting to sound robotic as I shook hand after hand. "The marriage thing could happen. Oh, I'm sure it will happen. I'm working on it." I noticed the hard edge to my voice, and I tried to soften it with a hug. It was time to start changing my answers to make things more interesting.

"Yeah, yeah, I know, my biological clock is ticking."

My cantankerous grandfather pulled me from the shocked naysayers and gave me a great big bear hug against his maroon jacket. He knew me a little better than the rest, and he laughed at my carefully molded expression. He was enjoying this!

"Have you kept a tally yet of everyone who's asked about your love life?" he whispered into my ear after the hug. Before I could answer, he pulled Jade to him and gave her the same treatment. Her hand went to her suddenly disheveled hair, and I quickly smoothed mine back too. Keeping count? Well, that would be interesting. Seven condolences, three setups, and four lectures. Not too bad.

"I know a perfect man for you." *Oh, garbage.* I turned quickly, seeing another potential mother-in-law wearing a jean jumper and a desperate look in her eyes. "You could really change him, you know." My eyebrows went up at this one. I've heard this before. "You'd be the perfect woman to turn him around, pull him from all those video games."

Wow. That kind of talk wasn't going to turn my head. The strains of music flowed over us. "He's perfect" wasn't going to do it for me either because I wouldn't match up. What would? Probably nothing. I might as well admit it now. Well . . . I did want someone I could trust.

I glanced down the line. The guys were spiffed up in their black tails and ties, their snow-white shirts a great contrast against their summer tans. They were getting their share of the ribbing, but not like I was.

My grandfather hit Christian's shoulder. "You jerk, why aren't you married yet? Still a menace to society."

Britton nodded regally at that.

"It's about time you did your priesthood duty." Spencer just grinned in response.

"You'll be cursed for this." Well no, he didn't say that really, but that was the gist. "What's the matter with you?" The men slapped Trevor in the back. "There are plenty of great gals here."

Christian laughed. "He's a preemie."

"Oh."

I noticed nobody offered up their nieces or sisters to my safe guy posse. My attention quickly swerved away. "Yes, well, Kyle isn't going to college," the desperate mother said. "He never did think very highly of himself, poor boy. Maybe you could give him some direction in life."

My hands tightened over my roses. There was no way that I was putting myself on the sacrificial altar for her son. That's what reforming a guy was. He'll change? No, he won't. I've learned that the hard way. No more selling myself down the river. No more being nice. I never liked being nice anyway. It went against every grain of my soul, but then I guess you know that already.

Suddenly, the Monsieur turned the page to his music and did the worst thing he could ever do. He started playing "Für Elise." It used to be my favorite song. I always made him play it for me. That is until I found out that Beethoven had loved Elise. So why didn't he go for her? He just decided to immortalize her in a song. It was stupid. And that's when I snapped.

"Well, my psychologist says there's nothing wrong with me, either," I told the poor woman in a forceful voice. "But just between you and me, I think there is."

"What?"

I smiled blankly and my next tormentor grabbed my hand. "You poor thing."

Well, no, not really. "Yeah, I'm still trying to get over my commitment problems," I said.

"I just can't see why you aren't you married." It was Jade's childhood friend. I hadn't seen her in ages.

It was time to make the most of it. "Yes, I ask myself the same question every night before I cry myself to sleep."

Her mother gave me another warm hug for that. I stared at Christian over her shoulder. He was making faces at me, and I tried to ignore it. "Don't let them get to you," her mother said. "You marry who you want to marry." I grinned in spite of myself. Wedding receptions are the only place where it's normal to get a hug and an earful of advice at the same time.

"This should be your wedding," my second cousin confided. Her blue eyes twinkled.

"Yeah, Rusty and I used to date before *she* came along," I said. "Uh-oh. Maybe I shouldn't talk about that." *Well, that was awkward.* She kissed me with a giggle and went on to Jade. She knew me too well to believe anything I said.

"Still holding out, huh?" my meanest guy cousin asked me. He was the same black-haired bully he'd been since we were young, only now he was taller than me. "Is no guy good enough for you?"

I smiled coldly. "Well, there is a guy, and once he breaks up with his girlfriend and starts going to church, I'm sure he'll date me. Things are a little complicated right now. Once he learns to love me, we'll be married though."

"Good."

His wife laughed. "You're so funny. Why isn't this girl married?"

"Well, I was just engaged last week." I turned to the next couple. "Oh, yeah yeah, I know. I should go to Texas . . . Oregon . . . Arizona . . . to find a man. You've been talking to my mother, haven't you?"

No, my mom couldn't make it, but really it was too much for her to take. It was such a bitter irony, always giving presents to other people's kids, presents she'd never see paid back at her own daughter's wedding reception.

My hand was still in my deaf Aunt Maud's before I managed to respond. "Oh, what do you mean? I *am* married. Oh wait, I'm not." Just before I was about to start fake crying, I was startled out of my wits.

"So which one do you like?" My eyes widened at my old aunt. She wasn't supposed to be so observant. Aunt Maud nodded at the line of best men: Christian, Britton, Trevor, Spencer. "If you could pick one, which one would you pick?"

"They don't want me," I said hurriedly. Jade quickly hugged her, giving me the evil eye.

"That's convenient for you," Jade told me, trusting Aunt Maud couldn't hear a thing. "Now would you stop being so snotty?" I grinned in response and she sighed. "I was a squirrelly girl too, you know. Take it from me. Don't let it beat you." That was perhaps the most shocking revelation of the night. First of all, I was not a squirrelly girl, and second of all . . .

My aunt pulled away from Jade. "All that money for law school gone to waste."

"Nonsense," Jade squeezed her hand. "I'll still be finishing school. I need all the education I can get."

"But the children?" our aunt sputtered.

"Especially then." Jade put her arm around her, leading her to Rusty. "When the defendant Tommy takes the plaintiff Sally's doll, Tommy will be tried without benefit of jury. After his statement and if the accused pleads guilty, by reasons of insanity I can only assume since he'll be related to Rusty, swift and sound judgment will be easily executed for a maximum sentence of at least eighteen years without option of bail. You happy?"

"Huh?" Aunt Maud leaned closer.

"Sounds like Tommy will be standing in the corner for a long time," I told her loudly.

"Oh, you will make a great mother," our aunt spouted. She glanced narrowly at the would-be father, and for once I felt bad for them being under such scrutiny.

"I'm different from other men," Rusty was telling a blank-looking guest. "I'm more observant, really. I make it a point to make other people's business my own."

"He's a businessman," Jade explained, grabbing his hand tightly. He grinned at her and they kissed. Excited shouts to cut the cake interrupted their sappy exchange, and Jade dragged Rusty off to take a picture with the cake, her hand tightly over his so he couldn't escape.

"I have just the man for you."

No, not again, but before I could face the next do-gooder, Christian was at my side. "Sorry," he apologized. Before I could ask why, he put his arm around me. "Hey, pumpkin," he said to me loudly. My smile froze as he grinned broadly at my mother's best friend.

Her hand fluttered to her pearl necklace. "Well, I see you already have a partner for the dance, Jacqueline." She left us, heading for the bride and groom. After one last heckle, she tugged them out to the gym floor.

"Oh, you've done it now," I whispered to Christian, carefully keeping the same expression on my face. "I'll be getting another call from my mom." Last time I had made the mistake of telling my brother that I thought someone was cute, my mom assumed I was suddenly engaged. I wasn't sure how it could get worse than that.

"Good," Christian said. "You should talk to her more often. Besides, I had to get even with you somehow." I met his eyes. He couldn't possibly still be mad, could he? He shrugged. "And maybe it was that weird smile you had on too. The one you get when you're cornered."

Christian would know. He had a lot of experience with it.

The Monsieur had stopped playing and now he was leaning dramatically against the piano, cutting an impressive figure in the shadows. It had been so long since I had seen him that I couldn't help but stare. When he twisted towards me, I looked quickly back to Christian.

Christian was shaking his head at the bride and groom. "Poor Rusty. You should've seen him today. I've never seen him so flustered. The funny thing was that he was trying to pretend to be calm."

"Now look how happy he is," I said firmly.

"Yeah, well, once you finally jump off the plank, it's great to know you're still alive on the other side." His eyes turned back to mine, and I knew he was trying to tell me something.

"Let's raise a toast to Charity," I said without thinking. His hand got stiff on my back, and I realized now was not the time to mess with him. "They never would've gotten together without her," I explained lamely.

Christian's steady eyes were on mine, and he silently offered me his arm. I hesitated. "C'mon," he said, finally breaking a smile. "Let's start some gossip."

I made a face, but at least it was better than looking like the picky girl who finally got what she deserved and got rejected on the sidelines. I let him lead me to the dance floor and he put a strong hand on my waist. The Monsieur had already sat back down and started playing some crazy Elton John song—something about love. It was actually very romantic, and I tried not to think about the words as Christian spun me into his arms.

Oh garbage. I had forgotten one thing. Dancing. It was my weakness, and it was the one thing that Christian didn't know about me. What were the odds that I would be doing it with him? And no Charity around to witness it. She hadn't even arrived yet, so what was the point?

He dipped me and my eyes sparkled. There was just something about a guy who could lead that got my attention, and he noticed it. I could see it in his expression. He hesitated before he spoke, "I like this part of you a lot better."

"What do you mean?"

"The part when you act like yourself." I stiffened, looking up at Christian, but he had no idea what he was doing. If I let myself go, I could really like him. That was why it was so important that I turn myself off, except . . . I laughed when he spun me, my skirt twirling around us. "Ah, there you are," he said. "There's my Jacks."

I frowned. "Ooh, Christian, don't you try to bully me with your psychological tricks. I should've known you'd try to play mind games with me. May I remind you that you're practicing without a permit?" And he did it so easily. That's what made me so mad.

"I'm messing with *your* mind? Listen, cutie, I don't know who taught you the dating rules, but there's one thing that everybody knows: when you're interested in someone, you don't give every hint that you aren't, and when you're *not* interested, you don't give every hint that you are." He pulled me closer and I floundered, not able to say anything without giving myself away.

"Look," I tried to gather my wits. "I have one goal with my social life right now. I figure once I can get off the phone without making my mom cry when I tell her about it, I'm officially successful."

"What are you talking about? Your mom thinks you're the greatest thing since CTR rings."

"She only told you that because she wants you to be a part of the family."

"She wants to adopt me?"

I laughed. "If anyone needs help, cutie," I easily adopted the affectionate term, "it's you."

He wouldn't let me change the topic. "There has to be some way to make your mom happy, and you. Who do you like?"

"No one." I shrugged. "I'm sorry, my heart just doesn't work anymore," I joked. "There's nothing you can do about it."

"Even a timid rabbit can see the bait. Who are you interested in? C'mon, you can tell me."

"You're just as bad as my brothers."

"No, I'm worse." He twirled me around and I had to agree. "Now, give me the lowdown before I torture it out of you." He spun me again just to back up his words. "We all know a nice girl like you shouldn't be alone." I glanced up at him. Was he teasing me?

"As far as I'm concerned," I said, "it's a miracle anyone gets together. It's like colliding two puzzle pieces that don't fit."

"And what are you looking for? The perfect man?"

I laughed. "Those come in short supply."

Christian winced at that, or maybe it was at the Monsieur's lounge singing at the piano. I couldn't be sure. "Now, he's a perfect example of the law of supply and demand," Christian whispered into my ear. "The supply of jerks are short, the demand is high." My gaze drifted to the

Monsieur, and Christian grinned crookedly. "Sorry, he's taken." My head lifted at this. "Don't worry, she's hideous. You're much prettier."

I smiled, but it was weaker than before. "Well, I guess anyone can be pretty compared to hideous." I tried to get a better look at the Monsieur, but he was still hidden behind the piano. He had told me that he was too busy for a relationship. He had lied to me. I could almost hear *hee-haw* noises in my head.

"It will be over in a month," he said. "They always are."

Just like I had been? "Why didn't you warn me?" I asked quietly.

He had no answer for me and I sighed. I never would've listened. Your whole life you have the fairy-tale story shoved down your throat, and then when real life happens, you wonder: yes, but who will save me? And then at times like these you realize you have to save yourself. You see, everything can be fooled—your mind, your heart—but not your fears. Your fears can't be fooled. Some people say don't dwell on them. Well, I say they're the only thing keeping me from making the same mistakes. If I had listened to my fears earlier, I never would have gotten my heart broken.

The Monsieur sang even louder at the piano and Christian's hand stiffened over mine. "Can someone please shoot me? Garbage, I can't sing, but at least I admit it." I pointed to his rubber band and he snapped it. He was strangely out of humor now, and I studied him closely.

"Well, maybe I'll go for you." The answer to his almost completely forgotten question had flown out of my mouth before I could snatch it back. Christian's gaze flew to mine. The Monsieur began pounding on the piano, almost like he was sabotaging us, and I cast him an angry look. As usual he was only paying attention to his piano.

"I don't want to be the consolation prize," Christian said. I turned back to him, and my forehead wrinkled. Why would he think that?

"She's throwing the bouquet!" Maggie shouted. I glanced up, seeing Charity had finally come, and I wondered if she was witnessing our little exchange. She was wearing her usual belts over a flowing skirt, and her right arm was covered in bracelets.

"Christian." I tugged on his sleeve, giving him back his own advice from the time we scrubbed down the kitchen. "You don't settle, you upgrade. You could never be a consolation prize, especially with me."

"What did you say?" Christian leaned closer to me and we hit heads. "Ow." My hand went to my forehead. It looked like I'd be spending the rest of my night icing my head, not catching bouquets. It was probably just as well he hadn't heard me. I didn't really mean it, right? But at the same time, there was something that made my heart race when he looked at me that way, right before we hit heads. I groaned. I should really lay off the dancing. I knew it was trouble, so what was I thinking?

Before I knew it, Maggie was tugging me into the mix of girls. Charity shoved next to me with a competitive look. "Did you just get here?" I asked.

"Yep, just in time to see you trick Christian into dancing with you."

Excuse me? Did she really just say that? Besides, it had been the other way around, but I couldn't let her know that. I kept silent and Charity readied herself for the bouquet. My fingers curled into a fist. Jade smiled over us and threw her bouquet over our heads. Charity blocked me with her right hand, her bracelets clanging together, and suddenly I forgot my aching head and turned competitive.

Dignity? What was that? I spiked the bouquet in midair volleyball style. Rosebuds flew through the air and plopped inelegantly to the ground. Maggie and Charity dove for it, but I quickly overtook them, tugging what was left of the bouquet from the ground. The roses were a little bent out of shape, and I stared at them. I didn't even want to catch the bouquet, right? But I did if the right one ever came along. Well, if that right one happened to be . . . what was I thinking?

I turned, seeing Charity help Maggie up. They were both laughing. I tried to catch what they were saying: *". . . always the way she is? . . . worth it?"* What? What were they saying? Was that a bonding moment? Worse and worse.

I came closer and they stopped talking, not hiding their grins very well. Maybe I had overdid it? I tried to push the roses into Maggie's hands and she shook her head. I glanced at Charity. "Take them." Even she refused them with a little laugh. What was going on?

"Huh." Britton pulled next to Christian, giving him a knowing look. "All the girls run for it and then they push it away when they actually get it. I wonder if that's symbolic."

Chapter 21

Really, seeing the amount we give in charity,
the wonder is there are any poor left.
—Jerome K. Jerome

Friday, July 3rd, midmorning

Garbage. I had no one else to turn to. Normally I'd have no problem with this, but Christian and I were on shaky ground . . . sorta. I just had to forget all that. After the second ring, Christian answered his phone.

"Christian, the clamp. It won't grip on the brake. The clamp!" It was all I could get out.

"Is this a real call or are you just trying to drive me crazy?"

Both? For some reason, I couldn't keep away from him lately, even if it wasn't business. "The brakes." I readjusted the phone on my ear, trying not to sound like I had been crying. "They're goners. And the clamps. It's gonna cost me $700, and I called my dad."

"You actually called for money?"

"I was going to." I took a deep breath so I wouldn't start sobbing all over the place. "But then he guessed what I was going to do before I could do it, and then he made some crack that I'd have to marry a rich man, and I will never marry a rich man, Christian! Never!" I didn't mention that my mom told him about Christian and how he had started lecturing me about him.

"What was I thinking?" I cried. "They have four kids in college. They can't help me. I've got to help them, and no one will take my plasma. You know I got a false reading last time I gave blood, and the magazine only pays me fifteen bucks an article. I have to get some sort of a real job, but how am I supposed to get there—"

Christian cut me off. "Get your car over here."

"I can't. That's what I've been trying to tell you. The starter died. I thought I could get away without the brakes, but I'm cursed. Either that or the mechanics sabotaged me."

"All right, I'll bring the hammer."

He hung up the phone. What was he going to do? Beat it to death? I wouldn't be surprised. I pulled my keys from my pocket. I had no idea how I was going to survive this one. I barely made enough to pay rent and feed myself weevils. You can't squeeze blood out of a turnip, 'cause this turnip didn't have a credit card. This turnip wasn't responsible enough for one.

And I was getting desperate. Car washes? You need running water. Cookies? Sure, I'd give up my self-respect, but I had no cooking skills. Lemonade? You need lemons, not to mention a fresh-faced kid. I guess I could push Maggie to the table, except she was sick.

Maggie, covered in blankets and surrounded by wads of tissue, pressed a glass of ice water against her forehead. It was too much dancing at the reception, I was sure. And she had fought the flower girl for the privilege of jotting down the thank-you card recipients. "Do you need my help?" Her voice was croaky.

I shook my head violently. "Sorry, I don't need any martyrs." I ripped open the fridge and stared inside. It was bare except for some green Jell-O. It didn't look like it was setting up. I poked at it, sending a ripple through the liquid surface. "What's this for?"

"Don't touch it," she called from the living room. How did she know what I was doing? My hand snapped back superstitiously. "Liza's sick," she explained.

"So are you."

"I'm fine." She interrupted herself with a coughing fit and I grimaced, heading for the door before she saw me cry. That would propel her off the couch, and the girl was too sick for such daring good deeds.

"Can we please give it to MaryBeth instead?" I said, thinking back on her Relief Society lesson. "I can't think of anyone else who would appreciate green Jell-O more than she would."

Maggie just groaned, and I threw on a pair of Converses with the backs missing. I definitely wasn't looking my best, but I went outside anyway past the crops and foosball table. I just hoped that I hadn't ruined things too much with Christian with that romantic talk. What was I thinking, anyway, telling him I'd go for him? I galloped down the stairs two at a time.

Why did my car have to break down now of all times? Besides the odds theory of course. The problem was that I could never quit while I was ahead because I was never ahead. I mean, I was supposed to be writing an article. Of course, I had no idea what the topic was going to be. To be or not to be a jerk, that was the question.

I leaned against the teal minivan. Was our plan even working? Sure, I had frustrated Charity, but was it enough to make her act? Would the nice guy win, or would Britton?

"You know this will cost you more than your car is worth?" It was Christian.

I took a deep breath, deciding to match his light tone, even though it felt so good to see him. "Well, it can't be that much then," I said.

Christian looked tired. He was wearing his glasses. I must have woken him up. It was just as well. They made him look pretty cute in an intellectual way. He handed me a flashlight and stole my keys. "It's at least worth more than a dozen cookies. I'm tired of apple pie." He threw the service idol casually into the backseat of my car when he clambered in to turn the key. No sound and the headlights were still working. "Yep, it's the starter," he said.

"You didn't believe me?"

He smiled, wisely not answering. His sisters had taught him well. He pulled up the emergency brake. "Where's your jack?" I got it out of my trunk just as he jacked up one side with a spare jack. He pulled the other one from my hands and raised the other side. "Don't try this at home," he told me, throwing some random cinder blocks behind the wheels. "At home you actually have real tools," he muttered. "Give me some light, will ya? Has it been smoking?"

I joined him at the front of the car. "No, no Word of Wisdom problems that I know of." He got underneath and I listened tensely for the worst. "There's still hope. Maybe we can donate its lungs." I let out my breath and he stretched out his hand. "Give me the hammer." I found it by the tire. It was just like old times. He always made me do something constructive with my energy. It made me feel less helpless.

"Okay, get in and try to start it," he said finally.

I gingerly sat on the seat, hoping my extra weight wouldn't crush the jacks holding up the car onto him. He started hammering from underneath, so apparently he didn't care about the danger. "All right, now turn the key," his voice was muffled. I took a deep breath and turned the key and felt it catch. It actually started! So if all else fails you hit it? He crawled out and started lowering the jacks. "Don't turn it off or we'll never get this piece of junk started again."

Christian's hand curled over mine and I stared at him. "We're switching places," he explained, tugging me out. He almost sat on me and I scrambled away. Why did his touch have this effect on me all of a sudden? I awkwardly watched him from outside the car as he shoved the seat back to give himself some legroom.

"Get in, hot stuff." He glanced at the gas. "Mercy, you like to cut it close, don't you? Good thing I live close by or we'd still have to push this thing home." He laughed. "Hey, maybe you're just out of gas?"

"Very funny." I climbed into the passenger's side, throwing the jack down at my feet. It was a strange place to be, and it took me a while to realize what was playing on the radio: the worst elevator music imaginable. Some love song from the '70s. The Carpenters maybe? I was cursed lately. "Um, I wasn't listening to that," I explained in my most guilty voice.

Christian's lips turned up at the sides as he drove me down the block to his house. His hand wavered over the radio. "This next song is dedicated to you." He flipped the channel and it landed on Britney Spears. Some love song about repressed feelings. What luck! His eyes danced as the poor diva sang, and I was just glad that I had caught him in a good mood, until he turned to me with a mischievous grin. "Are you hiding something from me?" he asked.

My eyes widened as he started to sing in his usual shower-singing voice. "Sometimes I'm scared of you, but then all I really want is to hold you tight." He didn't even know the words, and I tried not to laugh.

That's what I loved about him—I mean liked. To be honest, nothing felt as bad when he was around. Now he was singing in a shaky voice about treating me right. It was impossible for him to stay on one note.

"You make Britney sound good," I said.

"Who's Britney?"

I broke out in a laugh. He knew every band in history and didn't know Britney Spears? My feet kicked against the floor of the car and I held my stomach in pain. I had always wanted a man who could get me to laugh and who liked it when I laughed. But Christian? No, that was ridiculous. I abruptly stopped laughing. I couldn't think of anything more improbable.

Christian turned the wheel to park behind the Rambo House, completely oblivious of my thoughts. Britton would kill us both when he saw this new addition to his lawn. Who knew how long it would be staying? Christian gave me one last measuring glance before turning the car off. There was a chance it wouldn't ever be starting again.

He climbed out and leaned across the hood, meeting my eyes when I finally clambered out with the service idol. "Jack," he said. I pulled the jack from the passenger's side and thrust it at him. He shook his head at me, suddenly caught in a mischievous mood. "No, I meant you, Jacks. I want you." He smiled at my bewildered look and accepted the jack anyway.

"Okay, Jacks, here's the deal." He propped up my car while he talked. His long fingers worked quickly over the bolts. "How long do you want this piece of junk? Because throwing seven hundred bucks into it when you're not even sure it will last another year is a complete waste." He took the front wheel off the driver's side and groaned. "Yeah, the clamp doesn't work. Your brake pads are worn completely off on this side. It's been compensating. Didn't you hear the screeching?" He was holding some heavily rusted piece of junk, but it was attached to some more heavily rusted pieces of junk. "See that?"

I shook my head and pulled closer. "No." I got on my knees and put my face next to his, trying to get a better look.

Suddenly he was grinning. "What, are you blind?"

"What are we looking at?" How old were those things anyway? They looked awful. I tried to wriggle even closer until I was right in his face. "Are we even looking at the brakes?"

Christian met my eyes. "No," he said slowly.

"Well, you can't blame me." I turned to the mess of iron plates and rust. "They're not much to look at."

"Yeah." His hazel eyes took on an interesting gleam. "Especially when you're the distraction." And before I knew it, he leaned forward like he was going to kiss me. I almost didn't move away until I remembered myself enough to scramble back, my heart fluttering. In excitement? What was wrong with me? For some reason right now I could barely resist him. I was messed up.

"Christian, don't do that!" His lip was curled in satisfaction. I had given him the reaction that he wanted and he had completely turned the tables, but I wouldn't let him for long. He shouldn't play with me that way. This was more than forbidden love. Friends just didn't do that! But he was already hammering out the pins, thinking we were just joking. We were always just joking, but now . . . now I was having a hard time accepting it. And the worst thing was that he was giving me back my own medicine. It tasted awful because he just didn't mean it.

"I can jimmy rig it," he said, changing the subject, but I could see he was still laughing, "But it will mean you'll have to change the brake pads more often. We'll have to wait for a starter. If we can get a used one, we can get it cheap."

"Cheap?"

"Eighty bucks. Maybe less."

I whistled, but that was better than the three hundred dollars the mechanics had quoted me. "And the brake pads?" I asked, trying to keep my mind on other things besides Christian.

"Twenty dollars."

"Not bad." I would only be out a hundred bucks. But where could I get it? I started brainstorming again. Maybe eBay? What could I possibly sell? I could take out shares on my soul, but then Britton already had it for rent. "Maybe I could inherit millions," I said. But from whom? "I'm not related to anyone rich. I'll just have to marry rich." *Ugh.* I was parroting my dad's idea.

"Well, maybe you can con one of your rich suitors to take you out on a date first," Christian said dryly.

"I'm not that desperate. Although if he fed me . . ." I smiled, hoping to distract him from my money woes.

"What about your harvest?"

Maggie's crops on the balcony? "You knocked them over, genius."

"Then I guess I owe you." He offered me his hand, and I stared at it. The palms were strong and slightly calloused. I wondered if this was another trick. "Here, let me show you how to take care of yourself." He tugged me out of the weeds and we walked into Rambo House, going through what used to be Britton's pristine clean kitchen—until Maggie and I sabotaged it.

We had scattered a slew of girly items on the counters: scrunchies, cheap bracelets, nail polish. We had finished it off with desperate messages on the white board: *Christian! Why don't you ever call me back? I brought you some cookies again. Am I ever going to catch you home?* Just below the madness was a message I didn't write. *How are you doing, hot stuff?—Charity.* Hot stuff? That's what Christian called me. My lips twisted and I grabbed the eraser.

"Ever hunt for your own food?" Christian asked, turning from the sink. He had been washing the oil off his hands.

I dropped the eraser guiltily and collapsed into a high-backed chair, feeling like I was staring at my grandma's curtains. There were flowers on them. "You mean kill Bambi?" I asked.

He dragged a bag of bagels off the table. "How about the Provo Bakery?" My hand clenched over it. What was the catch? "Spencer dumpster-dove for it," Christian said.

"You have got to be kidding! Gross!" I almost threw the bag back on the table, but then I stopped myself. They looked normal enough. "That is *so* Spencer!"

"Hey, everybody's doing it."

"Yeah, well, if everybody jumped off a cliff . . ."

"Just a little cliff. Live a little."

"That's a contradiction. You can't jump off a cliff and live a little." But I was starting to warm up to the idea. Dumpster diving was the Provo joke, but as long as we weren't trespassing, it wasn't illegal. And it actually looked like the Rambo guys had found some pretty good stuff. "You really live off this?" I asked.

Christian shrugged. "I don't see how it's any different from pillaging DI boxes." I rolled my eyes, but I stood up, not wanting to show my excitement. "C'mon," he said. "It will get your aggressions out."

"I don't have any aggressions." But I followed him out the door, throwing the bag of bagels over my shoulder.

"Yeah right. Once you find a real job . . ." Christian trailed off, finally looking at me. "Have you applied anywhere *real?*" I bit my lip. I had tried every random place I could think of. Phone sale surveys got nixed in the beginning. It was against my morals. Placing donation boxes ended up being a joke. I was spending more on gas than what I was getting in wages. The flyers just weren't cutting it. The magazine . . . well, it was good for a résumé, nothing more. Any real place had about sixty applicants for the job. We were in a college town.

"Well, I tried Brick Oven," I said, "but they depend solely on tips. Nobody tips in Provo, especially so close to the school. I did try a photography place at the mall. We just ended up talking about why I wasn't married. They told me to try California. I think my mom put them up to it."

Christian put his arm around me, squeezing me to make me feel better. Strangely, it worked. "You know, you just have to figure out where to find the perfect opportunity. You can have tons of talent and energy and skill, but if you don't know where to put it, it's useless."

"And where am I supposed to put it?"

"Where it matters. Why aren't you running that magazine you write for?"

"Because I'm a peon. I'm a nobody there, that's why!"

"Well, change that." I suddenly noticed where we were heading. He wasn't taking me to some obscure dumpster, was he? We were going to the Deluxe, and I felt my face go hot. Only he could get away with doing something like this. If those hoity-toity girls caught me going through their garbage, I would look even worse than I did now. Of course, if Charity saw me with Christian . . . I still wasn't sure if that would be a good thing under the circumstances.

"Go ahead," he said. "No one's looking."

"Yeah right."

"I thought you didn't care what people thought of you anyway." His voice was challenging, and it hit a chord.

"I don't even know what I'm looking for," I sputtered.

He laughed. "Start light. Get some broken appliance for your modern art collection. No more depending on the overpriced DI bins."

I sighed. He really knew how to get me, and I lifted the lid off the dumpster gingerly, looking inside. Immediately the lid landed on my head. "Ouch!"

He tugged me away. "Mercy, you're accident prone. Remind me to never go on a safari with you. You'll get eaten by a lion the second you walk into the jungle."

"I'm not ready for that kind of commitment anyway," I blustered.

"Of course not."

"Well, with you it might be different." The reassurance tumbled thoughtlessly from my lips and I groaned. Flirting with Christian just came naturally, but it was caring about him that made things more dangerous. And I cared about him before the flirting even began. I had to remember that I had his best interests in mind, and nothing else.

He rummaged through the junk. "The trick is to never ever go into the trash bags. You go for the big stuff lying around." I stared at him. He was so cute with the sunlight shining over his face and the birds singing tranquilly over his head. The day was so beautiful, and just what exactly was he doing? *Garbage!* Come to think of it, what was *I* doing? Man, I was cheesy. This definitely would be a moment I would always remember because it was so crazy.

"You've got to love life just because you're alive." He breathed the afternoon air in deeply, and I thought I was going to burst out laughing.

"Wow. You're really looking on the bright side today, Pollyanna," I said.

"You're a college grad, Jacks. Whether you like it or not, the world is now open to you." He handed me a vase, and I realized it was the same kinda stuff I'd find in the DI box. "No matter what life throws your way, you've got to take advantage of what you have." He curled my fingers over it. "Now maybe you can make something out of this junk instead of destroying everything you touch." I looked at him closely. Was there a double meaning in that? Nah, not from Christian.

I caught sight of something shiny on the top of the pile, and I threw the vase back in and tugged out a candy bar wrapper, a Sprite bottle, a few Relief Society handouts, and old taffy. The Deluxe girls must throw their candy away instead of eating it.

Christian jumped down from the dumpster to inspect my findings. "What are you going to do with that stuff?"

I smiled a secretive smile. "You'll see." I would show him just how ridiculous this was. "You do have a birthday tomorrow."

He gave me a stern look. "You had better not be planning anything for my birthday, especially not with that junk." I laughed. Well, he had nothing to worry about. Nope. I was just planning on hooking him up. That's all.

I turned quickly away and started walking back to my apartment. "Don't do anything to my car until I get you some money," I said.

"Jacks, don't sell your soul to do it."

I stopped short. It was just a joke, but how come his jokes always hit so close to the mark? "Okay, okay, I'll try something real." I wasn't sure what. So far the only idea Christian had given me was to seize *Happy Valley* magazine in a guerrilla coup. Well, maybe I'd take his advice. He tugged the vase back out of the dumpster just as I waved to him, and he hid it behind his back. There was something about Christian. He just made me happy every time I talked to him. The world just seemed like such a better place because he was there.

Just the thought of seeing him again made me happy. My heart dropped at that. He wasn't harboring any kind of feeling like that for me. He liked Charity, and she was starting to like him, too. No, I had this under control. I just had to sabotage myself and everything would be fine.

I reached my apartment and leaned against the door, shutting it behind me. Maggie was crying in front of the TV. Not just a light cry, she had been sobbing. Her blond hair was matted, and the couch cushions were still wet from her tears. I threw the service idol on the end table and rushed to her side. "What's going on?"

She pointed to the TV. "It's just some commercial. It was just really good. I mean, 'Family—isn't it about time?'" My mouth dropped. "And then it made me think," she said between sobs. "Why are we so bad? Oh Jacqueline, let's just try to love her."

"Love who?"

"Charity. Why can't we be charitable to Charity? She's actually a really nice girl. I talked to her at the reception. She's nice. MaryBeth was right when she talked about loving each other, and I didn't listen.

I just talked and talked." She sobbed into her blanket. Wait, that was my blanket! But I surrendered it to her, especially after that startling announcement. "Charity's on a date with Britton," she said with another sob. Another one? But they had one tomorrow too.

Maggie just felt guilty, that was all, but the thought that we might lose sent a panic through me and I started pacing the room. I couldn't be losing. This was more than Charity now, more than Christian. I was trying to forget what I was feeling. Besides, this weird thing between Christian and me wouldn't have worked anyway—not under such false pretenses. I had only been flirting with him to win a bet. That wasn't the way relationships were made.

"Maybe she's one of those first-date kinds of girls," I said. "She'll never go on another one with him."

"This is her third, and they still haven't gone geode hunting yet!"

"That sneaky little jerk!" Of course, I was talking about Britton. He couldn't win. Charity wasn't taking the bait like she was supposed to, and it was time to step up the game. It was the only way to nip this thing Christian and I had right in the bud. We just weren't meant for each other. "I think you're right," I told Maggie. "We *should* love her. This calls for a slumber party. We'll have a ball with Charity. You make the invitations."

Charity would never come if it came from me, and besides, the cheesier and gushier, the better. Already Maggie was smiling in that hopeful way of hers, and I didn't suspect. No, I didn't suspect a thing.

Chapter 22

Let all your things be done with charity.
—1 Corinthians 16:14

Friday, July 3rd, late evening

The mattresses were piled across the living room floor. At Maggie's bidding, we had actually given Charity the magical mattress. It was the one Jade had slept on before she got married, which meant whoever slept on it would be the next to go. Yeah, we single sisters were a superstitious lot, and as far as I could see, the scene was set. Everything was going as planned—chick flick, brownies, and all—just like all the slumber parties from my youth.

"Imagine," Charity said just as the closing credits of *Pride and Prejudice* descended over us. She swung her legs and her red *Karate Kid* pajamas bunched over her knees. "Elizabeth loved him all that time and she just didn't know it." She smiled and I frowned. I thought I had been torturing her for six hours straight, but she loved it. I liked it too, but by all rights she shouldn't.

"No, she didn't love him in the beginning," I argued. "He finally proved himself to her."

Charity glanced at me. "Maybe we should watch *Taming of the Shrew* instead?"

What was that supposed to mean? "How about *Parent Trap?*" I asked.

Maggie gave me a warning look before I went and blew everything. "Girls, it's too late for that." She had managed to make a miraculous recovery just in time for the slumber party. In fact, she was completely rejuvenated. Repentance generally did that to her, and she attempted to tuck me in, her pigtails swinging. She looked like some fresh-faced kid. Now if only she had a teddy bear.

I laughingly pushed her off. "What are you doing?"

Maggie settled back into her pile of blankets and pillows. She had made a little nest for herself. "Would you turn out the lights?" she asked in her laziest voice. I tossed the blanket off me. Unlike everybody else, I didn't have cute pajamas. I just slept in my patchwork shorts and whatever random T-shirt I could find.

"Sure, why not?" I asked. "I'm only on the very end of this mattress pile." I climbed over the mattresses, digging my elbows and knees into everyone I crawled over. Maggie and Charity started screaming and laughing. "Let me get those lights for you, princesses."

I turned off the lights. "No more screaming, girls. I mean it, or I'll send your father down." It was a line I heard often, and I dove onto the mattresses, stealing blankets.

Charity choked on her laugh. "This is really fun. I don't normally make friends with other girls." Well, she wasn't now either, and I started feeling guilty. "Usually they hate me. Maybe I'm too much competition or something." My mouth fell open. What about Faith and Hope? Did she really have nobody? I really was a jerk, wasn't I? And Maggie said Charity was nice. What had they talked about at the reception? Whatever Charity said, I didn't believe it.

I leaned back. "Yeah, I know what you mean. I don't normally have friends that I like. Uh, I mean . . ." Maggie was listening, and I didn't want her to know how evil I was. "I just have a hard time keeping up with friends, that's all."

"Yeah, you can't remember half their names," Maggie said. "Like that time when you tried to introduce me to one of your old roommates."

"Oh, please. We were roommates before my mission. Everything back then was a blur."

"Then how come you remember every little annoying thing they've ever done?"

Kinda like how Maggie remembered everything? "It was impossible to forget," I tried to defend myself. "Take all the gossipers on the middle floor and combine them together and you still can't compare."

Charity giggled and Maggie hid a smile. "Quit gossiping about how much they gossip!"

"We're not gossiping. We're just laughing with them." I propped my feet on the couch, staring up at the sparkles on the ceiling illuminated by the streetlights outside.

Charity couldn't stop giggling. "They have to be here for you to laugh with them."

A mere technicality. "Hey, Maggie," I said. "Who were we laughing with the other day who wasn't here?"

"Oh," said Charity. "Britton." Her tone had changed. She actually sounded serious. I rolled my eyes, relying on the fact that she couldn't see me through the darkness. What was with her conscience lately?

Charity shifted in her blanket. "So, Maggie, not to change the subject, but are you dating anyone that I don't know about?" I stiffened.

"No," she said.

"Oh, so it really is like *Taming of the Shrew.* Your roommates must be married off before you can?" What? Was she trying to tear Maggie and me apart? I kicked the pillow far from me.

"Except there's no shrew," I argued. But who was I kidding? I knew what I was. Actually I didn't want to be the shrew. I was tired of trying to fight everything and everybody all the time. Sometimes I just wanted to relax. Despite popular belief, I wanted to make friends. It's just that it was really difficult sometimes.

"I understand," Charity said. "Mean girls can get away with a lot because they're pretty."

I felt my face get white and I sat up. "Huh?" Who was she calling pretty? She thought I acted nasty because I actually thought I was some sort of babe? What a revolting thought. That was definitely not me.

"I totally understand," she said. "We're very similar, same tastes and all that."

"Uh, no we . . ." Before I could completely give myself away, I amended my words somewhat. "Garbage." Charity snickered, and I tried to restate it, "I mean, mercy." Did I even have any words I hadn't borrowed from Christian? "What are you talking about?"

"Do you ever see Anthony anymore?" she asked.

Anthony? Oh, the Monsieur. It was hard to remember him as anything else. She was silent with anticipation, and I tried to watch what I said. What did this have to do with anything anyway? "He's pretty busy," I muttered.

"But he still likes you?"

"Sometimes he does. Sometimes he doesn't." *Mostly he doesn't.*

"Huh, so that's it then?" Charity asked. "You never completely have the guy, and that's why you want him. He's the only one immune to your charms and so you won't give up? No other guy measures up. I know where you're coming from." Why was she so obsessed with reassuring me of that? "We're two of a kind." My fingers tightened over my remaining pillow. *Please let it not be so.* I hadn't stooped so low, had I? "Not like it's any of my business, but how was he while you were dating?"

I didn't like how she was turning this against me. "Why? Do you want to date him?" Charity just laughed, and I listened for the Maggie intervention, but she didn't say anything. Maybe she was just as shocked as I was. Like I would ever admit what had happened anyway. The Monsieur never made time for me, never wanted to see me, never really cared, took me for granted completely. "Well, we broke up," I said finally.

"Then why do you still like him?"

My eyes widened in the darkness. "I don't."

"Are you sure?"

"I'm going for a nice guy now. *Nice,*" I stressed. That was part of the reason for this wager anyway—to prove that nice guys won. To go for a jerk would prove to everyone that love was hopeless. I couldn't remember why I cared. "Someday I'll find one I'm attracted to."

"What if he's not cute, just nice?"

What? My lips puckered. It was time to turn this against her. At least now we were official evil twins according to her assertions. "So then from one squirrelly girl to another"—I heard Maggie gasp at my supposed admittance and ignored it—"why do we go for the jerks? Is it poor self-esteem? Do we want to feel needed, or are we just bored? Maybe we just want a project."

"Because it's fun," Charity said. Well, I hadn't even considered that, but at least now I knew Charity was wrong about me. It had never been fun. Or had it? She was much more honest with herself than I was. By now I could see her through the darkness. Her eyes were open and she was looking at me. She rested her chin in her palm. "It's a relationship without any real commitment," she said. "What?" she defended herself in the accusing silence. "I'm not saying its right. It's just true."

But had that really been my reason? I wasn't a squirrelly girl. Before this summer started, I was just fine. In fact, I could've been married to the Monsieur by now and would've been perfectly content. And yet, in the end I was glad that I had been saved from myself. The unspoken accusation stung. Did that make me a squirrelly girl?

I forced a laugh. "Is that why you like Britton?" I asked. Yeah, that was a little too direct, but I was tired of getting thrashed here. It was her turn.

She tossed her pillow into the air, catching it. "He's intriguing, but then so is Christian."

I forced myself not to retort. Charity knew very well that I was the competition. What was she doing? Appealing to my better nature by claim staking? That was the only explanation for her honesty. And so far Britton and Christian were tied? I steeled myself. "You like him?"

"Yeah, don't you?"

I hadn't really claimed Christian. I wasn't sure why I was so concerned about that. "Well, he's a nice guy," I said, then flinched. To a squirrelly girl that was the worst insult of all.

"Yeah, but he's hot."

I stiffened. Christian wasn't just some piece of meat. Even though she couldn't see me that well, I shook my head. "No he's not!"

"Hot with a capital *H*."

"Can we *not* call him hot?"

Maggie laughed. "You call guys that all the time, Jack."

Yeah, so what was wrong with me? I was supposed to be making Charity jealous, and I was just making myself jealous. How was that possible?

"I guess I didn't think so when I first met him either," Charity said. *Of course she did.* I stuffed my face in my pillow before I could argue. "I think I had to be humbled to like him."

My head lifted at that. Christian wasn't good enough for her? "How were you humbled to like him?" I asked in a dangerous voice. Maggie recognized it, and I could hear her sitting up. I knew she would try to stop me before I did something stupid. Charity saved me the trouble.

She shrieked and suddenly dissolved into giggles. "Your service idol seriously gave me a heart attack!" It was on the windowsill casting a threatening shadow over us. "You ever think of passing that thing on?" she asked. "Sheesh, how long have you had it anyway?"

"It keeps turning up. It's like a bad penny." But now that she mentioned it, once again I found myself dragging over the mattresses like a half-crazed zombie. They shrieked under the weight of my elbows. I flipped the lights back on, and we winced at the sudden brightness. "I think I have an idea how to get rid of that thing."

Maggie was shaking her head at me, but I knew it was time Charity found out who she was dealing with. "Christian's birthday is tomorrow. Maybe we should throw a party for him with invitations. Really nice ones."

"Uh, I'm not sure that's such a good idea," Maggie said. "It's a little late."

I smiled at her. "Of course it is." I always started with the best intentions and ended up doing something I regretted. I suppose this would be one of those times. "Everyone get your slippers on. It's time to do a good deed."

Charity didn't move. "What ever happened to a good old-fashioned toilet papering?"

"We need the TP more than they do." I ran to Maggie's scrapbook collection, grabbing her fancy scissors and paper. Before long she stood over me, her hands on her hips. "Did that green Jell-O ever set up?" I asked. Maggie shook her head. "Good. Everyone knows that food means love. Go get it."

"That's for Liza."

"She'll survive."

"Maybe now she won't," Maggie grumbled on her way to the kitchen.

"So, Charity," I asked as I cut out the paper, "do you think that we should make the invitations to a *Pride and Prejudice* marathon or to a *Man-richment*?"

"For his birthday party?" Charity asked in an incredulous voice.

"Duh." One way to get a girl interested in a guy is to prank him. It shows he's fascinating enough to take an interest in. I've lost more than one guy that way when I marked such a man, except this was not my intention this time. Nope, I was going to do something even worse. Christian didn't want anyone to know about his birthday, and Charity was going to take the rap.

I wasn't sure how this fit into my plans, but it was the only possible explanation of how we found ourselves in the Deluxe parking lot in the middle of the night tromping around in our pajamas and slippers.

The invitations were beautiful, thanks to Maggie. Ribbons and bows trailed from the glamorous inscription. *In honor of Christian Slade, Britton Sergeant formally requests your presence at a* Pride and Prejudice *Party held at the Rambo House on July 4th. All day! Six hours of pure torment. Bring a hanky.*

Charity's eyebrows lifted, but she grabbed a few and started taping them on doors. "He's going to start getting ideas," she said dryly.

"Really?" I snatched another invitation from Charity's hand, peppering the doors with them. Every door in the ward was getting one. "What sort of ideas? That we're throwing a party for him? I hope he isn't *that* obtuse."

"You're really going to hold him to this?"

Nah, it was just a joke. No one would ever believe that Rambo House would be throwing something like this, even with the invitations, but I knew Christian would be annoyed anyway. And Britton? He'd try to get his revenge. "Won't it be fun?"

The damage was done at the Deluxe and the Rainbow Villa apartments, and now it was time for the riskiest operation of all— especially since I fully intended to get caught. "You got the Jell-O, Maggie?"

Maggie nodded. We fairly skipped across the deserted street and rested the green Jell-O on the Rambo House doorstep as quietly as we could. The TV was on, and lights were on in the kitchen in the back. I threw down the note: *A birthday treat for a birthday guy. Perhaps it will set up in time for your party tomorrow. Either way, enjoy the setup.*

Everybody else in the ward will. I placed a *Pride and Prejudice* invitation next to it.

I chuckled and glanced sideways at Charity. "Now, we've got to plaster these invitations on every door in their house."

"How in the heck are we supposed to do that?" Charity asked. "They're still awake."

"*They* are called insiders." I crept around the house, knowing exactly where the motion detectors were. I peeked inside. Britton and Spencer were on the couch, but I was looking for Trevor. Gone. Where was Christian? I glanced at the lit window above.

"Okay," I turned to Charity. "Trevor's AWOL. That means he's in his room. Let's get him down here." I pointed to the lit window. It just happened to belong to Christian. "Grab some pinecones." Christian had done this to me plenty of times, so I had no problem startling him in the middle of the night. My lip curled at the thought. At the same time I edged closer to a bush where I could hide when he pushed his head through his window.

Charity's eyes were wide. "You have *got* to be kidding. Haven't you heard of a cell phone? If we're going to do this, let's do it without getting caught." She pulled hers out of her pocket and I bit my lip when she found Trevor's number. How did she have his number? She wasn't even interested in him. There was more to her than I could put my finger on. And besides that, she was making things difficult. "Trevor, this is Charity. I'm on your back porch with Maggie and Jack. Get down here and keep it quiet."

After a moment, a laughing Trevor slid the back door open wearing striped pajamas. His eyes got big when he saw us all together. "You're working together now? Scary." I surrendered the leftover invitations, furiously thinking of an alternate plan. It was working too perfectly. Curse Charity's quick thinking.

"We want them on every door in your house," Charity said. "Can you handle it?"

"Wow. Beautiful." He turned them over in his hand and guffawed. "Sure. Just make sure this doesn't get back to me. Britton would kill me."

"Then we'd better get a souvenir from the house," I said, suddenly inspired. Even Maggie looked at me like I was crazy. "So it looks like we're the ones who did it. We're just keeping Trevor safe."

"Put the idol by his door." Charity grabbed it from me, starting to lose patience. I ran my hand through my red hair, thinking hard.

"Yeah . . . and . . ." I stalled, "give us a signal when you're done." Trevor nodded, and as soon as he disappeared inside, I turned to the Charity. "We have to knock on the front door as soon as he gives us the signal."

"That's too risky," Maggie complained.

"We're here to protect Trevor's good name." I had every intention of ringing the doorbell before Charity could get off the front porch. Maybe *accidentally* spilling green Jell-O all over her would slow her down too. No, too obvious.

Just then headlights flooded onto the driveway. We scattered all different directions, every girl for herself. I ran right into the motion detectors. The light blared over me and I winced, turning the corner only to set off another one in the back of the house.

The car door slammed shut. "Hey!" It was Christian and I groaned. This would've been perfect if I was Charity. "Emily?" That was one of his sister's names, and I breathed a sigh of relief. Good. At least I had mistaken identity going on here. Now if I could only keep it that way. He turned the corner, his shoes crunching over the gravel. I turned another corner just in time, but I set off another motion detector.

I tried not to laugh at my ridiculous predicament. He started running, and I quickly slid around another corner to the front yard, passing the green Jell-O setup. No motion detectors, but still no time to make a break for it to the street. He was too close. There was nowhere to hide but these walls, forcing me to pull around yet another corner and bringing me back to where I started.

I heard Christian laugh behind me. He must have stumbled over the Jell-O, but it wasn't the reaction I was expecting. "You are so caught," he said. Charity was supposed to get caught, not me! I wondered how long I could run circles around this square building, but before I could find out, I ran straight into a hard chest. Britton! His strong arms caught a hold of me.

"What brings you here?" he said in a sarcastic voice. His jogging pants were cut off below the knee, and he wore a wrinkled white T. It was the most dressed-down I had ever seen him. His razor-cut hair was a bit untidy, but he still had that soldier look.

"Can't talk, Britton. Gotta go."

"What? Afraid of getting caught?" It was a little too late for that, and I looked back, just waiting for Christian to turn the corner. "Nothing says you're up to no good like green Jell-O." How did he know about that already? Was he some all-knowing leprechaun?

"Listen, if I get caught," I whispered, "Charity will get desperate. She'll be all over Christian and you lose the deal."

"Let me get this straight. I lose if Christian goes for you?"

I met his eyes. Yeah, sorta, but not that way. After a moment's hesitation, Britton pulled me into the kitchen. "I'm a changed man since I've met you." I rolled my eyes at his obvious sarcasm. "This goes against everything I believe in."

"What? Helping someone in need?"

"No, allowing you in my kitchen."

"Thanks for the sacrifice." I ran through the house past Spencer and waved at him. "See ya, peeps." He looked confused, but he waved his remote control at me anyway. "I'm late for a sleepover," I said. "Gotta go."

"A slumber party," Britton sneered behind me, "commonly referred to as spying on the enemy."

"Why aren't I ever invited to these things?" Spencer asked.

"Maybe someday when you get rid of your commitment problems and ask me to marry you." I ran out the front door to freedom and tripped over the Jell-O. It splattered all over my legs, and I pulled back just in time to see Christian running after Charity. She was a red pajama blur in the distance, but Christian was fast. He'd have her in no time. I wasn't so sure I wanted that. Maybe it had something to do with Christian's amused reaction to the prank.

I fumbled with my cell and pushed speed dial. "Yeah," Christian answered breathlessly. *Lucky break.* The poor guy thought he could talk and run at the same time.

"You've got the wrong girl," I disguised my voice, completely forgetting his caller ID.

I saw him slow down and look around. "Jacks?" I ducked head-long into the bushes before he could see me. He only won if he caught me, not heard me triumph at a distance. I watched Charity slip away. Christian was safe for now. He leaned his head back. The wind had picked up, whipping the ends of his shirt. He searched the area. Except for the swirling clouds, everything was bathed in darkness. The shadows of the Deluxe and Rainbow Villa loomed even blacker overhead. The moon made an eerie light through it all.

"I was tipped off, that's all," I said. "I'm sitting in the comfort of my own home, and . . ." Oh garbage, he started heading that way. That's where Charity was. "Watch out for that dumpster." He slowed. I trusted his intelligence, trying not too lean too hard on mine. It only made sense that I wasn't at home since I could see him at this angle. He checked the dumpster and I laughed. "Unlike some people, I wouldn't be caught dead in there," I told him.

"That's cold," he said. Now he was really looking around.

"Well, nothing that a housewarming party can't fix." I clicked off the phone, and after a last backward glance at my poor hapless Romeo, I took the long way home, chuckling the whole way. I just hoped I had distracted him enough to stop him from heading me off at my place. The first thing I saw when I got home was Charity's angry face. "That was a close one," I said.

"For who?" she hissed, and I bit down a grin, though I wasn't sure why she was so angry. I had saved her, and even if she had objections to that, she had no idea it was me. I shifted, my shoes squeaking over the balcony. They were covered in green Jell-O and I kicked them off.

Maggie was smiling, still full of adrenaline. She leaned against the foosball table, her pigtails popping out on either side of her head. "Let's pretend we're playing a game. That way if they track us here we won't look guilty."

At least Maggie had mentioned it. That made it seem innocent. Charity's eyes narrowed at me. "How about I play Jack?"

I was still on a high. "You think you're a good enough player, huh?"

"No, but your boyfriend is." Which one was she talking about? "Oh, I never told you about that?" Charity smiled coldly at me. "Well, since you're the only one I can trust, let me confide in you." My eyes quickly flicked to hers. "The Monsieur and I went out last week. He was looking for you, but you weren't home. I was hanging out with Maggie, so he asked me out instead. Isn't that funny?"

My hands clenched over the foosball handles. Is that why she had been asking about him earlier? And she was hanging out with Maggie? What was this? Did she want everything that was mine? "Yeah, real funny," I agreed in an equally chilly voice. Mormon meanies. The Monsieur always had a thing for them, which made me wonder why he ever liked me. I didn't like to think about that too deeply.

I kicked off my slippers. "Sure, let's play."

Charity rolled her karate pajamas up to her elbows and threw the ball into the slot. It rolled to her side. The table was a little warped, and she whipped it straight past my taped up goalie and into my goal box. She gave herself a point, and I threw the ball back into the slot, determined not to mess up this time. As predicted, it favored her side and she hit it hard. I blocked it. "You've been practicing," she said.

"Hours and hours with my HE brothers. I can actually beat them now."

"Which roommate did you take out?"

"In what way?" I hit the ball hard and made a goal. She simmered while I gave myself a point. I glanced up at her. "Can't hate the game if you're a player, you know."

"I don't hate the game." The scathing tone in her voice left no doubt to what she hated, and she hit the ball hard, readying her men for my counterattack. We volleyed back and forth, shouting not-so-veiled insults.

"Girls," Maggie said in a shocked voice. "It's just a game." But it wasn't. Christian wasn't something to fight over. He wasn't. But we weren't really fighting. I was pretending, right? I was trying to act a part, but it was hard. Strangely, half of me felt jealousy very strongly.

"I'm sorry, I can't control myself. I just get so passionate about the game. Especially when I play Christian," I couldn't help throwing out. I had no idea why I just said that.

"Do you do that a lot?" she seethed. "He's pretty young, I guess. Younger than you."

"He's fashionably late, and only by a year . . . or two! It's the newest trend, you know. Like Ashton and Demi!"

"Oh, how cute. Well, you're the side dish, honey. I'm the main."
She shot the ball to my side. "How about we make a friendly
wager?"

"No."

"Why not? You like wagers, don't you?" I froze. Did she know? But
how? "I know what you're up to," she said. My hands froze on the
handles, and I let the ball slip past me. Did Maggie tell her? It could've
been anybody. The whole Bitter Boys posse knew about it. "You don't
even like Christian," she said, "but he's a challenge. Is that why you're
going for him?"

"I'm not."

"Maybe you just like Charity scams then." My eyes flicked
quickly to hers. Did she overhear Britton and me? What had we said
that might have given us away? It would've been too disjointed to get
anything out of it. "Is there anything else that I should be aware of?"
She hit the ball into my goal box for a winning point. "You aren't
going to give me sugar water for mosquitoes, are you?"

I pushed away from the foosball table. The jig was up. I avoided
Maggie's eyes. "You know, I was going to tell you something about
Christian," Charity said, "before we pranked the guys." Charity's cell
phone went off the same time mine did.

I answered mine, grateful for the interruption. "So does this mean
you're going to be jumping out of the birthday cake?" Britton asked
on my line. I tried to smile at that one, but it was very hard, especially
since I knew exactly who Charity was talking to now.

"No, Christian," Charity murmured into her phone. "We'd *never*
do that. Let's just say that we're anxiously engaged in a not-so-good
cause." Her eyes were on me.

"Looks like squirrelly girl is going for Mr. Nice Guy," Britton
said. "Better start writing your article." I frowned. He didn't even
seem to care he was losing. That probably meant he had a trick up his
sleeve. He couldn't give up! It wasn't fair! How would we know who
would've really won?

I tried to concentrate on Britton, but I found myself acting like
I've never acted before. I acted out of jealousy. Pure jealousy. I always
gave up and gave the guy to the girl, but this time I was sabotaging it.
But not on purpose. "Oh Britton, you're so funny," I said, laughing.

"Yeah right. What are you playing?"

"Oh stop. You wouldn't."

"Uh, you're not even making sense, but I guess that's not too unusual."

"No, no, I forgive you. I always forgive you. You're so scandalous."

At least Maggie looked interested in my conversation. Her eyes were wide, but then they usually were at night. Charity determinedly ignored us, but I took that as a good sign.

"Am I supposed to say something to that or just sit here stupidly?" Britton asked.

"If it comes naturally," I said.

"*Jacks*, you're wanted." Charity held her phone out to me.

"Yeah, give me Charity," Britton agreed. "Let me work my magic."

For once I wished he would. I gave Charity my phone and she gave me hers. "So are you throwing it?" Christian asked. It took me a while to realize that he was talking about the party.

I tried for a jovial tone. "No, you are."

"You realize I will drag you down with me."

I smiled. "Try to catch me first." I clicked off Charity's phone, and she followed suit.

"Well, you managed to sound so nice," she said dryly. "What an obvious act." We stared at each other. Maggie looked nervously at us. "That's one thing I learned on my mission." I let my surprise register on my face only briefly. Charity had served a mission? She *was* the ward mystery. How old was she anyway? "Never give up," she said. "That's what I learned. And just in case we get interrupted again, let me tell you why I like Christian. It most certainly wasn't anything *you* did. It's what he did. He's amazing. He's the coolest guy I've ever met."

I leaned heavily on the foosball table. "I helped you see it."

"No, because you never saw it. You let him slip through your fingers." She crawled under the foosball table to escape this ill-fated slumber party and slipped on the long hems of her pajamas, almost knocking our crops off the balcony in the process. I would've laughed if I didn't feel so bad. I had won the wager, but not the way I wanted to. But how did I want to? I just figured that she was mean and deserved to be played with. But I was meaner than she could ever be.

"I don't think anyone can help you," she said once she was free. "You don't deserve him."

She was right, and I wordlessly watched her leave. Maggie looked distraught, but she couldn't feel as horrible as I felt. I had made a mistake—a big one. I was the one who didn't know who I'd been dealing with, and I lost. I lost out big time.

Chapter 23

One of the serious obstacles to the improvement
of our race is indiscriminate charity.
—Andrew Carnegie

Saturday, July 4th, late afternoon

I had been staring at the computer screen for hours, and I only
had one sentence to show for it . . . and sometimes not even that
because I kept erasing it. I slipped my flip-flops on and off, finally just
resting my bare toes on the legs of my chair while I listened to
Christian's CD of sappy songs. He had completely overdone it. Each
song dripped with bitter cheesiness. Right now it was Enrique
Iglesias's turn to sing his woes to me, and since I knew Christian was
making fun of me, I was laughing. But that only made me think of
him more, and it sobered me immediately.

It was his birthday today, and Charity had officially fallen under
his spell. He wasn't answering his cell, and when I tried to call him at
home, Britton soberly informed me he was out. The fact that Britton
was still home meant trouble. He was supposed to be geode hunting
with Charity and he wasn't. Christian and Charity were both missing,
and I could only assume it meant that they were together, which
meant that it was true. I had won. At least I was completely free to
write my article. And Christian? He would be safe from the grasp of
the Bitter Boys—and me—forever. What had I done?

The screensaver came on. *Jacks is hot,* traveled all over the screen.
Christian!

"Mr. Nice Guy wins," I typed to clear the screensaver then back-spaced quickly. Was Christian really winning? It seemed like he was losing to me. Seriously, Britton really deserved to win in this case. I started a new headline. *Why Jerks Deserve the Girl,* I wrote. *Number one, they don't lead you on. You know who they are from the beginning, and you can be prepared to be miserable with them, at least subconsciously. Number two, no one likes Mr. Nice Guy anyway. They're usually whiners, always whining about why they don't get dates when they won't even consider the ones who really like them. Number three, It only makes sense that the jerk would win because what is he winning anyway? Jerks are attracted to each other, and therefore . . .*

My fingers hesitated on the keyboard. So why was I attracted to Christian? Yes, I was attracted to him. Not like it would do me any good now. He was Mr. Nice Guy, and I knew what I was. We didn't make sense.

I deleted everything and started again. *Mr. Nice Guy Wins,* I punched it into the computer with unusual vigor. Of course, had I ever stopped to consider that maybe Christian really wasn't Mr. Nice Guy? I stared at the screen. *Or at least Mr. Smart Guy,* I found myself writing, *and how do you define a jerk anyway?* I smiled, typing even faster. *A jerk doesn't see what's staring him in the face . . . a perfectly nice . . .* I erased that. *A somewhat nice . . .* I erased that too. *A potentially nice girl.* I bit my lip. *At least, a girl who's nicer than someone else, who we won't mention in this article because it isn't professional or it might be slander or libel or something.* I stared at it. Was this an article or was this my journal?

So really, I typed in quickly before I could erase it. *It isn't so surprising in this case that a squirrelly girl went for Christian because he really was a jerk in the end.* I sighed. Not really. But then why was Christian doing this?

I mean, who would go for some squirrelly girl like her? I wrote it, but I was actually just asking myself. *Even the Bitter Boys president said it would never work, and being bitter, you'd think he'd bank on the worst-possible-case scenario.* I mean, Britton actually wagered he'd go on a real date and give up his freedom and give into everything he feared in this miserable world because he was so sure I wouldn't win. Forget the tricks I played, I'm not *that* good! Forget her wiles. *You would think a nice guy would be smarter than that,* I wrote finally. *You would think I'd*

*be smarter than that. I mean, c'mon, why would anyone fall for Christian?
He's such a nerd! No one can possibly be that nice, and he's not. He's always
been a jerk! Please, no! That can't be why I'm starting to like h—*

My head collapsed onto the keys. Besides not being a very good
article, this really wasn't making any sense, especially when I lifted my
head and found *uyhhhhhhhhhhhhhhhhhhhhh* written all over the
screen. To make it worse, I watched the unholy article print out with
frustrated eyes. The way Maggie's computer worked, it would take
half an hour for the thing to come out. I shoved away from the
computer in battle mode and stomped into the kitchen. Charity
wouldn't get away with this. If I couldn't have him no one could.
Well, at least Charity couldn't. She might be nicer than me, but she
still wasn't good enough for him.

I kneeled on the kitchen floor, throwing pots and pans around the
place in a disorganized clatter. My brownies were cooling on the stove,
but now the kitchen was a mess. "What's this?" Maggie held up my
freshly printed article, "A cry for help?"

Her frown was completely out of place on her innocent face. Her
hair was flipped out and she was wearing light makeup, flowered
capris, and some free T-shirt she got for participating in something.
At her stern look, I desperately tried to remember everything I had
written. It wasn't too incriminating I supposed. At least for her
undiscerning eyes. Of course, if the jerk article got into the wrong
hands . . . I kinda laughed and she glowered. If Christian had seen
that then it would be the perfect ending to my evil deeds.

"Don't worry." She began ripping up my article. "We're on our
way to winning this one tonight! And Britton can ask some *fortunate*
girl to date him, and then we can all go on with our lives." She stared
at the ripped pieces with distaste and stuffed one in her mouth.

I was quickly on my feet. "Don't eat that. It'll make you sick or
something!"

"Jack, go get my list of things to do. We have to get rid of all the
evidence." I snorted. You know when you hear about those bad girls
who write everything naughty they do in their journals? I thought it
was just some weird old wives' tale, but here was living proof that
people did stupid things.

"I'm not eating your list," I said rebelliously.

Chapter 24

Behold, I do not give lectures or a little charity,
When I give I give myself.
—Walt Whitman

Saturday, July 4th, evening

I stepped over the green-Jell-O-covered porch with my chunky
wedge heels. I needed the extra power for tonight. No, I didn't need
to steal Maggie's most flirtatious skirt and raid the DI box for cute
shirts, but I did anyway. After a guilty exchange with Maggie, I
grabbed the brownies from her, balancing Christian's present in my
other hand. The brownies had to look like they came from me,
though I don't know why I even bothered. Everyone would think
they came from her anyway. "Is my hair all right?" I had worn it
long, and after too much effort it looked the same way it always
did.

Maggie gave me a weird look. "Like you care."

No, Maggie didn't care, and it was weird. She had been out doing
errands all day and had dragged me out the door as soon as she
returned without even getting ready. It was so unlike her.

"I just don't want to look like some weirdo girl."

Britton opened the door and smiled wickedly at me. "You've
brought offerings." His gaze traveled over the brownies, and he
opened the door even wider, letting us slip through.

"We're only here for the *Pride and Prejudice* party," I needlessly
reminded him.

He smiled dryly. "And perhaps something else. I couldn't help but notice our new lawn ornament, Jack."

"Yeah, it's your little present," I said.

"Well, it's not my birthday," he said. "How about we just put that thing out of its misery?" Misery? I looked past Britton to Charity in the second living room. Only she could pull off such an '80s look with her skinny jeans and plethora of belts. She was already in position, playing with her hair. Yeah, I knew what misery was. We were like players in the big chess set of life. Christian was playing with a karaoke machine looking like some surfer bum, and she was next to him, sitting on one leg with her high heels tipped flirtatiously off her heel. Come to think of it, girls always sat that way around him.

Britton turned abruptly from us, walking like a peacock with incredibly broad shoulders. How could he not with all those girls clamoring for his attention? We followed him into the living room. The party was already in full swing, and the house was alive with people. The first living room held games. Faith and Hope were playing *Girl Smack*—some joke of a game—with Betsy.

It was a miracle. The Deluxe girls were actually integrating with the Rainbow Villa girls. They wore princess crowns and were laughing at the questions on their pink cards. Hope turned to smile up at me. I couldn't believe she actually liked me now. Maybe I should finally figure out her real name.

I would've joined them, but Sarah and MaryBeth looked cranky. As soon as the two saw me, they started whispering behind the fairy wands they scored from the game. I made a wide berth around them instead. Nintendo was on in the office. The whole Bitter Boys Club was playing in there, the blue lights from the TV flashing across their serious faces. I swerved away from that, too.

We set our presents on the clunky desk in the sitting room, and I watched Britton ahead of us. He was easy to spot since he was taller than everyone in the room. He was wearing some black muscle shirt lined with different colors on the biceps and I laughed. Had he been working out lately? It was the first time I had noticed, and I quickly took my attention from him, perusing the room instead. Seriously, I must be going crazy. First Christian, now Britton?

It was pretty funny, actually. I had initially had my pick of who I wanted to date. Granted, those men were easily turned off, but as for the one I really wanted, there was no way Christian—or Britton, for that matter—would want me. Now *that* was ironic. I just hoped it wasn't the squirrelly girl coming out in me.

Lane Bryant, however, seemed safe from my grasp forever. Liza wouldn't stop touching his elbow or brushing his hand or hitting his arm. She glanced up at me and stiffened a little uncomfortably. I smiled back. Take your claim, girl. One down, how many more barnacles to go? Most of my unfortunate suitors had gotten tired of me by now, except . . . *garbage*.

Who invited Doug or Dan or David or whatever his name was anyway? Probably Britton. He looked mighty proud of himself. I wasn't sure how he knew him, but I wasn't surprised. It was just the odds. Of course, I was probably just overestimating Britton's underhanded ways. He might be evil, but he wasn't all-knowing. He probably didn't even know that I'd gone on a date with the guy.

My nameless friend looked like a director in his baseball cap and alternative rust-colored shirt. He was in, too in. I quickly ducked through the crowd. At least it was big enough to get lost in for the time being.

I could feel the fear in the air. It was the karaoke, and it was contagious. A couple of groups bobbed their heads to the music, but that was as far as they would go. I was sure there would be no dancing, and I decided to mix things up. Spencer was singing loudly off-key, wearing some high school football jersey. I marched to his side, stealing the mike as quickly as I could for my ears' sake if nothing else.

He kept singing, and I turned a charming smile on Christian. He returned it. "Jacks, you're here."

"Yep." I gave Charity a measuring look. "Now, I know you want some *Pride and Prejudice*," I said into the microphone. "And believe me, that will happen, but first this song is dedicated to the birthday boy." Garbage, I was even stealing Christian's mannerisms. He didn't look like he minded. "Hit it, Spencer."

With a grin Spencer switched the karaoke to number nine and I listened to the opening chords of David Cassidy's "I Think I Love You." What were the odds? Well, Spencer *had* orchestrated it.

I gave a self-derisive grin and decided to play with it. I certainly couldn't sing, but the war of the flirts had started. Even at this thought, Charity picked up her plate of birthday cake and tried to feed Christian with it. I stumbled over my words. Christian just laughed at her and she gave a small pout.

"Oh c'mon, girls don't have cooties." Charity tried again and fell into his lap. "Oh dear, I didn't mean for *that* to happen," she said sweetly. Even if she hadn't cast me that evil look right before she did it, I still wouldn't have believed her. To make it worse, Christian just helped her up. Where was Britton when I needed him? True to jerk fashion, he was nowhere to be found. Poor Charity was having a ball without him.

"All right girls," I said into the microphone. "Let's give the birthday boy a little loving. Betsy?" She turned from her *Girl Smack* game, dimpling, and I eyed her *Girl Smack* crown. "He needs a birthday crown," I said.

Faith and Hope were game and so were Sarah and MaryBeth with their catty looks. An unlikely mix of females surrounded Christian, making it almost impossible for Charity to get to him. "Only a true man can get away with this," Betsy said, sliding the *Girl Smack* crown over his head. He smiled wryly and gave me a warning look. I ignored it, hoping that would do the trick, except my plan was working better than I thought it would.

"How about a birthday kiss?" Faith asked.

I found myself unsheathing my claws. *Not even a hug, honey.* "Well, let's give him a little room." I tried to shove them away.

Maggie fought her way to my side. "What are you doing?"

"Strategy," I said without preamble. Maggie had seemed to accept that as an answer before, but now she just looked suspicious.

Charity pushed angrily past us. "You might want to keep the boy on a tighter leash. You don't want him to escape." Where was she going—to get more ammo? How much cake could she possibly stuff into him? She slid past me into the kitchen. And that's when *what's his name* stopped her. Dan or Doug or forget it. He glanced my direction just as he did it, and I ducked, which is kind of hard with a microphone. I smacked into Spencer's shoulder. Oh well, he was good for pretend boyfriend material. Except Christian's eyes were suddenly on me. *Ugh!* I quickly pulled away from Spencer too.

Maggie caught sight of my nameless friend. "Isn't he the one who . . . ?" I nodded. "Maybe you should warn Charity?"

"Why would I do that? They're perfect for each other."

"You're despicable."

Britton appeared out of nowhere and I wondered where he had gone. Probably just playing hard to get. I glanced sideways at him. "Seeking after Charity? She's over there."

"What have you done?" Maggie looked desperate. "Distract him," she mouthed to me.

I purposely misinterpreted her. "Distract who?"

Britton intercepted our communications and gave me an ironic grin. "I'll take care of this." He marched to Charity's side as if to save her like a hero from some romance novel.

"Now look what you've done," Maggie grumbled. "Britton is looking better and better."

"Well, in comparison." I smiled. "But if I intervened, it would just make the barnacle look attractive to her and that would've gone against all rules of the game."

"Are you crazy?"

Yep. I picked up the microphone. "Spencer just requested we start the birthday dance. I think he just wants to kick me off the microphone. What do you think?" There were some cheers at this, not particularly because they wanted to start a dance. They just agreed with Spencer. "Okay," I said, "but only if I get the first dance from the birthday boy."

Christian crossed his arms. He looked so cute with that birthday crown on all that scruffy hair. "Anything to get you off that thing," he said.

Spencer flipped through the CDs. "Just make it something that we can dance to," I told him. He nodded, taking out "Pump It" by Black Eyed Peas—radio version of course, it was Spencer's. Not exactly romantic, but I wouldn't have it any other way.

Christian smiled at me, bobbing his head. The poor kid had no rhythm, so why did that make him so cute? He placed the crown over my red hair, completely startling me. "Here, this will look better on you." He studied my face, then reached forward, tipping the crown to a jaunty angle. I let out my breath, not realizing that I had been holding it.

Suddenly Charity joined our group on our makeshift dance floor, dragging Britton with her. He didn't look like he minded. In fact, Britton and Christian made a hilarious dance team. Christian might have wowed me on the dance floor with his waltzing skills, but when it came to hip-hop, neither of them could dance. They made up for it in creativity, however. We all did. For a moment I forgot that I was playing a part until I found Christian's eyes on me.

"I love this mix," I told him, not sure why I was trying to break the mood. "I want to marry whoever burned it."

"I'll hold you to that."

He laughed at my startled face and I gnawed on my lower lip. What was I doing? Things were working *too well*, and I found myself getting nervous. What if he really liked me? Would it be worth it? If we really took this to another level, we probably would never be able to go back to what we were now, especially if we messed things up. It was like tearing into a fight not knowing if you'd win. It was courage, but it could also be called stupidity.

Whatever it was, I tried to muster enough of it to take his hand. All thoughts of success disappeared, and were replaced with self-doubt. Forget all that noncommittal talk. How could I even think he would like me enough to mess up our friendship with something more? "Sure," I found myself saying, "if you'll take me." At his surprised look, I immediately changed my tone to flippant. I was too nervous to show him how I felt. Why did I have to act now anyway? Why now? I could just enjoy the moment.

I glanced up just in time to see Maggie's shocked face. She stole my hand from Christian's. She dragged me to the other side of the room, almost as if she were trying to put some distance between us. "You're taking this too far. You're only trying to make her jealous. You're not *actually* supposed to steal him. You don't even like him, Jack! Go help Britton!"

I was way over my head and nothing I could say now would make any sense. It didn't even make sense to me. "She's fallen for him already!" I heard Maggie say. "We can just sit back and relax now."

Easy for her to say. I was aware of Charity's every move. The music had ended and everyone was pulling their presents from the desk to give to Christian. Charity had her present in one hand, and she squeezed Christian's arm with her other. "Open mine first."

I took a steadying breath, watching the Relief Society throw the presents around his feet. Christian just shook his head. "You really didn't have to." Charity shoved her present into his hand and he opened it, finding a picture of himself. "Yeah, you really didn't have to," he said more sincerely this time. Charity hugged him. "Look, it's even autographed." She had signed it, *One Hot Guy.*

Uh yeah, we're in the college scene. Nobody gives real presents. Trevor gave him an opened bag of Halloween M&M's. Liza gave him the plaster of Paris pig that I had thrown back into the DI box. Spencer threw in a free Internet access CD he just got in the mail. Betsy gave him an orange made up of different slices of oranges, made specially by the little punk girls downstairs. And then he got a tuner from Maggie. It probably wasn't meant to dis on his singing ability. Britton thrust a mirror at him. *Here's your dishwasher,* it said.

"Wow, thanks guys, I won't have to raid the DI box for a while now."

I exchanged glances with Maggie and pulled away from her long enough to put a fancy bag on Christian's knees. I had resurrected it from Jade's reception collection. It was beautifully wrapped in recycled bows and ribbons and covered in miniature wedding cakes.

Christian's lips curled up. It looked pretty, but opening it would be an entirely different matter. "Wow, I can't even contain my excitement." He made a show of ripping it open as if he had lost all use of his fine motor skills he was so excited. He pulled it out. It was dumpster-diving art.

"So, you told me to create something from what I destroy." I watched him closely. It almost meant more than what I was saying, although I tried not to give it any meaning.

"Garbage." He met my eyes, not even bothering to snap the rubber band. "What?" he told the room. "I used it in context." He held up the rainbow of crushed glass and wrappers and taffy, everything I had pulled out of the dumpster with him.

I had written, *Bless this home. It needs it.* "You can hang it on your front door," I said, giving Britton a challenging look.

"Hey, aren't those my beads?" Charity asked. Yep. It was just like the outfit Cinderella made from her stepsisters' discarded junk. No one had better tear it apart though.

Maggie gave me an accusing look. "There's a piece of the handout I gave in Relief Society." I shrugged.

Sarah scowled, seeing the taffy. "That's disgusting."

"Thank you," I said. Betsy and Hope laughed.

Christian actually looked impressed. "How long did it take you to make this thing?"

"I had writer's block." *And it got rid of the sudden aggression I've had lately.*

Fireworks spewed outside, and I noticed Spencer and Trevor were missing. They couldn't wait? "They're going to pay," Christian said. Everyone rushed for the door, but he stayed put. So did I. He just looked at me, and I didn't know what to say. Something had changed between us. I wanted to be more than friends. I didn't want him to break my heart. My mouth wouldn't move.

Apparently Charity didn't have that problem. She stuck her head through the opened door. "They're calling for you." She gave me an especially smug look because she had interrupted us. Christian stood up and grabbed me in a big bear hug—not exactly a romantic bear hug though. "Let's see what Spencer and Trevor are up to, huh?" He pulled away and Charity looked ready to kill me.

"Whatsa matter?" he asked her. He pulled her into a hug too, and now it was my turn to look angry. *Save your hugs, man.* It was suddenly clear what was happening. The poor kid had no idea that any of us could possibly be interested in him, and suddenly I wondered. Maybe he just didn't see either of us that way. Except Charity knew how to work the situation better. She refused to let go and hooked her arm around Christian's like some sort of koala bear. She smiled possessively up at him.

I turned away as they went out to see the fireworks. I lost. I pulled the crown from my head and threw it on the desk, listening to the fireworks explode over the street. I tried not to think of the symbolism. My reign of terror was at an end. Sure, *you're* happy about it. I finally got my just desserts. The squirrelly girl had lost. Well, I wasn't a squirrelly girl, but nobody really cared about what I really was. Did I even care anymore? What an obnoxious brat. What an unhappy person I was turning out to be.

Any war worth fighting had its pitfalls, but there was nothing worse than realizing that the cause you were fighting for had more than its share of imperfections. I thought I was right. Why else would I keep scaling this mountain? But what were the odds that once I reached the top, shaking, sweating, and bleeding, that I would see it was wrong? I had ruined Christian's life by throwing that woman at him, Britton was against me, and now even Maggie didn't seem to like me. I was out of control.

Spencer poked a cheerful head into the house. "Jack, come here." He shoved a sparkler into my hand and laughed at my attempts to keep the sparks from me. I rushed outside before I set the house on fire just to have Trevor throw snaps at my feet. I jumped back.

"Dance, cowboy!" he called. I smiled reluctantly until I saw Charity break through my bubble. I searched for Christian. He was setting up fireworks on the street, oblivious to the chaos he had unwittingly caused. Even Britton had joined in the fun, fleeing from the cars, sometimes flagging them away. It was something you could only get away with in a college town.

Charity couldn't stand not being the center of attention for long. If only she was a firecracker, she'd have all the attention she wanted and then she'd be outlawed after the Fourth. "Spencer," she said. "Give me a sparkler."

He happily obliged. Trevor threw some snaps at her feet and she didn't even flinch, but she did give a satisfying squeal. "Please don't! Stop! Don't! Stop! Don't stop!" Soon, she was doing what Charity did best, flirting with every guy around me until I found myself pushed out of the circle.

My hands clenched. It suddenly was a point of honor to get the attention back, and this time I turned to the Bitter Boys Club. Brock, Bryan, and Barney were watching the fireworks with watery eyes. They must've just pulled away from their video games because they were squinting at the sudden light. I wrote my name in the air with the sparkler. "Hey Barney, guess what I'm writing."

He awkwardly failed, and I was getting nowhere with him, which Charity could easily see. She tried to hand him a sparkler and he flinched away. "What are you doing? You could have burned me!" I tried to hide my smile.

"None of *us* have been burnt," she said.

"Not yet," I muttered.

"For now, *we* just do the burning," she said with a meaningful glance at me. "Of course, maybe if you were just a little better at the game, Jack, we wouldn't have our ward's Bitter Boys problem." She sighed deeply. "I have a lot of work ahead of me."

"Then go ahead, try it," I said before she could change her mind. "Change a Bitter Boy into a happy man."

"Can you?"

"Any day." I glanced at Barney and he shrank.

"Girls, girls." He tried to ward us off. "There's not enough of me to go around." He scurried somewhere safer, most likely to his video games . . . but no, it was to *Girl Smack* in the living room. Brock and Bryan were quick to follow. We *must* be scary.

Britton passed us and Charity turned on him with a predatory look that he easily interpreted. He lifted his hands, smiling slightly. I tried to get between them, knowing we were playing right into his hands, but I just couldn't let Charity play him too. "Back off," he said. "Even I have my lines." He stopped to laugh. "I have lines? I can't believe I just said that. But every guy knows the number one rule, girls. Never get in the middle of two chicks fighting."

"We weren't fighting," Charity said sweetly. My eyes swept to her heavily lidded ones, and I tried to read her mind. It was difficult. But it almost seemed like she meant it. Failure was so close I could almost smell it. I wanted to lose this bet. I had never wanted to lose, but I really wanted to now, and not just for me. I had already lost Christian. Well, I never really had him, but Charity was no good for him. If I had to lose, I would lose everything for him. I didn't even mind writing the jerk article now. With all my heart I wanted the jerk to win!

Maggie glanced up at us and her eyes widened, especially when Charity's hand snaked to his arm. I tried to pretend like I cared. Britton could take care of himself. I could see that now.

And then the worse thing happened that could possibly happen. Monsieur Romantique in all his glory strode through the clouds and flash of fireworks, the perfect backdrop to his dramatic entrance. He wore a sweater vest over a button-up shirt, the ends hanging over black tuxedo pants. It was some hot metro thing. The lights reflected off the blond ringlets in his hair, looking just like a halo, and he was coming straight for me . . . until he tripped.

The Monsieur lay flat on his elegant back, looking up at Christian. "Hey man, did you just trip me?"

"Yeah." Christian dimpled, kneeling next to him. "I've got something to show you."

"In a second." The Monsieur got back to his illustrious feet and headed for me again in that smooth way of his. Why was he going for me now when my defenses were down? I tried not to back away. He was the reason I hated the game. Why try so hard to break down the barriers only to find out that, once the walls have fallen, what you wanted wasn't behind it? I never wanted him. Right? Of course, he never gave me the choice. I never really knew.

Charity giggled behind her hand. "He's even cute when he falls," she said.

I turned in annoyance. I would try to steal any guy from her except this one. He never had been mine and he never would be. I wasn't sure what ate at me more: jealousy, anger, or disappointment that Charity knew what could get to me. She couldn't really like him, but that wouldn't matter to her. "Don't even go there," I said.

Maggie got to my side as fast as her legs could carry her, and she gave me a worried look. I shrugged casually. The Monsieur didn't hurt me. Well he did, but that wasn't the problem. It was just that the walls were just a little stronger now. How badly did I want to break them down? Wait, not for him! I drew back in horror at the thought. Had I actually been considering it?

Without thinking, I retreated back into the house, but the Monsieur kept coming like some sort of zombie in a horror show. I tripped over the *Girl Smack* game. The Bitter Boys were in deep with the Deluxe girls. They wore the tiaras on their heads like badges of honor. Without realizing it, I backed into Britton for protection just at the Monsieur reached us. The Monsieur looked his roommate over, impressed. Britton was surrounded by females. Even Charity had followed me inside.

"Ah look. Seven brides for one brother," the Monsieur said in a liquid voice.

"Forget that." Britton shook his head with a dry look. "That's way too much commitment for me. This is Christian's clan. I'm just keeping them warm." Maggie looked enraged.

"Thanks, Britton, that's thoughtful of you." Christian was at the Monsieur's side, looking protective. Well, he should be protective. We were best friends. At least we had that.

The Monsieur's deep blue eyes were on mine. "How are you?" he asked me.

There were volumes in that question and I tried to avoid it. "Couldn't be better." I glanced at Charity, but for some reason she didn't really look interested in stealing him. Great. If I wanted him, I could have him.

"Good." The Monsieur reached out and tugged my hand away from me, subconsciously playing with my fingers. I felt a thrill, out of habit, I suppose. I pulled my fingers away.

Christian crossed his arms across his chest. "I thought you were at some girl's party?"

"It was so crowded I had to sit on *some girl's* lap."

"So why didn't you stay then?" Britton asked.

Maggie gasped. "I've had just about enough of that, Britton. Why can't you just stop it?"

Britton looked confused. "What?"

"I . . . I . . ." Everyone's eyes were on her, and she lowered her voice somewhat. "I don't like you this way."

Britton was silent, looking at her.

"Have you *ever* liked him?" the Monsieur asked scornfully. He turned back to me and put his arm against the closet door, blocking me into a corner. "It's been so long," he said.

With Maggie and Britton occupied and me unwillingly so, Charity sidled next to Christian. "I say we liven this party up a bit. Ever play the *yes* game?" That sounded awful. "You have to say yes to everything I say." I froze. Things were getting worse.

Christian just snickered, but at least he agreed with me. "Sounds dangerous."

"What have you been up to?" The Monsieur was trying to catch my interest, falling back to such desperate measures as to actually asking me about myself. I watched the sickening scene over the Monsieur's broad shoulder. I wasn't sure who was stealing my attention more: Maggie and Britton fighting or Christian and Charity, until suddenly the latter had my full attention.

"Want to see what I can do with my left hand?" Charity's hand landed on Christian's shoulder. She had already moved her left foot and her right so that she was standing face to face with him. "How about my right hand?" A manicured hand landed on his other shoulder.

This was like the quarter game, wasn't it? Christian had to see through that, which meant he had to be interested in her. Except he seemed a little distracted right now. His eyes kept darting to the Monsieur.

"Want to see what I can do with my lips?" Charity asked.

"I've been trying to get a hold of you forever, Jack," The Monsieur said. Without thinking, I tore away from him. I told you I was wearing chunky-soled wedges, but that was the least of my concerns. I watched Charity's eyes slant in that flirtatious way of hers, and I shot over the *Girls Smack* game and tripped over the karaoke cords.

I wasn't quite sure what I was going to do, but before I could decide how I could suavely come to Christian's rescue, I tripped just as Charity lifted her finger to her lips and made some crazy sound. What? It was some sort of joke? But just as this registered, I was already knocking Christian off his feet. We landed in a pile of arms and legs.

"Jacqueline? What are you doing?" Christian pulled to a sitting position, regaining his wits somewhat to smile down at me. "Well, that's forward," he joked. He reached for me and before I could shield my expression from him, I looked at him. Yeah, I really looked at him, my heart completely in my eyes. Christian stilled. It was in perfect girl code and by all rights he shouldn't have seen it, but he did. It had taken him forever to break through the codes of my telepathy, and now I couldn't take that searing look in his hazel eyes when I *knew that he knew that I liked him.* Yeah, I liked him . . . and not just the way a girl likes her best guy friend. No. This *was* different and he had seen it in my eyes. I had given everything away.

"Wow, Jack," Charity's voice broke over us. "Did you honestly think this would get you a man?"

I gulped. Nope, I knew it wouldn't, but I hadn't been thinking. Nothing about this made any sense anyway. I tried for a light tone, "Just following your great example." I sat up, wincing at the pain in my ankle. *Great.* I was about due for another sprain.

"Last time I checked I wasn't signed up for the rugby team," Charity retorted.

"Wouldn't surprise me if you were," I said. Christian's eyes went back and forth from us in sudden understanding. "Since you can do anything," I allowed. "Except I still haven't seen you tame the great Bitter Boy into a man. Get distracted?"

"Uh, Charity," Christian quickly interrupted before she could give an angry reply. "Can you get some frozen veggies from our freezer? I think Jacks hurt her ankle."

She sighed overdramatically and flounced into the kitchen. "What are you trying to do?" he asked once she was out of earshot, "Reenact the Civil War?" He glanced up at the gathering Relief Society. They actually didn't look happy, muttering to each other. They still wouldn't let off. That was weird. "Or maybe this is Ward War One?" he asked. "We could call it the Battle of the Flirts. That might be fun. Relief Society Strikes Back?"

I tried to laugh, but it came out a whimper. "That's pretty funny, Christian."

His face was serious, and I tried not to crumble under it. He was the last person I wanted to see me like this. I wasn't the kind of person I wanted to be right now, but for some reason these last few days I just couldn't control myself. It was no excuse, but it was the best I could come up with. "Cattiness doesn't become you," he said.

Did it become anybody? I sighed. "I think I sprained my ankle."

"Why do you wear these dumb things anyway?" Despite his determination not to give me sympathy points, I knew I got him there. He began slipping my bulky wedges off my foot and it tickled my foot. "Just tell me what's going on." Christian asked me under his breath.

Did he just ask me that? I sucked in my breath while he examined my ankle. It was already swelling. "Nothing's going on," I said, glancing up at Maggie. She had stopped fighting with Britton long enough to find out what was happening. Instinctively, Christian lifted his hand in front of her eyes, effectively blocking our line of communication.

"Can you for once tell me without . . . ? Garbage!" Christian's hand ran to the rubber band, but he didn't snap it. He just pulled at it in a worried gesture.

"Oh, is Christian out of charity with . . ."

Maggie turned on Britton. "Knock it off!" And they were at it again.

"Just tell me, Jacks," Christian whispered. I was silent, trying to think of a possible explanation that didn't incriminate me too much. "There's some sort of weird love triangle going on and somehow I'm involved. Can you tell me how that is possible?" With some difficulty I kept my jaw from dropping. "C'mon, I'm not that oblivious. I have sisters," he reminded me.

"Well, I was overcome with jealousy when I saw Charity flirting with you. Anybody would be." The truth sounded stranger than anything I could make up, and I knew he wouldn't believe me.

"But you're *not* just anybody," he said.

I stared at him. Was there some deeper meaning to that? Charity came back with the veggies and threw the bag carelessly on my ankle. "There's something going on in the kitchen you should probably know about," she whispered to me. "There's talk." Her eyes glittered.

"What sort of talk?"

"Apparently Christian's the newest player in our ward, bigger than the Monsieur even. Not only that, he's a jerk."

I gasped, glancing around at the Relief Society, noticing the whispers that I had ignored before. Jerk talk. It smacked of it. Sour MaryBeth and Sarah of the middle floor gossipers were consulting seriously in their little group. I bit my lip in sudden worry. Did I start this? I had given them such high hopes, and now it looked like they had been jilted. Nothing would get a guy labeled a jerk faster than when he finally finds the girl he wants, except Christian really didn't. I glanced anxiously at Charity. At least I hoped he didn't.

"And apparently you're the biggest flirt in the ward." It was obvious Charity relished telling me, and she no longer whispered. "The way you broke the Monsieur's heart."

"He doesn't even have one," I spouted. I searched the room for him. He had already found another girl to flirt with, his arm against the door and almost around her, the same position he had been in with me just moments before. "I have a right to know my accusers."

Charity stood up, trying not to smile triumphantly in front of Christian. "Look in the mirror." She threw a paper onto my lap.

There it was. My article. My words coming back to haunt me, grammar mistakes and all. I quickly scanned it. At least I hadn't been stupid enough to write anything about the wager. Well, not in any recognizable form.

"Is that your article?" Maggie knelt next to me and I flinched, seeing she was done with Britton. She would soon be attacking me just as viciously when she found out what I had done. She glanced around at all the spectators and quickly turned up the music to drown us out.

"Yeah, but you ate it!" I said. This wasn't supposed to happen.

Britton laughed.

"Let me see." Christian tried to take it from me. I tried to hold it from him, which was hard with my ankle. It made Christian look like a complete jerk, attacking a wounded girl.

"I don't know how it got out." I sputtered.

"Everybody uses our computer." Maggie was almost hysterical. "You didn't just minimize it on the bottom of the screen, did you? You got rid of it, didn't you?"

I buried my face in my hands. "Liza!" She checked her e-mail at our place as often as she staked claims on guys. Of course she was nowhere to be found. *Convenient*. And without the whole story of the wager, Christian was the villain, not the victim. Why did she do it? How could I be so stupid? I was half-crazed at the time and Christian was going to hate me when this was through, but I *had* to clear his good name. I took a deep breath, the paper crumpling in my hands.

"Um, Christian, you were part of a wager." It sounded really funny coming out, and I tried not to laugh. It wasn't funny, I told myself.

"What do you mean?"

Britton sighed. "Look, Christian, if you want to blame anyone, blame me. I didn't think it would work anyway. We all know girls go for jerks. I was just proving it."

"No, please, Christian," Maggie said. "It's my fault. We just wanted you to be happy and we knew that Jack wouldn't do it unless she had incentive." That made me sound a lot worse than either of them, even though I wondered where that even came from. I met Christian's eyes, knowing I was doomed.

"Et tu, Brute?" he said without the accent. I felt my face go red. Normally he would've said it for a joke, but I felt my insides curl at the look on his face. I had hurt him, and I didn't realize how much I'd feel it in my gut.

Christian pulled away from me, pacing the length of the fireplace. "Let me get this straight. Maggie wanted to get rid of the service idol, and Britton wanted to further his bitter ambitions, and you did it, Jacks, because you wanted to write an article?"

"It was Britton's idea," I said, hoping that would explain it better.

Maggie shook her head at me.

It took me a while to notice Christian had stopped in his tracks. "You really did it for the article?" he asked. What? Well, I guess I hadn't denied it, but I didn't realize he hadn't really believed it. I felt awful, and I really hoped this wasn't the last straw. I had never lost such a friend. I didn't want to lose him, but I couldn't fix this. I started to feel sick. "You don't even get fifteen bucks an article," he said. "You could've at least sold me out for more."

Britton and Maggie shifted guiltily, but I was past guilt. This was like getting tortured.

"I know you won't believe me," I said, "but it was for you, not the fifteen bucks. Really."

"I would've liked it if you had told me about it first. Before putting me in the middle of some war with Charity. And your signals! Garbage, you're seriously bad at the dating game, Jacks, or did you do that on purpose? I didn't even get what you were up to until a few minutes ago. You *really* had me confused."

Christian stole my article from my hands and I sat very still, unable to run with my swelling ankle. He clenched it tightly, his eyes running over the paper. I wasn't sure how he would take being called a jerk, especially by me. He smiled slightly. "I like what you wrote on the bottom, 'uyhhhhhhhhhhhhhhhhhhhhh.'"

"My thoughts exactly," Britton murmured.

"I'll clear it up," I said.

"No." Christian folded the article. "It's one of us goes down or all three of you, and I pick me."

"No!" It was the most unified answer Britton, Maggie, and I had ever given. For once in my life, I felt really terrible. I mean really terrible. Of course Maggie looked stricken, but even Britton was tight-lipped. Christian stuck my article in the back pocket of his cargo shorts, and my hands itched to wrestle it away from him as if I could erase the hurt by burning it.

He shrugged. "What do I care what the Relief Society thinks of me?"

"Well, why should I care what they think of me?" I asked just as stubbornly.

"Don't fight with me." And he glanced at Maggie. She would care. Now I was torn.

It took me a while to notice the flashing lights and the sirens above the loud music. "Uh-oh." Britton glanced at the clock. It said 12:01. It was past curfew. "Scram. It's the cops." His lips curved up. "They're onto us."

This wasn't funny, but it really was. "Go out the back," Christian said. "I'll talk to them. They know me by now." He ran his hand through his hair. "What a birthday, huh?"

I cringed again. "I'm not running from the police," I said in a high-pitched voice. For one thing, I couldn't walk. For another, it was just the old lady next door complaining about the noise, and I was sure we wouldn't be taken out in cuffs. And for three? I didn't want to ditch Christian anymore.

"No one's asking you to run from the police," Christian said. "It's curfew. Get out of here."

I almost screamed when Dan or David—aw, you know who I'm talking about—stuck his face in front of mine. "Need some help?" He gave Christian a measuring look. Apparently more than the Relief Society held him in contempt. Luckily I noticed the jealous girl at his side. It was the ice princess from Relief Society. Clara. I'd recognize that CTR ring anywhere. The coldest girl in existence had invited him to Christian's party?

"I'm taking Suzy Q home as well," he said regally. Let me guess, that was her middle name? He with all of his social awkwardness had still beaten me. In all my pride and social ability, I was still single. There had to be a lesson in that.

"I've got her," Maggie told my nameless friend. Christian and Britton helped me to my feet. I didn't deserve such good treatment, and he certainly didn't deserve such bad.

Christian picked up the service idol on the fireplace and handed it to me, folding my fingers around it. "Next time you give it away, make sure it's for something good."

I put my arm around Maggie. "Britton," I said in passing. "Talk some sense into him." I was sure he would try. Maggie helped me hobble out with the rest of the girls and the lights from the patrol car reflected over our faces as we crossed the street to our complex. I turned back, seeing Christian talking to one of the officers. But this time Britton, Spencer, and Trevor had joined him. The Monsieur, predictably, was nowhere in sight.

I listened to snippets of conversation around me. "Oh yeah, I always knew he was a player." It was Sarah. "Such a jerk."

I groaned. The article had definitely gotten into the wrong hands. You'd think these girls would know better than to believe everything they read, especially if it was from me. How could they ever believe that Christian was a jerk? But it was such a juicy story that they swallowed it hook and all—if only I hadn't planted so much evidence against Christian. This was all my fault. I could honestly say I had ruined Christian's life. Well, at least his year. Maybe just his summer. Well, his birthday at least.

Everyone was talking trash about Christian, though some in an admiring sort of way. What if they knew the whole story? Well, I wasn't the only one who would be going down. Britton and Maggie would join me, not that I cared about Britton. What could I possibly do or say to make this better? I couldn't do anything, and that's why I am the villain of this tale. And now that you know what I've done you can stop feeling sorry for me.

"Hey, Jack," Betsy found me leaning heavily on Maggie. "What happened to the Monsieur?"

"I sent him running to his momma."

"Man, you're so cool. How can you be so old and not be married?" For once I realized that I seemed ancient compared to our little beehive. "Maybe you should go to Australia," she continued as if she hadn't just cut me to the core. "Australian guys are cute."

"Yeah," I said. "Maybe I'll go as a convict."

Chapter 25

Charity is injurious unless it helps
the recipient to become independent of it.
—John D. Rockefeller

Sunday, July 5th, evening

"Well, you're the reason the cops came, Maggie," I said. "You kept turning up the music." My ankle was propped up on the pillows of the couch. I spread my lime and khaki plaid skirt across my knees. I tossed the yellow teddy bear the Monsieur had given me in the trash from where I sat. It followed everything else that reminded me of him. I guess the nice guy finally won, not that it would do me any good.

"I did you a favor," Maggie said. She was dressed for the fireside, a little more somber than usual in a dark, fitted blouse and long skirt. Due to the circumstances I didn't blame her.

"Just like you did me a favor by letting the whole Relief Society in?" They kept coming until we had a full-fledged party. I should get hurt more often if this was the usual treatment. The love was pouring in: cookies, apologies from Liza, a casserole from MaryBeth . . . I didn't even know anyone in college could make casseroles. They actually cared about me? What was even stranger was that I actually liked these girls back, instead of out of some strange sense of duty, although it did take them forever to leave. The threat of the imminent fireside was the only thing that did the trick. I just didn't get it.

"They turned against Christian though." I flattened against the couch, knowing there was no way I could make it to the fireside in this condition, and I desperately wanted to see Christian. If only I hadn't fallen so far in his eyes.

"Your problem is that you stereotype everybody. They're just showing they're sorry in their own weird way."

Of course, and it was just another challenge that I failed. I failed them all, and I covered my face, realizing I could never be good enough for Christian. "The best thing now is to let Christian go his way in peace," I said mostly to myself.

Maggie sat heavily down on the chair next to her electric piano, tying the sashes of her shoes around her ankles. "Without you?"

"Yeah. I said in peace."

She sighed angrily. "Well, if you don't go for him, then I will. He's cute." I turned towards her. What? He was more than cute! He was Christian. He was . . . I turned quickly away from her, not sure why she was playing with me. "Maggie, this is serious. Can't you see I'm struggling here?"

It was her favorite line, which is why her next words surprised me: "Whatever. It's not the end of the world."

I gasped. The struggling line worked with everyone but me. It wasn't fair. "Yes it is," I argued. And there were things I wanted to do first, like repent!

Maggie began playing "As Sisters in Zion" in minor key, and that's when I knew I had overdone it. "Hey Maggie, I'm not mad at you."

"No, I'm mad at you!"

What? Maggie was mad? That was the second time in two days, and it was completely unlike her. "Hey, what's bothering you?" I asked. "You're never mad. Not really."

Her fingers hardly hesitated on the keys. "Why? Because I don't have feelings?"

My forehead wrinkled. Where did that come from? "No, because you're practically perfect."

She turned to glare at me and I groaned inwardly. I had definitely said the wrong thing. "Oh, is that what everyone thinks? Well, it's garbage! How would you like being the best gal pal ever with no one taking you seriously? But you don't have that problem. You take every guy and then they won't date the roommate. Yeah, you have it real bad! It's girls like you that give girls everywhere a bad name!"

I stilled. My fear was affecting Maggie? I had been hurting her all along, and I didn't even know it. It was the final betrayal of friendship. How could I fix this? "Well, you won't tell me who you like," I said.

"Not even after the Millennium."

That was hardly fair! "Why not?" Even as I asked it, I wondered. Christian? She had just said he was cute, maybe that's what was wrong with her.

The phone rang and Maggie lurched from the electric piano to get it. "It's for you." She threw it into my hands without even answering it and marched out.

I watched her leave, putting the phone to my ear. "You've been summoned to the council of Bitter Boys," Britton informed me in a deep voice.

I choked on a bitter laugh. This was beyond ridiculous. Was this some change in the terms of our agreement? The wager was over. Couldn't he see that? How long did he plan to drag this out anyway? "What? You expect me to hobble over there?" I asked him.

"That would be more convenient for us, certainly."

I hung the phone up on him and sighed. Maggie was still in her room with the door shut, and I didn't really want to face her. Not after I had been a complete failure as a friend. And maybe she did like Christian. I wasn't sure if I could take that yet. And what could Britton possibly have to say? But then again, maybe Christian would be at Rambo House, not that I should see him. I pulled to my feet, sucking in my breath when my foot made contact with the ground. I was sure I'd get over it.

I pushed my feet into my lime colored flip-flops and made my way to the door as quietly as I could. After closing it behind me, I leaned heavily on the railing, the breeze playing with the flares of my A-line skirt. Rambo House wasn't so far away anyway, and after dragging my feet, not on purpose I assure you, I was there. I opened the door without knocking and almost snickered at the dramatic scene. The Bitter Boys meeting was in session, and each Bitter Boy was there, minus Lane Bryant, thankfully. They sat in their stadium seating in dignified silence, looking like gangsters in their suits.

Their marriage wall with my love articles was strangely bare. "Hey, what happened to the marriage wall?" I complained.

"Britton tore it down. He was mad." I smirked, imagining the sight. *That was crazy. Was everybody crazy then?* I zipped up my hoodie, feeling the air-conditioning pour over my head. I shivered. I wasn't used to being cold anymore.

Britton came out from the back. His eyes flicked lazily over to my bobby pins, which were twisting my red hair all over the place. "Keep those on your head," he muttered.

"Don't worry, I'm running out of them, and I don't have money to buy more."

"Good." He wrinkled his nose. "Pun intended."

I tried to figure it out, but it was completely senseless. "Excuse me, but there was no pun there!"

Britton didn't care. He pulled his sleek black suit coat over his suspenders. "All right, let's make this quick. I'm in a hurry."

Barney leaped awkwardly to his feet. "What can I do to help you?" *My liege.* No, he didn't say that part, but he should have. It would have been more fitting.

"You can brush my teeth," he muttered sarcastically.

Barney disappeared into the back and came back with a toothbrush. He shoved it into Britton's surprised mouth. "Give that to me," Britton said in a garbled voice. He wrestled it away, brushing his own teeth, but then his eyes got wide and he pulled it out. "This isn't mine. It's Spencer's."

Barney ran to dispose of it, but Britton held it away from him, pointing at me with it. "Well, well, my arch-nemesis is late."

"I suppose you're going to the fireside?" I asked.

"Of course." He stared at me hard, unconsciously throwing the toothbrush back into his mouth. I winced for Spencer. "You realize, of course, that according to Shakespeare and every chick flick in existence, we should be going to this fireside together."

"Not according to me," I muttered, half smiling.

"Finally we agree on something."

I sat down on a couch, putting my foot up on the cushions. Bryan inched away from me, and I threw my flip-flop at him, giving him something to be scared about. "The Bitter Boys have made yet another victory," Britton said.

"I don't even know what you're talking about." Christian was safe from their clutches. He would get the girl and she would love him, no matter how twisted she was. "He won the biggest squirrelly girl in the ward," I said.

Britton snorted. "Nope, Christian lost her. Get her some frozen vegetables," he ordered one of his sidekicks. Brock ran to his bidding.

I sat up straighter. "Charity dumped him?" If she broke his heart, I'd get her . . . after I nursed Christian's heart back to health. He probably wouldn't want that though.

"Who said anything about Charity?" Britton said. "We all know the biggest squirrelly girl in the ward is you."

"Garbage!" I jumped to my feet, but I let out a cry of pain and opted for sitting down instead. "You said it was Charity from the moment we made this wager."

"No, *you* said it was Charity. I just didn't correct you, but I meant you all along."

"You idiot, you can't do that!"

"Why not? Even Maggie agreed with me." He was smiling now, though he tried to hide it under the guise of fixing his pink tie.

"Without my knowledge," I argued.

"Yes, and I thought it only fair that we clarified the terms of our agreement."

Now that it was too late? Now that I had lost everything? The bet and Christian? What were the odds? My face got hot. "I'm not a squirrelly girl!" I cried. *Not really. Not very often anyway.* "How many times do I have to tell you that? I don't give any guy false hopes. I don't put any guy on a back burner. I throw him into the fire before he can even get close."

Brock threw the frozen vegetables at me, sinking hard into the couch. "And that's just the way it is. The girl will go for a guy who is better looking who treats her like garbage."

"Thus the jerk wins," Britton said. "I want the article on my desk tonight."

Why was Brock even getting into this? I turned to him angrily. "Maybe she knows you would treat her like garbage."

"I open doors. I pay for food."

"Do you make her feel better about herself when she's around you? Seriously, everyone's so willing to make themselves out to be the good guy just to make everybody else the bad guy."

"Yeah?" Bryan cut off his brother. "What about me, Jacqueline? I treated you well. I made you feel attractive, and you wouldn't give me the time of day."

It felt very surreal, like I was Scrooge being visited by the ghosts of dates from my past. "And how long would that last?" I asked. "I've seen how you've treated other girls and how quickly you fall in and out of love."

Britton pointed to Barney. "Okay, now that we're being so honest, why didn't you like him?"

"Uh, we don't like the same movies."

Britton snickered. "Paltry excuses. Your heart was already taken by someone else."

"I am over Monsieur Romantique, okay? And even if he were never in the way, I still wouldn't—"

"We're talking about Christian." I froze, not believing what he was saying. "You were so caught up with Christian there was no way anyone else could get in. Even the Monsieur."

If that was the case then they had no argument. That would mean I had preferred the nice guy from the beginning, but for some reason I wasn't ready to admit it. "But that was just an act for Charity."

"Give us some credit, Jack. No self-respecting gossiper would miss how long you've liked him. The middle floor has been most assiduous in their reports. Maybe you should just answer the question that's on everybody's mind. Why are you still here in Provo?" Britton stared at my dumbfounded face then nodded. "Exactly."

He held up one of my magazine articles he had pulled down from the marriage wall and I stiffened. "Let's see, who were you talking about here? 'Give Me That Mountain: A Guide to Getting Lost While Hiking,' 'The Best of Foosball Trash-Talking,' 'Why Guys Like Baseball,' 'The Art of Dumpster Diving,' 'Guys Who Can't Sing,' 'The Nice Guy's Tips for Putting Up with Jerky Roommates.' Oh, I guess that one is about me."

I tried not to laugh.

"Ah, my favorite: 'What Happens When Hanging Out Is No Longer Safe? Falling for Your Best Guy Friend.'" I froze, not realizing how transparent I was. "Besides some articles on Harleys, Christian's your main attraction. You have it bad, Jack. You quote his favorite lines, you love his favorite bands. You stole his favorite habits, and you can barely touch him. And that's why the nice guy will never win."

My mouth opened, but nothing came out. I was a coward? I mean, I had always figured that once the right one came along I wouldn't be afraid, but Christian was *the right one* and I was afraid. Was that a sign? A sign that I was an idiot? I wanted to be with him. I trusted him, depended on him. He even made me laugh, but what good would that do me now? It was too late. Britton was right. He could never win. Not when I was so afraid of losing him.

"A shrink would have a heyday on you. Actually, come to think of it, Christian's going to be a shrink. Maybe you could save on doctors' bills."

I sunk back on the couch. "There is no way anyone is getting into this mind. I can't even."

"Unfortunately for you, we are of the same mind," he assured me. He sat next to me, almost throwing me off balance. "We're picky. Why? Well, there are plenty to pick from. Sure you want the right one, but there's no hurry. You're enjoying life now."

Yep, I was the little bachelor-rat. Well, it was better than being a Mormon Monk or Bitter Boy.

"Well, everyone's got to settle down sometime." That was a strange thing coming from Britton, and I studied him closely. Something was different. He noticed my leg was in an awkward position and he rested my ankle on his knee. It was a thoughtful gesture, and he smiled at me to distract me from it. "So if you like him, quit messing with him, because he's falling for you."

"He's mad at me."

"Mad *for* you. Here's a clue. It's the only freebie you'll get from me. You're the squirrelly girl he's always liked. It wouldn't have made a difference anyway. Compliments mean nothing to you. Nope, just anger. It's a well-known fact that we can get you to do anything if you're angry." He shrugged at my furious look. "Hey, even Christian does it. That's how Maggie and I pulled off this wager in the first place. Maybe it was after you agreed to go on that 'polygadate' with those knuckleheads when we realized how much you were willing to do for Christian."

Maggie and Britton? They were in cahoots? But why would she turn on me? Well, it actually shouldn't have been too big of a surprise.

We had done it to Christian, but to think that I was the one they were manipulating all along and not Charity? I could just imagine how he talked Maggie into it. *You must be cruel to be kind.*

Britton put his finger to his lips. "Or maybe it was the institute teacher." I shifted. Brother Baer? This was just getting worse and worse. "He *did* know how to crack the squirrelly girl, and it just *might have* been his plan in the first place." By now Britton was smiling broadly. "Maggie and I just couldn't pass it up. It was the perfect charity project."

Things were beginning to fit together. The prepping. The talks. I felt like an idiot. Everyone had manipulated me, and it was disturbing how easy it had been. "Well, at least Christian never used it for evil," I said.

"That's what you'd like to think," Britton said.

That was more than enough. "He's a gentleman in every way," I cried. "He never would've done that to me." The Bitter Boys exchanged glances at my adamant defense of him, and I ground my teeth at the insinuation.

"Well, Christian loves you. I don't." I felt myself go weak at the words. "Think about it. When you broke up with the Monsieur, he went straight to your side. Forget about the roommate he grew up with."

Christian couldn't love me, not like that. "No, he doesn't," I cried. "I'm nice but . . ." I broke into a fit of bitter laughter. "I can't believe I just used that line on myself."

"What?" Britton asked.

I breathed in deeply. "I'm nice, but a guy like that isn't going to go for me, no matter how much he likes me."

"Now he won't. No one is as good at messing up relationships as you are. You're worse than your own Iago."

I squinted. Othello's arch-nemesis? Britton had pinned it. "Look, that's not something I did on purpose."

"Really? But you broke every rule. You talked to him about other guys, you showed no marked attention, you were best friends for too long, but even after all that, he still tried to win you over. I just don't know how you finally lost him. Oh well. Maybe you should just go home and eat some chocolate. Oh wait. There's not enough chocolate in this world to fix your problems." My chin lifted at that, and he tapped it down playfully.

"Hey, don't worry. Love makes us all stupid. Or in your case, incompetent. After all, a heart can break many ways. I've experienced quite a few of them. The friendship will never be the same again. Of course, if you really liked him, you would jump in with everything you've got, but you won't. Nope, because you won't sacrifice anything for him. Besides, what if you find someone else more attractive?" He arched an eyebrow at me.

I gasped at that one. How dare he? As if I would be so disloyal!

"You're better off anyway. Can you imagine finding true love? The work, the constant heartache, the . . . oh," he guffawed, "I guess you can't. Sorry." He pulled away from me, standing up after he settled my leg back on the cushions. "It's time to give up. Join us. Become a bitter girl."

He hit a chord there. Everyone and their dog was telling me to give up, but I wouldn't. I didn't listen to dogs anyway. Britton was watching me closely, and I knew he had done it again. He really knew what made me tick.

"But he likes Charity now," I said. The Bitter Boys shuddered, and I wondered how many of their hearts she had broken. Could she possibly have broken my record? "And she likes him back," I reminded them.

"What do you care? You're not her roommate. Her tears against her pillow won't be keeping you up at night. And of course, being the girl you are, that should only add to his attraction."

Rude. Of course, maybe there was an ulterior motive to this. Had Britton fallen head over heels for Charity? Was that what this was all about? A setup to get Charity to go for him? It almost worked, and worse! I voiced the nagging suspicion in my mind. "But what if *my* roommate likes Christian now?" I asked.

Britton winced. "Leave her to me."

"Yeah right, she hates you too." If Maggie liked Christian, why would she try to set me up with him? Was she that selfless? The thought just made me feel even more awful than before. I couldn't be mad at her, even if I tried, or I'd be a hypocrite. And even if I was, hadn't I done the same thing to Christian? Sorta, and I didn't want him to be mad at me either.

"I'll take care of it," Britton said.

"Thanks." I had no idea why he was doing this, but I was grateful. Why was he being so nice anyway? Britton was an interesting man. He pretended to be a bad boy, but when push came to shove, he did what was right. "Garbage," I said, "with enemies like these, who needs friends?"

Britton looked uncomfortable at the compliment, even though it was double-edged. "This may surprise you, but I don't want to win our little wager."

"You'd rather ask a girl out on a serious date? Oh, how the mighty have fallen. I thought you were The Chosen One? The Bitter Boy Extraordinaire?" He laughed at that one, and I realized I had never seen him so human before. Maybe he was breaking the spell of bitterness over himself too. "And what are the demands of the Bitter Boys council?" I asked suddenly. In other words, how was I going to win this wager for us?

"You're the queen of flirting. I think you know what to do."

"Not really."

"Tell him that you like him. Be honest. Love is like war, you can't go in halfway." Britton glanced down at his watch. "Now gather your guts, we've got a fireside."

"Is it about charity?" I asked.

He smiled. "Maybe." He was crazier than I thought. The Bitter Boys slid off the couch and followed their great leader out the door, wrestling with their ties. Was it the fall of the Bitter Boys? Was it the fall of the squirrelly girl's reign? I desperately hoped so.

Chapter 26

To give up yourself without regret
is the greatest charity.
—Bodhidharma

Sunday, July 5th, evening

Britton dropped me off with some vile pep talk. "Remember, the weevils always rise to the top." He grinned wickedly and drove off.

I blanched at the memory, but for some reason the weevil cereal gave me courage anyway. I guess that's when you know you're desperate for encouragement. I hobbled up the steps to my apartment. How was I supposed to tell Christian anyway? Be honest? How? I had no idea what to say. My thoughts kept circling until I felt the confusion I always felt. I prayed that I wouldn't chase love away with my crazy bumbling, that I could open my heart, that for once I wouldn't let my fear get the best of me.

And for the first time in my life, I prayed to be humble enough to do it. Of course, I knew that meant trouble. You never pray to be humbled. But maybe there was no other way to accept love or rejection when it came. I knew I couldn't do it on my own. I had failed over and over again, and I knew that I needed some serious help. If I could just have a new heart, a new life, a new hope, to actually make a friend like Christian into my family.

What was I supposed to do? I wasn't getting any answers. Well, not the usual answers. I just wasn't sure what to look for, so how would I know what to do?

I opened the door to my apartment and my eyes almost bugged out. There was the Monsieur sitting calmly on my couch, his flip-flops propped up on Maggie's end table. The sleeves of his black blazer were bunched up over his elbows '80s style.

He swigged back a drink. He patted the cushion next to him. "Sit down."

I bit my lip. What was he doing here? Maybe I had played too hard to get last night. The last thing I wanted to do was remind the Monsieur that I existed. I limped to his side, wishing I had seen his parked Harley outside. Too late. He found my hand and tugged me next to him. He pulled an ice pack out of his backpack and put it on my ankle. "Heard you were using frozen vegetables," he said. Before I could defend myself, the Monsieur pulled out an ankle brace from his bag of tricks too. "Seems like you got yourself into a bit of trouble last night."

I shrugged. "It's just a dance-off injury," I lied.

"With Charity?" He took a long pull of his drink. "I like the present you gave Rambo House, by the way. Of course, you're much more beautiful in comparison."

I grinned at that one. Was he calling my art ugly? There was no telling with him. He always talked in code, especially when he thought I was too stupid to pick up on it. I wasn't even sure why he liked me. Whatever the reason, it sure wasn't healthy.

"The masters have worked backbreaking hours to recreate what God has created. Just the replica of it even. Life." He waxed even deeper, and my smile grew even wider, and suddenly he was transfixed. "But no artist can duplicate the beauty of your smile."

"So, you didn't really like it?" I asked. He looked blank. "You know, my dumpster-diving art for Christian?"

"Jack, I'm trying to have a heart-to-heart with you."

"It's okay," I cut him off. "No one can." Britton was right. My heart was untouchable because it belonged to someone else who just didn't happen to like me that way anymore. Only it wasn't the Monsieur like I thought all along, it was Christian. Seeing the Monsieur now made me see the truth. How could I be so stupid?

"I guess that's a compliment." The Monsieur pushed a long strand of hair from my face, peering into my eyes. "You refused every man but me. Was it just a lapse of judgment, or can I dare to hope it was something more?"

He was digging for some reassurance, and I couldn't give it to him. "It's okay, Anthony. You don't have to pretend to like me anymore. I no longer have feelings for you."

"Really? Because I do for you." I glanced up in alarm. Everything that I had hoped he would say and dreaded. Wait, dreaded? Yeah, dreaded. Uh-oh. I was proving Britton right all over the place. Had I really gone for the Monsieur because he wouldn't return my love?

"The problem is that I'm always on a speeding train." The Monsieur was about to get deep, and I braced myself. "Always racing towards disaster, faster and faster."

"Yeah, and you pushed me off!"

His hand found my chin. "Well, you don't want to crash with me."

I jerked my chin from him. To him I was a back-burner girl and always would be, even when he was declaring his love. "You pushed me off the ride before it got exciting." He knew that I loved the storm, the adventure—but did I? I couldn't even tell Christian how I felt.

"Hey, it's not me, it's you," he said, deciding to lighten the mood. He knew what I fell for, and I couldn't help but soften at the joke. "I mean, I can't get married," he said. "What if my wife gets fat?" What? Well true, I did eat a lot . . . hey, what a jerk! He laughed. "I'm teasing."

He offered me his drink, and I shook my head. "Sorry, I lost my appetite."

"It's about time." He snorted again, and I punched him hard. He didn't even know that I was angry for real. "Hey honey, you're always beautiful to me," he quickly reassured me.

I drew back in alarm at such talk. I was stuck next to the Monsieur with a bum ankle, racking my brain on what to do with Christian, and I found myself growing more and more vulnerable by the minute. C'mon, I needed some sort of help! I needed my mom's faith.

The phone rang and the Monsieur just stared at me until I got up to answer it. He beat me to it, pushing me roughly back on the couch. "Yo, Mom!" he answered. "Sure, I'll get your baby." It felt almost surreal as he handed me the phone and turned on our TV. I caught my breath. Maggie would have his head if she were here. No TV on Sundays. It was the only day to get any peace and quiet, and if she came in, I'd get blamed for it.

"What happened to Christian?" my mom asked testily. Darn her motherly intuition.

"Um, he's not here?"

She would take no excuses. "Well, then get him over there." That was my cue to hang up the phone, but I kept on the line. Anything was better than talking to the guy sitting next to me. "Look, that's not really why I called," she said. "I need to tell you something. I've been worried about you all day, and I just felt like I needed to tell you that I'm praying that you'll be happy. Don't go for a guy just because he's breathing."

What? The one time she warns me against guys was when I was suddenly feeling weak? How did she always know these things? "Okay, mom. I won't." I hung up the phone and cleared my throat. "Um, we don't really watch TV on Sundays," I told the Monsieur. "Maggie doesn't . . ." I was going to use her as an excuse, but changed my mind. "I don't like it."

He snorted. "Shhh. It's a replay. The Yankees are about to pitch."

"Why aren't you at the fireside?" I asked him.

"I'm sorry. I was looking at you, but I wasn't listening," he used my own line against me, but for some reason it was no longer funny. He laughed anyway. "I've actually decided to become inactive with you." His words trailed off at the pitch, and he cheered loudly.

I cupped my chin in my hand. I had completely forgotten what a jerk he was. I could never stand up for myself in situations like these, and it was interesting how challenges were designed especially for us. I listened to the laughter outside instead. It seemed so far away, almost like old times. I was stuck inside with the Monsieur while everyone else was having fun outside, and he somehow had my attention, and I was trying to be nice and kind and good and . . . bored.

And that's when my thoughts always wandered. They turned to Christian. I guess they always had with the Monsieur. I sighed. There was something different about a guy who goes for you as a friend rather than an object.

The Monsieur groaned as his team fell behind, and finally he just clicked off the TV, turning to stare at me with probing blue eyes. I stiffened, realizing he was giving me "that look" again. It used to melt me, but now it just made me sick because I didn't know how to fight it.

Christian and I had both made bad choices, hadn't we? And it was time to make a right one. I'd help him get over Charity the only way I knew how, but first I had to get rid of the "perfect man." "Isn't it curfew?" I asked.

"Nope."

"It's gotta be twelve o'clock somewhere in this world."

The Monsieur grinned and his arm snaked around me just as Christian walked in. The Monsieur couldn't have planned it better. Christian was still in his white shirt and tie. He had come straight from the fireside, and my heart fluttered at the thought. Did he actually still care about me then? Could he have forgiven me? His eyes narrowed slightly at us. If I hadn't been highly sensitive to him right now, I wouldn't have noticed.

The Monsieur nodded curtly at him. "If it isn't Heathen, er, Christian."

"No, you had it right the first time." It was in true Christian fashion, not jealous, just mildly cynical. He picked up the empty Dr. Pepper can from the table and rattled it. "Ah yes, the perfect scene, complete with devil pop."

"Oh, cool it," the Monsieur said. "It's devil free, not like you have a problem with it. I found a sale on it today."

Christian arched an eyebrow and glanced at me. I tried to defend myself. "I didn't go Sabbath breaking with—" I stopped myself before I sounded self-righteous.

"Yeah, I heard that you dropped by Rambo House, Jacks," Christian said. "It looks like you made it back okay. Are you?"

"Yes, yes, I'm okay. How are you?" Yeah I know. Lame. I couldn't think of anything else to say, especially with our audience.

"Yeah," he didn't answer my question and started moving to the door. "Sorry to interrupt."

"No." I pulled the ice pack off my ankle, attempting to follow him. "I'm not sorry."

Both Christian and the Monsieur's foreheads wrinkled. "I almost forgot," Christian's hand was on the doorknob. "I came to invite you to my brother's homecoming. It's today. Tonight. Right now actually. There's a lot of food. Oh, and speaking of handouts," Christian dug into the pockets of his burnt tweed pants and threw my keys on the table. "Twenty bucks for the brake pads, a hundred twenty for the starter. You owe me your firstborn now."

That could be arranged if he married me. I tried to think of some way to make that happen. Well, at least distract him from leaving. "I followed your advice," I said. "I have an interview with my magazine."

"As an editor?" I nodded and he grinned. "Good." He would've hugged me if the Monsieur wasn't there. I knew it. I got to my feet, but the Monsieur got in the way.

"Sorry, she can't exactly get around right now." The Monsieur offered me his arm. "Here, let me help you." He was such a snake. Such a charming snake, and I sat down just to avoid his touch.

There was only a ghost of a smile left on Christian's suddenly tight lips. "Like a dog to its vomit, kid," he warned me. *Garbage! Not Proverbs again!* He thought I was getting back together with the Monsieur! I would've stomped my foot if my ankle didn't prevent it. Christian headed for the door and I was losing him.

I said the first thing that popped into my mind. "I'm so sorry, Christian."

His eyes crinkled. "For what?" His gaze went to the Monsieur. "For tackling me?"

"No, for the bet. The article mostly."

He leaned against the opened door. "Oh, yeah. I'm sure it just adds to my attraction." He looked at me with penetrating eyes and I tried to will him to stay. "I forgive you," he broke into a grin, "but I won't forget you. See ya, peep." And with that half-serious joke, he was out the door.

No, don't! But before I could trip over the Monsieur to get to him, I noticed Charity waiting outside and she looked so dang cute! I squinted. Well, at least her hair looked really dark. She played with the ends of her white linen skirt. It was slung low on the hip with some sort of beaded embellishment on it, complete with matching sandals. Despite the jerk rumors, she had stuck to his side. She showed that much conviction at least.

She waved brightly at me, her chandelier earrings swinging. I knew none of her cheerfulness was feigned. She knew exactly who I was sitting with. "Get well soon!" she called. "The ward won't be as fun without you."

Christian closed the door. How could I have let this happen? I twisted around on the couch to stare out the window. Charity clasped Christian's arm as soon as she could get to him and I gasped. "What's going on?" the Monsieur asked.

"Nothing." I threw the ice pack to the side and started strapping on the brace he gave me. It made me look like some sort of apocalypse crusader. I didn't know what I was going to do, short of tackling her, but that was one thing that the Monsieur taught me: never to think too much, and I refused to now. I felt it was right. My heart was all for it, but my mind was giving excuses. I tried to push out the fear.

"Where are you going?" the Monsieur asked.

Away from you to Christian. "If Maggie sees you watching her TV on Sunday and drinking devil pop there will be heck to pay."

"Is that some sort of pun, hon?"

He knew it wasn't. "Yeah, and here's another one. Stay away from me."

"What are you talking about?"

"You're not healthy." I hobbled to the door and tore it open. The Monsieur wouldn't be happy until he shot us both in the foot, just so he could be sure I couldn't get away if he changed his mind about me later. "I want something healthy, you know?"

"Well, you're not going to get it by putting all your weight on that ankle!"

I slammed the door behind me and limped outside, hesitating on the balcony. I knew what I had to do, but how was I going to do it? Hey, Christian, you hate me, but . . . uh, sorry, I'm such a jerk and I don't deserve you. Did I have to say those things? It would definitely hurt my argument to take me back.

I glared through the dimming twilight. Charity was touching Christian unnecessarily on the arm, and I couldn't stop it without being socially unacceptable. My hand wrapped convulsively around the little plastic ball on the foosball table and I chucked it. It bounced across the pavement and they both glanced up. I ducked, hiding in the crops. This was crazy.

I couldn't play "maiden in distress." Even though I was, that would look too ridiculous. At the same time, I just couldn't give him up. He was a part of me. The good side of me, I mean, and he was walking away with her. What could I do? Declare my love in front of Charity? It would be impossible not to now. She'd be his shadow from now on if she could help it.

How could I step into the darkness if I wasn't sure there would be anyone there to catch me? My whole life was built around conquering fear. I couldn't do this on my own, and I was losing him. Christian and Charity were walking to Rambo House, and I kicked the wall with my good foot and retreated inside, meeting the Monsieur's eyes. "Well, that was fast," he said.

I leaned heavily against the door. I was losing Christian without a fight. *"I know not, save the Lord has commanded me."* That was the scriptures' take on it, but commanded me to do what? Follow my heart? What if I didn't know my heart? I just knew that I belonged with Christian, and if that was my answer I was taking it.

"Anthony!" I stretched my hand out to him. "I need you." The Monsieur stood up reluctantly. I dragged him outside, half-leaning on him, half-leaning on the railing. "If you like me at all you've got to help me!"

"I do like you. That's what I've been trying to tell you all night!"

"No, not that way. Don't you think Charity is hot?" Charity was playing with the three strands of her long beaded necklace in the distance.

He didn't even look. "I think someone else is better looking."

"Not true." I wasn't fishing for compliments, I was fishing for help, and I pulled him after me down the stairs, my bare feet padding uncomfortably down the stairs while I leaned heavily on the railing. "You know she's better looking!"

"Jacqueline." The Monsieur stopped me in front of the gossip floor and I squirmed uneasily. "This might not seem like the time, but I'm trying to tell you that I'm starting to have feelings for you again."

No, it definitely wasn't the time. "Whatever. If you like someone, you actually care." My words trailed off when I saw his suddenly vulnerable face. "Please, you don't really like me. Forget about that stuff, just help me. You've got to get Charity away from Christian."

"What? Why? You want your revenge on her or something?" *Among other things, but no, not really.* He glowered at me. "I'm not playing some stupid prank."

"I'm not." Christian and Charity were about to have some DTR. I knew it, and I was about to lose him forever, or at least for a very long time, and I had no time to waste. "I like him," I said lamely.

That shocked him. "How long has this been going on?" he asked bitterly.

"Forever."

"While *we* were dating?"

I groaned. "I just figured it out two days ago, okay?" That was a safe enough answer.

He studied the two in the distance. She was laughing and flipping her hair. "Yeah, Charity is hot," he finally conceded.

Good. The Monsieur was a perfect villain to the end, and that's why I knew he could help me. You could always trust a villain to do the right thing if just for the wrong reasons. Even now, Charity was getting into Christian's car. "Tell me how to separate them."

He was silent for a moment, his perfect eyes on me. Then he sighed. "Leave it to me. I'm only doing this for you, just so you know." He pulled out his cell phone and pushed speed dial. "What?" he said at my surprised expression. "Charity and I went on a couple of dates, okay?" He blanked me out, leaning against the pole.

"Hey, Charity." He gave a charming smile, even though she couldn't see it. "We've got a Relief Society emergency. Duty calls. Well, nothing the compassionate service committee can't take care of, but . . . uh really? Sounds perfect."

Oh yeah, he was good. I smiled, glad that the Monsieur was on my side for once until he closed his phone in disbelief. "She blew me off. She told me she'd meet me at the open house at Christian's if I happened to be there. Man, I didn't realize Christian's appeal. He's a dangerous roommate to have around."

I staggered toward the parking lot. "I've got to stop this."

"Jacqueline, wait." The Monsieur's strong hand landed on my arm, and he met my eyes pleadingly. I hesitated. "Wait." He tapped me on the nose and left me, rushing up to my apartment. He returned with my keys and something else.

He threw the service idol into my hands. "Cut them off at his brother's open house and do something meaningful with this, huh? Like this." He pulled me off my feet. I let out a startled cry, tugging my plaid skirt down, but I didn't have time to argue, which was just as well because he got me to my car three times faster than my sprained ankle would have allowed me.

He set me down on my bare feet. "Thanks," I said, confused at the help.

The Monsieur leaned against my minivan, laughing at me. "If he doesn't take you, I'll be waiting."

My lips curled up slowly. "Okay, don't move from that spot then." The Monsieur wasn't so bad. Well, when he wasn't going after me. I jumped into the minivan, praying it wouldn't make a fuss, and it actually started. Unbelievable. I really did owe Christian. I just hoped he wouldn't regret fixing my car after this. And the Monsieur? Who would've thought he had a heart? I mean a real one!

He hit the back of my car in farewell and I was off, trying to remember exactly where Christian's family's house was. About five blocks away, close to some school? I gnawed on my lower lip, trying to bite down my fear.

What was I doing? I could really get hurt this way. For a girl who was deathly afraid of rejection, I was making myself really vulnerable. Why? My hands tightened over the steering wheel. "Give me this mountain!" I said.

The children of Israel wandered in the wilderness for forty years, and they weren't able to live in the land of promise because they murmured. That's what Christian said. Was that what I was doing? I didn't take a blessing because I was scared of it? Of course, what if this blessing wasn't meant to be mine?

I listened to the faint fuzz of my radio. It only made sense that Christian had turned it to a good station while he had been working on my car. I made out the lyrics of Katie Cassidy's country version of "I Think I Love You."

What were the odds? I let my breath out. It was definitely our song. So, what was I so afraid of? Of course I wanted to love, but nothing hurt more, and nothing brought more happiness. What was I afraid of? Responsibility? Rejection? Real life? The Monsieur? What a selfish life I'd been leading up to now. I held back affection because I was afraid. Well, no more.

"Christian," I whispered, "this is for you."

It was the only way for me to be happy. And now I found myself rushing to his side, trying to get there in time before he made the biggest mistake of our lives. Even as I thought this, I felt my car slowing down, and I pressed harder on the gas with no results. I glanced at the gasoline light. It was on. Apparently Christian wasn't a complete martyr. I had completely forgotten I was way past empty. I pulled to the side of the road and rested my head on the steering wheel, knowing I was finally beaten.

Maybe it just wasn't meant to be. I mean, what did I expect to do? Rip him from Charity's arms? My hands were still shaking, and I sternly told them to stop. It wasn't as if I had to face my worst fear anymore. It wasn't as if I had a chance with Christian anymore. I groaned.

"What are you doing? You can't park here."

My head lifted at the voice of an angel. I saw his car parked behind me. Charity wasn't in it. Christian leaned against my door like some sort of miracle. I got a close-up view of his laughing face in my open window.

"I'm not stalking you, I swear," he said. *No, I was.* "I got to thinking about it," he said, "and I didn't want to leave you alone with the Monsieur. But I guess you're fine."

If being out of gas and my mouth so dry with what I was about to say was fine, then sure. Except for once I was out of words. How could I tell Christian how I felt? The problem wasn't expressing myself, the problem was getting him to respond the way I wanted him to. Oh garbage, that wasn't going to happen, but I couldn't let that stop me. I took a deep breath, and my words just tumbled out. "Uh, you want your rib back?"

He smiled uncertainly. "What?"

"I . . . well." I jerked open my car door and almost hit him with it. He grabbed my hand to stop me. His hand lingered on mine. Suddenly I couldn't concentrate on what I was trying to do or say or anything. "It's a good thing you know what I'm going to say before I say it," I said, "because there's no way I'm going to get this out. I mean, you know me better than anybody, even my mad smile. That's why I like you."

Christian looked confused, but at least he was grinning. "Because I can read your mind?"

"No. More!" I still wasn't making sense. I scrambled out of my car, my bare feet hitting the hot pavement, and I hardly even noticed the pain in my ankle. "I'm just sorry I ruined your life because of it. You're not a jerk. Well, not all the time. I'm more of one. Look, you've ruined my life too. I just liked it!"

"Are you confessing your sins or mine?"

I laughed. "Would you listen to me?" I tugged on his thick tie. It was the copper and chocolate twist one I loved so much. "I don't want to be a spinster anymore."

"Oh really?" He suddenly looked guarded. "Where's the Monsieur?"

"I told him the truth. I, uh, communicated."

His hand loosened on mine. "And it did the trick, huh?"

"Yep, like butter. He ran the other way."

Christian started playing with my fingers, making me lose my train of thought. "You do what it takes, don't you, to get rid of the guys?"

"No, just a couple. Christian, please. I know I'm crazy. That's why I need you. Nobody else is sane either! Britton's crazy. Maggie's crazy. Charity's crazy . . . the Monsieur. Even the institute teacher. He's crazy as a loon. And me, I'm completely done for. I'm really crazy for you, and that doesn't help anything." He was silent, and I took a deep breath for courage. "I love sitting on the porch with you and dumpster diving with you." He was still being too quiet and I searched his eyes. "And my mom loves you too." This wasn't working.

"What about you?"

I was dying. He still hadn't let go of my hand though, making this pure terror somehow worth it. These were the hardest words I could get out and so I nodded instead. "Pretty darn close." With my free hand, I tugged the service idol out of my car. "I'm just hoping this will make things better." I tried to hand it to him without hitting him with it. I was having a problem controlling my adrenaline-rushed fingers. "And I'm sorry that I'm laying all of this on you now with

Charity and everything, but I have to. I can't go another second without telling you how I feel!"

He smiled and pulled me closer. I could feel his warmth. "How about we call ourselves even then? I was just on my way to take out the Monsieur and pretty much do what you're doing."

"Humiliate yourself?"

"Yep." He leaned his forehead against mine. "It would've been worth it though."

Could he possibly feel the same way? I couldn't believe it. I listened to the dirty rumble of a motorcycle engine and before I could turn my head, Christian jokingly tilted my chin towards him instead, but he didn't have to. All my attention was on him.

"It is," I said. "It's worth it." I laughed in relief.

All of the things that had kept us apart before didn't matter now: exes, squirrelly girls, and least of all our friendship, because it was about to turn into something more. Besides, I could watch for the make and model of the bike behind his shoulder. It was a Flying Pan by the way, just in case you were interested.

"You know what my favorite part of your article was?" he said, "'A jerk doesn't see what's staring him in the face—a potentially nice girl.'" My lips curved up. "That's when I knew I had a chance," he told me. "I'm just sorry I didn't see it before."

"Me too."

"Well, garbage. Let's just kiss and make up, huh?" I blushed bright red, and his lips met mine, making me forget all about the source of that dirty motor as it sped away.

Epilogue

Every good act is charity.
—Muhammad

Tuesday, August 4th, evening (a month later)

Betsy was sitting in the pews in front of us, her tan elbow resting on the bench, and I shoved the ward directory into her hands. It was finally done. Now everyone could quit complaining. "Happy?" I asked in an undertone. We were in the middle of institute, and already Brother Baer was giving us the evil eye, but at this point I didn't care. He deserved what he got, the trickster.

She quickly flipped to her picture and winced. "Not really." But she laughed when she saw our fake Mormon ads. "Dating—isn't it about time?" She shook her head at us. "Quit rubbing it in our faces."

I glanced at Christian. Our fingers were interlaced, and he rubbed his thumb over mine. "Sorry," I said. We leaned back on the bench, smiling at each other.

"I don't think Charity will be happy with this one," Betsy muttered, seeing her page.

Christian fixed me with a warning look. "Jacks, you didn't?"

"What's wrong with it?"

Christian pulled the directory from Betsy and read Charity's caption. "'*Too many have dispensed with generosity in order to practice charity.—Albert Camus.*'" He turned to me. "I don't get it. Are you calling her a player?"

I laughed. "Your quote is even better." I flipped the pages with his hand and snuggled closer to get a better look. "I'm a nice guy, but . . . no, I am!" He groaned and I could tell Brother Baer would be calling on us pretty soon. "Shh, you're going to get us volunteered."

"That's Maggie's job."

Maggie glowered at us, and I bit my lip. She hadn't been very happy lately, and I knew it was something I had done. Her burning accusations still haunted me, but at least I was out of the way and she could have a chance with the guys. Just not with Christian. No way.

Suddenly there was a stir in the front of the room and Britton walked in late . . . seriously late. He cut a rakish figure in his signature Bermuda shorts and black T. I'm being honest. He did, and all the girls' eyes were on him, and all he had to do was pick one. Well, he *had* to pick one. After all, he had lost the bet, and some sixth sense told them he was now available. His eyes roved over them in disinterest until he found us, and he opted for the safer seat next to Maggie. Well, there happened to be an open chair anyway.

"You little vixen, Maggot, you saved me a seat?" He sat down next to Maggie without asking. "Now if only *all* girls were like you."

I swiveled at that. Britton had actually given a compliment. A flirtatious one, but a compliment all the same. Maggie didn't look flattered and she edged away, the blue silky material of her capris making it easier to slide down the chair. Britton shoved a hymnbook at her, and Maggie tried to take it from him, but he held firmly to the other side until she was forced to share it with him.

"I think they're perfect for each other," Charity whispered behind me as soon as the hymn was over. I stiffened, realizing she had been sitting behind us the whole time. I probably shouldn't have been so vocal about the directory.

I glanced at the two. Maggie was giving Britton annoyed looks, and he tried to look innocent. "I'm not sure I agree with that," I said slowly.

"Too bad."

Christian had already left to do the spiritual thought, completely oblivious to the evil lurking behind him, and now I was stuck with her. My gaze went unwillingly back to Maggie and Britton. "And just how are you going to get *that one* to work?"

"Put two and two together, Jack. The same way I got Jade and Rusty together. And Liza and Raine, you and Christian. I mean, I got a little help from Maggie and Britton this time, sure." Now I was dumbfounded. She couldn't be serious. "What's the matter? You thought Maggie and Britton were working alone? Or maybe you just don't think they're a good match?"

"Well, no." I felt my face go hot. I didn't think that her scheme had worked on me. I didn't buy it. "What about *your* graduation from the singles ward, Charity?"

"I'm waiting for a missionary."

"But you're . . . you're . . ."

"Twenty-five, and I have no problem with younger men, just like you." Then what was all that age talk? Had she planned this all to the last detail, or was she just that good? Of course, no one was as mean as she pretended to be. If anything that should've given everything away. She giggled. "You were a little more difficult than a lot of them, even with Britton and Maggie's help. I thought I had almost met my match."

But I had instead. Christian flipped his scriptures open at the podium. "It is not good that the man should be left alone." He looked so cute in his cargo pants, and no, I'm not biased! "'And the rib which I, the Lord God, had taken from man, made I a woman.'" He caught my eye and stopped in the middle of what he was saying to grin at me. Everyone groaned.

I couldn't care less.

"It's time to make another sacrifice to the wedding gods," Britton muttered. He pretended to be disgusted. "They like the redheads." Maggie elbowed him hard.

Charity gave an exaggerated sigh. "My work is never done." I swiveled to look at her, but she was gone in a flurry of Bohemian skirts and the jingling of bracelets. Before I knew it, she was sitting on an empty seat next to Britton. She snuck a friendly arm around him. Maggie stiffened. I couldn't believe it. Charity was so right. Maggie was head over heels in love with Britton! That's why she had been so irritated. That's why she wouldn't let Charity flirt with him. She didn't want the jerk to win because she was in love with the jerk. That was it. Forget the article, I was writing the book. What were the odds?

Brother Baer smiled secretly at the new love triangle, and my eyes narrowed at him. He knew a hawk from a handsaw, that one, and he started his lesson. "No hanging out . . ."

"Oh, we never hang out," Britton whispered to Maggie. "I always count it as a date, Maggot."

That would be truer than he thought. Once again, I wasn't sure what I felt about this, but then I broke into a smile. I liked it. Christian sat down next to me, and I grabbed his hand, my attention on the scene in front of me. My smirk matched our institute teacher's, especially when I saw Britton turn his full attention on Maggie. For a moment they both looked happy. Charity tried to get between them. Yep, those two wouldn't last long.

And who knows? Maybe Charity was destined to fall next. Maybe the Monsieur. Maybe together! I laughed aloud, seeing Brother Baer's crazy eyes on him too. The Monsieur was sitting in the front, intent on the lesson. He was taking notes and wearing glasses that I had never seen on him before. Actually, I had never seen him so studious, and there was no girl next to him he was trying to impress. Yep, he would be the next to go.

I giggled, and Christian met my eyes with his thick-lashed ones, giving me a strange look that melted me. What? You know I've always been an eye girl. "You're losing a bobby pin," he said unexpectedly, and he pulled it free from my hair with light fingers. Then with a mischievous look, he flattened my long bangs and pinned them back like some crazy hairstylist. "Perfect," he said with a touch of pride.

I smiled at him. I was sure I looked like a freak show now, but I could barely contain myself. I knew he'd appreciate the latest news for sure. And me? Well, I needed to assign one of my love columnists to write an article on why nice guys went for jerks. Or maybe why people weren't such jerks after all. Every fairy tale needs a villain, you see, but none of us were that good at it. The Monsieur stunk at it, and Charity? I shook my head. What a fraud. I'm sure Britton would soon agree.

Let me get this straight, girls. Fairy tales can never compare with real life because real life is much more interesting. There's no riding off into the sunset unless you count sitting on the porch with Christian watching the crops grow in the evening. And let's face it, Prince Charming can never compare to the real thing because the real thing . . . well, the real thing you can actually hold on to. Christian's warm hand slid over mine, and I leaned against him, playing with my notebook. I watched Charity work her magic. She was so gonna get it. After I helped her, of course.

About the Author

This last year Stephanie Fowers had a blast hanging out with her fellow Bachelor-Rats in her hometown of Kennewick, Washington, where she blew bubbles at the Sunbeams and moonlighted as a Primary bouncer.

But wait, there's more. Recently, Stephanie watched her niece's middle school perform a play Stephanie wrote—*Robin in the Hood*. She couldn't believe how well they pulled it off, and that they actually memorized their lines. Amazing! She also had an awesome time writing a *Macbeth* screenplay with her younger brother for his Shakespeare class. And if you think taking over a country is hard, try getting a bunch of high-schoolers to act it out. Everyone was incredibly fun to work with!

So far, her nieces and nephews prove to be her greatest fans. They give her much-needed input for her upcoming YA novels, children's books, and plays, and in the meantime she brainstorms ways to put all her crazy ideas to use. She now lives in Salt Lake City, where she volunteers to make movies and works with her friendly WesTech Engineering coworkers to support her writing habit.